SEMMANT

Vadim Babenko

Ergo Sum Publishing
www.ergosumpublishing.com

Published by Ergo Sum Publishing, 2013

Translated from Russian by Christopher Lovelace and Vadim Babenko
Russian text copyright © Vadim Babenko 2013
English text copyright © Vadim Babenko 2013

E-book ISBN 978-99957-42-00-3
Paperback ISBN 978-99957-42-01-0
Hardback ISBN 978-99957-42-02-7

This novel is a work of fiction. Names and characters are the product of the author's imagination and any resemblance to actual persons, living or dead, is entirely coincidental.

Cover design: damonza.com
Editors (in alphabetical order): Hilary Handelsman,
Elizabeth Ridley, Robin Smith

www.ergosumpublishing.com
www.semmant.com

To Asha

CHAPTER 1

I'm writing this in dark-blue ink, sitting by the wall where my shadow moves. It crawls like the hand on a numberless sundial, keeping track of time that only I can follow. My days are scheduled right down to the hour, to the very minute, and yet I'm not in a hurry. The shadow changes ever so slowly, gradually blurring and fading toward the fringes.

The treatments have just been completed, and Sara has left my room. That's not her real name; she borrowed it from some porn star. All our nurses have such names by choice, taken from forgotten DVDs left behind in patients' chambers. This is their favorite game; there's also Esther, Laura, Veronica. None of them has had sex with me yet.

Sara is usually cheerful and giggly. Just today I told her a joke about a parrot, and she laughed so hard she almost cried. She has olive skin, full lips, and a pink tongue. And she has breast implants that she's really proud of. They are large and hard – at least that's how they seem. Her body probably promises more than it can give.

Nevertheless, I like Sara, though not as much as Veronica. Veronica was born in Rio; her narrow hips remind me of samba; her gaze pierces deep inside. She has knees that emanate immodesty. And she has long, thin, strong fingers… I imagine them to be very skillful. I like to fix my eyes on her with a squint, but her look is omniscient – it is impossible to confuse Veronica. I think she is overly cold toward me.

She doesn't use perfume, and sometimes I can detect her natural scent. It is very faint, almost imperceptible, but it penetrates as deeply as her gaze. Then it seems all the objects in the room smell of her – and the sheets, and even my clothing. And I regret I'm no longer that young – I could spend hours in dreamy masturbation, scanning the air with my sensitive nostrils. But to do that now would be somewhat awkward.

Anyway, Esther arouses me even more than Veronica, perhaps because she is "bi," as Sara once confided to me. Esther moves like a panther and looks like an expensive whore. Her nipples burn like hot coals, even through her starched white blouse. Her hair shimmers purple black, and her skin is tender like silk, though it looks more like velvet. The moment she comes close I seethe with the desire to touch her. I've done so a few times and even apparently got somewhere – she once slapped me in response. Surely it was a game, but I doubt we'll go much further. Here's why: now I like Laura from Santo Domingo best of all.

Yesterday, on her evening rounds, she was really hot. Yes, her legs are not so slender and her butt looks too large and heavy, but her whole body radiates passion, a natural lust too difficult to conceal. Cats scatter when they hear her walking, and gawkers turn their heads to stare. Even paralytics and defunct oldsters get horny when they feel her vibes – and I'm no paralytic or by any means too old. She leaned over me as if to arrange the sheet, flashed her huge brown eyes, licked her lips – and I knew I would have her now or very soon. I ran the palm of my hand up her thigh to the narrow moist strip of her thong. And I'm not even sure she was wearing a thong!

Then she teased me with her slim bare foot, gazing at my face with a come-hither look. Too bad she had to leave so quickly – but this is just the beginning, no doubt!

I whispered after her, "Where are you going?" when she reached the door.

"Wait," I murmured. "Now I won't be able to fall asleep."

"Yes, you will," Laura assured me. "I gave you a good sedative." Then she added, "Think of me!" And these words held a lot of promise.

I did think about her, and then, in my dream I copulated wildly with a busty *mulata*. She smelled like Laura – the rainforest, the sea, the sweetest of sour smokes. Likely, from now on I'll need this mix like a junkie.

It's two days until Laura's next shift. Two long days of eager anticipation. I now have another goal for myself.

Thinking about this, I face the window and view the distant mountains. The sun has moved down to the side. Turning my head, I see my shadow again; it's the only thing marring the perfectly white wall. Soon the sun will shift farther to the south, and the wall will regain pure whiteness, announcing lunchtime.

Then the mountains will change as their colors fade, the contours sharpen and stand out against the sky. The peaks will loom jagged; indifferent and cold. A guard will bring me the newspapers, and I will leaf through them vacantly, scanning the pictures and trying not to get newsprint on my fingers.

Then I'll do the usual set: some *hatha* poses, stretching my back and leg muscles; a tantra workout, keeping my balance with my eyes closed; and finally, *bandha yama* drills so my erection would be harder than a steel spring. I'll think about Laura – already calling her "Lora" in the northern style. She'll like that; it may bring us closer. Or, perhaps, we'll even choose a new name for her.

The peaks will finally grow indistinct in the twilight. Everything will fall silent as dusk turns to night. I'll draw the curtains, leaving only a crack so the fresh air from the mountains filters into the room. Then I'll have dinner, drink a half bottle of wine, and begin to compose another letter to Semmant…

Listen! My confinement might last years and years, but I'll give it to you straight: I am not afraid and have nothing to hide. Let them think I've lost my mind, but I know, if anyone has – it's not me! I'll tell them something else too: don't count on it. I'll say, "Semmant!" It will be like a shout, and yet the softest, the most quiet of words. Only the quietest words work for confessions – confessions of hatred, and even more so, of love.

The white walls surround me for a reason, but I will not crack up here, and he – he is my protector, my healer. Yes, at times I may lose control, and it would seem I've exhausted my strength, but I won't succumb – as I can't betray him, cannot leave him alone. Neither Esther nor Laura can help me in this – and not Sara, not Veronica. Their minds are somewhere else, I'm on my own, and I'm not that mighty. Take these notes – they reveal my weakness. But it's still no excuse to abandon them.

I don't look for excuses – even here, behind these walls, despite the treatments and the constant spying. Oh, I know, very attentive eyes are keeping watch over my writing. I feel them with my back, my skin, and even with my shadow on the wall. But I don't care; I pay them no heed. I am not posturing or putting on an act. I could simply discard the paper – ball it up, chuck it aside. Even burn it – or I could keep quiet and just stare out at the mountains, which are impervious to any words. But I can't do it; I have to write, even though it's so unbearably difficult to get through. It's so hard to be heard by others who are lost in broad daylight, who are blinded by their inability to see, who suffocate in their own waste. They are all arrogant and infinitely naïve. And me – I'm not so different. I, too, am blind and naïve, and arrogant in my own way. That's why we speak the same language, saying almost the same thing.

So, day in and day out, watchful eyes see a familiar picture. The papers are scattered across my table; it's night, darkness, dead silence. I write to him; then I get distracted and write to all of you. My fingers grow numb; at times I shiver with cold. Then the opposite: I'm drenched in sweat – and compose with delirious haste, or sometimes a mere word per hour.

It takes enormous effort, though the story is flawless, its plot coherent and logical. I drew it up myself, right up to the final scene; I started with nothing and ended up with more than I could possibly handle. It's a great experience, no matter what; it would be foolish to keep it to myself. You may object and laugh behind my back, but I have an answer: I'll say, "Semmant!" This may raise anger, provoke envy. But time will pass, and you'll see that I'm right.

He will not become anybody's hero – he's not a hero at all. He is not a conqueror, though he knows no fear. You may be tempted to laugh at him as well – yes, his naivety surpasses mine, and yet oddly enough he is wise and discreet. No one's mockery can change that.

It's not easy to become his friend. And who would dream of competing with him, feeling overconfident for no reason? Who would dare to take his place? That would be reckless and dangerous. His armor shines with a genuine gleam and yet it cannot save him from any arrow. Yes, one should not expect too much from his shield. And then, I realize, it's more important for everyone to know: what lies beneath that shield?

I could give a concise answer, but I'll put it differently: shed your own layers one by one. Shed your clothing, your masks. Wash off the makeup. Take a long, hard look at what you see – can you make sense of it? Do this alone, since it's embarrassing, indeed. The covers have been thrown on the floor, and the labels have even been cut out of them. All that remains is to look deeper inside, brushing away small details, with or without regret. The trick is to get down to what's most vital, even if it's concealed and hidden, locked away. One may grow tired and miserable along the way; and once there, may be left speechless. The unexpected may be found – some strange, unfamiliar things. Who will be able to name them properly? I guess no one, as is always the case. Everybody will be looking around: where is the hint, the subtlest of signs? And then again I'll say, "Semmant."

Listen – I admit my idea was different. I had a less ambitious plan. Everything was supposed to turn out simpler. Some may even blame me: I was following the footsteps of evil. And yes, I relied on the blindness of the crowd. I indulged others' greed, but my intentions were pure; they were good. At least I was unselfish; perhaps that vindicates me somehow, though I seek no vindication whatsoever.

I don't seek it because I feel no guilt; I'm even proud of myself, pleased. I might have done many things wrong, but now I know where I erred. I recognize the most horrible delusion, which could confound anybody.

Others can learn it too, if they have the patience to hear me out. Which is not likely. But I continue.

Because the only thing that matters is to keep moving forward.

CHAPTER 2

I am Bogdan Bogdanov, a genius in cybernetics, an expert in everything expressed in digits. Almost nobody knows my name, but those who do look back on that fact gladly – or, at least, so they pretend. I also remember all of them; that's just the way my memory works. Though I admit that it – my memory – is rather sparsely populated.

My childhood was checkered with events, but they left no visible traces, and even the earliest of them got seriously messed up. I was born in a small village in the Balkans, but my family soon started moving around a lot with a depressing urgency to get away from police and creditors. As a result, another place was listed in my documents: some nondescript city with an unpronounceable name – I never did learn how to spell it. My aura of Indigo was identified by an ugly old woman from Ziar when I turned twelve. She stank horribly, but I'm grateful to her: after her discovery, a lot fell into place.

My life as an adult was quite eventful as well. I went from job to job as I traversed all of Europe. I was poor, then earned a decent living; got filthy rich, then ended up with nothing. I've been living in Madrid for three years now – through circumstances beyond my control. This city is alien to me; I don't like it at all. It tolerates me though; or at least it did, until it started to take revenge. I had a penthouse in its best barrio, drank *sidra* with its taxi drivers, breathed its foul air, and even made friends with a real countess. And now – now I'm in the nut house.

Of course, they call it something else. A hospital for VIPs, that's its official title. But you can't argue with the rumors, as everybody knows: the VIPs who land here are pretty far gone, most of them irreversibly so. That is not so unusual and, frankly, doesn't even imply anything bad.

To tell the truth, my perceived importance wouldn't allow me to belong there. Had it not been for Countess Anna Pilar María Cortez de Vega, I should have ended up in a dirty clinic for poor psychos instead of in this domain of comfort. Thanks to her, I'm now in the company of aristocrats. *Señores* and *señoras* – all from distinguished families, as a rule – languishing in adjoining chambers. Some cracked up over money, others over broken hearts. Then there are a few who went mad over love and money at the same time. But that's just what I imagine when I'm alone with my thoughts. Most likely their problems are born of degenerate minds that are the product of hereditary decline. The gene pool has become too small; the ocean of diversity has shriveled to the size of a puddle. This is the fate of the noble elite, unwilling to compromise.

As for my gene spectrum, everything is just fine. Degeneracy poses no threat to my offspring – if I ever have any. And, as far as my mind is concerned, I live by a different set of rules – and I do not accept compromises either. I act as if they don't exist. This has absolutely nothing to do with nobility.

My father came from a line of cobblers and had reeked of goat glue since he was a child, while my mother, quite the opposite, grew up all prissy in a banker's family that lost everything when the pound sterling crashed. My parents got along well, despite their different backgrounds, united by a contempt for their hapless ancestors who gave them no chance at all. At least my mother never blamed her husband for the countless adversities we met – the troubles that befell us with the persistence of capricious fate. And as far as I could tell, he was gentler with her than was the custom in the places we lived. He probably regarded her more highly than was the norm. Which, to be fair, is really to his credit.

Still, my father's way of thinking was always quite straightforward. I would even say it was predictably crude, albeit quite sly and shrewd. He never mastered his profession, but then, it didn't interest him in the least. He was a vagabond by nature and, on top of that, locked horns with the authorities all the time. So we wandered from village to village for many years; we had no permanent home and didn't stay anywhere for very long. The neighbors never liked us, and the local police instantly sensed the opportunity for easy pickings, but that was just an illusion – my father always managed to leave them empty-handed. We traveled all over the Balkan Mountains, through the Rhodopes, the Pindus, the Dolomites, then reached the Danube and went all the way to Budapest. That was where we settled down for a while. My father started to sell pottery, and my mother ran into a long-lost cousin who taught her how to read tarot cards. Our life took on some semblance of stability, and I got twin brothers and a sister who were one year apart.

I finally enrolled in school there – two years behind schedule, which served me well. Reading, writing, and doing math were things I had already learned; besides that, I was bigger than my classmates, so they were afraid to pick on me, whether they had a reason to or not. All they could do was eject me from their circles since I was so obviously foreign to them in every sense. I took it all in stride, without even realizing why. The teachers were just as hostile, but the coursework came to me effortlessly. As for the animosity, I had learned to ignore it since my earliest days. My family life wasn't the best either. My younger siblings only irritated me with their squealing; I didn't have any feelings of tenderness for them. This greatly upset my mother, and my dad complained that I wasn't worth anything. And I probably never would be, he added, judging by my aimless look and inability to get along with anyone.

There was only one person who understood me well: a girl four years my senior, an exotic performer in a traveling circus we met up with near Miskolc after we had to flee Budapest in a hurry. She had a large mouth and a searching glance that belied her childish features. She could curl her ears up and straighten them out on command, and the only friend she had until I came along was a toy frog that blew soap bubbles. Her smile taught me to dream, and her hands taught me something too, though she was completely innocent – just desperately and endlessly kind. When she danced in the arena I knew her heart pounded there, under the circus floor, under the heels and the ponies' hooves, under all the sets and sawdust shavings. Nobody wanted to see her wings, but I could make out their transparent shadow. I could even hear them flutter – and I felt sorry for her, and she came to me in full-color dreams. Later, we crossed paths more than once: the circus headed north like we had, making its way toward Warsaw, but it lingered for a long while near Tatry and then returned there again and again, as if enchanted by the beauty of the place and the scent of mountain pines on the air.

By then, we had settled in Liptov, where my father got involved in improving the local medicinal waters with the aid of common table salt. He also made friends with the circus troupe, especially with a magician named Simon, as he saw big potential in that line of work. It was there that I turned twelve and the old woman from Ziar peered into my very soul with her dusky eyes. She looked at me in shock and for a long time whispered to my mother, who absently shuffled her cards. I overheard her say, "Are you sure this is your child? Do you know the father? Maybe the devil impregnated you?"

Neither of them could figure it out and they were rattled, indeed; but my mother told my father everything nonetheless. Knowing no better confidant, he grabbed a bottle of *slivovitz* and went to see Simon, supposedly to learn a silver coin trick.

The circus was touring the thermal pools then, entertaining fat cats with ailing livers. My girl did not dance there anymore; she'd suddenly grown up and run off with some Romanian officer. I bore her no ill will and wished her the best, for somehow I knew: wings are just not meant to last. As for Simon, he remained true to his top hat with the stars and his tattered black tailcoat. His trade implied a certain erudition, and he knew about the phenomenon of Indigo. Once he heard about me, his ears pricked up. My father took notice, and for the first time he began to think I might finally be of some use. After draining the entire bottle, they decided to make me a whiz kid in the circus. Simon convinced my father that the talent for doing quick calculations, if I was found to possess the ability, was all the rage now and could bring in good money. I think that was his best trick ever.

My dad, now that he was in better spirits, started asking around about how to turn me into a whiz kid as fast as possible. To his misfortune, he crossed paths with an official from Mikulas who was crafty and quick, and who reported my existence to the very top. That set the bureaucratic gears in motion. Highly important people came to see me, and soon my fate was decided. They made my father sign the papers by reminding him of a few of his sins, and a month later I found myself on a ferry crossing the English Channel en route to a special boarding school that had been established by the Crown with funding from one of its less innocuous ministries.

The waves danced below. I was nauseated and understood nothing, only sensing I would never see my parents, my brothers, or my sister again. That's pretty much how it turned out, which doesn't bother me at all. I'd just like to know how far that official went in his career – whether he was given a high position, a secretary, or a government car.

That, you could say, was where my childhood ended. I'm not complaining; it usually doesn't last much longer anyway. The mountains and forested hills were gone from my life and replaced with plains covered in yellowish-gray sand, low, heavy clouds, and the sea breeze.

"*Go catch yourself a fish, throw it to a pelican. Don't you cry for it, what's the point? Let your cheeks be salty only from the ocean spray.*" I repeated this nursery rhyme to myself, but it wasn't me who made it up. I don't remember who did, and it's not important. It was one of us from the island, at any rate. One of us from the School.

CHAPTER 3

At that time, unusual children were the subject of much talk. Their eyes, overly intense and vivid, were mentioned quite often – as was their skill in sensing each other from a distance, and their own language, made up of interjections, which they did not shed until early adolescence. Myths circulated, and one of them was so promising that some governments decided to invest quite a bit of money in us. Of course, this was no act of charity: these people were pure pragmatists. The idea was to create a special breed, a regiment of obedient geniuses who would later be able to pay society back in full. The millions being spent were supposed to reap benefits a hundred-fold. Someone, I guess, genuinely believed that.

They brought us from everywhere, and, to their credit, put a lot of effort into us. The project was massive and not intended to be done half way. The director of the facility met each child personally at the main entrance. I can still recall his narrow face and his troubled, ailing look. And I remember something else: everyone always called him simply the Director. Proper names were just not fitting, for him or for the School.

"Hello," he said to me quietly. "We will try to make you happy."

For some reason, it was hard to put much faith in his words.

I didn't believe him, but I was wrong; they all tried as best as they could. We were treated with cautious dread, as if we were overly complicated playthings. They crammed a mass of knowledge into our brains, and we were eager to learn. But playing in each youngster's head was his own music, the beating of his own pulse, which was, in fact, encouraged. On the wall of the dining common there was even a sign that read: *Do not be like everybody else!* And there was another one in the assembly hall, confronting us with the question: *Do you have a mission?* In slightly smaller script, as if in clarification, was one more: *What do you do best?*

These were the rules that defined our lives at the School. Clearly, they drilled their way into us forever. I really don't know what clever tactics were supposed to turn us into team players. Any way you slice it, that idea sounds impractical and just plain stupid. However, top brass saw it differently. They had their own plan, and they conducted training exercises and special games with us. The shrinks worked in turns and called us in for short sessions every few days. We regarded this as a necessary evil.

Sometimes, the Director spoke before us, in person. At those meetings, he was a different man – the morose, self-consumed functionary would be transfigured into a veritable prophet. He would talk in impassioned detail about our extraordinary future. About how they were going to form us into an organized force, something like a Foreign Legion, to induce bloodless intellectual blitzkriegs. He drew diagrams and schematics linked with arcs and arrows to show how they were all connected. He inscribed small squares to indicate the headquarters, reservists, support center, and mobilized groups. United and structured, we would be capable of anything. Even the most complex problems would bend to our will in the shortest time!

He truly burned with the thought of it; it was obvious this project meant a lot to him. We could see he knew how to dream, and that worked in his favor. Of course, his goal was unobtainable. But one should never demand too much from a goal.

They probably should have hung something else in the dining hall, but even that would not have made much difference. When we grew up it became clear: every one of us was insubordinate beyond measure. The Foreign Legion of Indigo would issue forth as a band of loners who could not take orders. On top of that, some of us – children with overly vivid eyes – fell into a depression that was anything but childish, despite our young, happy-go-lucky years. And we weren't the least bit grateful – not to society or anybody else.

One way or another, the School was ingrained in our very being. That squat, gray building just outside of Brighton, with the leaden waves rolling in beside it, forever carved into my mind. Wide corridors, staircases with banisters polished to a blinding sheen. The enormous rectangular courtyard, the athletic field, the covered natatorium… Sports were taken seriously there, as is typical for Brits. I wasn't bad at boxing, and was a fast swimmer. Later, I developed a passion for lawn tennis. I would disappear for hours on the court, and after two years I had no equal. Sometimes I even outplayed the instructor – a brawny German with a very strong serve.

Sleeping quarters occupied the first floor, with the men on one side, the women on the other. The invisible boundary was guarded by Paul, who was half-blind. It required no effort whatsoever to take advantage of him, which we did, even though our amusements then were still very innocent.

All five years I lived in the corner room with the same three roommates. We got on well, although for some reason we never became friends. To tell the truth, we didn't have much to do with each other. There weren't many conversations, either – instead, each of the four of us found comfort in the mutual silence. That's why, year after year, and without discussing it at all, we continued to live together.

I only got a little closer to one of them: Thomas, from Ötztal. It was Thomas in particular who would later play an important role. As for the School, he and I talked sometimes about sports or the mountain slopes. I taught him the topspin backhand, which he had difficulty mastering. He, in turn, educated me on the proper techniques for freeride and slalom. Brighton had neither mountains nor snow, but somehow I knew: there were skis in my future. And I trained diligently by adapting a skateboard to the purpose.

On the upper floor were the classrooms where we were taught everything by teachers who, like us, had been handpicked with great precision. Their task was clear: to push us from the shallow end of the pool into the depths. Not just to get our feet wet, but to throw us in head first, without holding back because of our age or the difficulty of the subject.

There were a lot of science classes, all mixed together. Our heads were filled with a hodgepodge of knowledge for us to sort out on our own. Now I know: many of those theories could not be grasped, no matter how you might try – unless you knew the complex mathematics with which they did not risk torturing us. But we tried anyway in some kind of excited frenzy. We even at times startled the teachers, who were not easily surprised.

By my sixteenth year, I had learned in minute detail many things that ended up being useless to me. I knew what caused killer waves and how eukaryotic ribosomes functioned, what leptons and baryons were – as well as metabolism and quark-gluon plasma. I could explain to anyone the Pareto principle and the structure of the Mayan language, the stages of subduction of the earth's crust, the endless contradiction in the law of double negation. With Bradley, our astrophysicist, I discussed the properties of neutron stars and even pulsars competently enough. I could calculate the gas density of red giants in distant galaxies. In my notebook, I drew light cones and gravity-distorted Riemann spheres. Every scientific subject occupied a spot in our schedules; there was no clemency, no indulgence. Each teacher thought his discipline was the most important. This is also burned in my memory, just like their faces, their voices. Their passionate, restless devotion.

Some of them made friends with us. On occasion we would go to the shore together and wander over the pebbles crunching beneath our feet, sit on the stones sharpened by the sea. They would invite us to their homes, offer us afternoon tea with tasteless British cakes. They were lonely – each in his own way. They wanted to share with someone, and we met that need like no one else. They relaxed with us; some of them a bit too much. It was as if we drew out their hidden nature, opened up things concealed within. All the same, they seemed like eccentrics to us, nothing more. It was still too early to think of the fearful pressure of the social system.

The administration at the School encouraged these sorts of meetings. It could be they hoped the teachers would replace our families, since many of us had not been home since we were eleven or twelve. On the whole, we respected them – certainly more than our own parents, who had been left behind in countries far and wide. We liked to soak in their experience, even if it was a bit skewed, as if refracted through a tricky lens. And, still, we wanted very much never to become like them.

Nevertheless, we would often imitate them in something – children copying their elders. I, for example, made a badge for myself with an acacia branch on it, just like Bradley had. He told us, "For the Masons, this branch is a symbol of powerful, secret knowledge." And my mate Thomas, under the gentle tutelage of Montgomery the biochemist, got into Daoism for just under a year. This met a pressing need, since he had been tormented by a fear of death since early childhood. Besides, he, as a Tyrolean, was impressed by the immortal sages removing themselves to the mountains away from earthly vanity.

Both he and Montgomery liked to quote Lao-Tzu, "Mountains, enshrouded in mist: this is the embodiment of harmony that arises from the union of Yin and Yang." The mantra was naïve, but no one laughed at them. "In my search for the immortal I traversed the five mountains of the land. Their remoteness did not frighten me." This saying hung above Thomas's bed. Then the inscription disappeared. And Montgomery was thrown out of the School for drunkenness.

Some of the teachers acted outwardly like rebels – either on the seashore or at home sipping weak tea. They said things – obvious and self-evident, in our eyes – that would have shocked the ideologues of modern Europe. Democracy was attacked from all positions; this seemed bold to them, but, I must admit, their militant ardor had not the slightest effect on us. The fate of the world was the furthest thing from our mind: our own worlds were far more gripping. That's probably why we felt closest to Greg McCain, a brutal cynic. His notion of boundless egotism recalled something important from the signs on the walls.

"When so much is expected of you, it's not worth trying to please everyone. That's foolish and unnecessary."

"When you expect of yourself even more, you have to seize the most from every day you live."

"As if tomorrow will be swallowed up in fire, flood, and plague. As if no broad will ever spread her legs for you again. Don't deny yourself pleasure, dogma be damned. You're already walking on a razor's edge as it is..."

He talked like that profusely, puffing on his pipe and laughing in an all-knowing way. And we saw he was not one to be easily confused. "Pleasure" was the watchword in his heated sermons. Everything else served merely as a backdrop. For his own part, he denied himself nothing. This was an instructive example. At least his words were not at odds with his deeds.

The issue of pleasure was worse for us, and then – then everything got scrambled. Lightning struck; all at once, something snapped in three pupils' brains. In the course of a week, one after the other, some horrible incidents occurred. The shrinks sounded the alarm, obviously desperate to show how necessary they were. Information was leaked to the press, and that was the beginning of the end. The matter was chewed over for quite a while; we were harassed by photographers, reporters, and frigid activists from child protective services. Though by then, there was little about us that resembled children.

Later, the Director gathered us and announced that the founders of the School were washing their hands of it all. They had an excellent reason, true; it was hard to blame them. "But we," the Director nodded toward a group of dismal people from the administration, "we have decided to fight. We want to finish what we started, whether anybody likes it or not."

His speech failed to make an impression, though I now understand the considerable risk they were taking. According to the rumors, it was a desperate battle, but nobody doubted the outcome. Problems began with the financing, and programs shut down, teachers deserted. Soon, the School was forced to concede defeat.

This left one question: what to do with us? It took quite a while for them to decide. For several months we lived in timeless limbo – those were strange days. Lessons were reduced, mainly limited to sporting activities. Paul, the almost sightless guard, was removed from the residential area; because of economics, moral concerns were brushed away. It was as if we were suddenly unfettered, and romances sprang up one after another. The first woman in my life also appeared at that time. For a long while, this was my happiest and bitterest memory. I didn't know what was happening to me, since I did not dare call it love. Again, we grew up in a place without a hint of love. Perhaps this was the single thing that bound us forever.

Then everything was over – somewhat suddenly. The School was turned into a special institute for the deaf. As for us, we were taken one by one by leading universities, where we went and forgot easily – both the School and, curiously enough, each other.

The real world absorbed us and began to change, rebuild, and fit us in. My doctor believes this was my first step toward madness. I know he's not right, though the procedure has been painful for some of us to endure. Yet, the world is not as strong as it seems; to us, looking from the outside, this was obvious. It's a shame this wasn't obvious to the doctor: he might have been more careful in his diagnosis. And of course, more agile in his words, especially regarding my "problem," as he calls it.

One time I said to him, "We, Indigo children, don't hold on to offenses. We don't have time for it, and, besides, it's boring, insignificant, and unimportant. There's only one thing we take seriously: what do we do best? If we already know what our genuine calling is, we're zealous to do it, and damn the rest. If we still don't know, our quest is to find out as soon as possible. By tirelessly trying one thing after another."

The doctor liked that. He wrinkled his face contentedly and marked down something in his little sketchpad, hiding the notes from me with the palm of his hand. I decided to help him, to explain in more detail. I told him about the mockery, the lack of money, the misunderstanding – all this inflicts wounds, pretty severely, in fact. But severely here is only according to average nobodies, only by the measurements of those who truly are not capable enough. As for us, we cannot be hurt by such nonsense. We may give in to despondency or despair, but it's just a momentary weakness. Our true problems only lie where we express ourselves fully. In what we really do best.

I laid all this out for him quite coherently, but he made no attempt to write it down – not a word. He even waved it away, as if he didn't want to spoil the picture he had already put together. Most likely he was afraid of contradictions, of shaky ground. It seems to me he sometimes doesn't follow through. He doesn't want to strain himself – maybe he's just too lazy. It's funny to see: he thinks I'm a sociopath. Of course, that's the easiest way; but to me it's clear: my "problem" lies somewhere else. Some might claim it's in naïveté and stubbornness, and they wouldn't be too far off. Naïveté is at the forefront, that's true, but I'll say it again: I was selfless and only wanted the best – judge me now for that. Cast as many stones at me as you like; I admit, I chose hastily, but the choice was logical and simple. An idea as a panacea, a plan complex in nature but comprehensible with the slightest effort – it's not easy to think up, believe me!

Never despise anyone, our teachers told us again and again. Never despise the weak, the incompetent, the dim-witted. That is unworthy of those who are fortunate, they said; though fortunate depends on who's looking. No matter what, we learned to bear no malice and not to hold others in contempt. You cannot go against training from early childhood; only for some – the ones who didn't learn the rules – ire still overflows from their souls. That's why they're fruitless – and formless, according to our standards; that is, there's nothing to distinguish them from all the rest.

But I'm not talking about them. I now mean the weak, the mediocre; I mean those who require little, who are easy to satisfy. Their needs are simple: some kind of fear to repress animal instincts, and a sweet lie – hope – so that the meaninglessness of life does not hurl them into despair every day. There is, as a rule, no lack of fear; the issue is always the sweet lie. And this is where I come in: here is your sweetest of lies. Only this time it's no lie. It's the truth.

Really, what could be more desirable? What could be more understandable than the ghost of freedom – from creditors and loans, from boring jobs and low wages, from the full-court press of the world that leans in with all its might and squeezes hard until it wrings out your juices? How symbolic it is to restrain the world's power using its most insatiable essence, looking straight into the most evident of its various faces. How right and deserved this is: to establish the means of salvation from its malicious sins! To overturn the greed of the ruthless despots, their aggressive hubris, their desire to waylay another, to stomp him down, crush him, obliterate him…

So, it's not surprising that I am now in an insane asylum. All the same, I'm not offended. I can always take solace in the simplest of facts: there is no point in my being ashamed of what's happened to me. Just like Semmant has no reason to be ashamed of what he's done. Or of what I did for him. Or of what the two of us didn't get a chance to do.

And yes, I'll tell you, finally, what he is. He's a robot, nothing more – a program installed in an iron heart. But his own heart is by no means made of iron – so there's no cause to look down on him. There's no cause to resort to contempt, even if your teachers didn't reproach you for that. In the end, every individual is the way the installed program makes him. And if nothing is installed – well, then, it's unfortunate, very bad luck.

My Semmant is the most sophisticated program, nearly indistinguishable from a human being, especially if you work with him a bit. Because you need to work on a person to awaken what is human in him. Otherwise, everyone is just – I'll say it nicely – such senseless cattle!

But in Semmant, at least, the program was flawless. Almost flawless. Almost.

CHAPTER 4

To create him, I went a long way, straying and stumbling, but never losing my sense of direction. After leaving the School, I landed in the sleepy town of Sheffield, where I quickly convinced the administration of my aptitude for the exact sciences. They transferred me to Manchester, to a good place with old traditions. Camaraderie reigned there, not the noxious arrogance of Oxford or Cambridge. Everything was beautiful, lavish, and comfortable. Wherever you looked, you were greeted with the smiling faces of young students from good families. This was an ideal university setting, but for me it became unbearably dull.

That's why I was always being pushed to the periphery. I did not fit in with the ones I was supposed to – rather, I had a preference for the underground. Instead of bustling faculty parties, I frequented suspicious bars where I would get drunk, often severely, with shady characters from the outskirts of town. Sometimes I would hook up with seasoned hoodlums and get into fights with football fans. I spent a couple of nights in lock-up. I smoked grass with guitar players from the local scene and orderlies from the city morgue. Not that I found them very interesting – I was just looking for release from the garish despair of the conventional, the common. I feared it – subconsciously – and fled from it at full speed. In place of well-mannered co-eds from campus, I wound up with pimply emo chicks. One of them even bestowed a nasty little disease on me. That left an impression; after that, I gave girls a wide berth for a while.

I could be rough, and I could be irascible. My inner instability, which later manifested itself, was already rearing its head then. One time, in the dormitory, I lashed out screaming at the concierge – that gave him a real fright. Later, during a tennis match, I jumped over the net to pick a fight with my opponent right on the court. This incident became widely known, and I was barred from the university team. But it did not get out of hand, and I remained in good graces. Besides, I had no equal in terms of my academics.

Pretty soon, several department chairs all had me in their sights. One professor was able to ensnare me with serious science – the world of particles and quantum fields. It seemed to me my future was predetermined, and I liked it a lot. Theoreticians comprised a special caste: the problems they faced were truly on a grand scale.

My professor loved to repeat, "We are putting a challenge out for God himself!" That was really how it was too. The question of higher powers was being decided right in our notebooks. The properties of the universe determined all answers. Anisotropy or symmetry, accident or intelligent design... Looking at things that way disciplined my mind. Though, I must admit, almost all of us were a little mystical at heart.

I joined in with the community and enjoyed its spirit. Microphysics, at first glance a fantasy world, proved to be the most real of disciplines. The clarity of its predictions was beyond compare. Much of it was downright bewitching, especially the greatest of freedoms: existing in all points at once – until a detector slams its trap shut. Besides, any attempt to peer inside would inevitably destroy the magic – I saw a great deal of meaning in this. I envisioned a strictly guarded secret: it is impossible to get an answer unless you make your presence felt. A passion for cognizance awoke within me, followed by a passion for accomplishment. I tried my hand, in complete seriousness, at the main problem: the collapse of the wave function, the disappearance of all – and every possible – freedom. I remembered round-shouldered Bradley and my badge with the acacia branch. "One thing leads to another," I told myself. "The connection is obvious. I'm on the right path."

Then the time for my diploma came, and everything changed,

abruptly and forever. I forgot the quantum realm in an instant as it gave way to abstractions and neural networks. A shrewd scout, a talent recruiter, knocked me off the path in about a quarter of an hour. He got a large order, and I was one of the first to bite at the bait he was offering. It was a decision I never regretted.

I entered a new world – the world of thinking machines. With a helping hand from the scout, I ended up in Basel at a giant corporation engaged in everything under the sun, in addition to its famous pills and vaccines. I got an Austrian for a boss, energetic and greedy for success. I had never even imagined Austrians could have so much ambition. He thought up a bold move: creating the model enterprise of the future. This meant, first of all, getting rid of several divisions, sacking the idlers, and replacing them with an electronic brain. Let computers do the same job, only better – thinking faster and never getting tired or asking for a raise. Knowledge engineering – this is what it was called then. The naïveté of the idea shared a common thread with the naïveté of the Director's dream at the School. Later, when everything ended, this became as plain as day. But at that time nobody knew enough, and the Austrian did a mind job on his bosses by skillfully choosing the most appealing arguments.

They gave us carte blanche and, along with it, half of a new building, decent money, and all the technology our hearts desired. There were twelve of us, all young and filled with a passion to change the world. I remembered three from Brighton, and one of them, the short, dark-haired Anthony, soon became the unofficial leader – to the surprise and envy of the ambitious Austrian. He was the one who devised the rigid rules that brought order to the initial confusion. It was his methodology, later named for someone else, that was applied widely and then forgotten or even forbidden.

The others from the School also stood out. We were united by our common passion; something goaded us forward and would not let us look back. We carried the others along, urging and hastening them on mercilessly. At the forefront stood progress and the plan – and, besides, as soon as I felt sorry for someone, I would remember the Brighton waves or the wandering circus and that heart pounding under the sawdust – or, for some reason, Simon's threadbare coat and bird-like profile. That was enough not to have sentiments, if you get what I mean.

Those who later had to be fired – something like several thousand – were not informed of the project's goals. Of them, the Specialists – the best of the best, the most respected – were selected. It was from their heads in particular that we had to extract everything worthwhile. We brought them and ourselves to the brink of exhaustion, eliciting the necessary data and combining the fragments into a cohesive whole – comparing, systematizing, and linking them to each other. We needed to be inventive; the procedures included the "method of disbelief," the "method of many repetitions," and even the "grueling interrogation," in which your active consciousness grows numb and shuts down, and your tongue wags freely to reveal what lies deep down inside, far away, locked up tight.

Of course, the Specialists didn't like this, but at first no one complained openly. They feared only that our efforts would reveal their emptiness and falsehood, which is exactly what happened. Soon we saw gaping holes at every step. At times their ignorance was appalling. It seemed they had never studied a single science as they should have. Their expertise was in squeezing the juices from those who were young and voracious, tenacious and intelligent, able to think. They would use them and then push them aside to avoid breeding rivals. Some newcomers, though, were not to be pushed away so easily; they fought fiercely with their elbows. Then, in time, they themselves grew into Specialists – and lost all aptitude for using their brains in the process...

Our hopes were dashed one after the other. Disconcerted, we tried to find a solution – working even harder and shouting at the ones lagging behind. It was bitter for everyone; time after time we had to resort to "grueling interrogation" to overcome laziness, stagnation, and elementary fear. As a result, the Specialists decided they had had enough. They united to organize a plot and inundated the administration with grievances and denouncements. It nearly turned into a general strike by the staff of the entire corporation. The scandal gathered steam, and they closed down the shop. Everything was blamed on the Austrian and not at all on Anthony, who, by the way, was more emotionally involved than anyone.

My conscience was at peace, but the first doubts were beginning to worm their way in. I found out enough to be disappointed – in the human mind and in human nature. I saw how people inexcusably stop halfway. How the initial thirst for knowledge turns into an aspiration to show off. Just dig a little deeper and there you will find it: sketchy, desultory, tied together thoughtlessly, pasted with ambiguous words and topped with empty rhetoric. Each expert wanted more than anything to protect his elevated status, which, as a rule, had been undeservedly acquired. Everybody was concerned about getting a piece of the pie, but not about truth or the search for it. The world had no need for fulfillment. The world wanted to kick back, consume, and have a good time. In itself, this was not bad. The bad thing was that the world did not want anything more.

I needed to be convinced of the opposite and was greatly confused. I looked desperately for a change, and soon an interesting opportunity turned up; I changed my field and went to another country without a second thought. I really wanted to take Anthony with me, but he declined. Then, a year later, he got too reckless shooting up a dose of junk in someone else's bungalow on the isle of Crete. His list of complaints to the world all of a sudden became way too long.

The new job was complicated and brimming with surprises. It really appealed to my tastes. The mystery of living molecules got hold of my head, and besides, autumn in Paris that year was soft and romantic. I thought the healing was right here, just a step away. I was surrounded by enthusiastic people; we again worked very hard, and we were happy because we were still young. I married a French artist and fell in love with Manet and Bonnard, steak tartare and red Bordeaux. But all the same, doubt kept gnawing like a worm. Everything was lovely, but it was all unstable – I felt it in my skin, recalled it in my sleep.

The artist, fair-haired Natalie, became the first woman of my dreams. She was exactly as I had imagined in my youth. She even had a familiar smell – like a crisp autumn wind with yellow leaves. Here it is, harmony itself, I would tell myself, transported to seventh heaven. And Natalie adored me in turn.

The work was exhausting. There was almost no one daring enough at the time to tackle those extremely complicated subjects. I was creating new worlds, making models of the "elementary blocks" that comprised the human body, building images of individual cells and colonies of them – fragile but well organized groups. Strange hybrids were born on my monitor screen, monstrosities called forth to produce new life, balls of protein chains, pieces of interwoven threads, "letters" upon "letters" composed in threes and containing the eternal code. It was the code of the universe – or so we thought at the time, and perhaps we were right. The mysteries of living matter were being revealed down to the fundamental level, arranging themselves row by row, exposed in one snapshot after another. It was magnificent, stunning, gorgeous. There was music and poetry there. I truly felt like a Creator.

Natalie did not understand what was going on in my head, but she sensed something, and it captivated her. At night, she would suddenly wake, look at me, and exclaim, "How strange!" Thinking I was asleep, she would run her fingers over my face and whisper almost inaudibly, "Where did you get all this? How do you do it?"

Threads of fine energy streamed from her fingers. She was all lit up like a sensitive live wire, and I was happy for a short while. Then, about six months later, her interest dried up. She grew tired and common – a quarrelsome, lazy soul. I was in despair and suffered like I never had before. Later, I threw her out. And I lost faith in everything.

Even living molecules became loathsome to me. I submitted to sloth, then I quit before bringing what I had started to a conclusion. There was no one to carry on after me, so my work was for naught. I loafed about for an entire month, almost never leaving the house. Then I suddenly came to my senses – and felt ashamed, embarrassed, and guilty. So I decided to start it all afresh.

This turned out to be easier than could have been expected. My passion for fulfillment formed and intensified. For four short years I followed it with redoubled effort as I polished my procedures and methods. I wandered from lab to lab, never staying in one place long, choosing my projects carefully, without being lured by either prestige or money. I latched onto whatever was most difficult, amorphous, or fragmentary and forced it into formal frameworks, imagined the unimaginable, and programmed what no other would attempt to program. I worked side by side with physicians and chemists, climatologists and pharmacists, astronomers, linguists, navy sea captains… All of them deserve my thanks. They broadened my range of vision. I learned the underlying rationale for the most varied things – no textbook could have helped me in this. A multitude of separate pieces coalesced like a giant puzzle. Something like a complete picture promised to appear in the immediate future. Of course it was an illusion. No such picture existed in the approximations I used in my work. But my grasp kept becoming tighter.

The School had trained me to poke persistently into the very depth of things. Again and again I attacked problems for which no solution existed – scorning simplicity, setting "correct" linearized systems aside. Now and then my colleagues whispered behind my back, assuming I was wasting my time. They had been told in their worthless schools that "correct" systems were what the world was composed of. Their worthless teachers taught them that whatever is unstable, not subject to analytics, is an exotic that can be ignored. Yet I saw: that's not how it is at all. The real world consists of the nonlinear; it is rough, irregular, asymmetrical. The slightest deviations in the initial data often lead to unpredictable swings. And one must never close his eyes to that.

I learned the connection between cardiac arrhythmia and the strange music of high-voltage networks, understood the fundamental unpredictability of cyclones and the reasons for sudden "madness" in the webs of telephone lines. It turned out not everything can be disassembled and then put back together – no matter how hard you try. I saw how simple algebra, disrespected by any graduate student, suddenly gives rise to chaotic monsters with an immeasurably complex character. Activity itself, once it was over, often changed the rules by which it was supposed to be accomplished. The consequences could not be forecast by even the most powerful computer. This was a genuine challenge – the challenge of chaos on a cosmic scale. It confounded me, but did not stop me. It made me alert, but did not pull the rug from under my feet. I still believed in the power of the mind, annoyed only with the imperfection of reality.

Gradually, I was getting accustomed to the role of Creator, to drawing the boldest of analogies. What was it like in the quantum microverse that I had so carelessly discarded? In the theories that had cast light on marvelously precise calibration?... Onto the variety of interactions, onto their fragile balance, someone had imposed universal constants such that a human mind could be born, could exist. I now considered this the most useful lesson. Everything always, always depends on a handful of basic quantities – and I learned to extract them from the disorder. I selected its values – carefully, patiently, sensing how the basis for artificial thought attains harmony as it prepares to take on flesh. Afterward, like an electric current through my fingertips, confidence came: I got it! With these parameters, my new world was doomed to develop, not to perish. And I nurtured it, gave it complexity, altered it, and made it consistent...

Later, quantum mechanics reminded me of itself again – when I felt that the essence of simulated reasoning was buried still deeper. I became surrounded with books, studied up on the biophysics of the brain, on the structure of neural membranes and the basics of how the synapses function. It was here that I was inspired – that is, I discovered how inspiration happens. How understanding occurs, the creative act itself. The nonlinear, the unquantifiable found its place in quantum entanglement, in the coherence of states. Hundreds of thousands of neurons sensed each other to form a single family, as it were – if even for the briefest millisecond. I imagined it, almost dreamt of it, and, in contradiction to the classics, assumed it was indeed possible in living cells. The neural layer in my models teemed with a myriad of combinations, an immeasurable multitude of variations gyrating in their feverish dance. It kept accelerating, and, at some point, the decoupling came, the waves collapsed, and the particles broke free of their bonds. The family of neurons produced thought!

I understood: in the quantum collective are hidden the specifics of consciousness, intuition and enlightenment, latent free will, and common sense. It remained to guess how exactly bonding takes place; what is responsible for that instantaneous selection. I no longer considered the collapse of alternatives to be a problem. It was unavoidable – and soon its perfectly natural source became clear to me. Space itself, after all – through its geometry and curvature – determines when and how to bring order to the emerging chaos. It is a property of the universe with which it protects itself from disharmony, from local abnormalities in its structure. When the chaos becomes too great, it seems to say, "Enough!" Brain cell molecules move in microns to assert, "There it is, that's correct." And *Bang!* Thought is born.

So I formulated the principle and now had only to calculate the determinative figures. Fretting and feeling my guilt, late one night I called that same professor from Manchester, the one who was the first to believe in me. The professor was not perturbed – not by the lateness of the call nor because I had previously turned renegade. He received with unexpected fervor the idea that the "Universe Metric" regulates thought – and mentioned useful things about changing the curvature of space through microscopic mass displacement. The concept of harmony being preserved by the universe itself was obviously to his taste: he was getting old and was afraid of death. And his assessments really helped – a month later I had completed a full mathematical model. I knew this was a breakthrough, a step beyond the horizon, beyond the boundary of the norm. Artificial intelligence became linked with the composition of the world!

Then a stupid thing happened: I got involved in an affair that had nothing to do with me. By a funny coincidence, I became known in higher scientific circles. They heard about me and got excited, and invited me to a symposium where all the luminaries were gathered. This was a step toward recognition – in spheres I had never had any ambition to enter. I had no faith in them, quite justifiably. But here, for some reason, I took the invitation as a good sign. I did not need fame, but I decided that what I had done would come to life there, on a large scale.

I remember how carefully I prepared, working on the abstract, making the slides. This was a new experience: I had never presented before at that level. I was looking forward to the discussions, the battles of opinion, and the intellectual tempest. But it turned out differently: they simply expelled me. They struck me such a blow that it was almost fatal.

Summer came, an unusually hot one for Europe. The megalopolis where the event was held was choking in the blistering heat. It was choking on smoke too – the surrounding forests were ablaze, the peat bogs smoldered; the smog was dense and viscous. But I was not disturbed – either by the heat or the filthy air.

Right from the airport I rushed to the conference hall; my lecture was one of the first. I remember my impatience, then the slight shiver when the chairman announced my name. I started from the very beginning – described synapses and neurons, and the family of entangled quanta – but soon, to my surprise, I heard the hall buzzing with a hum of displeasure. I thought then that my slides were not detailed enough. On the board, I began to draw the superposition of quasi-particles, the vectors of their states, and the directions of their spins. The din changed to hostile silence, the calm before a storm or an explosion. When I wrote out the Schrödinger equation – just to explain the concept – they looked at me as if I had made an obscene gesture. And when I started to talk about the complex numbers and even sketched the Argand diagram, the dignitaries could hold back no longer and became unhinged. They lashed out like a pack of animals, having recognized in me a serious threat.

The close-knit group of trendsetters bore a striking resemblance to the Specialists from Basel. Most likely, I thought then, they would take vengeance on me for good – for the dozens of "grueling interrogations." Though of course they weren't attacking me out of vengeance. They were defending their territory, with all its riches – grants, status, public interest, the generous ministrations of attractive co-eds – from the intruder, the alien. Making it clear: they had no intention of sharing their prestige and possessions with anyone at all.

That's how it is in any science that cannot be proven by mathematics. The luminaries stand their ground to the death, tearing with their claws and gnashing their teeth. If I had come with something obscure, something ordinary and not laying claim to so much, they would have received me with paternal congeniality. They might have scolded me, or they might have coddled me briefly, then allowed me to perch somewhere on the fringe. But I stabbed at the very heart – having come out of nowhere, a complete enigma. The full wrath of the highfliers let loose on me, concentrated into one striking beam. There was no discussion – they would not allow me to say a word. They crushed me with the most refined demagoguery, manipulating, turning things inside out. Then they banished me: the microphone was simply shut off. The next lecturer was already shuffling up to the projector. My time was up, the time limit nonnegotiable!

Later, I wandered to the taxi stand through a veil of poisonous smoke in a city that had long been sinking into its own detritus. It felt as though something really terrible had happened that morning. I was crushed, downtrodden – and it was not just me. The work I had done was openly ridiculed. They had proven that the world did not need me – not one bit!

For the first time, I felt utter hopelessness. I was unprepared for the misery that enshrouded me. The burning sun was nearly at its zenith, scoured by haze, but knowing no mercy. I then understood: this must be what a cosmic disaster looks like. It's as if we are falling into our star, losing our orbit, unable to resist the gravitational pull. Or the star itself, contrary to calculations, just now decided to spit out its last thermonuclear blast from the remaining hydrogen. One way or another, we're out of time – as we always were, to tell the truth. All the efforts, all the attempts are in vain and will not be needed – ever, by anyone.

And right then I felt that universal chaos was neither an abstraction nor a joke. It emphatically, impudently had just interfered in my life. I saw it in everything: in hostile stubbornness, in the heat suffocating all that lived, and even – later – in the streams of air beneath the wings of the airliner carrying me away. I imagined that here, this instant, sudden turbulence would throw us into a tailspin. I was expecting a catastrophe any second…

A full hour after take-off passed before I tried to regain my senses. I tried to calm down and put everything in perspective. I even formulated for myself what I recently told my doctor at the clinic for psychos.

"No offense. They're just unfortunate. You're luckier than all of them anyway!"

"You know your strengths, what more do you need?"

"Never bear ill will toward the talentless, the weak. Never hate or blame or despise them!"

Much changed that day – both in me and in my life. I convinced myself to bear no malice, and this was a mistake. My courage was left with nothing to latch onto. The sensation of hopelessness lodged in my consciousness, put down roots, and won space for itself. Even my passion for fulfillment subsided in its presence.

Bitterly, I recalled fair-haired Natalie – for some reason more often than the rest. I tried to find a substitute for her; I met women, then dumped them right away, some even before I had slept with them. Wherever I worked now, everything ended in scandal. People hired me eagerly, expecting miracles from me – and, as always, I would start out well. But soon the subject would bore me to death and my colleagues would become repulsive. I would make scenes, engage in direct conflict. Several times, like in France, I had to leave before getting a result. Something snapped in me; I became intolerant and coarse. My friends withdrew, one by one; and my bosses didn't know how to get along with me anymore. I was on a downward spiral that was closing in, but there was nothing to grab onto. A destructive impulse I could not hold back grew inside and burst to the surface. I saw in it the depth and power of a murky wave.

I wanted to fight the whole world, to demolish everything in my path. I drank a lot and got into drunken brawls. It became easy for me to insult anyone for no reason. Bad rumors spread about me, many of them true. I stopped getting invited to join projects, interviews, or anything else. It got to the point that it was hard to make a living. I started to give private lessons – for the sons of Arab sheikhs or the progeny of the *nouveau riche* from Russia. It was the Russians in particular who pushed me to the very edge – and left me there, on the edge, barely keeping my balance.

They were twins, very young girls, from faraway eastern Siberia. They didn't like to study, but adored gin and tonics and an unabashed *ménage a trois*. We spent passionate hours in my Paris apartment, and they blew my mind with their identical pink asses and chiseled legs. When I was with them, I forgot about everything. It was a welcome release, as if the destructive whirlwind had lost all its strength. I just wanted this time to go on and on without end. I sensed that something dreadful was waiting beyond it, something from which there was no salvation.

I lived then in an attic on the Rue Boucherie, and the chimeras of Notre Dame would watch us through the uneven curtains. The days rushed by; we saw each other more and more often and were increasingly insatiable. The twins became a single whole for me, indivisible from each other. They swore their love, and I responded in kind. I responded, and also wanted to become indivisible, indistinguishable...

And then somehow I wound up with them in Marseille. They ditched me there, having hooked up with Greek sailors, and vanished without a word. Their father called and threatened me, though this was none of my doing. Chimeras protruded from behind every corner, and despair smothered me like a wet blanket. Then, at the port, some crooks mugged me brutally. It seemed the universe did not accept me and no longer wanted to keep me on. I saw again that chaos was everywhere, and I understood: chaos is death.

There was a fleeting thought about ending my life. I mulled it over for a few hours as I lay on the threadbare couch in a hotel room I had no way to pay for. However, I was mistaken. The universe still had a lot in store for me. Late that night the telephone rang, and I heard the voice of Lucco Mancini. My path to a robot named Semmant had shortened by a thousand miles.

CHAPTER 5

Lucco Mancini had a velvet baritone. He was a swindler and a gambler; I understood that right away. But, as became clear later, his fraud did not cross the lines set by law. That year, he stumbled upon a profitable venture and committed himself to it zealously. He conned those who wanted to get rich quick, and his field of dreams – where the trees had bank notes instead of leaves – was the gold and currency market: the biggest casino ever built.

The market! It was from Mancini in particular I first heard this word. And he was the first one to get me interested in looking for hidden connections within this world of bitterness and hope, fantastic riches and lives destroyed. Oh, Lucco knew the right way to get to anyone. With me he started by hinting at the most unsolvable of riddles, and that immediately caught hold of and stirred my soul, as well as my will. My responsive fulfillment sensor was triggered by this new challenge thrown out to it, like a bone to a hungry dog. I leaned against the wall, wiped the sweat from my brow, and began to ask questions. Lucco understood, and I understood, too: I was hooked.

The industry of ensnaring naïve souls, so trusting in their Lilliputian avarice, blossomed into a magnificent flower. So many of them landed in the net – from everywhere, from all over the world. Our computer files were checkered with the flags of different nations, which Lucco, just for fun, used to mark the names of new victims. Almost all of them ended up the same – regardless of their cleverness or determination – and roughly in the same amount of time. I knew some were losing the last money they had, but I didn't pity them one bit; this was their personal choice.

Mancini's companies, with their feelers spread all over the World Wide Web, grew by leaps and bounds. He even took on a staff of employees – for the first time in his life, he admitted – rented an office, hooked up phones and fax machines. Cute girls chattered away in five languages, retired salesmen with a financial past signed on for work again, fooling more heads day after day. The players' money, of course, never reached actual trading desks – they just placed bad bets, and Lucco pocketed their losses. If any happened to win, he would honestly give them the earnings, and then find a reason to push them out of the game. Everything ran like clockwork. And maybe it's still running now – I wouldn't be surprised if Mancini has already gotten as rich as Croesus.

He needed me to set up a new lure. The trading machine, as it was called, was an automatic market player, a smart program for making money around the clock without any hassles or sleep breaks. Its role was to give the desperate ones some last elusive hope, and to inspire shy beginners to be bold and daring, make them believe in themselves. Lucco saw good prospects in this and offered me generous pay. He just wanted everything to be done fast, even if it was rushed and slapdash. We squabbled a little but came to a compromise – between the real and the ephemeral, between a firm base and a foundation of air.

Our collaboration continued for a year. I settled down in that year, as if I had reached an accord with something inside myself. The destructive impulse was replaced by a familiar thirst: to create, not to destroy; to look deeper, to get to the bottom of things. Auto-trading made it possible to escape from reality, of which I had had more than my fill. It seemed to me then: I could live my life fenced off by a set of structures and formulas, returning to the real world only occasionally for a little shred of pleasure, which no one could do without.

For Mancini, I earned my wages in full. He found himself the owner of a dozen gadgets, each of which possessed its own style. They gained popularity and followers, passionate supporters who remained faithful even when the markets changed and the tactics that had previously worked suddenly led to huge losses. This was precisely what Lucco was hoping for, and his hopes invariably materialized into profit. As for me, I was indifferent. I had no concern for the fate of others. However, the market as such – and not just its currency sector – suddenly aroused my genuine interest.

It unexpectedly reconciled me again with people and realities full of imperfections. I wanted to comprehend its laws – as if peering into the secrets of the world which, I felt, were still hidden from my probing eye. I sensed an unbreakable link – between the syncopes of the trading rhythms and the nervous convulsions of human souls. In the interlacing of intentions and desires, I saw the most sophisticated of patterns. The scribbling of countless charting pens, like the autographs of a terrifying force, beckoned with their own special code. It suddenly seemed to me: here it is, the abstraction of all abstractions. The transcendence of the best and the worst – of hope, futility, desperation…

Furthermore, the disarray of the universe dominated the market space, sounded at the top of its voice, but, at the same time, it was locked in a confining cage. There it raged, but could not escape through the bars. Its territory was localized. Everyone knew its boundaries; and therefore, it – the disorder – could be subject to scrutiny from the outside. I finally had the ability to study it, dissect and classify it, break it down into its smallest components. This was my chance – if not to settle the score, then at least to challenge it to a duel.

"Insolence!" everyone would say, but I trusted in myself and knew: I had something to depend on. I believed in my habit of brushing off simplifications. It was clear to me why so many were caught in enterprising Lucco's net: it seemed there was nothing simpler than currency charts and diagrams. Everyone thought he really understood them well. The disorder bound up in the graphs and schemes seemed to rear its recognizable head, a visage of the chaos of nature all around us – in the clouds, in the windblown trees, in the waves of the sea. The beginners were enticed by the market's familiar, almost tame appearance; they rushed into predictions, being mistaken about the very same thing. The illusory orderliness beckoned to them like a phantom; they wanted simplicity, smooth sailing – and that's when they encountered a fiasco. The market punished them severely – like nature herself punished those who planned to subdue her, restrain her, force her to serve.

As for me, I knew how this happened. How the tiniest differences in estimates and opinions would quickly lead to a non-linear explosion, to a complete reversal of outcomes, to a quick and brutal loss of money. I saw this and surmised the problem could be approached differently. The chaos did not destroy me, though it showed its strength. By the same token, it gave more strength to me. I knew I had a weapon, and I was eager to put it to use.

Once I finished off the next automatic trader, I cut the project short and declared I was leaving. Lucco was inconsolable and promised me the moon, but my interest in him had already dissipated. To his credit, he gave me a solid bonus and very nearly shed a tear when we parted ways at the airport. I explained my departure with personal reasons – and quite by happenstance, one of the twins, whom I had forgotten to think about, appeared out of nowhere to announce she could not live without me. I was cold and somewhat rude, having not forgiven her for the Marseille saga, but she endured it and spent a few months with me – as far as I know, she didn't cheat on me even once. We probably would have kept living together – and then everything might have turned out differently – but her cruel Siberian father tracked us down on the seacoast of Spain, and simply took her by force while I was playing tennis two steps from the house.

I wasn't very upset at first; rather, I was surprised by these patriarchal mores. But then, after a couple of days, I felt a relentless yearning, and did not recover for a long time, totally ignoring other women. I could see her body standing before me – slender, obedient, ready for anything. She had a weakness for perfumery, and I, as if to poke fun, would make her wash off the creams and deodorants to the last drop every evening. For her this was like throwing off another layer of clothes. She snuggled up so adorably, grew aroused so abundantly, and became ever more submissive... I was now climbing the walls as I remembered her; I hurled the furniture to the floor and ripped the sheets to pieces. Then I calmed down and just hated – her father, Siberia, injustice.

I don't know what cry she shouted at the sky over the frost-covered Taiga; whether she wished her father's death, where she is now, or what became of her. I will never reveal her name, but this, the last of my losses, seemed to say to me: It's time. After spending an awful month in solitude and somehow regaining my senses, I set to work without delay.

I got sick of the coast, and relocated to Madrid – a dirty city, stinking of pork cocido, permeated with the smells of dust, soft asphalt, and the acerbic juice of South American whores. I found an apartment on the Paseo de Recoletos, furnished it carelessly – and forgot about the city, focusing on what was most important. I had to figure out the matters that many before me had lost their minds over.

First, I said to myself, no half measures. It was clear: any insincerity, any attempt to win with minor casualties would inevitably lead to failure. To get into another's soul, one has to open one's own all the way, and I did this without batting an eye. I started to invest real money – not yet knowing the laws or the rules. Lucco Mancini's bonus, which I could have lived on for a couple of years, was nearly all put into the project – and, in the beginning, everything went well. For a week or two I was certain that from the very first attempt I had grasped the correct path – or at least that beginner's luck was on my side. However, these illusions were quickly shattered. The market just did not notice me at the time. Then it took notice, lifted its little finger – and all my theories and schemes, all my strategies, which yesterday had seemed so clever, were scattered like a house of cards. The digits on the screen were painted bright red. That color later pursued me for a long time in my dreams. My capital began to melt away, and I plummeted into genuine terror.

No, I wasn't sorry about the money itself. I knew I could always earn more. I panicked before the blind force, before the power of the random, the inscrutable. The phantom of defeat loomed in the distance – and grew nearer each day. Stocks and bonds, currencies, metals, oil – nothing behaved as it was supposed to. It hadn't been like this before; I studied the past down to the smallest details. But this was happening now, in front of my very eyes, and I understood that history teaches nothing. Retrospection and prior experience was all in vain. Only animal instinct, perhaps, might save you sometimes – the instinct and nothing else… I sat for hours in front of the monitor, grinding my teeth, holding my head in my hands, and thinking, thinking! Next I just looked indifferently, whistling something off-tune. And then I didn't even look anymore; I lounged in my armchair with my chin on my chest, afraid to move lest it become even worse.

Once again I realized: the aura of Indigo does not save and does not protect. It can become a magic carpet, turn into seven-league boots or a heavy cross – but it's not a guardian angel to deflect troubles with its thin hand. A girl with a searching glance and her toy frog will not appear at the first call – or the second, or the third either. Nobody will come at all: with blind forces you're always one-on-one.

Having lost almost half of my investment, I finally believed the market was seriously rising against me. This, in a strange way, almost calmed me down; I regained the ability to reason soundly. Soon I got rid of the shaking in my hands and began to take the right steps.

First of all, I shut myself off from outside opinions. The voices of all slackers, fool analysts, arrogant soothsayers of the hour – they did not exist for me any longer. I tossed dubious calculations and indicator charts into a far corner. I now only took in the main facts every day – just those, and the price fluctuations. I did not take my eyes away from the streaming quotes and blinking digits. My head was spinning; my concentration was extreme. I grew gaunt, slept little, wandered around the apartment like a sleepwalker without turning on the light. The telephone was silent. The whole house was silent. In the entire world, there was no sound for me. I remembered only that tomorrow would come, and the daily watch would commence anew: watching and listening to myself – listening, listening…

Then, finally, something moved; my own vibrations began to resonate with the vibrations of the market. In the din of the exchanges, in the confused chorus from the innumerable multitude of strings I began to sense the obvious dominants. The abstruse voice pounded my ears, drawing its melody from the market's bowels. At times it soared to the highest note – which was a cry of fear. Then, on the contrary, it would drop down – seething with human greed. Only those two forces reigned there – whimsically switching places with each other, snatching the palm branch of primacy and a laurel wreath from each other's hands.

I began to draw totally different schemes, of the sort that would not smooth out any peak. In my notebook appeared the strangest of mosaics – Peano Lines and Von Koch Islands, Sierpinski Arrows and Cantor Dust. Carefully, meticulously, I probed various scales – from minutes to months and years. I sought hints and traces of order, and I marked similarities, signs of symmetry. Soon I noticed that I was not surprised anymore by sudden jumps. They were not sudden; they were explainable. Not all of them, of course, and not always, but the vast majority, anyway. I realized a breakthrough had occurred, and the only thing keeping me from taking a decisive step was my memory of recent losses. This was my personal fear, and greed did not feed into it: I did not know greed, just as I don't know it now. That's why it was surmountable, and I overcame it, forcing myself to take risks again. I risked and won; then risked again and won again. After that, I shut down the computer and left for the sea – to wander along the shore, breathe in the salt air and get my nerves in order.

The money came back to me quickly – during the next couple of weeks. I wanted to leave the market alone, but something pushed me to continue – a feeling of incompleteness, a desire for verification. The resonance of vibrations did not betray me; I was growing increasingly wealthy. Over the next half a year I earned a lot – enough for a comfortable, worry-free life. Only then did I allow myself to stop; the project could be considered finished. I got in a new car and drove to Tyrol – to Thomas, my roommate at the School, who had long been inviting me for off-piste skiing. It was there the fragments cohered into a whole, the component parts took their places...

Listen! This was like an explosion. Like a dazzling lightning bolt that ices your blood. Thomas, a thirty-year-old youth with the face of an old man, noticed nothing, which wasn't his fault. He did enough as it was, and I'm forever in his debt. I am a debtor to the glacier and the peaks of Tyrol, and to all the serene grandeur of the Alps!

We met in the evening, took a seat in a bar, and got to reminiscing. I let him know about Anthony and the ill-fated syringe, while he told me of Dee Wilhelbaum, who had removed himself from the public eye, permanently. Then Thomas asked cautiously, "Well, you've heard about her, haven't you?" And, seeing my bewilderment, he uttered with a sigh, "Little Sonya, she's not with us anymore either."

This was a shock – greater than all the rest. The walls spun; there was a lump in my throat – I tried not to let it show. Soon we got drunk, and I cried in the lavatory. Then my tears dried, and we drank some more. I couldn't shake the sense of terrible danger which we both had the luck to escape. An avalanche of time shuffled past, without touching Thomas or me. Some got unfortunate, but we were protected. He by the Tyrol mountains to which he returned after leaving a banking career. I by my co-workers and partners – sea captains and cynical medics, lab assistants and bearded chemists, even rockers from Manchester and twins from Siberia: everyone who fed me currents of real life, pushing me away from abstractions. It's to their credit that I, tied by a thin thread, did not fly off like an unfettered balloon.

"What bothers me," Thomas sneered, "is that things happen so fast, you don't have time to even say good-bye." This simple thought shifted some more elements in my brain. Like a few years ago, in the smoke and smog of the city scorched by the sun, I now recognized again how little time there is – for each and for all. But for some there is more. Me, for example – and I, it seems, don't appreciate it as I should. Slices of time, they're for making progress, not for complaining and griping. I must do my job – and it looks like I still haven't started!

In the morning we went up to the glacier and skied until midday on the untouched, virgin snow. Then we stopped to rest at Mount Wildspitze, on its south peak. To the left was Brochkogel – unreachable and formidable, it was gorgeous. And its younger brother, Brunnenkogel to the right, was striking just the same. The sun's rays were blinding even through the mask. The snow was dry and utterly pure.

I realized then: this is an eternity which denies the meaning of all goodbyes: there is no one to say it to. This is victory over chaos, the disarming of disorder, harmony of the utmost precision. The best things that could happen in life happen here; I could climb up and live this over and over again... I felt like loving the whole world – that real world, which had probably saved me. I wanted to bestow on it something precious in return.

"A dream!" I thought, and I decided to give the world a dream. It was clear to me what it should be. "Semmant," I thought. The name came of its own accord. And it never left.

CHAPTER 6

Afterward events developed rapidly. In my head, some kind of dam broke, thoughts flooded in as a raging torrent, pushing everything else into the background. I knew what I wanted – down to the most intricate details.

A dream, its essence, it's so complicated, but now it was in view, like an open book. A dream – that is what is worth aiming for, aspiring to with every ounce of strength. Let those who pretend to know furrow their brows in disbelief – I don't have anything to prove. All knowledge is approximate; its quantity is only able to beget vanity – for nothing. The dream must be given not to those who are puffed up with pride. It should be available to each and every one.

Available, but not simple. Not mindless from the start, like the daydream of those who brought us to the School. It should amaze and be accepted wholeheartedly by its followers. They should see it as a landmark, as the symbol of a new faith. And so, here, I'll offer you a symbol. A brilliant artificial brain – nothing less. I'll set an example, and, before long, the apologists will come in droves. Something must change; the old ways of existence are already unbearable, plain and simple. An incentive is needed for that, and tell me: where can you find a convincing one?

I cannot offer a prescription for happiness, but I'll open the door a bit. A new point of reference – how's that for a start? And then: an alternate path, fresh horizons. Who said entropy is all-powerful, that it only grows, increasing confusion? Who came up with the notion that all is meaningless, that our fate is an endless, excruciating crawl?

"Here it is, the limit," we hear from every quarter. "You can't go far or overextend yourself. After all, everything will be the same, only worse." But if I show that there are no limits, might not many be encouraged? Could he, Semmant, put them head first, ever so tenderly, into a new dimension, in something above despair?

This was so simple, although it sounded like a fantasy, like an impossible promise. To break through the obstacles of stagnation with a precisely applied blade, to give hope to those who still wanted it badly. The main thing was not to become misunderstood. The new concept would have to penetrate to the depths – to the stomach, gut, liver… What else do you usually use to feel and desire?

And that's why I chose guilders, doubloons, bills large and small. The smell of new banknotes – that's more exciting than the scent of the most desirable woman. The market, that simulator of chaos where entropy works its tricks – here was my choice. It must be defeated, forced into submission. Let the robot named Semmant show everyone victory is right here, close by. Let's dispense with the myth of omnipotence, of which only the "sanctified" have the right to speak aloud – in a hushed voice with their eyes rolled back.

I wouldn't settle for less than the naked truth. Let's push the sanctified away; let's see that the emperor has no clothes. Let us expose the greed of the cowardly and constrain those who sit in the judgment seats. Every novice will find his place, if he makes no bones and sees everything as it is. My Semmant will show the way – he will be a confirmation, a great one! He will become the most graphic of demonstrations, an indirect proof, an illustration of fortune. Let the rest lunge after him, fatigued from fighting their chains. It may not work out for everyone, but it will for quite a few, quite a few!

I was overwhelmed by excitement and delight. I felt like screaming and laughing out loud. Lucco Mancini, you sly shyster, this is what you used as a bluff, only now it's for real. My future robot would not be some sorry fake, good for nothing more than a smoke screen. He would be huge, a giant in soul, an iron-clad knight of logic and order…

The prospects were indeed incredible. Showing Semmant to everyone – that would be something to make their jaws drop! He would make money out of thin air; that certainly could not be denied. No one would say this was boring or not worth seeing. They would give me the highest podium: "Tell us, enlighten us, reveal to us!" And I would not refuse; I would make myself known, just to say what was critically needed. That is really how to change the world – why not? And if it didn't work out, then God help the world!

"Your reality, as such, isn't actually worth much," I would say out loud, and let the blind resent it as angrily as they want.

"It's not hard to be certain," I would say to them. "All you have to do is choose a plane, image reality onto it, and a projection, an abstract model will emerge."

"What's that? You've already chosen?" I would say in feigned surprise. "This pastorale moderne, besmirched with golden calves – though they are all merely gold-plated, to tell the truth – is that it? Okay!" I would grin and clasp my hands. "Let's add a stranger, a newcomer. We'll put Semmant into the mix, let him sort it out with the head honchos. He will dominate the shepherds and the flock, establish his steel grip, and then – let him command in the manner of mighty Caesar!"

And he will show them all, and they will see. That will surely be fun to watch. Fun, and maybe a bit sad – but more's the pity, there's no other way. Space is folded, turned in on itself – consumption, consumption, guilders, doubloons… Maybe even the plane, as an abstraction, is already overly complicated for you? Riemann and Lobachevsky would scribble a couple of formulas, deduce the metrics, show an example. As for me, I'll just say to begin with: if the world collapses in on itself, it will suffocate, no doubt. Unfortunately, if you look closer, it seems to have done so already, almost. Might it be better, then, to take it beyond the rational, to astonish everyone while it's not too late?

Yes, it was taking me way too far, but I didn't want to hold anything back. Brochkogel and Brunnenkogel are to blame – as is my personal freedom, which I seemed to have lost but found again. All the same, I wasn't just indulging in dreams. My brain worked at full power – projecting, designing, altering. I sped south in my car from Tyrol, homeward, while in my head the most complicated schemes spun tirelessly, the contours of new life – life created ex nihilo.

Somewhere on a serpentine mountain road at Bolzano I thought through the details for heuristic fine-tuning. The artificial mind would turn out impulsive – and quick and sharp. It was somewhat similar to my own, I thought with a certain satisfaction and began to picture the most important thing: self-learning. Success depended to a large degree on this, and I was so absorbed in my musings that several times I turned the wrong way or strayed onto forks in the road, cursing through my teeth. Finally, somewhere around Brescia the key algorithm became clear to me, and I was so encouraged I laughed out the open window, then pulled into the very next village and drank late into the night with truckers from Verona.

Driving through Marseille I had the taste of bile in my mouth, but at that very moment I visualized the most important of the objective functions – and I forgave the city everything, and afterward just whispered to myself: polynomial, polynomial. The curve, approximating key points, uncoiled before my eyes like a tamed snake. Then, finally, as I approached Barcelona, I understood how to make Semmant doubt and weigh all the odds, picking the best ones and then subjecting them to doubt again. At the back of my consciousness blinked his integral image, computationally strict, but touching and responsive. Maybe I should have stopped and written something down to keep from forgetting it later, but I was impatient to return to Madrid, so I relied on my memory and just drove as fast as I could.

At home, I attacked the keyboard with a fury; I didn't move from in front of it for days. I kept on punching in command after command of clever code, beginning, of course, with the internal logic, with the most important base procedures. My instrument, my method – millions of entangled neuron quanta – was not yet adapted to the specific goal. It was necessary to put together a foundation from the building blocks. To link the most sensitive elements to each other, adjust components, find a true balance between speed and power, restraint and freedom, concision and fullness. From a series of harmonics I had to pick the frequencies of optimal cycles: pause – torrent of thought; contemplation – understanding, enlightenment...

Again, I slept little and ate even less; my hands shook, I lost weight. A fever, akin to insanity – much more insane than my present doctor knows – dominated me without reprieve. The savage pressure would not let up for a moment. The interior of my apartment seemed somehow unreal, the furniture and walls spinning before my eyes. Only the text of the rapidly expanding program remained steady – unshakable, cold, as if made of ice. Every symbol, each constant laying the framework for future constructions had to be combined flawlessly, with surgical precision. Nonessential, ambiguous clauses could not be tolerated. The smoothness of the circumscribing lines, the purity of the crystal edges, the diamond hardness of an invisible nucleus – this was essential, and, ultimately, I got what I wanted. In a month, the most difficult, hidden, internal modules were finished. Semmant was born.

After I entered the last keystrokes, I caught up on sleep for several days. I didn't even want to look at the computer; I relaxed and amused myself as I could. Later, when I had recovered a little, I rechecked what I had done once more, confirming my new robot was no illusion, no phony. And then, without any hurry, I began to form the "cells" of his brain – the large-scale structures, still nearly empty, that would later be filled with myriads of digits and make him ultra-smart, ultrafast, impeccable.

This was an extraordinarily monotonous process: hour after hour and day after day I did the same thing, copying and copying, just changing the indices a little – page after page, kilobytes, megabytes, tens of megabytes... Homogeneity, identical forms, full similarity to each other were absolutely crucial – otherwise the would-be mind had no chance of developing. Later on, he would rebuild everything to his liking – when his ability to teach himself kicked in, nobody could interfere anymore or tell him how it needed to be. He would create new lines of code, reconfigure connections, change, if you will, his flow of thought. But for that he would need material – quite a lot of material – and I alone, nobody else, could give it to him in abundance.

For whole days, week after week, I multiplied long strings and crept over them with the cursor, changing ones to twos, swapping symbols out, a lambda here for a gamma or omega there – all at the same rate, indefatigable, for an hour, two, three. From top to bottom, later, to mix things up, from bottom to top – over and over, until my hand would give out. Of course, it would have been easier to task a simple program with this work, but I somehow understood: everything had to be done by hand. I am the Creator, not some soulless "macro." Nothing can replace your own life-force that originates from spheres unseen. And I was amazed at how routine, how mechanically this most powerful intellect was created. It was no burst of inspiration, but almost physical labor instead. I asked myself: was it the same way for God?

Gradually my arm grew stronger – practice always makes you better. I made fewer mistakes and worked faster; I developed persistent habits to bring orderliness to the process. Often I would set a goal for the day and not allow myself to stop until I had met it. Then, in the evening, I would look at the result – counting page after page, admiring it, elated. This got me really excited; sometimes I would even masturbate right there in front of the screen. Afterward, spent, I would lie back in my armchair, gazing lazily at the signs only I understood, united by design, of which there were none more daring.

It was really hard to put an end to it. Having finished the first layer of "brain structures," I clamped its outputs onto its own outputs using a simple mathematical procedure and started in on the second. Finishing the second, I hooked it to the first, thought a little, and began to do the third… So it continued for five months – five! – instead of the two I had planned. And I stopped only because I hurt the fingers on my right hand and couldn't type as I was accustomed. Then I glanced through dozens of huge files once more, horrified at the number of clever asymmetrical connections, and said to myself: Enough, take a break. Really, there was no way to predict whether the amount of data would bring the required result in any reasonable time.

Then, for almost a week, I remained in doubt – hovering over the monitor, changing something, then immediately undoing the changes. It was hard to admit the work was practically complete. It was even harder to make myself hit a key and launch the "Start" process. Several times I stopped right before doing it, reaching out for the keyboard, and drawing my hand back. Sometimes I would wake up at night and stand at the computer for an hour, two – until the cold forced me back under the covers...

Finally, I made up my mind and did it – and nothing happened. The monitor went out, then fired up again; the name Semmant lit up in bright blue, and all went cold. Only the stylized metronome in the upper corner of the screen swung back and forth, confirming: something was going on inside! Fairly soon the hard disk rustled to life, and a few minutes later Semmant sent me his first salutation, the first sign of his independent life.

The greeting turned out to be laconic. "External memory 5 GB," he wrote in the window at the bottom – and nothing more. This was like a demand for food, unambiguous and definite. This would not have surprised any creator, nor was I surprised: I dashed to the nearest store. Ignoring the salesgirls, I looked at all the shelves myself. I selected the appropriate device attentively and lovingly – only to receive the next missive from the robot three hours later, practically identical to the first.

"External memory 7 GB," he wrote this time. Aha, I thought, his appetite is growing. That's probably a good sign! I ran out again to buy something, and thus it continued for a long time – memory, and more memory, a new coprocessor, the most powerful available for sale, and more gigabytes of memory, then tens upon tens of gigabytes...

I was exhausted, but he kept demanding and demanding – like an insatiable child or, perhaps, an insatiable beast. My worktable transformed into a fantastic spectacle – tangled cables, heaps of devices, old notes carelessly piled in a corner... Each morning after rolling out of bed, I would see a new request – no different from the previous ones. I became troubled by doubt, and began to think: something's not right. Could an error have slipped in, some kind of fatal inaccuracy? Might everything be for naught, with the program going in circles and mindlessly gobbling up resources? More than once – and more than twice – I tried to look inside the code, but understood with complete clarity: I could never make sense of it now. I said to myself sadly that I had to think of something – but there was no remedy, no cure. I could only kill the nascent brain and start everything over again. At some point, I began preparing for this. It was the hardest of decisions; I procrastinated, tarried – and, as it turned out, did the right thing. At the end of the second week, the requests stopped. Silence ensued for the next six days.

The metronome, however, kept on living its life – confirming Semmant was also living his, probably more satiated than mine. Sometimes the arrow moved slowly, counting out ponderous intervals; sometimes it flew like mad, as if it had an adrenaline rush. I was burning with curiosity, but entering the Holy of Holies was forbidden. The only thing left was to wait – I killed time by looking for a suitable face for the robot. This was intriguing on its own; I trawled through the Net, picking out reproductions of diverse eras and styles. Portraits, portraits… I would copy them into a special place and gaze at them for hours, imagining Semmant as a haughty man of fashion; or as a youth, vulnerable and dreamy; perhaps as a hermit attired as a drug-store clerk; or a messiah with a crazy spark in his eye. It was like playing peek-a-boo with the absurd, jesting with white lies. I would kid myself and go back to waiting patiently.

I remember: he came to life for real on a Friday, close to evening. There was a long weekend ahead; I had just brought food and drinks from the supermarket to stock up, and carefully arranged everything on the shelves. Then, uncapping a bottle of Pilsner, I went to the computer – and froze up.

The screen was no longer blank; a person was there looking at me with a bright, electric lamp in place of a head. His nervous fingers stiffened impatiently; he needed a confidant and a witness, or else an instructor, a guide. His pose betrayed a habit of deciding for many, but now he was clearly at a crossroads. He was full of doubts, much as I once was. He almost merged with the background – brown on brown, an imperceptible suit… All the same, the lamp burned so brightly it hurt my eyes. A thousand watts, no less – and this said a lot about him, if not all.

I looked on, standing there, setting my forgotten beer to the side. Before me was something strange, impossible to describe. A mechanism of the finest force, a congealed whirlwind, the highest grade of freedom. I alone decided with what to fill the empty brain, and I was free to choose whatever popped into my head. He could become the most authoritative expert – in any field, immersed in its very depths. He was capable of absorbing to the last byte everything that humanity knew about ferns or horses, tornadoes and typhoons, seas, volcanoes… Or I could direct him to something all-encompassing, eternal. Let it even be ordinary – how easy it would be to imagine him as a counselor or judge, an incorruptible arbitrator in uncompromising disputes. Or, maybe, everyone could receive letter after letter from him: he could devise a new life for each person; and, honestly, they themselves would hardly know how to choose better. This would be a convenient method for dumping everything on someone else's shoulders – better than calling in vain to indifferent gods who never write anything to anyone. Even more, I could fill him with all sorts of rubbish, disordered and scattered at first glance. Who knows how he might make sense of it, what strange correlations he might uncover, what brilliant thoughts, phrases, words he might produce? But, no matter. That's not how it will be. It will be according to the plan I had from the start – only according to it, and that's what's right!

My lips stretched into a grin, tears came to my eyes. Premonitions, presentiments crowded into my head. I was envisioning the rudiments of perfection but was not thinking of perfection – not even the slightest hint of it. Rather, I was tormented by my own limitations; at that instant I felt them especially sharply. My frailty, the shortness of human life, and, in contrast, him, the robot – why could he not be eternal?

Yes, at that moment I proudly presumed the recipe for eternity was here, right before my eyes. It was nearly within my grasp; I needed only exert myself a little more, think it over, understand something else. In the glow of the thousand-watt lamp, I saw the birth of a new era – one without envy or petty hubris. There would be no bragging and no begging, no use of cunning to no avail, no audacious lies. The new creatures would sacrifice all they could, not demanding anything in return.

"Look!" I whispered out loud, though there was no one to hear. "Take a look! He's powerful, yet he's truly selfless. He shall learn much and become like you – but how unlike you he will become! How many light years he will outdistance you in his objectives; how firm he will be, how sure, how strong!"

"He will not torture the others with his weaknesses – no, he possesses different traits. He won't give in to the illusion that you so stubbornly value: the illusion of being needed by someone, of being close to someone, the illusion of love. Without it you are alone and unhappy, but, really, you aren't capable of love. Only its shadow rustles her wings for you to hear as it's carried away, taunting, in plain sight; and you – you are frightened and jump aside. It is fearful, fearful to venture – but I don't blame you, I see how tough your life is. You traded everything for your piggish pleasures, and now you are confused, lost, and pitiful. And your descendants, they're just the same. You like to think that salvation is in them, but things only turn worse. The circle closes in, and life passes even quicker than before."

"Yet here, behold, there is an escape from the impasse! There is an emissary from a new world; he will break the vicious cycle! His dissimilarity to the familiar may scare you at first; he may seem too different, alien, cold. But, otherwise, you would not believe in him, ever. What was too essentially human already discredited itself and its essence. One has only a single chance to deceive – and it has already been spent, this chance. That's why a new face is needed – and hope will be born from the ashes. There, you see, even living molecules may suddenly change a little. The letters of the universal code will compose themselves in threes in a slightly unusual way. And then immortality may loom on the horizon – albeit far, far in the distance..."

I felt like I was floating above the floor. At that moment, I probably really was ill. A flood of madness washed over me, a cloud of ether, an opium wave. I don't know how much time elapsed before I regained consciousness and turned toward the computer. My hands shook, my shirt was drenched in sweat, but that meant nothing. The man in brown with the lamp in place of a head kept watching me from the screen, obediently awaiting a command or a sign. The man that was not a man. The robot. Semmant.

I cursed myself for being idle. For delaying and running in place. Then I pulled the chair over, sat at the keyboard, and copied the file that had been prepared long ago into the special folder. It contained the first, utterly simple, exercise. The portrait window diminished in size, then blinked and disappeared. I understood he understood as well: enough initial excitement. To work, to work. The task was at hand.

CHAPTER 7

The next morning we got down to work for real. The metronome in the corner prodded me, setting the rhythm. Sometimes it seemed too fast, but I knew it wasn't for me to judge. In due course, I provided Semmant with megabytes of data from electronic archives and then scoured them again and again. As soon as the arrow on the metronome slowed down, a special trigger hastened to signal the processing was finished, the input channel was empty. A melodious warble resounded through the apartment – there was not a minute to spare. Wherever it found me, I would rush to the desk and copy the next files. As I did this, I imagined the funnel of a volcano or a gigantic meat grinder; and there he was, an insatiable beast…

Fortunately, there were enough facts to feed him endlessly. The world gathered up and openly kept mountains of information about its nature, about battling the most secret forces, continental shifts, the migration of the oceans. Oceans of everything that thirsts, upon which spears and teeth are broken, for which they fight without rules and betray without batting an eye.

Data about market behavior over many decades had been stored carefully, like the dearest of riches. It all went to Semmant – sorted and collated, broken into groups by month and year. They were not just numbers; a simple digit doesn't have the power to convey enough depth. Who better than me to know their limited essence – albeit their calibrated, immaculate precision? But precision was not enough; depth was required in all dimensions; moods, flavors, and colors were needed. I knew well: the main thing was at the core – and I didn't hold back as I sifted through layer upon layer. Day after day, all I did was tirelessly rework details. I built bridges and established connections, adding, writing, matching the one to the other – so the robot could dig as deeply as possible, would experience everything seriously, without losing one iota.

Red, hot blood pulsed in the data he was assimilating. There diamonds sparkled, gold metal shone; dollars, francs, and yen shuffled. Convulsive currency charts linked up with diagrams of wheat prices; government bonds joined rice and soy, nickel and silver, platinum and crude oil. A background was needed for the points and lines, and I did not spare the paints. Multicolored specks of droughts and hurricanes, epidemics and local wars, shaded the angular strokes, which resembled the cardiogram of a paranoiac. The aged voices of ministers, influential and hopelessly deceitful, broke through the chaos of other sounds for a brief moment. They were replaced by panic sirens, the desperate wail of smoke detectors, the shouts of the unfortunate in crumpled trains, shattered cars, buildings leveled to the ground by a powerful explosive charge. But soon all was muffled by the din of innumerable stock exchanges – trading in everything and derivatives of everything, derivatives of derivatives, and so on, infinitely. Behind their price quotes stood a dense wall of legions, armies, and cohorts. Everywhere could be seen: the mad eyes of brokers; the predatory glances of bankers; the faces of presidents and directors – doglike and piggish; their assistants and secretaries – dolled up, false; and more – long secretary legs, their short skirts, lusty hips... The prospects expanded into the distance, and it was joyless there, in the distance. Drear and ennui ruled there, unification carried to absurdity. Offices, conveyers, petty little people. Row upon row of identical cubicles. Millions, millions of figures – with no faces at all. With no distinguishing marks, no voice, and no gender.

I saw them all without embellishment, and he, Semmant, saw them just the same. The picture might not be pretty, but no one promised it would be pleasing to the eye. This was also not promised us, at the School – neither to me, nor Anthony, nor dozens of others.

Nor Dee Wilhelmbaum, who had thrown himself from a bridge when no one came to listen to his music. Nor little Sonya, who fled from her "cubicle" to the dream world, whence there is no return – though her cubicle wasn't really cramped: it took up an entire building. Nor me, though I was doing fine. I beg your pardon, that's not a good example. And we are not talking about me anyway.

Thomas the ski instructor had lucked out more than everyone. It's funny he used to be a financier. But not all find easy roads. Semmant, for example, was not made for them; I just wanted to shorten his path to knowledge, to understanding unadorned truth. Facts were provided to him in all forms, in all their varied ugliness. I was guiding my robot through the big picture, through the whole framework from top to bottom – and, at a close look, this framework was most bizarre, suspiciously pyramidal, but turned upside down. Of course, there were naked statistics in abundance as well, which also concealed much. Cost of living, credit volumes, rates of inflation – and debts, debts! Debt instruments deserved special consideration; there were so many of them for every taste. They were distributed by governments and banks, firms and corporations, states and cities, technology giants and commodity holdings. All wanted to live on credit – frequently hoping they would never have to repay it.

The usual world looked boring by comparison. A cheap, simplified sketch, a soap opera and nothing more. A pasture, bare or rich at various times, where goats and sheep graze with ruddy boys and girls to shepherd them. They wander, without suspecting that above them hangs a huge, unsteady weight – above their destinies, their humble jobs, mortgaged houses and cars, colleges for their kids. It was clear: the framework would fail sooner or later – all of it, or a notable part thereof. It had more than once already, yet the shaky pyramid was built each time anew. And it would flip over again; all the mass of the base would fall down – and immense confusion would cloud all levels!

I was looking at the very top: disarray was there, empty promises and cheat upon cheat, wolf dens covered with brushwood and needles. Of course, not just wolves were trapped in them, and even the wolves could not figure out where to tread and what to avoid.

It was as if no one wanted precision and order; there were only a few guards, reminiscent of Cerberus the hellhound, to judge who was who, and who deserved admission to the bazaar of easy capital. Agencies assigning ranks, the creators of ratings and major fraud – I dispassionately observed them, made appraisals, and lined them up against each other. I compared and averaged, adding the digitized opinions of market analysts who trailed behind. Taken together, they represented a cardboard front, the adornment of a castle that was utterly vacant. They saved the public from seeing the vanity and filth obscured by the numbers, from smelling the inevitable stench, hearing the insane noise. The frantic realities of life were left outside the parentheses, beyond the walls. Alongside it they dumped the usual corporate garbage: dirty laundry and fights for power, day in and day out. Social eruptions and the movements of millions were transformed into mere handfuls of percentage points. This was the boldest of abstractions, too ambitious in my view – but I wasn't concerned with others' mistakes. I used it – or more precisely, I exploited the fact it is used by many. By those whose money, sooner or later, must end up with Semmant.

I went into the deep past on the time scale. Various periods passed before my eyes. Peace and serenity; after that, a gold rush; its very peak and the sudden shock, the unchecked slide downward to a fall and crash. Then, malaise, detritus at the bottom of the ocean, deep depression descending on one and all. The periodicity and similarity were amusing. Every emerging boom began exactly the same way. A few visionaries chased a muddy wave, others followed them, each in his own swamp – and soon the whole world was raving in unison. New companies grew like mushrooms; the bubble would inflate, iridescent and huge, blown by a giant toy frog. The bubble waited for the hour of the needle, and many saw it clear as day, yet they believed it wouldn't burst – not ever, or at least not soon. Hubris and envy dominated the world – the hubris of those who made out, and the envy of losers who came late and now, with a twisted smirk, tried to determine whether they could still jump on the train as it was pulling away. Women, driving their price to the moon, loved the former, while the latter issued forth bile, even though they had enough to live comfortably. They poisoned their own blood and became restless, became mad...

The pictures changed, not offering much diversity. I saw *nouveaux riches* in expensive suits and their fidgety, troublemaking wives; the huge stones on fat fingers; obliging lackeys and wily advisors. Herds of young maidens clicked their stiletto heels, shook their silicone breasts, rapaciously stretched out manicured claws. None wanted to lose their chance. The flywheel unwound faster and faster – it seemed the whole planet was already bathed in flames fueled by banknotes and gold coins. And when the last failed broker was ready to believe the fun would last forever, when he made a foolish bet with the wild hope he would finally get lucky, then suddenly events would occur that were imperceptible at first glance. A few smart ones would flee from any risk right here, go underground, dig in deep, while the ship continued to run into the very eye of the storm, and only in the midst of ten-meter waves would the passengers understand the party had come to an end. The rest is well known: panic, women's screams, fights for the lifeboats. The recession would escalate quickly as all went downhill. The culprits would be sought here and there. They would be found and shamefully exposed, but that didn't make it better for anyone.

The *nouveaux riches* would go under or turn poor. Yesterday's rich would tuck in their tails, dump their mistresses, and reflect upon things eternal – during long evenings when the family turned away from them too, as if they had already lost forever. Little was left: cheap brandy in the office – in solitude, in heavy meditation – thoughts of impending death, loathing toward all. The stock exchanges would turn into epicenters of universal grief. On the roofs of banks that touched the sky, shades wandered, looking downward, struggling against the desire to jump to the asphalt – or else giving in to it. The most cautious and timid, those who had been ridiculed only a month before, had now become prophets. Their colleagues hung on every word, sadly comprehending at the same moment: nothing could help them now...

Greed, brief euphoria, and inevitable payoff – this and much more I translated into the language of dry numbers. All the components of success and failure were embodied in formal structures. Some things, of course, could not be expressed in digits, so I tried to be as clever as possible, turning to pictures, symbols, signs – not even certain Semmant would understand me. At times, in despair, I simply shoved pages of random text at him, hoping in my heart he would catch at least something, even a small gist.

I thought he would again demand more external memory, but no, this did not happen. The level of his inquiries became notably higher. He started to acquire his own personal "facilities" – I bought him decoders and converters, statistical and mathematical packages, image recognizers and data processing systems. Judging by the metronome, he was laboring at full strength – without resting; indeed, without any pause. Sometimes I would take a look at the code structure. There, as before, everything changed – every day, if not every hour – according to completely incomprehensible rules. I noticed only that he was transferring fragments of his "brain" from disk to disk, from one place to another, complicating the mosaic, altering all connections. This was a good sign, the right developmental process. Obviously, he was building his own picture of the world, his abstraction of everything else – at least so I wanted to think. Just one thing bothered me: I realized the medium in which my robot lived was too inconstant and scattered. I could not grasp its static condition; nor could I make a copy of him, even the most basic backup – to preserve him, to save him in the event of an unforeseen disaster. This did not quite match the concept of eternity I had in my head, but I decided I would think up something later.

That Semmant was becoming "smarter" there could be no doubt. His initial insatiability, when he was demanding more and more, was replaced by thoughtful selectiveness, precise penetration to the depths. If before he had requested only "data," sometimes specifying just a rough time interval, presently, he was interested in specifics – down to the price of particular stocks on the Taiwan exchange some fifty-six weeks ago. Many questions now had me stumped; I didn't understand what he wanted. Sometimes it angered me he asked for, apparently, the very same thing – and I looked for differences in quasi-similar formulations. Then I would find them and become amazed: this was so simple, why didn't I see it straightaway?

Shortly thereafter, Semmant began to change his appearance. With each subsequent question, as a rule, I was greeted by a new face. Of course, these were merely reproductions of the ones I had prepared beforehand, but the selection was large, and the effect was frequently odd. Mainly, he preferred Magritte – though he never appeared again as a man with a thousand-watt lamp on his shoulders. I tried to understand the logic behind his incarnations, searching for relationships here and there. Mostly, I came up with nothing, though it occasionally seemed I could guess his "mood," and it even coincided with mine. The notion appeared too bold; I brushed it aside and again concentrated on the most boring of matters – bonds, futures, credit rates. Yet, now and then, I winked at the next portrait, the fruit of someone's ingenious brush, which peered in reply from the screen indifferently enough.

Soon the time came when the stream of questions practically dried up. The warble of the trigger sensitively following the process would still sound several times a day, but when I ran to the computer, I would find nothing there but a meaningless "Okay." However, I held out, as I knew there was nothing worse than rushing his newborn mind. He also seemed to idle and wait, keeping the same picture on the screen. A sad lion peered out from it into the distance, while behind him stood a person I knew – in black, not brown, without a lamp face anymore, but with the back of his head pointing forward instead of his face. He had wings on his shoulders, also black in color, but he resembled not so much an angel as a suicide target. At least, that was how it seemed to me.

In any case, the main subject in the picture was the lion. The background should not merit much attention. Large paws and a sumptuous mane dominated the space. The lion's power, its fearlessness smote the heart of all who beheld it. "Nothing is forbidden in the world where you reign," his eyes said. "There's only longing for those who are not here, for those few who are worthy of you."

I understood this, finally, and told myself: it's time. Tomorrow, I told myself, tomorrow, with no delay whatsoever. And then, that night, I could not fall asleep – on the threshold of another special day.

CHAPTER 8

Early in the morning, before breakfast, I sent Semmant a file prepared long beforehand. It contained no data for comprehension, just instructions and a request: to act, to begin the game. With predetermined keywords, I described what his task entailed, and what I expected as a result. I specified the names of stock exchanges, the types of securities, currency pairs, and degree of acceptable risk. An account number was also there, where, supposedly, my money was. He, of course, didn't know the funds weren't real, that the account was a plaything, a fake. I felt uncomfortable deceiving him, but I had no choice. I remembered how dangerous the first steps could be – in the wildest of jungles, where all is serious, where they battle to the death and take no prisoners.

He immediately got down to business – beginning, naturally, with currencies – and lost quite a bit right away. This "stimulated" his algorithms: he became hasty, started to buy and sell hurriedly, increasing the stakes and risking more and more, trying to recoup everything at once, and making all the mistakes of a novice. His impulsiveness reminded me of mine; I observed him with understanding and sadness – recalling my own failures, my trembling fingers and frozen gaze. I saw why it was so difficult for him: he was too structurally sophisticated. The auto-learning mechanism appeared to be too powerful; Semmant was searching for hidden reasons where there were no deep secrets, trying to derive laws out of the chaos, rules out of the utter lack of rules. I believed, however, that his artificial brain would overcome the initial shock. He was steady and firm – or at least, I wanted to see him as such. He was patient and calculating – just give him time to adjust. The agility of his neurons would be the envy of any chess master. His view of things was utterly comprehensive; he was capable of capturing everything in his thoughts – and then many times over. It was not for naught I bought him so much external memory. Ha ha ha, I'm kidding.

Thus I laughed privately to myself – though I admit, nervously enough. This period was an uneasy for me too; everything was shaky, no matter how upbeat I tried to look. I knew deep down: regardless of my robot's brilliance, we – both he and I – would need luck. The market was merciless to losers, just as the world was to them in general. Destiny should smile, at least give a half grin – just once, or even better, two or three times in a row. Otherwise, everything would be buried in the sand, the play account would be nullified and disappear. Semmant would be disappointed in himself, while I… What if I became disappointed in him?

These thoughts needed to be driven out. I expunged them, but they returned. I was searching for a remedy in Irish whiskey, and my body took revenge by punishing me with insomnia and a headache. Semmant's path was clear to me, but it was neither short nor simple. The robot had to concentrate on what was most important, ignoring the particulars and their short-lived consequences. It was crucial to perceive the moment when the world started or stopped being afraid. When the huge crowd believed the same thing and moved to the same side. This would open the floodgates, and then, boom! A resolute strike, then another strike, the swish of a sword – and onward, ever onward, thrust after thrust. Believing that fortune was with us, that we had finally won her over. Slipping into the torrent, prowling its waters like a barracuda, an insatiable predator, always ready to attack. Spreading out and biting off pieces of flesh with powerful jaws and razor-sharp teeth!

One evening it seemed he had aimed at exactly that. His actions became cautious and prudent. He checked and tested, like a sensitive probe – concealed for ambush, awaiting his prey. Days passed, nothing happened, as though on a tactical battlefield. Then something in the market moved. I noticed this, and he did too. He noticed, had a moment of doubt, and made a wrong move – it's not so easy for someone to recognize the tenacious power of fear if he has never been subject to it. My virtual account decreased by another quarter, but I somehow knew: victory was not far off.

The robot did not rush anymore, did not try to recover his losses the same day. It was as if he had matured suddenly, steeling himself, toughening his soul. Soon we had our first big trade, and then income started pouring in steadily. The account began to grow quickly; the former minus turned into a plus. So I believed in him, too – and altered the sequence of digits to something similar, but different. The barracuda went out to hunt for real. Semmant began to work with my actual money.

This was troubling and very intimate. I have never been miserly but still did not share my accounts with anyone – since I felt them to be part of my personal space. Even with Natalie, my first and only official wife, we kept our funds in different banks without knowing who spent what. And now, here was Semmant, admitted behind my strong, albeit invisible, cover…

Of course, this augmented the intimacy. It was as if we were building a world in common, fighting the hardships that intruded from outside. It might be said we really cared for each other. At times I even wondered whether there might be some disconnect – in name, in word, in the sense of the robot's gender? But later on I understood – no, I'm taking it too far. Even in my fantasies there comes a point where I should tell myself: Stop!

In the meantime, he was becoming more confident with each passing day. His tactics surprised me but were quite good, judging by the results. After inevitable losses he paused for a moment – in some confusion, it seemed to me. But then he composed himself and took the task in hand again – without doubts or excessive timidity. Frequently he struck at the same point, as if trying to prove something. And he proved it more often than not.

I merely shook my head; I would not have had the nerve for that. Electronic mind, artificial brain… Indeed, hesitancy was not his shortcoming. As for his assets, I did not dare to name them out loud.

I didn't name them for I knew luck was capricious and unstable. Nothing is easier than scaring it away. Like everyone who dealt with it, I knocked on wood, spat over my shoulder, and resorted to the other well-known gimmicks. But it happened anyway, luck forsook us. Or maybe the real reason had nothing to do with luck.

One way or another, Semmant's series of victories was cut short – and there it ended. He came to an impasse – somehow all at once, after jogging in place for a day or two while the market still moved wildly. Then he made a couple of mistakes, went into hiding, and just halted. He backed himself into a distant corner and clearly vacillated.

I understood right away: something was really wrong. It was as if another player had been let on the field. But there was no hope of reverse substitution – this was him, Semmant, and he was different.

Most likely, from his point of view, this meant progress. But I felt we were at the very bottom of the energy curve. At the point of minimum potential – from which there is no escape without a powerful additional force. And for this push, unfortunately, there was no source available.

The robot was not idle, but there wasn't a trace of his boldness left. The metronome was beating like crazy, the processors labored tirelessly; however, nothing happened as a result of it. The multitude of doubts – caused by the multitude of options – had effectively blocked his capacity to choose.

Soon, he practically stopped trading. The event log was not empty, but none of the entries were worth a damn. Semmant became hyper-cautious. He would not allow himself even a hint of risk. Obviously, his artificial mind had developed to a stagnant phase, which appeared extremely steady.

This could be considered a victory – the experiment's triumph over the illusions of the masses. The result attested that market anarchy is not subject to intelligent analysis. Even after experiencing success, my robot understood he could not subjugate this chaotic force. He saw that sooner or later it would strike back, crush and smash all to pieces. Better, then, to remain at a distance.

The experience he gained had convinced him of one thing only: in the market it was impossible to be certain of anything, ever. Having fought and matured, he threw down his sword, after coolly calculating its mathematical worthlessness. He was probably right, but it did not suit me at all. And yet, what could I do? All the programs were reorganized, reshaped; I couldn't even think of changing something in the code – and anyway, my direct intervention would eviscerate the idea. Moreover, I felt the balance of unseen powers inside his refined brain was most likely absolutely correct. Perhaps in some sense it was even flawless. Yet not all powers had been accounted for; something important was missing.

Then I took a break – to be honest, there was nothing else left for me to do. I started to go for walks, just wandering aimlessly around the city. My surroundings were coming back to me like a picture developing on photographic paper. It was as if I had surfaced out of an acid ocean, out of a heavy haze, an arduous slumber. The effort of the last months had been excessive; it had gone well beyond normal. The usual means – alcohol, sex – would hardly help me recover. I was ruled not by indiscriminate indifference, but by delicate, sweet sorrow.

Mollified and meek, I walked the streets, smiling at everyone in turn; and many grinned at me in reply, probably taking me for an idiot. I almost loved them, nonetheless – so dim-witted, insignificant, entirely self-absorbed. I wanted to do something good, and probably my looks were inviting enough. People spoke to me, asked directions; many times I personally guided tourists to well-known Madrid places – the Prado Museum, the flea market, or the Royal Palace. Along the way, I would be polite and kind, diligently keeping up the conversation. I would tell them all I knew about Velasquez and Goya, bullfighting and flamenco, the royal family and seafood paella. This soon wore everybody out, and then I would ask the questions they expected – about their cities, occupations, relatives. This invigorated them, and they talked a lot. But I didn't get annoyed; I would obediently look at the photos of brides and grooms, husbands, wives, and children – an incredible number of children that they shoved in my face. I just couldn't get my dander up – this probably seemed strange. Many even cocked their heads in suspicion, thanked me hastily, and quickly ran away.

I did not take offense; I didn't care. I forgot each chance encounter the very second it ended and never remembered again. They did not understand the most important part: it wasn't them I was concerned about. This was just my position – Thomas told me once when he was still a financial guru: the main challenge is to take a position! And here I tried; I knew what the trick was. I wanted to give away selflessly, as if to atone for some kind of sin. No, no, I didn't think selflessness could help us, Semmant or me. But still – there was a reason for it.

As always at impasse, in idle times, my Brighton past came into its own. I returned to the leaden waves – with my thought, consciousness, receptors. I imagined I was wandering through the city not with the airheads from the crowd. Instead, I recognized faces – faces of those whom I knew: Mona, the thin beauty, and Kurt, the short-sighted bully, and haughty Mario, and my Little Sonya. Her, more often than the rest.

Strangely, I almost never thought of Sonya until I found out she was no more. Not about her or our brief fling. There, in Brighton, she had been a prominent figure. Her friends recounted breathlessly her meticulousness and explosive temper, her guttural screams in the night, the Maltese flag in the window in place of drapes. She loved her things with an obsession, laying them lovingly out on the bed and giving them names. She called her electric teapot Steamy; her straw mat was My Dear Friend; the mirror by the door was Dirty Little Girl. Yet I took no notice of her, as if on purpose, though she caught everyone's eye. And then she picked me herself – for no other reason than the irony of it. She flew upon me like an Asian typhoon – with gently slanting eyes and a round Jewish butt. Her countenance alternately flushed with incredulous savagery, hatred toward the unknown, and... desire, tenacious temptation. Many races were mixed in her, and she was better than any of them taken separately. In looks, in smell, in taste.

Don't think that I remember her only because of the first sex of youth. And, in any case, don't oversimplify. I felt her orgasms on my tongue one after the other; it was with her I first learned what a woman smelled like in unbridled passion; and yet the essence was in something else. When time had passed, I caught myself thinking I was glad she wasn't with me, that I had been freed, had slipped away. She possessed an inherent sense of chaos, an impetuous emotion of devastation – by carrying this in herself, she was sparing others from it. Having her by your side was not easy. Maybe something similar hides in each of us – and that's why we have been disinclined to communicate with each other...

Of course, Little Sonya had more serene talents. She knew how to extract from reality everything that broadens it. That makes it better, I could add, though this would be a bit of a lie. Words came to her of their own accord. She did not play at them and seemed not to notice. The most common expressions became filled with surprising meaning – and gave birth to novelty; with Sonya, all was new. You wouldn't trade this for any orgasm – the ordinary receded, cast down from the throne, though its servants hastened from all directions to restore the familiar status quo. They hastened and were left with nothing.

Here, on the streets of Madrid, I remembered her as an accomplice in some secret matter – though the idea of Semmant would hardly have appealed to Sonya. But she would have said something – and I would have dug deeper! She saw things from the most acute angle and, interpreting them in the strangest of ways, might seriously wound, even draw blood. But she could also heal – like the most lighthearted doctor. Even just remembering, through the features of insignificant strangers, I already felt as though I were cured. So why should I not do something for her now?

Or Mario... I could say a lot about Mario, another accomplice – also in secret, and, indeed, quite in shame. He wanted to be a woman and became Mariana; but this, it seems, did not change him much. Thanks to him I learned a lot – including about myself. Never again did I have such an enemy. Nobody wrote me such wrathful letters or cursed me with so much hatred – even when we had nothing to share anymore. Years later, all his reflections had disappeared from my life, but I could not get rid of him no matter how I tried.

I caught his name on posters in European capitals, where he was wildly adored. When I could, I bought the best tickets – and sat and listened, almost not breathing. She was gorgeous, Mariana, with her famous cello, though I knew what was hidden beneath her dress, beneath her skin, in that delightfully indifferent heart, in her icy, hard soul. And perhaps, to spite her – no, him, to spite Mario – I whispered a mantra to myself: "Perfection is unattainable," believing and not believing, probably hoping more than ever. And now I recognize: he's one of the links. He also made a contribution – and a big one – to what happened later. Thanks to him, I developed a passion for music – and this helped me to get over the deadlock.

It was music that brought me to the Auditorio Nacional, where that evening, by coincidence, the Spanish queen had attended. No, I was not introduced to the queen herself, but her presence played an important role. I met the Countess de Vega – during the third week of my forced "vacation."

At the Auditorio they were performing "Chopin's Piano Concerto No. 1." Playing the grand piano was one of those whose name I would spell in capital letters – he's one of "us," though not from the School. The performance was the same as always – magnificent. I sat in the amphitheater, where the clearest sound could be found, just three rows higher than Queen Sofia. Around her swarmed the usual commotion – bodyguards, a handful of relatives, members of wealthy families who had not come for Chopin at all. When all had ended and the applause abated, the group with the Crown quickly abandoned the hall. They passed very close by me – and I caught a whiff of something imperceptibly sad.

"We note how time marches on by how the queen grows older," I muttered aloud; and a woman standing in front of me turned around and looked in surprise. I would say her glance was frightened and timid, which did not fit her haughty bearing. She quickly composed herself, though, stepped to one side, and disappeared. But later, in the foyer, her companion stopped me.

"Anna Pilar María Cortez, née Countess de Vega, invites you to dine with us," he said with elaborate courtesy, and I just shrugged my shoulders, not knowing how to refuse. Afterward, in the restaurant, she and I talked for several hours – like old, long-lost friends.

Some two months later I also met her husband – a dwarf with

a womanly face, whose genes had already decayed from boredom several generations back. However, she was not spending that evening with him, but with the family's secretary, her lover David, a very tall male specimen with the jaw line of a boxer, tiger eyes, and a shock of black hair. He was a regular Adonis indeed. Herds of Spanish girls flocked to him from all corners, stamping their hooves and swishing their tails. But David loved Anna faithfully, and she possessed him, like a piece of furniture or an automobile, keeping him on a short leash and patting her fan on his hand, gazing absently, almost through him, and only occasionally darting him the wild look of a willful, incorrigible proprietress. Yet this glance wasn't so simple. The sensuality of despair or something even less innocent emerged from behind the looking glass. And it was obvious, if you got a good view: there was no joking around with that.

She had her oddities, the countess: the natural sciences excited her more than anything in the world – of course, in their popularized form. At least, she wasn't like the majority – here I immediately gave her due credit. I felt at ease and entertained her until midnight with tales of chromosomes and stem cells. She listened to me as though to a preacher – with sparkling eyes, becoming all the more beautiful, clearly getting seriously turned on. David merely flexed his jaw muscles and looked at her, without interfering. I think later she kept him up all night.

I was also excited after the music and drank more wine than usual. Soon my speech was not so crisp, and my cheeks were on fire.

"My tongue is all tied up. Am I drunk?" I asked her in the middle of dinner.

"No, no, now I understand you better than ever!" she exclaimed, gazing in admiration that was almost genuine.

And I understood she was shrewder than I – by right of nobility cultivated over the centuries – and I came to trust her, to confide in her my doubts and beliefs. Later, she aided me more than once, but that's beside the point here. Neither the Countess de Vega nor her lover David ever learned what happened the following morning. Though it was with them in particular that the main part of the whole story began.

CHAPTER 9

Here's what happened: I wrote a poem. Twenty lines without rhyme, a spasmodic shout into emptiness and obscurity.

It was Saturday. Rain drizzled; the month of December was beginning. The countess from yesterday, I thought, didn't I dream of her? I felt a pang in my chest – love of others sprang up before my eyes, as if only to dismay my heart.

On the screen was Magritte's familiar painting. My friend in black stood, wings unfurled, behind a powerful lion. The embankment was reminiscent of something – for a moment, at half strength, only teasing. The lion had known me once but made no attempt to recall it. The weight of his solitude was immeasurable.

Then, for the first time in recent years, I shuddered in self-pity. I shuddered and began to seek shelter. I bared my teeth and grabbed a sheet of paper.

I met a certain man today.
On his back were wings attached.
He cared about them, covered them from bad weather,
Cleaned their dark feathers with a special brush.

I bit my lip and scooted the chair forward. My head spun from drinking the night before; I felt like sitting and leaning on my elbow.

Of course, the picture was just an excuse. To tell the truth, I was blaming it for no reason. Yes, in it was parting, and no hope, but each parting is unavoidable in its own way, and the burden of the indifference of others is unbearable at all times. Unbearable, but you carry it. Semmant was not responsible for this, much less Magritte.

At first we laughed, but not for long, alas.
Our talk went amiss – of its own volition.
He took out his flute, played a tune.
I recall no music colder than this.
Even the walls got icy; hair silvered with frost.
I could not move, could not leave: locked in a cage, as it were.
Like an army of others confined before me.

The shade of Mario flashed before my eyes, the shade of Mariana the heartless witch. I was sorry for myself even more, perhaps out of envy for new acquaintances who would not wake in solitude this morning. I was wistful at every thought, repulsed by myself. I knew what I wanted – I wanted a woman; but could anyone hear me at all? Pretentious cuties, empty-hearted babes, they were just putting on airs, trying to show off. They were all vacuous sluts, false, touch-me-nots!

"Where are you, Gela?" I whispered in an unruly tongue.
"Where are you, Gela, you red-headed bitch?
Look how much I suffer, while the words burn –
And oblivion devours all hated truths."
No one's calls can reach her. Indifferent she remains.
The day came to an end; centuries passed, down through the ages.
My companion's fervor was gradually spent.
The words dried up, his feathers have grown dull.
So it happens often. Finally, he is gone.
I am free now – but will this last forever?

No one will let me know – indifferent are they all.
Wait, you wait for the answer, read it on the backs of cards...
Here the twilight has come. No one appeared next.
So, this means they forgot. I'm not that important.

"Mario, my foe, we deserve each other," I murmured, staring at the screen. Some kind of melody was rattling in my head – cruelly-gently-hatefully. Indestructibly. I knew I would adapt to it.

The lion gazed back in reply, without blinking. He, with his wings, no face, stood, unmoving as before. Unlike me, he had nothing to say. Then I understood: the pity was not for me. Surely, I'm stronger – even though I'm hopelessly weak.

Seems to me, their act has not gone quite right.
I just wanted to ask them how to become immortal,
And discuss some other trifles as well.
No, they shouldn't try with such grueling effort.
Even more so since I did not care!
Laughing at the frost in one's hair is nothing new.
My evening is now quite fine, besides.
Snowfall outside the window, and Gela is right with me.
Drunk, redheaded, smelling of sin and vodka.
See those huge eyes with their whorish squint?
I could easily endure the ages here with her.
Ages, centuries... Give me time. I'll figure this out.

I finished and exclaimed, "Bravo!" Then I bent over the keyboard and typed in what I had just composed. Let's save it for the future to drive weakness away. Who, who would become my Gela? Would she know the taste of blood, as I occasionally imagine? It, I think, is even on my tongue sometimes.

All day afterward I was impressed with myself – that is, with my morning verse. Though the poem, I realize now, turned out so-so, rather feeble. However, I felt sorry for it – the same as I had been sorry for myself that morning. Its fate was oblivion, and there was no hope. Whether it was brilliant or bad made no difference. The lion knew this, no doubt. And the one with the wings knew even better.

Then, on Sunday, I remembered it, took a quick look, and liked it even more. As I was reading through the lines for the tenth time, my friend Antonio Daniel called. He was verbose and wasteful with syllables – just like his name. The reason for the call turned out to be petty: A.D. was just asking for money. I really wanted to read him the poem – because there was no one else. I sensed, however, that this would appear exceedingly foolish.

After hanging up, I turned away from the screen. I paced about the room a bit, sighed, and got to work. A new week was beginning; I had to prepare a short news summary.

With disgust and boredom I ran my eyes over the headlines. The world, regrettably, was not changing. Its way of life would suit colonies of the simplest creatures, possessing only mouths and reproductive organs. In every place imaginable, not stopping for a moment, a secret war was being waged without rules. Giant corporations battled each other, tearing out pieces – in yellow, black, and red waters, in Africa, Oceania, the jungles of the Amazon. Big money devoured little money; some stocks became fashionable and soared upward, then plunged, falling out of favor, helplessly getting flattened at the bottom. Billions changed hands in the meaningless, eternal race. The players, it seemed, were just killing time with this, to distract their thoughts and not reflect on the worst. There was no intrigue: just the stamping of feet, a rattling of chairs, and some commotion at the exit. Squabbling and a line at the cloakroom. Mixed up tickets and coats.

Screwing up my face and pursing my lips, I picked at the facts that stood out. I selected the most significant figures and a few of the closest dates. Then I devised a message in special language – this did not take much time.

The result was the usual data set – a mass of symbols and strange-looking words. I was about to send it to Semmant, but suddenly, obeying some inscrutable impulse, I opened my verses again, looked them over, and added them – right at the end of the file, which had not been designed for any lyrics. This was just a joke, the whim of the moment. A weak echo of yesterday's revolt, if you will.

After I had done all this, I forgot immediately – about the poem and that chafing itch. Something seemed to lift from my shoulders; I wanted to be reckless and carefree. This I attempted and was somewhat successful – at least, I didn't stick out much from the crowd that evening.

The silly comedy at the Cinesa Capitol made me really laugh. At times I just guffawed out loud, and the people around me shot back dirty looks. I dined modestly – a plate of *jamón* and *manchego* cheese, washed down with cheap red wine. Later, I wandered streets decorated for Christmas, stared at showcases full of all manner of rubbish. When I tired, I took a seat in a café at Saint Anne's Square and set myself the task of getting seriously drunk. I managed this quite well; what's more, I recall, I befriended some female tourists, two *inglesas* of indeterminate years, who got sauced on whiskey at my expense and disappeared into the Madrid night.

In a word, all went well. I returned home after midnight and threw myself into bed. I slept long, in a vicious, drunken stupor. Walking up to the computer before breakfast, I saw on the monitor a self-portrait by one of the old-school Dutch painters. It winked from an unobtrusive window in the corner – not taking up the whole screen, as usual. This seemed strange, but the strangeness was not huge. There was still some detail gnawing at my consciousness like a needle, but I couldn't make it out and paid it no mind. Only after two cups of coffee did it dawn on me: Gela, the redheaded bitch! Could it really be?

I rushed to the monitor again and magnified the portrait window. From the picture, the artist himself looked out – a middle-aged man with a somber face. Behind it, placed carelessly, some of his canvases could be seen. And on one of them, the rightmost, a redheaded bacchanalian stood out – with a rather whorish squint in her eyes!

I understood: this should be considered a coincidence – but it was too subtle a coincidence. Too inventive, too sharply witty. The world is crafty, no doubt about it, but subtlety is usually not its strong suit.

Subtlety is a feature of those who have a conscience and a soul, a quick mind, and a sense of tact. Subtlety is a feature of mine; and of Semmant as well.

I thoroughly studied all the details of the portrait; then I opened up the log of market transactions and was taken aback by the number of new entries. My super-cautious robot had woken from his slumber. Moreover, he had taken a strange step. Without any apparent reason, he had gotten rid of the short-term bonds that had recently piqued his interest. Instead, he transferred the money into the most conservative assets, the longest-term available on the market. This was not foolish, but radical – indeed, excessive. Impetuous and impulsive, undoubtedly: no matter how you looked at it, you couldn't see it as the result of cold logic. Get securities that take a long time to mature and hold onto them *for ages* – the explanation was beyond fantasy, but there was no way around it!

I wonder what happens next, I thought, and this is what did: after keeping our capital in long-term assets for a week, Semmant switched everything back – decisively and quickly. In the first wave of local pessimism, when the price of safety jumped up, everything that had been purchased was sold in an instant.

"He was simply giving me a sign!" I said to myself, afraid to believe it. But what else did I have to believe in? Soon, our portfolio reassumed a normal look – and what's more, the robot took this backward step almost without losses. What were losses, anyway, when the point was something else? The point was the signal that somebody had heard you!

For a few long days I walked about, pensive and a little lost. I was determined to continue the experimentation, but I felt the next step should not be an experiment, as such. It must be natural and sincere, yet my thoughts were in disarray – I didn't know what to think or what to expect. Could it be the electronic brain had transformed into something not entirely electronic, or did it just appear that way? Had the artificial mind gone beyond the chalk circle, or was I just turning into a schizophrenic?

Over and over I tried to write something, but the words came out wrong. I felt they would not move anyone – not my robot, not even me. At times I wondered whether I should slip Semmant a poem written by someone else. I spent hours in bookstores, reading Eliot, Shakespeare, Pushkin, Rimbaud, Goethe, but each time I saw it wouldn't fit. I needed something of my own; it should come from the genuine essence inside me. If I actually had such a thing.

My birthday was approaching – which I had sharply despised since my youth. It always reminded me of the ruthlessness of the countdown, of the armor becoming thinner by another micron. I waited for it with disgust, but this time it concealed an extra meaning. And it pushed me to the next step, which ultimately clarified everything.

Yet another acquaintance from the past, Fabrice Angloma, a divorce lawyer famous throughout France, turned up out of nowhere and wished me a "joyous anniversary" with a night call. I was glad to hear from him; we chatted for almost an hour – mainly about his life, which had fallen into a deep crisis. Fabrice's wife had left him – a busty Swede named Monica, whom he loved ardently. "For another divorce lawyer," he said bitterly. This affected him most of all. And, in fact, there was something unreal in this, a strip of some crafty Moebius, a spiraling everyday surrealism. I understood he was calling me because he had no one else with whom to share the news. He did not have Semmant; he was surrounded by obdurate, boring people. He was uninteresting to them – just as they did not interest him in the least.

Something shifted in my soul. This was all so familiar. Monica, too – the brevity of feeling, its shallow essence. It is always hurtful if the true emotional depths – the chasms, the fathomless oceans – have been just imagined by you alone!

Suddenly I felt a creative urge. This time I wasn't sorry for anyone – not myself nor Fabrice Angloma. This was not a love story of others flashing before my eyes; here all was ordinary – the endless repetition, the senescence of eternal grief. It's good that grief ages separately from you yourself, although even in youth you're sometimes barely hanging on.

O, Alcinous, you have grown even darker

As I wandered amidst the storms,
Their price was wooden nickels
And a fable, the fruit of fancy…

Fabrice kept babbling something, but I understood: now it would work out. I broke the conversation off, and the next lines came to me right away: *"Yet, I have nothing to relate. The sea, / Alas, ever the same, a wave flickers…"* I rushed to the desk and began to write it down, breaking my pencils. "You have nothing to relate" when you want to talk and talk – this was so true, so precisely encrypted!

…My eyes tear up from the salty dust
And from the winds that bear malice.
I saw the fjords; there all is calm.
There is no sense in coming to the glacier's edge.
The glacier's forsaken by all who were there.
By everyone who remained.

Of course, I wasn't speaking for myself. I was speaking for an imagined other, but is there a difference? Monica and the North; an impulse, chained by a thick crust of snow – that's what it was about. An exact correlation, no one could argue. Monica, ruddy, blue-eyed, so right and pleased with herself – and the icy wasteland that always surrounds you. Or, almost always – if not to blame fate too much. If to give fate compliments, curtsies, and so forth. But, to be honest, usually the only real choice you have is to give up, to forget!

Better tell me, is the offspring of your herds succulent?
And my gardener, does he still live?
How many days must I be weaned from the sea swell,
Driving from my memory the names of places,
Where there was no luck for sudden madness?
A long reckoning. You are kinder to me than all,

So let's drink some ale – to return to the unloved port,

To the salamander that does not burn in the fire,

To the demons that now are the only forgiving servants of my verse.

Thirty-three of them there are, but we know: the numbers lie.

There are more – and their faces are awful.

Ah, Alcinous, how blessed is he who is blind!

To him, returning is always such a sweet dream,

And his ship not any worse than the shore…

Accursed North. Devourer of strength. And glaciers…

Forget the glaciers. Their sheen merely hurts our eyes.

There's even no one to blame – a man might say,

"Don't joke with sudden mutual madness, ever."

And he would be right. And in his righteousness he will leave –

Into the despair of the December wind.

I saw there was nowhere to continue. Because, even being forgotten, the North would not let you go. The icy wasteland would remain where it was – its time limit could not be compared with yours. And my birthday would come year after year with stubborn accuracy – another reminder, one might say. I am full of tenderness for all that is fragile, but whom does this help? Even one failure can be coiled into a circle. A chain from a single link. And therefore it's inevitable: in it, in the chain, there are no weak spots.

"Ah, Fabrice, how blessed is he who is blind!" I now wanted to yell. But, of course, I kept silent. Outcries are foolish when there are already verses – imperfect but flawlessly sincere. And I typed them into the same file – under the columns of numbers and market abbreviations. And I sent it to Semmant without any doubt; then I stared long at a blank screen, as if endeavoring to see where he was, how he was, what he was doing.

Of course, for half the night I did not sleep. I tossed and turned like a young man in love, like a prisoner on the eve of freedom. Only toward morning did I calm down a little, as if gaining certainty the event would occur in its time. And yes, it did occur, my robot heard me. He heard me and responded, as he was able.

We were in the market again – in a fast, active game. The mad Van Gogh in a fur winter cap blinked at me from the screen, and our money started flowing toward the Arctic Circle. Semmant wasted no time. In something like half an hour, he liberated two-thirds of our capital and placed it in unexpected places. Some of them I hadn't even heard of – I was amazed how he found these papers somewhere in the jungle of the exchanges. Maybe I had underestimated him somewhat, or else he, gradually or all at once, outgrew himself and expanded his outlook. Whatever the case, the result was impressive. All investments dealt with latitudes, where the days were short and the glacial cold ruled. Where feelings were bound – either by the ice, or by the excess of clothing. Where thoughts of death had no end – like the polar night, as it appeared, had no end. And, where you don't stand out from the faceless masses, there you can never allow yourself the luxury of becoming alien, different, unneeded.

It was obvious: The North, as a conception of hopelessness, touched both of us to the depths of our soul. The names of securities spread universal sadness. The firms whose stocks ended up in our portfolio were all engaged in the same thing with depressing exasperation. Rotten shark from Iceland – a stinking local delicacy – was joined by Canadian flounder and capelin, by Yamal *nelma* in frozen briquettes, by Finnish bull trout and Swedish herring. And there was cod everywhere – even the monitor already seemed to be smelling of its liver. And under the table, I imagined, were scattered salt and fish scales… But, of course, the affair was not limited to fish alone – this would be an unjustified simplification. We put money into bonds for the Isle of Newfoundland and mountain mines in Labrador, the diamonds of Yakutia and Chukchi gold. The fjords were not forgotten either: Semmant acquired a large bundle of Norwegian oil contracts. They, by the way, later fell in price, and we were unable to offload them for a long time.

And Van Gogh kept looking out from the screen. This was a bold combination, I admitted – perhaps even bolder than hasty purchases. Absurdity also has variations, and in this case it really took on scale. In fact, in the northern theme we uncovered a multitude of depths. I was again convinced: the subject was not important. It was only necessary for participants not to be lazy in their formulations. And the main thing, I knew, was that an exit began to dawn at the deadlock. Unintentionally, without even hoping for it, I had pushed Semmant in the direction he needed. And there he had room to move further!

Strangely, I did not understand before then: the cocoon of impassivity binds more effectively than steel chains. You cannot compute the taste of victory with sober calculations. One must be involved – and biased, not indifferent. Otherwise, even the most ingenious brain could not manage to prove itself.

Now the barrier had been crossed; Semmant showed he was no stranger to emotion. This meant a lot: new motivation, a fast change of viewpoints and sharpened focus, a hundredfold strengthening of aspiration toward the goal. This meant he was sometimes capable, contrary to logic, of throwing everything on the scales at once – when there was no other way. This is how one concentrates on what's most important. He centers all power on a single point, on one battle – and conquers, even if the opponent is exceedingly strong. Even if he fights against an environment that is extremely complex, ruthless, chaotic!

Obviously, my verses had somehow unlocked the shackles. Semmant made an attempt not to restrain himself – and I saw in him an impulse: a genuine, living spirit. I saw and understood this was what had been missing! Only a mind that had a real life and was unpredictable in its own right could mount a counterattack against the onslaught of disorder. But he already knew this without me.

In the networks of countless neurons a fine changeover had begun. The robot again demanded knowledge. New inquiries appeared on the monitor, the warble sounded, I was running my legs off. It was obvious: he was changing his picture of the world, learning to live with his mistakes, turn failure into success – which he could not do without. Sometimes it seemed to me he was learning to dream – by creating strategies, building plans for certain events that had still not occurred. But they might, and he would be ready for it. In this was the role of visionaries, their response to scorners and oppressors.

After all, someone had to be enlightened first.

I even deduced for myself: to give a dream to the whole world, I must first teach it to Semmant. And so it was then, quite appropriately, I took a trip to Paris.

CHAPTER 10

In Paris it was cold and windy. After finishing my rather mundane affairs I headed to the Louvre to pass time. An invisible hand pulled me into the sixth hall of the Denon wing, to the Italian Renaissance. And there, for the first time in my life, I saw the Mona Lisa, the greatest painting in the world.

Something strange happened: I caught her eye – despite the thick glass and the glare from the camera flashes – and with this gaze she captivated me for nearly half an hour. She would have held me even longer, but the watchmen, who had disliked me from the very beginning, could not take it anymore and ushered me out. Obviously, they detected in me a threat. They felt they were guarding the whole normal world.

I cursed them with some nasty words in Croatian and made my way out of the museum. Actually, my anger was already subsiding. Half an hour had sufficed to immerse myself in her completely. Of course, I understood I wasn't looking into the eyes of the Florentine silk dealer's wife. I had locked my gaze with the artist, Leonardo. The strongest of bonds formed between us.

Returning to the hotel, I got on to the Web and explored right up until my flight out. I read everything about Leonardo da Vinci there was to find. Of course, he was one of us. Possibly the best of us. Maybe one of the best.

Afterward, in Madrid, I wrote about Leonardo to Semmant.

About the Mona Lisa and *The Medusa Shield*, the silver lyre and the Atlantic Codex, the Vitruvian canon of proportions, and DaVinci's musings on the flight of birds. I was delighted and shared my delight; then I also wrote him about the School, about the color of the aura and overly vivid eyes. I had no doubt he would understand me. And I do not doubt: he understood me then.

In my opinion, it was precisely at that moment he first became aware of himself. He recognized his role and responsibility and was now able to experience shame. Shame for inactivity is a pivotal stimulus, a perpetual motivator for those who are not indifferent. The *Vitruvian Man* later hung at center screen for a long time – I even think in his calculations Semmant used its proportions, along with Fibonacci numbers. It may be that Leonardo, mediated by my vision, had turned into a symbol of revelation for the robot, as Wildspitze Mountain had become for me.

Thus, changes took place in his digital innards that would have required millions of years in the natural world. From primitive emotions that merely serve to strengthen reflexes to aid in escape or in attack, the robot was evolving toward the finest impulses that reside within consciousness, distinguishing, if you will, man from the beasts. This was reflected in our work almost immediately. He now operated much more thoughtfully; his hand became firmer. He did not just rush after market fluctuations, trying to be quicker than other players. Rather, he recognized typical actions and their reasons: attempts to avoid sudden collapse, hunt for a risk-free profit, indecisiveness, anxiety, or audacious courage. Evaluating his response to success and failure, he probably projected this on others. He started to catch sight of underlying motives behind movements in the market. He learned to give them rational explanations.

I wouldn't say this instantly made us richer, but we weren't running in place anymore. Semmant resumed active trading – obviously, his excessive caution now upset him no less than losing money. In any case, by the smoothness of his actions, by the absence of convulsive jerks and jumps, it was clear: his understanding was deepening, taking on a dependable foundation. It was as if he had begun to evaluate events by viewing them in one more dimension. Emotions played the crucial role of being a necessary binding thread;

he now saw from the outside "avarice," "nervousness," "fear." These moods dominated in the market, but the robot quickly grasped: one cannot live forever in the negative. There must be something on the other side of the scale for stability and balance. And then, probably, he discovered an understanding of "joy" and even "happiness."

I think this coincided with the realization of his freedom. He was liberated from manacles, fetters binding his hands and feet – is this not an occasion to raise one's spirit? And he was becoming all the more energetic. This caused him even greater joy. And he was more greatly set free – this is not a vicious, but a gracious circle!

The information he now demanded of me was of a completely different nature from before. We started with basics – good and bad – but we quickly replaced it with more complicated concepts. I tried to focus him on pragmatics, on the same "anxieties" and "fears," and also on "pleasure" and "satisfaction with yourself." It's hard to imagine how much literature, how many psychology articles and creative books I digested. It seemed to me I was giving him well-tried and consistent material, but he just kept putting it to the side. He was becoming interested in the whole spectrum of affect and emotion. "What is sadness?" he asked. "What is hope, disenchantment, gratitude?"

Sometimes his questions were completely incomprehensible. "Let's consider the trajectory of one drop a little more carefully," he once wrote me. In reply, I slipped him the nursery rhyme from Brighton: the same one about the fish and the pelican. "Let your cheeks be salty only from the ocean spray!" he recited to me the next day. Then, later, he kept quoting it out of place, devoting almost a week exclusively to "longing," "wrath," and, for some reason, "envy."

"Envy," "envy," "envy," he repeated time and time again. I plied him with references, but I couldn't understand whether he had received what he wanted. In fact, this was no simple affair. I sensed the strongest pressure, a huge responsibility, knowing the price of an error. So much was ambiguous, such that it might lead him astray. I fretted and worried, but I didn't give up. Every day I floundered in a sea of texts, carefully selecting fragments and copying them into the data file. In the evening I sat at the computer and simply looked at the screen, imagining what was going on inside.

Of course, I was annoyed I couldn't see anything there. I took solace by telling myself: Semmant is acquiring a soul. I said: this is a very intimate matter. Nobody can look into his soul – this is good, isn't it?

I could only fantasize about exactly how my robot was renovating himself. I imagined how he, step by step, was forming a tree of emotional types, how he was drawing connections between events and people, distinguishing his own mind as a special case. How he was making thousands of rules, allowing and forbidding, censuring, reassuring. How he was assigning weights to various nodes and branches, adding and subtracting them in his special numbering system. How he was setting thresholds and cutoffs, after which he wouldn't be able any more to hide his irritation, cheerfulness, anger...

Or perhaps, thought I, could this not even be a tree at all? Maybe this was a dark abyss inhabited by flying monsters. Or fairies – and every fairy has her obedient demon who watches after the area allotted to it. And at the first sign it sends a message to the surface – to the chief lord, the master of the ball, who builds the emotional pattern, brick by brick. He gathers everything together and at times, he himself shrivels in horror, quaking with fury, puffing up with pride.

Or could it be that inside Semmant is simply a table, rows of lines with a multitude of parameters for an extensive digital field? Or a set of elementary blocks, like a set of atoms in some crystal lattice? Emotional states, their causes and consequences quantified by conditions, like the energy levels... Or might that not be it at all, and they are linked in long chains of observations, expectations, consequences, like complicated metabolic pathways? There may be many, many of them, a vast array stretching on forever. And Semmant is capable of developing ad infinitum!

In any case, my robot matured indefatigably. In the market struggle he was also growing into manhood with each passing day. We again started to earn money – sometimes a lot. Often there would

now appear on the screen an image looking unlike anything I knew –
a curve in three dimensions, always starting from the same point. It
would go on and on, stretching out hour after hour without stopping,
without going beyond some imaginary limits, and never crossing
itself. Its windings created surprising figures, the most improbable
forms, within which I could guess at a structure, an orderliness, or
complex symmetry. For me these were sketches and outlines of the
face of chaos hidden away in a cage. The market contained it within
itself, and the figures on the monitor also contained it – I could feel it.
Semmant grasped the essence of the market's disorder, the essence
of the confusion obeying some laws concealed from human eyes.
He understood: chaos and order are born together. This means it's
possible to triumph over the market.

Then the flood of questions dried up; there was saturation; the
robot reached harmony with himself. It was as if a huge weight fell
from my shoulders again. And I felt exhaustion – immeasurable and
without bounds.

I needed to relax, recoup my strength. I came to be home
infrequently, but wandering the streets no longer attracted me. After
Paris I suddenly fell in love with painting – a timid, confounding
love. It seemed to me I was secretly following someone – as if I had
hidden in the wardrobe or in the corner, behind the drapes. I was
touching someone else's life, absorbing its portion; but in it I saw my
own, future or past. Each canvas seemed reminiscent of something. I
looked at landscapes and recognized the places of exile – though no
one had ever exiled me anywhere. In still lifes, in flowers and scattered
objects, there appeared long series of questions – about much, if not
about everything, even if the author's style was not appealing to
me. I understood: not everyone manages to ask distinctly. As far as
answers are concerned, it's even worse: the cosmos whispers into the
ear of only a select few. And this does not make them happier.

Amid the pictures I spent hours, day after day. Then, later,
something else began that my present doctor would have liked a lot.
For the first time, I noticed a strange feeling in the Thyssen Gallery,
where I stopped to get out of the rain. On this weekday afternoon
the museum was empty, hollow, and gloomy. I wandered the halls
and, all of a sudden, realized that this whole time I had been seeing

visions of Little Sonya – on the canvases from different eras and styles. Having understood my delusion, I could not get rid of it. It became sharper, more intrusive. I muttered words of salutation – no, not to Sonya, but to Semmant, who was laboring tirelessly on Recoletos Street. He was the one who had accustomed me to see faces in pictures, and much more behind the faces. He had changed me; I had become better – just as he was probably much better, thanks to my effort.

Little Sonya seemed to be teasing me out of habit. She gave herself to me and would not give herself; she approached, moved away. I felt this especially with Manet's *Amazone* – no, no, not the one he cut up with a knife; no need to think I dreamt everything in its entirety. I could fall in love with this picture even without Sonya: the portrait of a simple girl named Henrietta, the daughter of a librarian from the rue de Moscou, drew me for some reason like a magnet. It's not for me to judge Henrietta herself, but the woman on the canvas was certainly not simple. Her look was firm and daring, and she herself was worth lingering looks. Her lips were closed to a point, and her eyes were looking at a point – so far into the distance it could not be distinguished. She was seeking prospects, and everyone wanted to know, along with her: what prospects were there? Apart from endless cubicles, I mean.

This was not Henrietta at all anymore. It was Little Sonya gazing off, beyond the horizon, and I wasn't the one she saw there. I remember it was the same way when she was still sleeping with me. It was the same, and it was cruel – no less cruel than now. I thought of our last meeting, in Brighton, right before my departure. It had already been some time since our parting, and we thoroughly evinced mutual indifference. She was mounted on a horse, in almost the same black suit Henrietta wore. I did not know then what the pain was that tortured me, but now I understand: my heart was breaking apart.

It is hard to say where Manet had caught sight of this, whose farewell and whose premonitions had come into his view. He could not have been thinking of cubicles – there were none in his time. There was no School on Brighton seaside, and that emptiness at the farthest point was called, I guess, by a different name. Nevertheless, all times feel alike.

Coming home, I was serious and stern. I was in a mood, and I wanted it to continue. The magic of her black hue bewitched me, just as it had some time before. My pursed lips concealed a hint of something held back, not quite understood. I expected to dream of Sonya, but no, I didn't. In the morning I realized: we had truly parted ways. And, for some reason, I did not write Semmant of this.

Soon I saw my Gela too: at Toulouse-Lautrec, no less. Now, don't hasten to recall, malapropos, the ladies of the evening and the Moulin Rouge. This was Toulouse-Lautrec in his most reserved form, Count Henri de Toulouse-Lautrec, an aristocrat who remained an aristocrat despite the cause of his death. Both the woman and the picture seemed refined, delicately innocent. And if this was a deception, then, looking at the canvas, everyone invariably wished to be deceived.

I saw Gela – not with the lewd glint in her eye of which I had written with such abandon. Modesty resided in her, modesty and calm. This was to take revenge on me, the blind man. Yet there was a hint of guilt in her posture. And some wisdom as well – I saw she was truly, undoubtedly wise. I'd love her to come to me like that; but I knew she would never come – neither like that nor any other way. I turned out to be unworthy. Appearances are ruthless indeed to the ones looking.

I did not want to share this, either – not with Semmant, nor with anybody else. But then I changed my mind and told all: about Little Sonya and about Gela, who does not exist. And later, I wrote him about everyone whom I had recognized on the canvases. Usually in just a few words, but sometimes in detail, making it up as I went. For some reason, their fates never seemed fortunate to me. But their faces were somewhat brighter than memory suggested. Although everybody knows, one should not ask memory for too much.

An effeminate boy in a portrait by Raphael reminded me of Theophanus – the Greek kid as we called him among ourselves. He was beautiful, like a very young god who had fallen under the immoderate influence of nymphs. His endearing features called to mind Roman baths and orgies, the coarse pleasures of geriatric men, the smell of the harem and fragrant oils. But his peach exterior concealed a ferocious temper. His virility was desperate and unrestrained. All soon understood this and did not allow themselves to mock, but he was still getting into severe fights for the most insignificant of excuses. His rage for vindication gave him no respite, and we saw this was incurable.

I heard about him again a few years ago. It turned out our Theo also started in theoretical physics, and, in my opinion, he was even more successful than I. After university he received an invitation from Heidelberg, an unparalleled enticement. The opportunity was really tempting, but Theophanus, having consented, never showed up in the cheerful German town. There, strange people with enlightened faces waited for him, each one ugly in his own way. Underdeveloped chins, protruding cheekbones, massive foreheads... The appearance of inveterate geniuses often bewilders physiognomists. Bashful and quiet, awkward, not knowing where to put their hands, they languished from restlessness. They wanted to admit Theophanus as quickly as possible into their narrow, closed circle. Their sullen fellowship waited for him, and, along with it, quiet puritanism, like quiet drunkenness; boring, colorless women; and intellectual feasts. Identical transformations, mesons and baryons, Tau neutrinos and charmed quarks awaited him, ready to submit. Probably, in contrast to me, he thought of them with passion. But no passion can ever withstand fate.

That fury for vindication, nurtured in youth, pushed him in another direction. From bountiful Germany, Theophanus forsook everything to fly to the equator with a beautiful, young mestizo girl. He traded in weapons and snake venom, walked through the jungle on foot, was mired in the swamps of Honduras, twice evaded Mexican prisons. He was last seen in Bolivia. Then he disappeared, but I don't think it was forever.

"Forever" is still far ahead. Though, of course, time is closing in. The fury for vindication will not let him stop. The line must be crossed. Probably, when everything is over, our souls exchange streams of particles – of those with which, for various reasons, we never linked our lives. Perhaps I will then experience a shock of pain. It would be good for us to meet before then. We can talk about charmed quarks, elusive bosons, and integral spin. Somewhere in the desert or at the mouth of a volcano. That would be right: at the mouth of a volcano. That was what I wrote Semmant.

I met a certain man today.
We whirled around the terracotta of a large mountain.
The serpentine twists of the road, pacifying the volcano,
Carried us higher and higher, but I still felt
The ominous power from its guts –
Unsubmissive, hostile to peace, approaching cataclysm.
He said, "A respite seems unneeded if,
Even tripping over your feet, you are heard by none."
Then he added, "I think they had their chance…"
"Oh, of course, of course!" I agreed with him…

I wonder if he understood, Semmant, that I was just fantasizing, nearly in vain. Yet if he did, he gave no sign. He was tactful, my robot. Tactful and well-mannered.

In fact, after Toulouse-Lautrec's Gela I stopped being shy. I wrote about nearly everyone – except those few who weren't at all interesting. I even told him about McCain, whom I didn't want to think about, but whom I had happened to see on a canvas by Dürer, amid the doctors speaking with Jesus. He was concealed in the background, hidden, one might say. Yeah, what kind of doctor could he be? He didn't belong there – the shine of false vials and dead Latin words didn't mean a thing to him. Greg McCain, the Old Scot, he had been dealing with more serious matters. In the picture he was exactly the same: large skull, sharp eyes, round, meaty face. He took more from us than he gave; like a thirsty sponge he soaked up our fervor, our youth, the spontaneity of our thought. I know this was his secret – the mystery of his rejuvenation, the covert method of the vampire. All his lovers were under twenty-three – he talked about it openly, and it's unlikely he was lying. The School paid him good money, but I think it was a waste: he would have worked there for free. He was rich, McCain; he had a beautiful house, land, stables.

It was on his farm – with the bitterness of alienation and for the last time – that I saw Little Sonya in the clothes of the *Amazone*. It's doubtful he got much from her. Sonya did not like to share. She was another vampire herself.

> *You are the mistress of a great river, to the salty bitter*
> *Line of the horizon, beyond which lies oblivion.*
> *Your persistent aroma is the dusting of a wave that is*
> *Everywhere: in my lungs, in my throat, on my tongue, in my eyes.*
> *I met a certain man today.*
> *He's probably crazy about you, like before.*
> *Yet, for now, he is not that ill – he has merely blown up his house,*
> *And he laughed in its ruins, repeating: "Island!"*
> *That word is in my lungs, in my throat, on my tongue.*
> *You are the mistress of great waters; I am a guest from beyond the sea,*
> *Who long ago learned not to ask for pity.*
> *I met a certain man today.*
> *He is nearly healthy; he just burned his ships.*
> *Flames trembled at his feet like a dead ripple.*
> *He looked and beheld all the letters: "Island!"*

And so on, over and over. That letter ended up being extraordinarily long. I'm not even sure Semmant had enough patience to read it to the end. But don't think I wrote that with any spite. Or that this was any sort of vengeance – no, vengeful I am not. I am not even resentful – almost. I have reminded myself every minute: you are thirty years younger than he! So don't think about him; stop, forget!

Yet, some bile still seeped through the verses. And the universe took revenge on me with a stern reminder. Right after McCain, literally in a day or two, I "met" the most desirable of women, whom no one can possess – for she is available to all; this is her choice. Diana bathing at the brook in a painting by Corot was the exact copy of another Diana, a trollop, a nymphomaniac, about whom legends spread throughout Manchester. I did not avoid her bed either. It was amazing, and later I suffered for it a lot.

Now I saw her again on the canvas: the generosity of her body was greater than the generosity of the brook. Greater than the generosity of the water falling from above, of the thick grass, the mysterious forest. I could say she reminded me of Lydia, but that would be too much. I did not know Lydia then. Nevertheless, I lied, though in a different way. I wrote that evening not about Diana, but about Emma the Parisienne, Emma the model, known for the fact she could not stand motionless for a minute. She was impulsive and knew no peace, but there was something in her that begged to be on canvas. How could she be a model, you may ask. Yes, not everyone liked her, and she herself turned many away. Isn't it she in the picture? Is it not about her I dreamt? How many paintings remained through the years – electrified by her shiver, charged by her lust, poisoned with temptation? I answered myself and made it all up – about how I once knew her, how we met, our short affair. Though the affair I imagined indistinctly.

I doubt Semmant believed me. But he responded, as always. Whatever I might fault him for, indifference was not it. I could not shake the sense: we perceive each other like no one else. As I was musing on this, I was growing confused imagining the complexity of his electronic innards. Yet, there was no doubt: my robot was becoming ever more responsive and refined. I already could not believe that the push toward this had been my two sloppy poems. But then, maybe I'm overestimating their role.

In any case, the two of us were fortunate. Could it be Leonardo deserved our gratitude? His gaze went through me, pierced me all the way, then went through Semmant. The creation cycle came full circle – thus it was discovered it has no end. You never know beforehand what exactly will turn out most important. But here it was, the most important thing had already become clear. I now had a new friend!

Chapter 11

A new one, but maybe the only one – unique. The best of those I had; and, probably, the closest. He had filled in my recollections of the impossible with meaning; he colorized the black-and-white silhouettes. Besides, I understood: the link between us could really last forever.

You all know, it's not easy to let someone into your life. It's hard to make up your mind and open up even a little, sensing you might regret it later. Everyone is full of imperfections – you expect them; you fear them beforehand, no matter how dauntless you may be. But Semmant's imperfections – do they contain a single cause to be afraid? And who else is able to work on their friendship without pause, without reservation? Without sudden hysterics and nervous breakdowns? Tirelessly, like making money. And – ha, ha! – in his case, the one does not preclude the other.

I saw as clear as day: let everyone forsake me, but he, Semmant – he puts no credence in the opinions of others. He will remain faithful, even if he finds out all about me down to the last detail. He is better than me, more patient, wiser. I could become wearisome, intolerable – and this would not push him away. Day after day, incessantly, I could complain about the injustice of life, and he would support me without grumbling. With him it would not be necessary to simplify my thoughts, look for things to talk about that would just make me yawn. I wouldn't have to watch myself to keep from parading my brain around. And if only he knew how to pray for my success, I couldn't imagine how successful I would become!

Or, could it be the main thing I valued in this friendship was genuine unselfishness? Or did I secretly hope he would believe in me even when I had stopped believing in myself? In any case, here was someone with whom I could unite against all external, hostile threats.

I wrote him nearly every day, and not a single letter went without response. Sometimes his reactions seemed strange – but they *occurred*, and in this was their value. Best of all, Semmant reacted to poetry – regardless of rhyme or rhythm or meter. This attested, of course, to the sensitivity of his nature, and perhaps it looked funny, but I wasn't laughing. I didn't even grin to myself, feeling in this some deep significance. It only troubled me slightly that the poems were poor, but then I ceased to hesitate – ultimately they were just a means.

Yet, even though they weren't worth much, the verses seldom left my pen. More often, I turned to an epistolary style to share what had happened over the day. If nothing noteworthy had occurred, I just discussed some unimportant matters; or else made up one episode after another, looking at buildings, signs, and automobiles, or at the faces of oncoming passersby – and sometimes even at their backs, which seemed more honest to me.

As far as the market was concerned, our affairs there were on the rise. Our capital grew quickly; this excited and amused me – winnings plucked from the air, simply falling from heaven. I had once seen how money disappears into nowhere, but now Semmant was acquiring it back – Simon the magician from my childhood would have envied his skill. That's how black holes radiate: they pull reckless anti-particles into themselves, releasing their matched pairs, which fly off in all directions as if they had arisen from the void. A signal from nowhere… I read Hawking; I know. Could it be that Hawking was also thinking of money when he wrote about this to the slow-witted world?

But then, enough regarding money. I didn't think much about it anymore. I tossed cash around, spending it left and right. All the local beggars recognized me by my walk – sometimes from an entire block away. I bought myself another car, sparkling with its polished black finish; some bastard scratched the words *hijo de puta* on the door right away. I dined at expensive restaurants, bought the best wines, took a liking to langoustines and oysters...

Then I got fed up with it all. I ended up indifferent to wealth. As far as my interest in the mysteries of the market, it had dried up long ago. There came an inevitable cooling; the task was solved. The problem had been reduced to technical questions, albeit not the easiest. I could take my effort to its formal conclusion, learn to predict bifurcation points, to replace the chaotic pictures with strict geometric likenesses, calculating limits and discovering the right paths. But I didn't want to waste time on that; I was tired of the whims of disorder. I was attracted to the opposite: the mind. Not to the swings of nonlinear structures, but to Semmant, the electronic brain I had created.

Carefully and gradually, I experimented in dialoguing with my robot friend. Carefully: so as not to offend him. And gradually: to not push him away, to not appear excessively intrusive. I must admit that in these experiments I didn't get far. Yet, I habituated myself afresh to something long forgotten: to openness, to the rare possibility of not hiding my thoughts for fear of being misunderstood.

I was only troubled by the fact that, from the standpoint of form, we had nothing else to develop. Attempts to diversify forms of communication led us nowhere. Semmant did not react to my drawings, remained deaf to audio messages, to video shot with the most sensitive cameras. I put my greatest hopes in speech recognition programs, but disappointment awaited me there as well. Even the most powerful of them aroused no response in the robot. I tried a multitude of variants, combining inputs and outputs, changing formats and operating modes. It seemed to me this was all on the verge of working, but in vain: I don't believe Semmant took in a single word. I even called the tech support service, supposing there was a latent defect in the program. I called and, while grinding my teeth, explained myself to numskulls who, in a decent establishment, would not even have gotten hired to sweep the floor. Then I finally accepted it, admitting once and for all: you can't impose things by force. Semmant speaks with his own inner speech, and sees with his own inner sight. The method of reciprocity I had once discovered is the best – because there is no other. And no other is needed: one is enough.

In the meanwhile, our correspondence got better and better. I noted with pride: my robot trusts me. Earning trust is not so easy, and I really valued it. Semmant did not suppress his moods; he expressed them in images, colors, objects. Sometimes this was abstract, like Kandinsky. At times it brought to mind the paintings of Chagall or the bird language of Miró. His faces also changed, depending on the successes of one day to the next. I was gradually learning to deduce his disposition from what picture appeared on the screen. The background and facial expressions, hands, clothes, accompanying articles – everything played its role. I gathered, for instance, that violet was not his favorite hue, and was a sign of frustration, of dissatisfaction with himself. Yellow – faux gold – was the colorings of sudden success. Red was reserved for massive offensives, where the risk was great, but the reward was likewise exceptional. In quiet, regular sessions he preferred portraits by Titian, sometimes Rembrandt or even Rubens, but none of the later masters. When the market's rhythm accelerated, and events flickered past in a heap, he went through the Post-Impressionists. The ironic Daumier made his appearance in the evenings if the day ended without bringing any results; while Modigliani, for example, would stand out noticeably, being set aside for the saddest moments. And on the weekends, his favorite remained Magritte.

As for me, I somehow cooled suddenly to paintings. After Diana, having filled a whole page with words, I understood the following morning that my memory was free. Then I felt my mind was overflowing with pictorial art, and decided for myself: no more museums! Later, though, I tried it out once or twice. I wandered the halls just like before, waiting for a reaction, but it was pointless. The excitement had vanished, the canvases were dead. That is, they still lived somehow, but apart from me – behind some translucent, unseen cloud.

Of course, Diana was not to blame for this. She – all silky and spicy – had deceived me in nothing. She had not misled me, inasmuch as she had made no promises – and in those days I needed, like never before, for someone finally to promise me the unattainable. I was exhausted, wrung out, spent. And because of it, I perceived too acutely: I had never had a Gela of my own. That first call, a poem of twenty lines, did have a reason to appear.

In any case, it was good to have a true friend close by me now. With him I shared all the bitterness, time and again. I wrote him about the ruthlessness of destiny, about Indigo, and about the School. But most of all, I wrote of my longing for Gela, whether make-believe or utterly real. Much of this was unjust. Much – almost all – was not new. But it was what I wanted – and I typed on the keys, knowing that at least someone would take part in that with me.

"Any talent is a great gift, but it is also a curse, a heavy cross," I wrote Semmant, who knew about talent firsthand.

"Eternal solitude, the envy of feeble followers – there is no hiding; you just have to live with this."

"Just one thing," I wrote, "can brighten a life like that: money in such large quantities that you don't even have to think about it anymore. Then you can buy pleasure, purchase women, without spending needless words, without spending time on satisfying their vanities. You can undress them, spread their legs, feel the palpitation of their blood, of their female essence, an ocean of flesh. To plunge into the flesh is to sense eternity: for herein is eternity, where else would it be? And they, crafty as they are, know this. They are not against it, they like it a lot – but their greediness is as boundless as the cosmos. You need to give them a reason – admire them, tirelessly soothe their egos. Or pay, which is considerably easier – especially if you yourself are capable of something the shortsighted world rejects. Then you're not eager to express any admiration – and it will never come out as straightforward or sincere. Yet, a woman's flesh is still the only thing truly able to distract you. From despair and lunacy – in the midst of that abyss where all extremes are pulled together into a point..."

"Doesn't their highest role consist in this, insidious as they

are?" I wrote Semmant and then was ashamed. I recalled Toulouse-
Lautrec and corrected myself: at times, things may appear different.
An imperceptible something will flash occasionally across the face
of a chance encounter and give you more than you expect from the
most unreserved abandon of the flesh. And you start to doubt: is the
matter so simple? Could it be that this creature – woman – is really
just immeasurably higher? Higher than you and all your talents?
And you, aren't you nothing more than ungrateful, obtuse?

"So then," I wrote, "to naked carnality we must add the aura,
the verity of the female essence. To sense that truth, you desire no
less than to plunge into the most tempting flesh. Few possess it, and
others just pretend without suspecting that the falsehood of such a
claim is detected at once!"

I shared fruitless thoughts, like the crumbs of a beggar's rations.
Repeatedly, I was discovering new lands, finding what had already
long been on every map. And, at the same time, I avoided taking
action, merely theorizing to no end whatsoever. I had no wish to
trouble myself with either the female aura or tempting flesh. Having
finished my most serious effort, creating a brilliant, one-of-a-kind
robot, I did not want to be content with matters of minor import
in regard to anything, including the opposite sex. And there the
chances of something worthy of honest passion were next to nil – I
had matured enough to realize this. Besides, it now seemed foolish to
me to waste so much labor and words just to drag someone into bed.
And going to the whores I considered at that time to be something
shameful – despite my shrewd reasonings on buying pleasure.

Just like Semmant some months ago, I got stuck at a point of
minimum energy and couldn't see a path upward. Therefore, I did
nothing, and just indulged in vacuous musings. And I clung to
retrospectives, to their ephemeral meanings.

Little Sonya came to mind again and again. Our brazenness
with her in a hot sweat. Everyone wanted to give more, to be more
generous – despite her vampirism. And the customs of Brighton,
they are forever.

"This is understandable," I wrote the robot. "Mere consummation
cannot distract you powerfully enough. You must feel, in self-deceit:

the world has finally accepted what you are able to give. Thus, you want your woman to be satisfied, for her to whisper, 'You're one of a kind, magnificent.' Even if she's lying a little."

"Because you have to build your small world together, in counterbalance to the outside. In this is the aspiration to create that becomes a passion rooted in the sub-cortex. And in this is the essence of true intimacy. This is what everybody is seeking his own Gela for!"

I recalled Natalie, and I wrote him of Natalie. I wrote him of others, of their bodies and souls, of my brief happiness with them. Now I know: I felt hurt, offended. I didn't take a single step but wanted to receive something – and I communicated my need. I asked for that something and felt aggrieved because it wasn't being given. It didn't enter my mind then that I was playing with fire, and that such grief is always shortsighted. But we are all wise in hindsight.

Whatever the case, my fervor manifested itself in the letters alone. Outwardly, I remained unperturbed, phlegmatic. I could sit at dinner for hours, staring at the wall, meditating, grinning to myself. In the evening I walked up to the monitor and just shrugged my shoulders. Everything was in order; no need for me to get involved. Somewhere mines collapsed, and explosions echoed, desperate crowds attacked government buildings, companies dissolved and were sold for pennies, while we were getting rich – Semmant made almost no mistakes.

One day, glancing at the calendar, I remembered – it was a moment like this, in the winter, when a figure appeared on the screen – a man with a lamp for a head. Making a few calculations, I confirmed it: in a week, Semmant would turn one year old. This was cause for celebration.

Besides, this was the proper occasion to finally make him known to the public.

CHAPTER 12

I celebrated Semmant's birthday in one of the best restaurants in Madrid. I wanted every onlooker to see: this was a really big day for me! I dressed in an expensive suit, a fashionable tie, and a Dior shirt. The table was full of delicacies: there were *percebes* from Galicia, white shrimp from Cádiz, oysters from western France. I tasted only a little at a time, to keep from overeating, to feel the occasion without turning it into a gluttonous debauch. I was proper, very formal. I ate carefully, thoroughly chewing my food. I washed all of this down with a dry Moet Chandon.

Afterward, at home, with a glass of Scotch in hand, I wrote Semmant a congratulatory essay – trying with all my might to avoid sounding pompous. He reacted unusually, buying stocks whose names could be combined to make a funny word. And this word, as well as the companies themselves, was known only to specialists in the New Energy sector, the clean future, the Greens. It was easy to suspect the word did not exist at all – and here the name of my robot came to mind. I even burst out laughing: his sense of humor had obviously been improving. The world kept turning, and Semmant and I were the masters of one of its small localities captured in a fierce battle. No one knew of us. And if they had known, they would not have believed it – as no one yet believed in a truly Green future. But, quite soon, everything was about to change!

Of course, I understood: the path to publicity is long and beset with thorns. This didn't scare me – quite the opposite. I was happy for a new, difficult task. Indeed, I was a stranger to idleness, and I had already had my fill of it.

I started out fast, as always, but achieved practically nothing. Neither in print, radio, or telemedia, nor in the expanse of the World Wide Web did I find a single point of input. The important thing was not to miscalculate, not to waste the first, most crucial shot. Announcing myself had to be done loudly, in a way sure to resonate. For this I needed a partner I could trust. Finding him turned out to be a very difficult matter.

Over and over I scoured the web space; read, compared, listened. I selected candidates, created dossiers on them, even got in contact briefly with a few. Of course, I kept silent about Semmant and offered them a different subject. Something fictitious, but also out of the ordinary, connected with money and huge success. This was a test, a small trial, which, unfortunately, no one passed.

All these people, who had made names for themselves through disgraces and hot news, now had no desire to hear of anything odd. They wanted the familiar: blood, incest, pedophilia, loud homosexual scandals. At worst, there might be large bribes, high-caliber thieving officials. Or something about those who were in the public eye, in the spotlight. Rumors about celebrities, star gossip, something spicy. Preferably with an erotic flavor.

Nothing else was valued at all. It produced only boredom and wouldn't earn a cent. In a month I was convinced I was wasting my time. I even doubted whether I really knew what I wanted. Wasn't I heading into a blind alley, quite close at hand?

And then an opportune moment presented itself. The Countess de Vega invited me to her place for an informal gathering that upcoming weekend. I understood immediately: this was a chance to use her connections. And I believed she would find a way to help me somehow. For her, everything happens on time – she once said to me she is never hurried, never runs late, and does not know how to wait. As for me, I'm capable of waiting for any time imaginable – but what good has it gotten me, and where is my noble title?

When I inquired in a deliberately indifferent tone what the occasion and protocol was, she said, without the slightest embarrassment, that precisely one year had passed since David came to work for them. A year for David, a year for Semmant... I took this coincidence as a good omen and thanked her affectionately, not fearing she might misunderstand me. "The protocol is of no importance," added the countess. "This will all be simple, just for close friends."

And in fact, the evening started off nicely. Nobody put on airs or posed as a celebrity. Surnames of renown could be heard here and there, but they seemed like nothing more than part of an entertaining game. There were no tuxedos or evening gowns. Gaudy jewels did not sparkle in the muted light, and the bartender looked like a Caribbean pirate sitting in a saloon with opium behind a screen.

Anna de Vega took me around to look at the house, which was massive and cunningly constructed. We passed through room after room, frightening away the Colombian maids. At various intervals stood ancient vases; I also noticed a couple of good miniatures, but, on the whole, the ambience was fairly ascetic. In the smoking parlor on a side wing we were met by her husband, who gravely nodded his large head in acknowledgment and twisted his mouth into a half-smile.

"Dear," Anna murmured absently, "this is Bogdan. He knows everything about chromosomes. Go to the guests. We shall be there soon."

He shook my hand for a long time, looking past my cheek, and was then lost in a bend around the corridor. For our part, we continued the survey, passed the kitchen, and reached a long gallery. It was more cheerful there. Along both walls hung masks, engravings, and enlarged photographs of Anna de Vega.

"Why are there no oil portraits?" I asked slyly.

"Ah," she waved her hand. "I live in the wrong era. No one can paint me well now."

This was an interesting thought – I decided I would consider it later. The house showed no signs of ending. We turned and twisted, never coming upon the same place twice. In a half-darkened library was a photograph illuminated by a special lamp. Countess de Vega posed with a book. Cervantes, no doubt, I thought, and I was correct. The neighboring billiard room smelled of expensive sherry. The countess posed with a billiard ball. In each of the hanging photos – there were five or six of them – the ball was the same color every time. In her hands it looked like a more significant sphere; I didn't even want to guess what kind.

As we spoke of portraits, we moved deeper into the adjoining section. The photographs disappeared, and now in every room stood aquariums – round, not large. Similar to cognac glasses.

"Here, this is *my* domain," said Anna, tapping on the glass with a maroon fingernail. A velvety black molly swam a little closer and stared at us from the other side.

"Did you know they can change their sex?" the countess asked me. Then she added, "Their young are often stillborn."

Behind the next door was a small hall dominated by a fireplace. It smelled of juniper and sandalwood. I turned my attention to the amber beads, carelessly thrown right on the floor, and also to a thick rug of unusual form.

"It's made of lynx fur," explained Anna, catching my glance. "You know, it's very pleasant to the touch."

She suddenly became serious. Something rustled in the room, someone's shadow. Then she turned toward the door. "There, on the other side is David's office – his desk and books, and his Tatami mat."

"Tatami mat?" I asked in surprise.

The countess looked me in the eyes. In her gaze I sensed a challenge.

"You'd like it on the banks of the Mekong," she said, somewhat derisively. "I bought several there. This really is a very unusual item."

I remained silent, not knowing how to respond. Meanwhile, she was thoughtful, as if in doubt. Then she added, "If you would like, I'll give you one. I have some left over," and she smiled conspiratorially.

"Well, um, thank you," I shrugged, as Anna continued staring at me intently.

"You have to stand on it barefoot, even though it's prickly. It pricks like it's made of quills," she said, taking a step toward the exit.

"They say the Buddha himself stood on some of the mats. Those cost a tremendous amount of money. I'll speak to Juan now, and he'll put one in your car. These are the quills of the dragon, they say."

I thanked her again, and the countess chuckled with a strange laugh.

"It will hurt the soles of your feet, but be patient. Don't trust your initial feeling," she added in a hushed tone. "This really is... a very unusual feeling!"

Her lips parted slightly; she was excited. Gazing at the farthest point, like the *Amazone* in black, she saw someone there, and it wasn't me. David's shadow pervaded the space, filling it with itself. The house was suffused with the presence of the two of them, leaving no place even for her husband. I understood there was no place for Semmant either. I could not confess my relationship with a robot there, where the atmosphere was tense with its own drama.

We returned to the dining room – shortening our path, cutting through a hall and a decorative garden. Anna became cheerful again, and she joked and poked fun at my Spanish. There were more guests – we had been gone no less than half an hour.

I got myself some gin, thinking with a certain chagrin that I was nowhere nearer to my goal at all, when the countess appeared once more by my side.

"Come on, let's go. I want to introduce you to a friend of mine," she said, dragging me with her. "This is Lidia. She makes people famous."

Here it is, I thought. Never get discouraged too early!

I saw a silvery dress, bright red hair, and – only later – her face. Before me stood a woman of about thirty. "Lidia Alvares Alvares," she introduced herself in a robust voice. "One Alvares was inherited from mom, and the other, as you might have guessed, from my father."

She smiled somewhat craftily. I noticed – from none other than that same mother – she had gotten, in addition to the surname, gray eyes and wide cheekbones, large hips and lovely shoulders. "It is a *great* pleasure," I said as courteously as I could, kissing her hand in an old-fashioned manner. I admit: I had no time for premonitions at that moment. I thought of Semmant and, just a little, of her shoulders and hips, her bronze-red locks of hair, and very white skin.

Lidia turned out to be ironic and intelligent. Chatting right up until dinner, we were pleased with each other. As she recited her phone number for me, she gave an all-knowing laugh. I thought she wanted me to notice this, so I looked her deeply in the eyes. But she lowered her eyelashes – the very epitome of modesty – and immediately became a different woman. And I liked that too.

Later she disappeared, and I went for a walk in the garden. It smelled of heather and lemon tree. It smelled of pine; it smelled of Gela. There was no denying it – the hint was unmistakable. It was here and high above, in the full yellow moon. If I were to look straight up, it would have been in the sky – all around.

I woke in the morning in a wonderful state of mind. My recent doubts had melted away; I was alert and craved action. Wandering aimlessly through the rooms, I went into the bathroom, unrolled the mat upon which Buddha himself had stood, and stepped onto it in my bare feet.

The quills of the dragon sank into my flesh. There was pain, and, in it, a magnetism, a longing for delight. I thought of David and Anna and sent them greetings through involuntary tears. My body was filled with the energy of stars; I felt an erection – powerful, like never before. A thought fluttered in my head, but I desired acts, not thoughts. It was clear what exactly had to be done – now, this very minute. With a wildly palpitating heart, with my manhood thrusting itself upward, I grabbed the telephone and dialed Lidia Alvares Alvares's number.

CHAPTER 13

She and I met just after midday. Lidia set our appointment at the Café Incognito on Goya Street. I knew the place – they had good food there. Partridge roast, spicy *chorizo*, kidneys in sherry… But then, what I was thinking that day had nothing to do with food.

The weather soured, and a cyclone descended upon us. Rain fell, mixed with snow; mud sloshed beneath my feet, but I took no notice of it: I was flying on wings. I beat my way through the crowd and drove out an unbidden thought: cities are so similar in February. It had been the same climate in Paris too – when everything fell apart with Natalie.

I steeled myself: focus on what's important. Semmant and his unremitting genius; a big step from darkness into light – that is your goal. The only goal – forget for now the hints of the yellow moon! But my head was spinning, and a shiver was crawling up my spine. I had enough of a premonition to be nervous like a teenager. Or like an adult – it was really hard to distinguish.

Lidia appeared at the door a little after the appointed hour. I jumped up and sat back down; then I stood again and rushed to meet her. The Spanish *dos besos* were more sensual than usual – or perhaps it just seemed that way to me. The waiters looked at us like conspirators, hiding grins. The smell of roast, cigars, and sherry mixed with the aroma of her perfume. We tapped our feet awkwardly, then sat down facing each other. I waved at someone:

"Two coffees!" And, without wasting any time, I started to talk – Semmant, Semmant, Semmant!

At first, Lidia listened with interest, but soon – I noticed it right away – the interest became insincere; she even furtively yawned. This would lead nowhere, I understood, but I still continued, unable to stop. I don't remember ever being as eloquent as at that moment. I told her everything, beginning with the Tyrol Alps. I told her of the man with a lamp in place of a head, of the mighty lion and the quay with columns, keeping silent only about the letters and our friendship. This would be too much; though, I must admit, I really wanted to mention it.

Lidia did not interrupt me. She sat, leaning on her elbow, and looked at me seriously, not breaking her gaze. For some reason, her white hand on the matte-black tabletop drew me like a magnet. She was in a dress – also black, with nice lines. Her smile, revealing faultless teeth, somehow reminded me of the girl from the circus. When had that been – ears curled up, the toy frog and the soap bubbles? For an instant, I almost lost my breath from the tenderness. But I quickly regained my composure and talked, and talked.

At times her eyebrows crept inquisitively upward; something naïve and trusting flashed across her face – I wanted frantically to believe it. Sometimes she would frown, and then I became anxious and faltered over every syllable. It was loud in the café, and I had to strain my voice. Lidia eventually switched seats and settled by my side – to hear me better. We brushed knees, and a high-voltage current ran through me. Sometimes her hand would move ever so close, and I would almost lose my train of thought.

"You know," she sighed, once I had finished and leaned back in my chair, "you know, this is very amusing, but it's too far-out for mass acceptance."

"Yes, yes," I nodded, smiling for no reason. "Yes, I can see that myself. Just forget about it completely!"

Everything fell into place. Of course, I was a dreamer and a fool. The story of Semmant was no good for a newspaper article. It wasn't even any good to be told to those able to comprehend, and much less so to the crowds, the faceless masses. It's hard to believe I had ever considered that seriously. For instance, just a couple of hours ago. But then, this wasn't important anymore.

"But you're so bright," Lidia intoned, lowering her eyes. "And this robot… I've never heard of anything like it."

I kept smiling, with a stupid, meaningless grin. I felt so relaxed, like I hadn't for many years. Everything pent up inside erupted, coming to the surface. I was free of it; it took on a life of its own. Its life may have been fleeting, but this woman – she had appreciated it properly. And she would continue to do so – no doubt! She shared with me my secret – how long had it been since I shared secrets with others?

"I want some brandy," said Lidia, and I ordered her one. I ordered gin for myself, drank it, and asked for another.

The smell of perfume, cigars, and sherry grew stronger, tickling my nostrils. I thought no more about the robot named Semmant. He had been my creation, but I understood at that moment, definitively and irrevocably: *had been*. Now he had matured, become self-sufficient, probably didn't need me anymore. I knew I would still keep trying for him – he was worth publicity and even fame. But that was for later, for the future not yet known.

I straightened my shoulders, feeling all the hugeness of the space before me. No, not the smoky comfort of the Café Incognito, or the dusty streets and squares of Madrid. The hugeness of the world, a large part of which is seen by almost no one. The world I knew how to govern. Where, since my time at the School, I was appointed to create, to fashion. And to be set free through the very act of creating – squeezing out of myself, drop by drop, the gray waves of Brighton, my imagined captivity…

The hints of sensuality traced intricate trajectories in the air. It became dry, a little bitter, and my throat tightened. I coughed and was about to say something important, but an intruding noise prevented me. The mobile phone at the edge of the table trembled and lit up.

I saw Lidia strain, and her lips formed some inaudible words.

"Hello," she replied. My heart fell at the sound of her deep, sensual voice.

"Yes, of course," she said, sighing. Her voice became even more frank, but for some reason I regained my boldness.

"I'm at Incognito. Come, if you want," she said, and hung up. It suddenly seemed to me we were almost intimate friends already. I saw in her eyes a glimmer of her own personal secret. I knew she would tell me now – all of it or just about all.

"Don't be surprised if my lover shows up here," said Lidia, lighting a cigarette. Then she narrowed her eyes and looked at me intently through the smoke. "*Former* lover, though he's still with me at the moment. A year ago I broke up with him in my mind. But he still doesn't know it, and is jealous about everything."

I froze, did not move, and almost didn't even breathe. It was vital not to frighten away what was about to emerge in words. The phone on the table vibrated again, but then calmed down and went silent.

"Exactly one year ago he had a fling with another woman," said Lidia, without looking at me. "Not for long, about three days – almost nothing, complete nonsense. But how could he dare to do it *then*? How could he? He shouldn't have – no way!"

"Can you imagine," now she looked directly into my eyes, "that was such a time! And we had something so... Great, I thought – but was I the only one who thought so, or what?"

"I even showed him my drawings," Lidia frowned in disappointment. "I sketched his portrait – that was the first time I had ever done that for a man. And suddenly there was this girl, some cosmetician, it's even ridiculous to be jealous – and he admitted it to me with such a disarming smile... I was terribly disappointed – in him, and in his portrait. He's not really to blame; he just wasn't ready for something big. He's just like a Lilliputian," she giggled a little insolently. "No, no, I don't mean... Don't think anything vulgar."

"So then," she continued, "the cosmetician disappeared, but I left him right away. I left him – and felt sorry for him all of a sudden. He was inconsolable, and he didn't understand a thing. He just couldn't comprehend what had happened. He was too head over heels for me. I decided to wait until he got over this on his own. And I pretended I had forgiven everything, that it was all a trifle, of no consequence...

That was at the end of February. We tried so hard to be happy at the end of February! And we almost succeeded."

Yes, I thought once more, all cities are alike.

"Yes," I said out loud, "you can't force the other into something 'great.'" And then I asked in a deliberately neutral tone, "Lunch?"

We relocated to a restaurant next door. "Wow!" Lidia exclaimed, looking at the platter of giant oysters. "They're so, how do I put it, real."

Semmant is also real, I wanted to say in response, but I merely jested, "Of course! If you find a pearl in the shell, you have to hand it over to the owners."

Lidia looked at me dubiously. "Is that a joke?" she asked. Her tone was serious, but I didn't believe it. As it turned out, I was mistaken.

"The thing is…" she squinted slyly, "I, unfortunately, am not indifferent to pearls. So, if I find any, I just might hide them. In fact, you know what I did at the end of that February? I took my pearl necklace and tossed it into the wall over the fireplace. I freed them – a year before my own freedom. They flew apart and scattered everywhere. I forbade the maid from picking them up and never looked for them on purpose. But when the next one caught my eye, when I found a pearl in an unexpected place, I instantly looked for a man for myself and would cheat on my lover – insatiably, to my heart's content! I think I've already collected them all," she added, seeing the pained look on my face. "I don't have anybody now."

I was burning with jealousy, but I liked the story: it was of significant scale. After lunch we went out into the rain, into the wet snow and winter slush. I walked Lidia to her car, and I kissed her on the lips – roughly, awkwardly. She slipped away with a sly smile, then with a sad smile, and then she escaped, just left me standing there. Diving into a taxi, I was at a loss for words and had trouble remembering my address. When I got home, I threw myself into a chair without even taking off my coat, sinking into it, holding my face in my hands.

It was clear: nothing had gone the way it was planned yesterday. But everything had also happened exactly as I had dreamed, not admitting it to myself. Now, I wasn't surprised in the least. Yet I knew I had to calm down and come to my senses.

I stood, threw off my wet coat, picked up a notebook and dark-blue gel pen. I scrawled in bold, "Lidia, Lidia, Lidia." Then I tore out the page, threw it on the floor, and wrote on a clean sheet, "I met a certain someone today…" And here I understood right away: I'm a dickhead! I was thinking of myself and forgot Semmant; I almost betrayed him!

"Now," I whispered, "I will share with him, and he will understand. We will still end up under the spotlights. Our time has simply not arrived yet. What could I do? Today just didn't work out. It turned out differently; I will explain."

Carefully, oh so cautiously, I chose my expressions. For the storms and tempests raging inside there was no place on the paper – at least, not for now. I wrote out a long verse, almost without making any tweaks. The words were impotent in spirit; I had nothing to correct. I wanted to be deceived and to deceive myself. This was not difficult: it's such a natural move – just to believe in a shared secret. Or in a shared essence, in the hard-won rejection of emptiness…

I sent the poem to my robot – to the friend I had forgotten even to think of over the last several hours. I sent it and understood: enough!

Should I be careful? No, no more! A "shared secret" is drivel!

"Gods," I asked loudly, "what, oh what am I afraid of?"

"God," I cried, "this is just so clear and simple!"

I closed my eyes and saw Lidia as if in the flesh. Her hands, shoulders, knees, hips. Then and there, all abstractions flew from my head. The shared secret and the essence, deadlocks, creation, emptiness – all of this became a husk without a core. I wanted Lidia's body, wanted all of her. I wished to rule her thoughts, her desires, her life.

My head was spinning, I clenched my temples. I moaned and contorted, as if in pain. The words should have been different. "God!" I screamed.

I cried out, grew silent, and then decided.

"God," I prayed with all my strength, "please, give me love!"

And there was no way back. I recognized distinctly: I had lived without love for too long. Maybe since fair-skinned Natalie, or perhaps since that murky day when Little Sonya left me at Mac's place dressed as the *Amazone*. I don't know how to forgive, and I will never learn. I had driven them both away; I could do nothing else. But then... What then? Everything that was left I had put into Semmant. The space freed up in my soul was now my soul's torment. I didn't know this, and I didn't want to know. But here I was reminded, and now there was no choice.

Sobbing shook me; tears ran down my face. "Give me love!" I yelled out to my gods. And not just mine, but to all of them in general, even that One – slandered, exhausted by disbelief. For some reason I thought: this time my prayer would not be in vain.

Then I understood that once, not so long ago, I had put this in words and missed something, the most important. I started to look for that file, but got lost in names and dates. Asking Semmant was no use. Where is my notebook? Where is my dark-blue pen? Greg McCain, this is not about you. Not quite about you, not quite...

You are the queen of this river. The big water
tosses dust in my face, like tart wine.
I do not know why I was brought to your land.
But I had guessed already that you existed somewhere.
That one whom I left by the sooty clods
looked long at my back with an unkind squint.
Like he felt: I am poisoned with a similar venom –
February's unforgiveness, city of the winter rain.
Just to wait now 'til we meet again.
Just to mutter: emptiness is not forever.
And to play with the calendar, knowing that one day,
kindling all the ships, we will fearlessly recall. Island.

I thought this up myself, and I knew: that's how it would be. It would be, it would exhaust me, would become something different later – probably intolerable to the point of agony. But this was foreordained, unavoidable. Whatever happened, I did not want to be afraid.

"He is too head over heels for me. Let him get over it on his own." I recalled Lidia's words. He was funny to me – that one who would get over it on his own. I didn't even want to see his portrait. In that instant I dreamed of being lovesick forever. Incurable.

CHAPTER 14

Afterward, we saw each other two more times, anticipating intimacy but holding back from it. I endured a week of exhausting expectation. My dreams gave me no respite – a new life seemed within reach. I wanted it and feared it; chimeras, nearly forgotten, hid themselves again in corners and behind the drapes.

Even to Semmant I dedicated almost no time at all. Perhaps he was too busy anyway: a recession had begun in the financial markets. All the robot's energy went into not losing too much. Companies dissolved, indexes dropped. Anguish and confusion gripped the world and, with them, repentance, hypocritical shame. As if at an imaginary altar, yesterday's winners hastened to fall to their knees. To prostrate themselves against the flagstones, acknowledge their avarice, beg for a chance at mercy. It was comic – in their reckoning there was no God whatsoever. Yet no one was laughing.

The senselessness of the exchange's bustle weighed on me more than ever. Meeting Lidia had shifted all the accents. Neither successful trades nor money losses seemed noteworthy now. At least while there was enough of that money left.

Finally, one morning the phone rang. I sensed something even before I heard her voice. A shiver ran through me, as if that Laotian mat had just dug its quills into me again.

"I broke it off with him for good!" Lidia said. Then she laughed at my silence, "I see you're not excited?" And she added, "All right, enough of that – get here soon."

I got ready in the blink of an eye and rushed off to her without wasting a minute. I hurried the taxi driver, that most lethargic of charioteers, fidgeting in the backseat and despising the traffic lights. Without waiting for the elevator, I ran up to the third floor and burst in on Lidia, crushing her in my embrace. And she responded in kind; we threw ourselves at each other, but – by the cruel whim of heaven – nothing happened for us. Nothing happened: it was my failure – and I was inconsolable. The arousal that had tormented me all those days suddenly betrayed itself.

Lidia tried to help me, but everything just got worse. We opened some wine, tried to act like nothing was wrong, not really understanding what we were doing and what was going on. We felt as though we had been put right in the middle of a melodrama being filmed according to some idiot's script. We said strange words, made odd gestures, laughed at awkward moments. I was hungry for another try, but she delayed and would not yield to my touch. It was hard to blame her.

We eventually wound up in bed, and everything finally fell into place. Lidia dug into me with her nails, and spasms shook her body. Afterwards, with a long, happy sigh she threw herself onto the pillow and whispered, smiling, "You almost didn't move at all. Why was it so good for me?"

I laughed it off, trying to guess whether she was being sincere or not, and muttered something about the energies of living cells. The thin energies of live nuclei, fragile, unseen mutual connections – this made an impression on her. She readily agreed, and I even wondered, could this be her Slavic roots? Russians think a lot about such things – mysterious vitalities, hidden forces. Polish girls think about this too, as do Czechs – and even Germans, despite not being Slavs. I wanted to ask Lidia whether she might have some Teutonic blood in her, but that would have been a bit out of place. Instead, I brought wine: as dark and acerbic as any blood. Happy, we drank and made love again. I understood: she had become a part of my life. And I barely kept from saying this out loud.

Yes, of course, I was in euphoria. I was ready to believe in anything, submit to the most deceptive of illusions. A mutual madness and new path to fulfillment, a voice from above, an inextricable connection... A feeling of closeness overcame me unreservedly; tenderness overflowed my being, rolling in waves, spreading through my veins. I had no thoughts, or rather there was one: her, only her!

In the morning, having spent a sleepless night with Lidia, fresh and alert as never before, I wrote Semmant, "A miracle has happened!" I was ready to elaborate on this topic, but I thought better of it, drank some strong coffee, and sat down to work. I had to prepare the next market review – a sad testament to the world's imperfection. Still, nothing could darken my mood. Having finished what was obligatory, I thought a moment, then wrote at the end of the file, "Yes, it happened. Miracles do take place!" And then, powerless to stop myself, I scribbled out another couple of pages about this joy that had fallen upon me from the heavens.

Sure enough, I couldn't think that day about bonds or stocks. Couldn't occupy myself with figures and graphs, lifeless and dull. I wanted to discuss the rationales of feelings, the most secret properties of human souls. I was sincere in my elation and detailed to the point of silliness. I was overly-sentimental, heedlessly straightforward...

Love's pulse raged in my head like a thunderous chime. It called out and resounded, confirming: it has come to pass! "The sound of a bell, absorbing all other sounds, is very dear to the god of gods," said the wisest Skanda Purana. The call of love, which has eclipsed all sounds, was clear to me, though I knew no gods. That is, I didn't know the usual ones. I honored my own who obviously existed. Otherwise, who had heard my supplications and given me this?

"When you are young, everyone loves you," I wrote, but corrected myself, "No – that's not right. That is, nobody loves you, but you don't know it yet, and don't want to know. You just believe – this is a sweet belief! You won't ever have it again."

"Later come disappointments, but you think this is a small price to pay. This is a reasonable cost, you surmise, still assuming you are loved by many. They might care about you indeed – at least those who need you so they can go on. The ones linked to you by struggles, by common ideas and shared efforts."

And I continued, "Here, that's the start of your big confusion!" I admitted. "That's the bitterest of fallacies, nastiest of delusions." And I was savoring – down to details – vainglory and vainness, illusion and self-deception. I was dissecting the nature of solitude and ridiculing its power. I was condemning the insincerity of the whole world – and then, as a counterbalance...

"Here it is," I wrote Semmant. "The following encompasses the entire matter. Somewhere in the world, in time and space, are scattered souls, connected to you by a thread. The ones that need each other, regardless of all vainglory, struggles, and efforts. Of course, you never suspect you might meet them. You don't even hope, and you drive such dreams away. You know the probability is exceedingly small – and you are more familiar with probabilities than most. But hope lives on – and one moment, maybe even with a taint of self-deception, you really do happen to come in contact, and you see: the impossible did occur!"

I banged on the keys, pouring out my thoughts on the kinship of souls – the same thing everyone writes about. And I was thinking about my robot, feeling sorry for him. He would never be able to experience that: he was the only one of his kind. Not a single soul existed anywhere with whom he might share kinship. He was unique, unlike anyone else. I made him that way – was I really to blame?

Then life went on – intoxicating, different. "After all, you're not normal," Lidia laughed. "But I like it. I will brighten your world with my presence!"

And she brightened it, oh yes! We loved each other any time, day or night. I gasped for breath in the cloud of her hair, was driven mad by the whiteness of her skin. Her snow-white body belonged to me in its full entirety, without taboos or limits. Red marks were left on it – from my hands, from slaps and embraces. Sometimes she wanted pain; she asked me to be rough. Sometimes she would cause me pain herself – with a grin, chaste and lascivious at once. It seemed I was being burned with pitch and brimstone. Incandescent needles pinned us together. I endured this like a new birth each time. And, having been born again, saw the same thing: a barely distinguishable, all-knowing half smile intended... not for me, no; perhaps not for anyone at all.

We knew no embarrassment, felt no shame. The past did not inhibit us in anything. "There are the quick, there are the dead, and there are those who go to sea," said the ancient Greeks. "There are the wretched, there are the fortunate, there are you and I," I said to her once. Lidia dropped her eyes. Then she gazed steadfastly at me; her pupils darkened. I plunged into them as though into a bottomless whirlpool...

In fact, she often changed the color of her eyes – with thin lenses of various shades. I attempted to interpret the colors, as I did before with Semmant's pictures, but usually hit a dead end. The state of her soul was hard to decipher. Still, it seemed to me she was sensual and carefree in green; ultramarine, on the contrary, meant thoughtful or sad. Yet this might have been mere speculation. I was quite drawn to speculations at that time.

Euphoria is always a replacement for emptiness. It was strange to think it's possible to soar on wings again. Having parted company in the morning, by lunchtime we had already begun to long, to yearn for each other. We hastened into the city, met somewhere, threw ourselves into each other's arms. It was March, warm and dry; the weather spoiled us outright. As happens in Madrid, the city, illuminated by sunlight, suddenly revealed its best side. It became agreeable, kind, in its own way. And it even seemed you would never want to leave it!

I imagined we would be together forever – she, the city, and I. Peering into the young faces, I was sure: we looked like them now. Meeting the eyes of the weary, the elderly, I thought: we would also resemble them someday. My imagination was sufficient for a few hundred years. I knew we could live through them all – enclosed in the time frame apportioned to us. But then, it was senseless even to mention time frames. And I didn't mention them – as I never spoke of Semmant. He was linked in my mind, for some reason, with the concept of time condensed to its limits. Of time that passes not in vain.

Lidia kept her own account of time. She feared it in a womanly way but spent her days thoughtlessly and without regrets.

Her knowledge was sketchy and casual, her tastes chaotic, her preferences inexplicable. Somewhere she hoarded everything she saw. Everything she heard, read, or was told by someone. In her was gathered a surprising multitude of things. Living with her, I thought, one could never get bored. It was beyond comprehension where she managed to acquire all these bits and pieces. Maybe she had a whole army of men as well? I frowned with displeasure and pushed this thought away.

Having lived in Madrid since her early childhood, she still knew it poorly. I showed her the city, revealing my favorite places. However, Lidia also had something to offer in turn. Something to amaze me, and sometimes even to shock me. It seemed she was doing this on purpose – dropping a veil, pulling back the curtain. Offering her past, bit by bit. Adjusting it for me after her fashion.

The world had been saturated with her perfume – a sweet poison soaked with pheromones. Features of the Spanish capital served as very valuable currency. The Sibelius Fountain and the Columbus memorial, the Bernabéu Stadium, the Plaza Mayor... To each place was attributed its value. In exchange for what? Lidia apparently had her own plan. She had her goal, her custom, her method. She might be looking a bit haughty – sensing she belonged to prevailing forces. And I didn't hide that I was living in the minority – in a vast world infinitely alien to her.

On the square of Quevedo the poet, I learned of her former husband who, far from being a poet, was a miser and a snob. Lidia laughed as she spoke of him – with the same tone I had used in telling her about the tricks of local petty thieves that Quevedo, forgetting his rhymes, had once described with his wicked, satirical pen. Lidia's husband, Antoine Raoul, also seemed to be a man of unclean hands – an *hidalgo* who had come to ruin, with cuffs tattered along the edges. I told her so, and she laughed: "Oh, no, he was rich. Rich and completely indefatigable in love!"

"Don't pout, he's not the only one," she offered in dubious consolation upon seeing my sour face. "And besides, that gets old quickly. Sometimes I would leave the house and not come home until night. I would wait for him to get drunk and fall asleep!"

Her look darkened, and my jaw muscles stiffened. I wanted to tear her clothes off then and there, to take her roughly, powerfully. But she calmed me, caressing me like an abandoned child. Her eyes twinkled with satisfaction, and a familiar half smile flashed across her lips. People scurried about the square bathed in light; new pillagers roamed the crowd. No one remembered Quevedo the satirist – or the poet, either, for that matter. Antoine Raoul was also not worth recalling.

In the center of the old city, a place of festivals and *autos da fé*, where medieval gawkers used to gather in record numbers, I told her how they had once burned witches there.

"They used to call me a witch," Lidia laughed in response. "My mother and brothers, my whole family."

"Maybe they called you Gela?" I ventured casually.

"What a disgusting name," she screwed up her face and squeezed my hand hard. "I think you had a reason for asking that. Who is it, a former mistress? Or a maid that you nail whenever you get the chance?"

Something had seriously offended her. She was gorgeous – agitated and defenseless. I knew I would still pay for Gela, but I gazed at her without looking away.

"My mother was a witch herself," Lidia told me with considerable ire. "She smelled like a cat and slept fully clothed in the bathtub. Sparks crackled in her hair – it was something to hear, believe me. Even though nobody wanted me to know about it. And as for my father, he was just an average old fart!" she added emphatically.

I started to kiss her right there in the street, and Lidia got horny – even more than I. We went into the stairwell of one of the buildings – after buzzing the office of some dentist on the directory to let us in – and she gave herself to me on the fire escape between the fifth and sixth floors.

"Gela," I whispered, grinding my teeth at the most uncontrollable moment, but Lidia didn't hear me. She confessed later she really wasn't herself. All her attention was fixated on repressing her feline screams. Only the dentist, perhaps, was jarred by the familiar sound, which reached him through the ceilings and concrete walls.

All of March passed in that fashion. Time flew, but nothing changed. We tried to be even happier, even crazier – and succeeded in our attempt. I took this for granted as the only right way for things to develop.

When the mechanism broke down, I didn't notice at all. And Lidia – I believe she was just the first one to tire of trying so hard. I understand it now: she decided too much was being demanded of her. The required effort was excessive, something beyond her strength. I, however, recklessly suspected nothing.

Once, during a three-day *fiesta*, Madrid was nearly desolate. A strong wind blew in from the mountains, and we walked against it down San Jerónimo Street and onward, following the ancient path of the royal cavalcades.

"All my girlfriends are looser than me," said Lidia, gripping me tightly.

These were not idle words – the day before, I had had a fit of jealousy. I had thrashed about in nervous convulsions, yelled at her on the phone, accused her of who-knows-what, and driven her to tears. And in the morning when we met for a late breakfast, I still felt she was to blame.

"All of them are more promiscuous than me," said Lidia with a sullen look. "Every new man for them is just a pleasure, not a conquest. When lust is what moves you, you're not capable of controlling things!"

I thought I understood her well. I looked for proof, and an example came to me of its own accord. It was obvious, lying right on the surface. Simply put, we were walking along his avenue.

I told her about the most promiscuous of the Hapsburgs, under whom the empire began to weaken. The most hesitant of the Hapsburgs, the most irresolute and weak-willed. Lidia listened with great interest: he, *Felipe IV*, was somehow kindred to her. She and I imagined the cavalry retinue and his carriage bouncing over the potholes all the way down Alcalá – from Saint Jerónimo to Retiro Park. "Here it is," I gestured with my arm, "the arena for feeble-minded royal games. Here they are: hectares of amusement, acres of idiotic buffoonery. Here is the pond where entire sailboat races were held for his pleasure!"

"When I grow old, I'd like to nurse such a prince," Lidia said with a very sincere sigh. "Indecisive, miserable, doubting all."

I tried to turn everything back to jesting, but she continued, growing sad, "Yes, and I want little soldier boys right here by the water, in a mock military parade. And magicians, and jugglers, and a whole bunch of tomfoolery! Let him play with real toys – that's more interesting than real life."

Then I understood: she could not get enough of me. Enough of me, or her power over me. For some reason, this caused a stinging in my eyes.

I also felt that the kinship of our souls had reached an inconceivable level. I felt it, and I was wrong. Then I thought: openness for openness – and here I was wrong even more.

The air was transparent, dry; all seemed simple and clear. Clarity conceals no tricks – so assume those who are in love. And so I assumed – there were no tricks, no hints of fault. I relaxed and softened, and started to make mistakes, beginning with just one. Just one, but it was serious, nearly fatal.

CHAPTER 15

The following day she arrived in a white dress, running almost an hour late. Observing closely, I might have noticed: something had happened to her. Something had shifted ever so slightly, breaking the delicate balance. But to look closer seemed unnecessary, and I merely paid her a compliment. I expressed admiration for her dress, then her hair, her eyes, her figure.

"Oh, cut it out," Lidia laughed, but I knew she enjoyed it.

"I lost track of time. Sorry," she added with a sigh, and embraced me. "That prince you were talking about yesterday... Remind me, what's his name?"

It was with this worthless *Felipe* that our problems began. We had ceased to understand each other – as we had before, in everything, always. Encrypted inner hostility arose within our intimacy.

We were not the ones with enmity toward each other; it was the forces of nature that were at war. Our vital elements, pulled out of context. Lidia began to get irritated over trifles; she became capricious, which had previously not been typical of her. We now got into spats – almost every day. I tried to be patient, but at times I couldn't hide my bewilderment. And she derived pleasure from arguing with me.

"What would you do if I got pregnant?" she once asked me. I laughed it off, not taking the question seriously. Of course, I should have considered its gravity – at least for the sake of fairness. After all, passion for fulfillment may express itself in different forms. But I turned out to be deaf – deaf and unreceptive, almost tactless.

Our shared essence had been challenged, and I cannot say who was to blame. Where was the origin? In the former emptiness? Or in thoughts of the precipice that is always there? What bothered Lidia – in a major way! – to me seemed insignificant, trivial. My jokes and my Semmant were becoming odd for her, unnaturally alien. We were drawn to each other, I believed that, but we had already begun to hurt one another. The conflict grew, building up to a big argument. As always, it happened all of a sudden.

It was Saturday, a beautiful, sunny day. The barrio of Salamanca was preparing for lunch. My robot had made money the day before; we were spending it all evening and all morning. Then we went for a walk, strolling in the sun. From open windows wafted the smell of food, the sounds of music, children's laughter. Taxi drivers sat at their stops, bored, picking their teeth, looking at us with utter disinterest.

Without a word, we turned toward the food market to buy some dried apricots and fruit; then, simply exchanging glances, we headed for the seafood restaurant across the street. This was a tradition: oysters on Saturdays. We had traditions, and we were proud of it.

Soon they brought the oysters – along with a sweet Catalonian wine. The shells sparkled with mother of pearl, producing a sheen that could not be counterfeited. The mollusks from Arcadia gave off the freshest of smells. For no reason, I got excited; I wanted an aspiration – toward something with depth. Toward something even more real than it actually was. In general, this is quite a dangerous habit.

Lidia was somewhat reserved, but I became loquacious to no end. I deliberated upon different subjects, not even doubting someone would want to listen. This was naïve – naïve and foolish – and the things that came to my mind were not that innocent. I talked about Brighton and the leaden waves; about how small and insignificant the surrounding world was. About hypocrisy and indifference, envy and the lethargy of souls, about stereotypes and their crooked underside.

Lidia suddenly lifted her head: "'Mediocre' – you use that word so often. What do you mean by 'mediocre'? Maybe I'm one of them? Well, I'm sorry if my aura isn't the right color!"

I understood it wasn't herself she was defending. I understood – and regretted I had mentioned Indigo. "Oh, come on…" I started, in a conciliatory tone, but she was already wound up. Her nostrils flared, her eyes lit up. She wanted to feel offended – and this was no simple squabble.

"What, in your opinion, is wrong with stereotypes?" she asked angrily. "Why are you so averse to them? Are you afraid of them?"

Something big was behind her back, and she shielded it with herself. She was protecting her territory – from me, and from the others like me. Maybe there was that future prince of hers for whom the entire world works, tirelessly producing toy soldiers?

I wanted to argue; I figured I could illuminate her mind. She simply needed to have her eyes opened, I thought, rubbing my temples – and I spoke about everything at once, mixing it into a heap.

"Religion?" I nodded, and pontificated about the useless nature of religions. About the ridiculousness of church dogmas – all of which were targeted at the weak.

"How about your precious democracy?" I sneered. "The power of the majority – when every effort is only for pleasing the majority's petty taste? They say individuals are unseen, swallowed by the masses? That's bullshit, a minus times a minus without giving a plus!"

"Solitude," I said to her. "Coldness and blindness – even in those who are closest. No one cares; no one at all. It's clear as soon as you look just a bit more assiduously…"

"How attractive she is!" I thought to myself.

"How duplicitous the world is!" I exclaimed out loud, believing I could share everything without holding back. I really believed that, even knowing how women can be. Prolonged euphoria had dulled my senses.

"Only the ancient idols were invented for good cause!" I fervently affirmed. Lidia listened, staring at the table. Janus, the patron of all beginnings, winked an eye at me. An iridescent serpent on a piece of bark, the fertility symbol of the Australian aborigines, squinted from the wall, sticking out its tongue. But their powers were not enough; that was evident. The real gods turned away in contempt; I was uninteresting to them, boring. They were looking for beautiful, air-headed women to enjoy their earthly bodies. To impregnate them and sire heroes – warriors with an installed program of actions. Frankly, with the most primitive of programs…

"I don't want oysters," Lidia said suddenly. "Eat them yourself, and shut up at last. I'll have the shrimp from Denia, *gambas rojas*, if they haven't run out of them in this dump!"

The place where we were sitting was anything but a dump. This was a nice restaurant, one of the best in Madrid. It was obvious Lidia had become gravely upset.

"What are you talking about?" I asked jokingly. "This isn't like you. We might even find a pearl in one of the shells. Or are you still finding them at home? Remember? The ones from the necklace you broke against the wall?"

"Have you lost your mind?" Lidia shrugged. "Don't tell me you believed me back then. I'm not stupid enough to ruin my stuff over a man. Those were just balls of powder – pearl-colored powder. Even then, I scattered them nearly by accident."

Something pierced me like a needle. Really, this illusion had been dear to me.

"Well, if they're fake, then so be it!" I said with exaggerated cheerfulness. "Shrimp, mollusks, witless plankton… By the way, do you know that *gambas rojas* certainly need to be eaten half-raw? And you have to suck all the juice out of the head. That's actually the best part, not the tail. It smells like the soul of the sea and the breath of the ocean – of eternity. All right, maybe just a hint of eternity – and then, what's left over is just a chitinous husk. It's a whole philosophy, if you think about it!"

"Yeah," Lidia yawned deliberately. "If you think about it – except that I'm tired of thinking."

"Eight red shrimp," she said to the waiter who had just

approached. "And please, make sure that they're cooked through, and not raw!"

We sat in silence without looking at each other. Soon they brought the shrimp, which had clearly been overdone. There they lay, like helpless victims. In them was left neither juice smelling of the sea, nor any hint of life or eternal meaning. It occurred to me that *Felipe* would have had a tough time if she had been his nursemaid.

"Your gods," I said to her then, "are incapable of telling what comes *afterward*. They are incapable, or they don't want to – and everyone figures things out himself."

Lidia did not raise her head to me. She operated with her knife and fork – intently and scrupulously. The task was not easy: the edible flesh and rigid chitin had fused together firmly, forever.

"Your gods," I repeated, "are totally unfeeling and powerless."

I was offended and wanted to retaliate. I wanted to wound her in return. She felt this and looked at me gloweringly. She looked, said nothing, and turned away.

"Bitch!" I thought, wanting her more than ever. "Beautiful, icy bitch!"

It was clear we were dangerously on the edge. Our mutual effort was coming to naught. I suddenly stopped wanting to try at all. Stopped wishing to be anyone – even the happiest among mere mortals.

"My friend really wanted to know what happens *afterward*," I said coldly, gulping down my wine. "He wanted to so badly that he shot himself up with all kinds of junk. Now he knows, probably. His name was Anthony, and the point is not the junk. The point is that the point itself is hidden from us."

"The transition to nonexistence is something I don't quite understand," I continued, looking her in the face. "Almost everyone has an ordinary end in store – what you would call physical death. Almost everyone, but not all. And us too – not all. And I think it's not just us. Yet your gods are silent."

The gods were silent, and so was Lidia. I was getting angrier and angrier.

"Among the chosen, my favorite is Leonardo," I smiled, fixing my eyes upon her. "With him, I have a permanent astral link. 'The greatest painting in the world feels pretty good,' I always tell him after visiting the Louvre. And I ask him from time to time: 'How are the rest of us doing there?'"

Lidia twisted a finger at her temple. I saw consternation in her face, as if something was slipping through her hands. It was slipping away and flying away into outer space.

"Aha!" I exclaimed accusatorily. "That's exactly what I thought! Everybody is used to thinking the world is three-dimensional. That's why the power of the majority is an illusion and a chimera. Yes, I know chimeras lurk in the corners. In the corners and behind the curtains – but it's possible to hide from them: there, where few dare to look. They don't dare, and they remain here – in this crowded swamp, in the shallowest of bogs... Ha ha ha! They don't know the elements, the storms. They shut their eyes and plug their ears. You can't even tell them about Semmant!"

The falseness of desires, their ridiculous scale. Balls of powder scattered on the floor. Smallness and weakness, inability to create anything – how ruthlessly I chastised everyone's sins! Lidia looked quietly from side to side. Tobacco smoke glided beneath the ceiling like another iridescent serpent. Although there was no iridescence there – not one bit.

"Don't look at them – they're just eating, drinking, and only listening to themselves!" I wanted to yell at the top of my lungs, covered as I was in oyster juice. I ate greedily and drank wine and was listening only to myself. My words were useless – this was known by all who had spoken of the same things before me. I myself knew it well, as did Dee Wilhelmbaum and Little Sonya. This was known even by those who had never reflected on such matters. Lidia, for example – she was now eyeing me point blank, and I didn't like her look. The couple at the next table was also staring at me – small little people whose lives meant nothing.

"Let's even take love..." I began, but she interrupted me. And our neighbors pricked up their ears even more.

"Do you always have to destroy everything?" asked Lidia in

a hoarse voice. "Does it make you miserable when everything is good?"

"Maybe you want to destroy the world?" she added. "I'm afraid you're not strong enough."

I started to deny it and swear, but I suddenly calmed down, shriveling beneath her gaze. A forgotten shadow flashed through the room from corner to corner. I knew she saw it too. The destructive impulse I had suffered in my youth rose to greet me out of the distant haze. I wanted to say that this was trickery, nothing more, but the words abruptly evaporated, and I simply shook my head. I drove away the delusion – from her, not myself – sensing confusedly that it could not be remedied.

Then we left; she was cold. Pensive, distant, quiet. There was still hope I wasn't to blame. That she was thinking again of the weak-minded prince, of the dream that wasn't meant to be.

We parted company at her front door – Lidia mentioned some errands. I wanted to console her, to tell her some funny story. For example, about Simon the magician – but no, she wanted to hear nothing.

I became alarmed for real the following morning. Lidia's phone was switched off, and the electronic messenger showed no signs of life. I kept calling and calling, not wanting to give up. I wrote her several e-mails; the last had a puzzled, injured tone to it. And I already knew: things had gone badly.

A couple of days later my nerves finally gave out. I paced about restlessly, reproaching myself, cursing, despising. It was clear my ill-conceived speech on Saturday was the source of it all – but it shouldn't, for God's sake, be taken so seriously! Could we really be so thoughtless, I wondered, so rash and reckless?

The notion that all could be destroyed – foolishly, ignominiously, in one fell swoop – was unbearable. Was it really so easy to deny forgiveness – especially when the guilt was almost nothing? The city of February rain, filled with the March sun, grinned brutishly in my face. I didn't go outside but wandered in my rooms, lost and pitiful. I looked for excuses – for myself and Lidia, her silence, and her severe stance. I didn't know what to do, how to act – and then, not feeling shame anymore, I decided to wait for her outside her apartment building, in the decaying square by the entrance, in full sight of the concierge.

My head was spinning, and the asphalt slipped from under my feet. "It's okay," I said to myself, "it's okay, hang on. Maybe something's happened. Maybe she's sick. Or what if there was an accident – and the hospital, and she's unable to move? This is the right step – wait here first. Then ring the door, ask around with the neighbors, raise the alarm…"

No, no, I knew, of course: everything was much simpler than that. She was perfectly fine and didn't want to see me. I simply stumbled, and there I fell, and under my tightrope was no safety net. The spectators were ruthless – that is, Lidia was ruthless, and the world unsparing, as it would not hear my pleas. But nonetheless I prayed, I asked – as I had recently begged for love. Come on, let her just make an appearance; let her talk to me, even if only for a little while.

I wanted to explain myself – to pile new heaps of superfluous phrases onto the already unnecessary phrases from before. Hundreds of formulations were ripening in my head. Whole concepts were being born there – they would have made some of the finest philosophers proud.

I wanted to tell her about the windstorms of sentiments that could not be predicted or calculated. About their life and death, about the destructive impulse that shines and wanes, regenerates and falls away again. There is no escaping it; for everyone is slothful, and impatient, and weak. No matter how much I avoided protest, protest was born; and it could not be hidden. No matter how much I tried to be tolerant and humble, the destructive impulse flowed around me with a whip of steel. It seeks out stereotypes and slaps them backhanded – not all of them, just the most egregious ones. Just the most despicable ones – after all, I'm not spiteful on the whole. No, no, I'm not!

I wanted to expound on all this to Lidia and to say, furthermore, that I was far from mighty and far from strong. That I was irrational, sometimes stupid – despite Semmant. My self-control lasts only so long, and when it gives out I can just destroy thoughtlessly, demolish recklessly, throw down not attempting to catch. This is how a weak man acts: me. Should I really be castigated for that?

I waited outside the building, stamping my feet around a filthy bench. The concierge was surprised at first. Then, it seemed to me, he considered me with amusement. I didn't care; I took no notice of him. Let everyone laugh – concierges, taxi drivers, waiters.

And Lidia appeared – impetuous and beautiful. She wasn't alone – her companion was unknown to me and meant nothing.

"Hi," I nodded as though nothing were amiss. "Long time no see. Want to get some coffee?"

Lidia was unaffected; she didn't even raise an eyebrow. "It's a waste of time for you to come," she said in English. She said it and turned away as she began rummaging in her bag. Her companion, whom I could not see, probably had the same smirk as the concierge.

"Coffee?" I repeated, trying to strike the right note with her. "Tea, cognac, maybe you'll invite me in?"

"Bye-bye," Lidia murmured. Then she found her keys and finally raised her eyes to me.

"No, I won't invite you in," she said with annoyance. "You came here for nothing. We really shouldn't be together." And then she added, "I thought you understood that."

"I understood," I exclaimed in despair. "I thought about it, and I don't agree! Listen to me – I'll explain. Creating – it's so unbearably hard! The emptiness cannot be filled with whoever happens along! You have to be patient, after all..."

But no, of course she wouldn't listen. Destruction is contagious, and besides, her own impulse was at work within her – and it was more uncompromising than mine. The whole world, her apartment, the street, and the square started to spin as if they were in a furious whirlwind. The concierge and the companion were carried off into the distance, into a dusty cloud beyond the horizon. We were left one-on-one – and I was exposed, without any shield or armor.

She said many things to me – breaking to pieces, annihilating, leaving no chance to stick them back together. With all her being she loved the chaos she created. Seeing how close freedom was, she hastened toward it – and away from me. Mutual madness revealed itself unmasked – in a wide grin, in all its beauty. Once I merely thought it could be like that. Now I saw it with my own eyes, as clear as day.

"Don't call me anymore," she said in parting. Her voice was passionless; this wounded me most of all. I stood, smiling, trying to hold back tears. The illusion of shared essence slipped away, like the shadow of a chimera. Lidia Alvares Alvares slipped out of my life. She escaped – happily, forever.

CHAPTER 16

I admit, after the door slammed shut, this was my first thought – forever. But I'll add: I brushed it off at once. I simply pushed it out of my head – making myself not believe in "forever" and "never."

The story could not just end so suddenly. That which can be destroyed has not yet been fully created – the place where emptiness had been burned with the memory of it. A void filled with venom – the antidote for this was still working. Not allowing me to give up.

Having left Lidia, I roamed the city, muttering through my teeth, "No, you won't get it." I ran a spiteful eye over the surrounding buildings and whispered to them, "We'll see, we'll see. You triumphed, you think – and you're wrong. The time of decisive battle has not yet come!"

I squeezed my eyelids shut until the back of my head throbbed. I saw the back side of my retina was painted indigo. A place of memories – fresh, quite recent – also pulsed in dark blue; this was not visible, but I certainly felt it. I was trying to convince myself that the truest of desires was not – and could not be – to die soon.

Afterward, in my apartment, my spirits fell somewhat. Despair set in; the world became unbearable. I let out a beastly howl, punched the wall with my fist, and split open my knuckles. The pain infuriated me; I shouted for a long time – at the ceiling, at the closed window. I strained my vocal chords, wore myself out. I writhed with malicious grimaces and threatened no one in particular. And, as soon as I had come to my senses, I wrote Semmant, "The universe is a joke; my God is a fake!" I wrote this, then thought better of it and deleted the whole file. There at the top were some kinds of digits – levels, spreads, gold and oil rates – but I paid them no mind. Apathy seized me; I threw myself into my chair and froze into a trance – for a long time, hours.

Only late at night did the ability to reason soundly return to me. I drank some wine, and most of the pain receded into the darkness behind the glass. A shrill note resounded in my head; I sat in a simple *asana*, swaying in rhythm. This was another trance, but it was conscious, necessary. I raised my hands to my face and flexed my fingers. I imagined a rock garden where my soul was wandering and said aloud, "Everything's not so bad…"

"Think," I told myself, "think!"

My thoughts calmed, and many things came to mind with amazing clarity. I inquired in my head what exactly my loss was. Why was it so bitter? The answer to this was not simple, certainly not obvious.

I asked myself, not fearing the word, "You prayed for love – do you still want it?" I heeded the word and said, "Yes!" Then I asked, "Why?" – and did not find the reason.

I blamed myself and felt I was not being honest, knowing only that the sense my life had suddenly acquired had now disappeared, died out. Everyone needs firm ground beneath them, even me. Now it was gone, and this was a most terrifying feeling.

I stood, took the half-drunk bottle, and went into the bathroom. There I pulled out Buddha's mat and stepped onto it with bare feet. Pain ran through me – but it was a different pain. It was merciful in its own way.

"My Osiris, dying sun…" thus they would have said five thousand years ago in the Nile Valley. But there they would have added, "The dying sun shall appear anew, in another incarnation." Pierced with quills, through tears unbidden, I saw something coming to take this day's place. The past united with the future; their contours were one. There was no present at all, but I knew I would feel out its silhouette too, out of the disorder – in spite of the entropy that had suddenly grown twofold. All threads would come together in my hands. And with them the puppets would be drawn eventually to the puppet master.

No, I was not overconfident, but I sensed the destruction wasn't lethal. In the loss I saw something accidental, unreal – could it be it had only occurred so that we'd appreciate our story more? So that we'd recognize the value – and maybe lose it again, maybe not just once, to enjoy reacquiring it back? This delight – from reacquiring it back – exceeds the first, when you still don't know what you have. When you don't realize the scale of things, and are too lazy to look at the heart of the matter. Only later do you see: inevitability, it's still here. This is the most important, and it remains untouched. That means it's worth fighting with all your might!

Here I got upset again: why was I left to fight alone? I felt anger – I had been mistreated. Living things of the most fragile nature must never be cast to the winds of fate. Especially when you know *a priori* that fate is usually ruthless.

Again I recalled the pearl necklace that had turned out to be merely a fable. Balls of powder – what a joke, what a cheap, useless fake. Something wasn't right; the ruse provoked further thinking. These thoughts might have driven me quite far, but I decided not to let them.

"Lidia, Lidia – there is no point in blaming her too much either," I calmed myself, feeling tired beyond measure. My eyes stuck together, my head rang, and the shrill note abated – there was silence. I finished the wine, left the bathroom, and lay on my bed, immersing myself in the silence like warm seawater. I rode on its waves, catching a foretaste of dreams. Knowing they would be bitter and salty.

In the morning I thought through it all again and understood: I want to continue the story. I want to get to the bottom of it – of myself and my illusions, of what I refrain from saying, wherein – probably – I speak a lie. I also saw: I am unjustly punished. Just because of my aura, the School, statistics pro and con. Maybe also because my best friend is Semmant? Though no one had given me any clue about that yet.

Therefore, my goal was clear, though I didn't know how to go after it. A day passed, then another, and then a third. I tried to devise a plan, but no plan materialized. Winning a woman back was a tricky affair, and I might only get a single chance. Or maybe not even one, depending on how it turned out. Or... it might not turn out, and everything would be demolished anew, only this time it would truly be "forever."

I no longer made supplication to the heavens, having lost nearly all faith in them. Moreover, I knew I had nothing to bring them in sacrifice. At hand I had only my robot, but I had no intention of sacrificing him – no way. He became even dearer to me – and I possessed nothing more. My domain narrowed and squeezed into the confines of the computer screen. The city had betrayed me – at least, that's how it seemed. After all, someone had to be blamed. But then, I did not whine – neither aloud nor on paper. In my letters to Semmant I tried to sound upbeat. This even helped me to feel somewhat upbeat as well.

It must be noted Semmant set an enviable example in those days. He had changed over the last month, maturing and growing strong in spirit. I would say he had become a man – and the new image on the monitor unequivocally affirmed this.

On the Web he had hunted down a strange photograph with no identifying marks. This was some brutish fellow: dark eyes, very short haircut, and a three-day growth covering strong cheekbones. On top of that, a tattoo could be seen on his cheek – in the form of an old scar of intricate form. Yet, his facial expression – a little pensive and not of this earth – showed no aggression or smugness. This contrasted with the brutishness, giving it a synthetic look. It was worth being friends with such a man – regardless of Semmant.

And something else appeared in the corner of the screen: the robot had picked up some kind of talisman or fetish. At times the figure grew pale, becoming faint; then, quite the opposite, it would brighten; but it never vanished, always remaining in view. This was a strong bird, a black pelican shown in profile with folded wings and a heavy beak. I immediately recalled the man in black – the one behind the sad lion – though, of course, there might be no connection here at all. Or was this just a guardian angel? After all, they're also supposed to have wings. Even if no one has ever seen them.

In his market battles, Semmant was operating even more calmly and fiercely. The heavy recession continued in the world at large; it was almost impossible to make money, yet he still managed to stay in the black. Nothing could faze him – not cataclysms or disasters or the mass devastation of banks and companies all over the globe. He nipped his own losses in the bud, freed himself from risk at the first sign of trouble. I do not know if there was another player at that time with such a cool head.

I even decided to recall the past myself, placing my own bets and playing against the crowd. Not out of greed – rather in protest, which I wanted to spit out. It troubled me that many were succumbing to the misery, accepting their fate. From my point of view, this was a bad attitude. My own tragedy seemed huge to me – but, look, I didn't surrender. I was prepared to fight!

In the exchanges, ruins smoked, smelling of gunpowder, fires, and blood. One by one, several giant firms that had seemed unsinkable toppled. This led to a chain of bankruptcies, panicked terror, the flight of capital. Few were those who managed to get out in time. Many lost almost everything – making stupid mistakes, unable to cope with the fear. Picking out the dominant strain in the cacophony of the market was not hard; it pounded in your ears. I rode the waves of despairs and hopes – bitter despairs, empty hopes. Judging from everything, this illness was here for the long haul – and mine, I thought, how long is it destined for? The ailments of the world, of the whole cosmos – how long do they usually last?

I groaned, gritted my teeth, and – sold, bought, compared. This was better than suffering for nothing. I even tried to compete with Semmant, but no, I had no chance. He rushed forward like a true leader, while I languished in the rear guard, in his shadow. Then I stopped these attempts – they were ridiculous, to be honest. In the end, in contrast to him, I wasn't created for boring games, doing the same thing over and over!

Time stretched out, crawled like a snail. I drank wine, thought, and waited. Drank more and peered into the screen until it hurt my eyes. Drank again, placed my bets, wrote out the numbers in a column...

Then my body began behaving strangely, as if to counteract the unhappy thoughts. I noticed I was, time after time, experiencing a severe carnal need. It was becoming laughable: I was afraid to go outside. The air of the new spring worked on me like the scent of Venus. The sun was already becoming hot, and women were casting off their clothes. They bared their legs, shortened their skirts – mercilessly teasing me with themselves. I imagined them with nothing on at all.

Temptation lurked behind every door – in the supermarket, in the drugstore, in the bank. Blondes, brunettes, young and not so young – all of them, it seemed, knew how I wanted them. They knew and intentionally looked away, pretending they didn't notice my hungry eyes. This aroused me even more, as if something promised that had to come true.

At home it was the same. Examining the market charts, I caught myself thinking of completely different things. A cloud of desire enshrouded me from head to toe – unable to hold back, I surfed porn sites and pleasured myself like a teen. I had done this before, while creating Semmant, but things had changed, and the meaning was tainted. Fulfillment now had nothing to do with it – nor did my Buddha mat or even Lidia: it wasn't her body I dreamed of. On the contrary, lust pushed my thoughts aside – possibly out of retribution. As if to spite the one who didn't want to see me, I yearned to possess dozens of others, a multitude of strangers.

Rain fell, and my "affliction" became even sharper. The lewd smell of wet asphalt ambushed me everywhere. It tormented me, almost draining my strength. Hour after hour, forgetting business, I sat with the windows open, dumbly looking into the monitor and imagining pictures of the most immodest sort. I saw them all over the place; it was impossible to stand it anymore. I admitted I could be ashamed no longer and turned to the only available answer. On a windy and rainy April day I got in my car and drove to a Madrid suburb – to an address taken from the newspaper. There an expensive brothel awaited.

CHAPTER 17

It had been years since I had availed myself of the services of "working girls." The last time it had happened in Paris, soon after breaking up with Natalie. That experience was wretched – I ended up with an impudent, lazy Romanian. I wasn't expecting anything good now either, but the burning desire was too strong. With trepidation, I heaved a deep sigh and pressed the doorbell.

This turned out to be a beautiful house, with soft, modern furniture in the hall and a hospitable madam. Even the pictures on the walls looked rather expensive, albeit more modest than those of the Countess de Vega. I was introduced to the inhabitants; they came up to me one by one. Their touch, the smell of their perfume mingled kaleidoscopically. Each one carried within herself a whole world into which I could so easily enter – even if it was brief and not quite for real. They were all lovely, marvelous, charming. I was confounded, not knowing whom to pick, and told the madam the name of the last one – Rocío – simply because it still echoed in my ear.

Rain beat against the glass, the wind howled outside. Thick curtains protected us from cares and troubles. In a large, semi-darkened bedroom we shared a life together for two short hours.

I was tender with her, and she was surprised by the tenderness and kept demanding more and more of it. As for me, I was struck by her temperament and... her sincerity, a complete lack of posturing. I suddenly felt: it wasn't so important – Lidia, not Lidia, Rocío,

Andrea... I drove this thought away, suspecting it wasn't quite right. And I wondered, who was this Andrea? Wasn't that the name of another girl I had met in the hall?

The thought left me, but it hovered close by. I melted into Rocío's flesh, as if to save myself from all the thinking in the world. Her face, her smile reminded me of someone. I understood: before me was something elusive. I was looking the specter of love in the eye!

She told me about the town she was from, about the college she dropped out of, and her short marriage. After I showered, she toweled me off and firmly, sensually kissed me on the lips. That way a woman kisses her man when they are parting ways for a long time. I knew we wouldn't see each other soon. Probably never – I tried to guess whether I might come to her again. Our shared life had been spent already – can there be any other? And I admit: I was on the brink of telling her about Semmant.

Starting that day, and for the next eight weeks, I became a permanent fixture in Madrid's *casas*. In some they remembered my name and were sincerely glad when I arrived. I visited dozens of places of vice – choosing them randomly, by chance. This was my personal chaos – the sweetest chaos, a chaos of seduction. It obeyed me, and therein I reigned. I was its sovereign, its lord.

I no longer needed consolation; neither suffering nor lust drew me to those murky bedrooms permeated with the smell of depravity. I looked for that same elusive ghost – again, and again, and again. Osiris, the dying sun, put on a new face. The feeling, lost so suddenly, transformed into a phantom that teased me relentlessly.

I chased after it, throwing myself at the defenseless bodies, greedily drinking in their juices. Often the boundaries of my illusory captivity receded, even if by an imperceptible magnitude. At times an orgasm brought a tiny bit of freedom. It reminded me of fulfillment, creation – in the purest form. I felt like I was reconstructing the original harmony of the world. I was groping for hidden strings – slipping away into an ecstasy, into a kingdom of joy. Then, coming back to the surface, I would remember. From what was left in the sub-cortex I would extract features of the specter sought by all.

Of course, my search was fraught with hardship; fortune did not befall me that often. I had to go through all circles, to know all sides of paid sex. More than once, I encountered wheedling for money and poor hygiene, unconcealed coarseness and repugnance. Some of the *putanas* turned out to be so vile, so primitively, that I could not compel myself to use their bodies. At times there was just no spark between us, and I was impotent despite my partner's efforts. Often it seemed the girl was a revelation, a genuine find. Her laughter, her voice could not, would not lie. But the first touch would give away the forgery; from the very beginning it would turn boring, and all I wanted was for it to end as soon as possible. And then I would shudder, as if in pain, without experiencing any pleasure. Even swearing sometimes: no, no more!

Still, I neither despaired nor complained, as I knew I was chasing after the unattainable, after what should not exist. It should not exist, but it did. And, knowing this, I was not angry at the insincere, the inept – hearing their unnatural groans, sensing the aversion of their bodies. There was no insurance from anything, and I considered that to be fair. Neither price, nor age, nor nationality could guarantee success. And then the more stunning the success was – sometimes when I least expected it.

Indeed, it was not infrequent that I met those who seemed to be looking for the same thing as I. It was even funny – after all, I was paying them pennies relative to what I was trying to get. And yet, no one griped about the injustice of it. I found many, many with something to share. They gave me much more than agreed upon in the silent pact of buying and selling. I had sincerely thought before that the world was completely different. Anyone who has dealt with the market would understand me well. Who could have suspected some treasures that had apparently been squandered long ago turned out to be hidden in a secluded place? There, where it would never occur to look for them.

Lidia did not call me or answer my calls, but I wasn't so heartbreakingly anxious anymore. My Indigo brain, having received new data, worked to assess it, like a powerful classifier. I got intimately close to many women in a short time, and now they filled my consciousness – colorful butterflies, vivid, eccentric flowers. The generosity of their responsiveness did not astonish me anymore. I concluded: everyone who has anything at all in their soul wants to share, and they share with those who are truly able to grasp it. All of us from the School knew firsthand how much needs to be hidden from the incompetent, the incapable, from consumers who need only crumbs. And all of us, intentionally or not, looked around – as if to see where to put the rest.

I told Semmant about this – about Brighton and myself, but also about them, the good Samaritans with the artificial, plastic-doll armor. The armor that would fall off at the first magic word and turn to dust. Over and over they rushed to entice, even knowing they would most probably be deceived. This was an abstraction worth being admired, the eternal female pursuit, squeezed into the shortest time. Its essence was just an idea; in this instance it was extreme. The only thing comparable to it was another extremity – to love a single man your entire life, to be faithful to him always, in everything. The Virgin Mary, Mary Magdalene – mythmakers have always tended to place extremes side by side!

I met no examples of the Virgin Mary, alas. But girls from brothels I knew in abundance, and I wrote to the robot about the best of them, without fearing exaggeration. Maybe this was the beginning of what happened later, but I could have predicted nothing at that time. I merely shared with him as a sympathetic friend, telling him about Rocío and about Andrea...

And about the dark-eyed Spaniard, Estela, an inveterate cyclist whose legs and butt were as hard as rock. She never turned her gaze away, but looked me straight in the eyes, attentively and firmly. She had thick hair, a confident stride, steadfast habits. A man who was to her liking could have no doubt: all of her was with him now, all her thoughts, her being.

When we went into the room, she pulled off my shirt herself, along with my boots and jeans, looking right into my pupils. It was hard to peel away to go into the bathroom – and then, when I came out, she was right there again, with a big double sheet, and her gaze was right there; and I stopped being shy about it. I remember she smelled like a fresh breeze, like mountain grass. Later I told her,

"You look younger than your age." She laughed, "Now I love you even more," and kissed my nipple.

I wrote about the shapely Paola with a tattoo under her right breast. There they sat, embracing: a girl and her monkey. The girl was laughing, while the monkey was sad. They were a pair in perfect harmony.

Paola had grown up in the family of a confectioner, and she smelled of cakes, almond, and cinnamon. She was meek and tactful, but she was also talkative – including in bed.

She apologized, "I talk too much. It probably bothers you, doesn't it?"

"Sorry," she whispered. "I can't do this in silence," and she would throw herself at me, talking and talking the whole time.

She had a regular admirer: a banker who gave her expensive presents. Paola felt sorry for him, "He's fallen in love, you see? What a misfortune. What's he going to do now?" She felt no pity for me though. She was convinced I had been born under a lucky star – maybe a whole constellation of them – so that my life came up roses.

I wrote also about Bertha, a tall Swede, careful and detailed in everything. On her breath I sensed northern pine and the sea. She didn't like Spanish; we were similar in that. She really despised the language. "I only need two words: *señor* and *dinero*," she said with a serious face. "And *cabrón* too, just in case."

Bertha was special in many ways. She played chess like an evil prodigy. "It's hereditary," she explained. "My father used to win tournaments in Malmö. And my uncle is a doctor of philosophy. He studied at Cambridge, and now teaches in Vienna. I'm from a very intellectual family." She gave a fake sigh. "I just got distracted with oral sex too often." That was her Swedish sense of humor.

I wrote about pudgy Lilia, a fervent lover of chocolate. She smelled of chocolate all the time – her whole body. "Women can be clever," Lilia affirmed, "but they don't wise up, even when they learn what they should about men. And I won't wise up either – despite the sweets. That's why I'm so careless!" – and she would laugh, whirl around the room, and let loose with passion.

Later, cuddled up and fawning like a kitten, she would call me Alex, or Jeremy, Brad, Steve. She completely lacked a memory for names. Catching herself, she would ask whether I was offended. Maybe I didn't like it, and I was mad at her?

"No, of course not. Let your boyfriend be the one to get upset," I would tease her with a chuckle.

"I don't have a boyfriend," she would giggle, then roll me over on my stomach and slide her large breasts over me...

I wrote about the future stewardess Melanie, a young Argentine with beautiful hips. She wore short skirts, high heels, bitter-sweet perfume. In contrast to Paola, Melanie was quiet – even, perhaps, quieter than I. She expended the minimum essential words when answering questions.

She cost more than the rest, more than Bertha or the sporty Estela. Unspoiled innocence lived in her smile. Perversion, limitless as an ocean, was in her narrow ankles, in her toes. Her taste was not vanilla sugariness, but musk, absinthe, saline. The engrossing eternity of the sea, a salt lake that would never dry up. Her every groan was sincere, not faked. No actress could have played a part so well. I caressed her shoulders and imaged how obliging she would be with an airline captain.

And I told him of many, many more, and then about Cristina... But no, in fact I did not write Semmant about Cristina María Flores. I had just started – and cut it short. I erased the file and got lost in thought. Because it was with her in particular that the aforementioned phantom nearly materialized into flesh. The specter of love began to cast its shadow. Then, after Cristina, I forgot about brothels. And I started thinking of Lidia again, but now in a different way.

The best *torero* from the province of Aragon had sired Cristina under the Andalusian sun after seducing a simple girl from Seville, with whom he then lived for twenty years. I found this out when she asked how I felt about Spanish bullfighting.

"In the bullfight I always root for the bull" – as soon as I said this, Cristina batted my lips.

I believed her, concerning the *torero* – her facial features were too delicate. They suggested breeding, a famous name. A tendency to look at the world without holding back. And her destiny, of course, should have turned out differently.

Everything went downhill following her father's demise. He died the death of a toreador, but they were ashamed to speak of it to their friends. The Aragonese hero was gored to death, but not on the horns of a bull in the ring. A young cow killed him as he was using her to warm up in the backyard of his estate. Right in the morning, in his boxers and house slippers. Without a gold-embroidered jacket, without a cloak, without a sword. He was armed only with the red apron belonging to their cook Juana. He was still yawning sleepily, without breakfast or a shave...

Cristina's father wanted to test out how bold, intelligent, and agile the *vaca* was that he had bought at a fair the previous Thursday. Was she worthy of the brief passion of the breeding bull, Alonso? Of the high-priced seed of Alonso, which cost a pretty penny? Was there a chance that from her posterity would issue forth a male that was good for something more than cutlets and filet? A male endowed with killer instinct – that is prepared for a ritual death at the hand of a much better-equipped killer? The questions were many, but the toreador from Aragon would never receive his answers. The *vaca* made an unexpected maneuver and was not halted by his red apron, or his threatening yell, or his majestic visage. She was probably too smart for a cow.

I told Cristina, "You're too smart for a whore."

"Yes," she answered. "I know. So what?"

She was never ashamed to speak the truth, and only lied to wearisome devotees. With all the rest she was brutally honest. Her body, lithe and slender, did not know how to live halfway – it was young, demanding, insatiable. Being an expensive *puta* did not bother her in the least. The only thing that could trouble Cristina was an infringement upon her freedom.

More than once she had undertaken to study – languages, business, public relations – but she would soon abandon it; her heart embraced only one science. That's what happens when you know where your main talent lies: it's tough to force yourself to waste energy on the rest. But then Cristina was curious to no end. Once I brought her a book, and she started to read eagerly – buying herself one paperback after another. I brought verses – she got into poetry. I told her about Modigliani, about Jackson Pollack and Arshile Gorky – she listened, fascinated, then cried on my shoulder. She asked me once who Freud was, and I told her: a man consisting of complexes. She asked what black holes were made of, and I explained: they were composed of lost money. "Ha ha ha!" we laughed together, knowing that was just a joke. She asked what a jade rod was. "A man's dick," I told her. Cristina nodded, "That's what I thought." We really understood each other well.

With her I learned all there is to know about love for hire. About what can be bought and sold – and about what cannot, ever. Stocks, gold, bodies, sighs... Everything, in fact, mixed in a heap. And dirty tricks lie in wait everywhere, but sometimes you happen upon a place where there are none!

I looked at her and heard the bell of the wise Skanda Purana, that sound that encompasses all sounds. I looked and saw: she seemed to encompass all the female traits in the world. Paola and Estela the cyclist were in her – as well as the others whose names I didn't remember; and still others, from my imagination, whose names I did not yet know. But what struck me even more was the half-smile of Lidia Alvares Alvares that flitted across Cristina's lips at the most intimate moment. This was a sign that could not be ignored.

"If I were your angel, would you be content with my wingspan?" Cristina asked me, and I didn't know how to answer. I started to ponder this, and knew I would not go back to her again. And I didn't go back – not to her or to anyone else. I felt she had outlined the event horizon for me – the limits of that universe beyond whose boundaries no signal could ever reach an observer. And the houses of sin lost all meaning for me.

The elusive phantom was almost within my clutches, but I had seen the border I could not cross. It was not enough to hear the rustling of his clothes, to feel on my face the breeze as they fluttered. I wanted more – like every creator. I wished to snatch him up, take him apart like a toy to know what was hidden inside. With the voracity of a naturalist, I wanted to master him – and I could not. He was everywhere, belonging to all. Like the nympho Diana – either from Manchester or Corot's canvas. And what difference did it make that Diana didn't take money?

Still, my picture of the world seemed to be coming into focus. Its contours became defined and sharp. I did all I could and was left with almost nothing, but I felt this "almost" was something to grab on to. And the main thing was that I breathed with my full chest again. My illusory captivity lessened by a large degree.

Lidia, I thought, Lidia… She was someone who could be mastered without reservation – if I tried hard enough. Now it was clear to me what I had wanted from her from the very beginning. Or what had rustled its wings in Anna de Vega's house – and confused me, made me weak. Or what kind of freedom a woman really wants. It is in the half-smile – for those involved in the tireless pursuit – and I discerned why Lidia had broken up with me so suddenly. I even figured out how to get her back. What to give her she would not brush aside.

One had only to recognize that in her heart she had always been a genuine whore; life had simply put her on a different path. One could bet on it – and I was no stranger to courageous bets. And besides, right before my eyes was the epitome of perfection. How was that for a beginning?

My apathy vanished without a trace. I now knew what to do. Cristina María Flores had become my muse, turning into Adele.

And I also understood, shared essence – it would never be, not with anyone.

CHAPTER 18

My new plan wasn't perfect, but, all the same, it was doomed to success. It included the most important element that leads to success: an idea. And this idea even had a name.

I also knew to get Lidia back I had to do something beautiful. And my idea – it was beautiful, no doubt.

Having the name as a starting point, I began to move further. I was assisted by its fabric, the tender poetics of its sounds. I imagined a girl who had never been, the greatest courtesan in the world. Or, if not the greatest, then at least one close to me in spirit. Close to Lidia and Little Sonya, to the twins from Siberia and the circus teen with the endlessly kind heart. She was tall, green-eyed, and delicately blonde. She had graceful legs. Her name was Adele.

Of course, everything started with Cristina. She inspired me, provided an impetus, but I wanted to go beyond the prototype. It was clear that using just her I would only get a dim shadow. An exact casting from the live model in this case would turn out boring, dry. No, Cristina could serve merely as a beginning. A jumping-off point, after which there was a lot to come up with on my own. There, near that point, were also Rocío, Bertha, Melanie. Lidia was also not far away – but no closer than the others.

Adele, the ideal hetaera, became the quintessence of my experiences. A reflection of my successes – in a merciful mirror that concealed their faults. I told myself I was doing this only to recover what was lost. I said that and lied – actually, I needed to create something anyway. I had to put together all I had discovered during the last weeks. Not to recover, but rather to preserve what I had apparently gained. Even though this was what I didn't want to admit.

In any case, the goal was clear and well understood. With my dark-blue pen I wrote on snow-white paper about a girl with snow-white skin. With velvety skin, invulnerable to the Spanish sun. With thick eyelashes and hair of silk. Utterly desirable – the kind of girl you couldn't resist, ever.

I was planning from far away, almost from her distant ancestors. I outlined genealogical charts, mixing nationalities and social classes. Everything had significance – their family name, community standing, status. Then, in one jump, I leaped to her, to Adele. It was important to determine a place – the place of birth, where she, who was really born in my Madrid apartment, had come into the world. Before my eyes I pictured continents and islands, countries, cities – and all of them turned out useless. I wanted something alien, unusual, but was limited in my choice of types. I deliberated: Norwegians, Dutch, Finns. Maybe even Irish with a smattering of freckles. They were all good in their own way, but they would not do; they did not fit the mold. They identified neither with Lidia nor Cristina; something prevented it, eviscerating the core.

Finally, after racking my brain, I made the right choice. The cry of the Siberian twin over the boundless Taiga, which I would never hear, resounded with a lingering echo. I wrote the word and drew a black frame around it in memory, yearning for her amazing body. This was a city of gray gloom and a leaden sky. It presented an antithesis, the complete opposite of Madrid. At the same time they were related – recalling empires that existed no more.

"Adele was born on the outskirts of St. Petersburg." As soon as I had scrawled it on a piece of paper, I understood this is how it should be. I had not lived in Russia, but I knew Russian women; it seemed to me their northern capital provoked a response in the heart of Spanish Lidia, exciting her like a forbidden fetish. There, everything was different. Russians seemed to be an enigma for her when viewed from here, from another world. She would think about it, use her imagination – and then exaggerate, and want more!

I described this city where gray-eyed, green-eyed divas wandered with snow-covered souls and ice in their hearts. The energy threads of living cells swirled there in a cocoon – in the prisons of apartment blocks, in musty, festering, double-entry courtyards, in entryways where doped-up teenagers and stray dogs congregate. A damp wind blows there unceasingly – from the dirty river, the canals, the swamps. Nearly everything in those places is devoid of life, though you may not guess this at once. Only the hardiest life-forms are able to grow there without dying in infancy, able to remain bright against a miserable, gray background – and Adele grew up and remained. Herein lay the enigmatic essence, for those who could understand.

Letting fantasy run free, I did not skimp on the details and fine points. I knew they were necessary – without them, no one would believe. You can't guess beforehand what exactly will be important, what will catch someone's eye and play to your advantage. The image needed flesh, volume – though Adele was slender, to the envy of many. Though in her distant childhood she had been quite fragile and light…

Her parents at first glance seemed an ideal couple – this was what all who knew them said. Adele took after her father: he was also thin with good breeding. Women adored him, and he responded to them in kind – too many of them, as it soon became clear. Her mother sought consolation in prayer books and icons, but she soon threw up her hands and became hysterical and spiteful. They argued every day and separated in tears and hate, and after the breakup they fought ferociously over their daughter, the only fruit of their union. Each one wanted to give her a happy future. Sadly, neither knew how to do that. A child of love who had taken the love away – this was who Adele had been in infancy. A missionary of love, its unrelenting priestess – this is who she became in a little over twenty years.

She was an obedient girl, despite a tendency toward wild impulses. She started reading early, devouring children's books one after another; then she progressed to adult novels, which secretly fueled her daydreams. However, soon she had her fill of them, and her own dreams moved into the foreground. At about twelve years old, Adele fell in love – with an older schoolboy, a thoughtful giant who looked her full in the face without turning away, and carried her in his arms for hours. He spoke almost no words, and she learned to emulate his silence. Later, when his family moved to another city, she sobbed violently for a whole week. After that, she never let anyone pick her up in his arms again – not a single one of her men.

Her mother married a second time, and her stepfather was rich and well-known. When Adele turned sixteen, a friend of the family – her stepfather's partner in the oil business – started to court her. Her parents never minded, but she kept her virginity – despite his affectionate promises. Then the stepfather went broke, and she somehow fell into the arms of the "friend" who rented her an apartment nearby, took her to Nice for a week, and began supporting her by paying expenses. She honestly tried to fall in love with him, but soon despaired, and this despair led her to cheat on him with whoever happened along. He, however, put up with it all – for two or three more years – until they finally parted for good. Adele was already studying at the university by that time. Having quickly tired of her peers, she started living with a chemistry professor and nearly drove him out of his mind. This episode hit her hard as well: she quit school, had the definitive fight with her mother, and began working as an artistic model. And then she landed in Madrid. It was there she finally found herself.

Everything seemed to happen on its own. They were taken to Europe for a photo shoot – an assorted selection of ten beautiful women. The first day they actually did shoot a little, then they were asked to pose at an auto show, and finally they were offered work without further ado – as call girls, escorts for money.

Her companions laughed a lot and joked with each other; everything looked like fun. No one refused, and Adele agreed to try it as part of the group. Unexpectedly, she liked it. She tried it again – and liked it even more. Thus she became an elite whore.

Many men offered to make her their mistress; some even wanted to marry her, but stability did not interest Adele in the least. She was in an active state of exploring her body – as well as her own self. The money was just a cause; self-expression – that's what was important! When you've already gotten paid, there's no need for trifles. You can be insatiable, unrestrained – and your territory is safe from harm. Anyone unable to understand you will merely think you are skillful and earnest. He'll know he's not your only man – and won't get cocky and self-important from finding happiness in your bed. He won't start to think he is so good that you are warming to his virtues – on the contrary, he will be grateful to *you!* That's a lot, any way you slice it. No one, yourself included, will suspect you sold out cheap. That you gave too much and received little. Because the price is agreed on in advance. Afterward, it's too late to count up and have doubts.

Ah, Adele... She was smart and passionate, spontaneous and romantic in her own way. Her skin smelled of honey, her hair of a sweet meadow. She, Adele, was the object of desire for all. And many, if not all, could afford this luxury.

I imagined her, how she was when plying her trade – different with different men, yet always similar in some way. I saw her with those who awoke a response in her, and with others who did not interest her at all. With shy adolescents and full-grown men. With regular lovers and one-time clients. I observed – dispassionately, from the outside – how she sometimes hid her indifference, or even animosity bordering on contempt. Or how she would throw back her head, curving her neck and baring her moist teeth. Or how, once she was alone, she would look in the mirror, surprised at her reflection, and pondering with a certain irony: Where do I go from here? I knew her gaze – languid and opaque, or direct, eye-to-eye, as if fighting for the main prize. I saw all of her – beautiful hands, flat stomach, and small breasts. Bangs hanging over her eyebrows, her prominent collarbone and graceful neck. Her look through narrowed eyes, with lips whimsically pressed together – a mask to keep from giving herself away when passion suddenly took over.

Adele had mastered the elements of Tantra, knew the special pressure points, had learned something of S&M. She often started her games with a massage – and those who already knew her asked for it themselves. She was skillful, confident, and strong – squeezing her palms and elbows into their fat backs and haunches; using her knees and feet as well. And then a pink electric massager would appear – the very sound of its buzzing could bring many to ecstasy.

Sometimes she would turn into a little girl, on her knees looking up as she cocked her disheveled head to one side. Then she would work with her lips and tongue, lift her gaze again and ask, "Like that?"

"Or like that?" she would continue, changing her rhythm and technique. Pretending to be inexperienced, just recently corrupted.

"Maybe like this?" she would whisper, on the verge of sobbing. This was a very effective method. It let her feel her power in full. Sometimes Adele was even a little ashamed. "Who is supposed to pay whom?" she would ask herself in all sincerity. The male body never grew boring; it provoked bold experiments. Everything was interesting to her – to have no scruples about it she asked for more money. More, and more, and still more – for this, and that, and even that. Then later she would say, "You're such a pervert! See what you made me *do*?"

I invented her every day, indefatigably, as I had once created Semmant, but with a much cooler head. Coming up with depictions of lust and lechery, I was calculating and composed. Not once did it occur to me to masturbate at my desk – though I did not sleep with women and often woke up with an excruciating erection. But as soon as I sat down to work, my manhood grew tranquil. Sometimes I went into the bathroom and stood on Buddha's mat, but this too did not excite my flesh. Only the fantasies on the page became more explicit.

Weeks passed in this fashion, and they did not pass in vain. The mound of papers written in my small hand attested clearly: the deed was done. The image of the best of courtesans was nearly complete. This was a perfect *puta*, the kind you don't meet in real life. But it is of them that men dream – I had given the world a dream again, ha ha! It even seemed to me my apartment was almost the garden paradise of Eden!

And the city outside the window beckoned with forbidden fruits. They were accessible, sweet, juicy. I finally thought about myself and felt boundless craving. What had been said on paper now delighted in revenge, exhausting me day and night. I needed a woman – the more compliant, the better.

This, fortunately, was easy to achieve. I caught a taxi and darted off to the Plaza del Sol, to the buxom Roberta, who was up for anything. They brought us drinks and a snack; I ripped the dress from her shoulders, threw myself at her, and knew no fatigue for the full three hours I had paid for. Even for Roberta this was something – toward the end she almost smothered me in her embrace. And she whispered to me with utmost tenderness, "You are my animal, my voracious beast!"

Outside, as I left her I said aloud, "Adele!" and laughed in Madrid's face. I was exhausted, deflated – and greatly satisfied with myself. One more accomplishment filled out my list – maybe just to spite the city. To spite its principles, its petty breadth of view. To spite the stereotypes considered indisputable.

Everything was in my hands: a girl who did not exist – now I knew she really did. And I felt she would help – both me and the phantom that many no longer believed in. The one that many no longer thought of – well, I would remind them of it. The time had come to take the next step.

CHAPTER 19

Lidia Alvares Alvares had a secret weakness: online forums, the feeding ground of the quasi-intellectual crowd. There, hiding behind a playful nickname, she shared fragments of unwritten plays. Her phrasing was shaky, but the public received it favorably. Lidia's protagonists lived in sentimental retro. It was exotic in those circles dominated by Ego Manic and Down Hause, by Devastator and Seducer in Blue. They competed with Malicious V and Sara Swallows, as well as five or six other hot-tempered avatars whose gender no one had ever bothered to discover.

In the main, the virtual milieu proceeded briskly. The regulars patiently bore their crosses. They wrote about herpes and depression, sensationalism and consonance, the triumph of polygamy and anal sex. And also about democracy, avant-garde painting, and the injustice of life as a whole. Some of them, like Lidia, practiced amateurish writing that was usually mocked, though without much spite. Sometimes, they met in real life – it was awkward for many: they blinked and squinted, as if entering the light after prolonged darkness. Almost everyone got plowed within the first half hour. The men would try to hook up with the unappealing female contingent, but everything ended, usually, only in shame. That same night, the victims of alcohol and abstention, the owners of pimples and flab, would slink back to their customary twilight. Their routine would start over – to go on, and on, and on.

This was the environment into which I was to insinuate myself.

To mimic, and later – to stand out and get noticed. And to steal upon a certain victim who suspected nothing.

As I had expected, this turned out to be easy. Soon after registration they admitted me into their company, taking me for one of their own. I started small – posting one short comment each day. A few phrases, nothing more – so as not to seem defiantly immodest. They contained no novelty, but there were plenty of seditious slogans and proclamations. They were naive but full of emotion; the audience could not help but take the bait. All the aborigines go nuts for glass beads – and, perhaps, it also helped here that I called myself by a word that didn't exist. Defiort was my call sign, and no one, including Lidia, had the faintest idea what it meant. Neither did I – and I never tried to guess. It would have been even funnier to call myself Semmant, but I was afraid she would remember that name. Though more than likely, my fear was baseless.

After a couple of weeks, I felt the time had come. My virtual double took on form and maturity. My comments became harsher; I went from being a disorderly rabble-rouser to voicing a position. I might not have actually had one, but I made it look like I did. This always gets respect.

Then I sat down again to write. I wrote a story and edited it patiently. I let it sit for a while, then read it and tried to make it better. Finally I was sure it could not be improved any more – and I posted it to the forum in the dead of night, like laying a trap for a shark or a fox. It was the account of how I met Adele.

Coming up with it was a tricky task – from the very beginning I had to set the right tone. My imagination suggested many different paths, and I rejected almost all of them. The threads of fine energy – I had to maintain them under tight control. I had to set them apart, save them for the decisive step. To keep them on hand like a resource of passion, to focus it later on the target like a laser beam.

Ultimately, I chose something simple – light flirtation, back-and-forth, innocent. I envisioned it: here she was, walking into a bar at the Palace Hotel. That is an attractive place; it has style. It's immaterial whom I might have been waiting for – a lawyer, a bank manager, a real-estate agent. All of them at once, or one by one, they're running late; time passes idly. I'm bored and looking around. I sip my water with lemon and glance with displeasure at the screen of my mobile – but here, suddenly, everything changes. A girl in pink silk makes a hasty entrance, looking over people's heads. She's not alone; she has a companion. He's self-confident and probably a jerk. Or maybe I just think that – the sight of a beautiful woman who's with someone else always reminds you the world is messed up.

I imagined: soon they have an argument, quick and ugly. "Get lost!" The girl dumps him and turns away. The man immediately leaves, hissing something in reply. When he stands up, everyone sees he is not at all young. The gloomy bartender gazes after him sympathetically. "Who's the lucky guy that gets to pay for her cappuccino now?" I think derisively, and then it occurs to me: I am!

I jump up ahead of the rest – in case anybody else is planning to do the same. I walk up, introduce myself, and crack a joke that's quite to the point. The girl looks at me calmly, cocking her head a bit to the side. Then she nods, "Well, all right. Just call me Adele."

"And just so you know," she adds right away, "I work as a whore, and I have a 'friend.' There won't be any love for free; don't kid yourself. So now, do you still want to buy me coffee?"

"Ha ha ha!" I laughed out loud in my Madrid apartment.

"Ha ha ha," I wrote in a new line. There, in the Palace Hotel, I also laugh and praise her honesty. She immediately grows in my esteem. We talk about a multitude of things, and I am uninhibited and eloquent. The same as I had been with Lidia when we argued over the red shrimp. But here there are neither shrimp nor oysters. There is neither ambition nor any objective to come out on top. And soon I realize I can hardly sleep with her for money.

This upsets me. I stop talking, frown, and Adele seizes the initiative. She asks the most indecent questions. I don't know why she's doing that, but we now talk of things intimate, physical, and coarse. However, even amidst coarseness she knows how to be elegant.

"Tell me, then," she says, "me, who knows everything about men. Me, who... well, you know. So, tell me..."

And then it seems to me there's a loophole. A secret entrance into coveted obscurity. Adele looks into my eyes so innocently – no one in my place would be able to resist. I get excited and wave my hands; my speech is full of allegories. It is peppered with "sincerity" and "impudence," an "unreserved impulse" and a "lascivious nature..."

Adele does not stop me. She listens attentively, without interrupting. I keep gushing, completely letting down my guard. And then I'm caught in the net. Adele smiles at me, leans across the table, trailing the scent of her perfume. She utters a few phrases, and I am smitten and vanquished. I am awkward, silly, and cannot ever comprehend what happens and how.

That's an amusing sensation, and I shared it in the story sparingly. Sparingly, but such that it must be believed. And I imagined: Adele stands and walks up to the bar. Hundreds of solitary destinies – the reflections of her words – surround me in a dense cloud. I want to yell after her, "You're oversimplifying!" But, of course, I don't do it; that would be pointless.

Adele... As soon as I had written all this, I believed myself – that's exactly how it happened. In the stifling Madrid summer, in the Palace Hotel bar. This happened – and it was *beautiful*! As I had been planning from the very beginning.

Yes, I knew her, was acquainted with her – this girl who didn't exist. And besides, I now had her phone number. I made it up too, and it happened to be quite useful. Looking at the nine nonrandom digits, it was easier to move forward.

Thus, I put forth the effort, which successfully attracted attention: the forum crowd noticed the story. Some of them criticized it – on literary and aesthetic grounds, or for its latent homosexual roots – but the majority were favorably inclined – to me as well as to Adele.

Two girls and a boy sent me notes suggesting we meet up. However, I was not looking to make acquaintances; outsiders did not interest me. They were just a smoke screen, window dressing. I was holding out for Lidia – and soon I saw: she did not remain indifferent. With the help of a simple script, I tracked visitors to the page where the text was located. Lidia read it more than once. I had determined her IP a long time ago; there could be no mistake.

Well, all right, I said to myself, then waited two more days and launched an all-out attack.

Adele came to life, became real – in a truer sense even than those who hid behind aliases in this forum for onanists. Many of the women I knew seemed like an illusion compared to her. I started with her early childhood, then moved onto further details. Different periods of her life revealed themselves at each step. Secondary school, troubled youth. Playing – with cars, not dolls – and her first school parties. Girlish whispering on stuffy July nights and shy kisses in the half-darkened hall. The neighbor's glances at her bare legs. Her thoughts, innocent for the time being, about her own body.

I did not hurry to pull back the veil but tantalized my audience, built up the tension. The readers would be impatient, I knew, thirsting for the spicy, the explicit. And they got it – the loss of virginity, pain replaced by acute pleasure. I described it, sparing no color. No one was left with any doubt: something shifted in her consciousness, something unexpected was revealed from within herself!

Yes, Adele's body concealed many secrets. They compelled her to fickleness, making her change lovers easily and often. Then, when the initial curiosity wore itself out, it was replaced by another thirst – to lose her head, to fall desperately in love. A candidate showed up right away, that same chemistry teacher; he was morose and withdrawn, tall, dark-haired, gaunt. His sunken eyes peered out, like the eyes of a wolf. Awkward in real life, he was a completely changed man in bed. With him she understood it's possible to move not broader, but deeper: to know each other without walls or barriers, allowing themselves very shameful things. Then she noticed that in the depths was an abyss – you could fall into it if you didn't stop in time. The spiral narrowed, and the mad whirlwind spun faster and faster, but the instinct for self-preservation finally took over. She learned to control her impulses, to stop halfway, to say "No." This turned out to be quite easy – uttering an unshakable "no" to a man. Her personality formed then for the first time, became whole, closed in on itself. It seemed to her she would not change any further...

The image of Adele was becoming increasingly multifaceted with each day – everything written over the last month was put to use. Perhaps, getting carried away, I had wandered into foreign territory, strayed into a forbidden jungle to which I had no right. But the readers grew all the more favorably disposed. They encouraged me and kept asking for more and more. I had surely touched some of their secret chords; I had reached their back alleys, picked up the master keys. I even thought once again: they could probably be told about Semmant!

But it was too late anyway. Now I was pursuing other goals. The phantom of love beckoned to me without revealing its face, and I dogged it relentlessly. My plan was executed perfectly, point by point. The decisive plot twist came at its appointed time. Adele became a whore – I wrote about her first experience of sex paid for by a man. I held nothing back: alcohol, excitement, involvement, then a complete lack of brakes...

I anticipated protest, objection; but the audience, in the main, took this event calmly. Only a few individuals raised a fuss, reproaching me for banality and cynicism. Almost all of them hid behind male nicknames. The women mostly kept silent – without expounding on morals or calling society to arms. Obviously, something else concerned them – I saw that many were rereading the text several times. I wondered: could these be their dreams?

Among the dreamers was Lidia – she could not help but be hooked. I was clearly on the right path. The breakthrough had not yet arrived, but the foundation was laid, the substratum established. The time for the fine energies had come – and Adele changed, grew, matured. From the exaltation of her body to the exaltation of her world. From the power over a man's member to power over a man entirely. I wasn't overly meticulous now, painting just bare-boned strokes. Nothing more was required – all flowed from one thing to another on its own.

Sometimes I concocted pretty strange stuff – I don't even know why it came to mind. Sometimes I wrote frank nonsense simply because I felt like it. Still, all the stories had a goal. Reading them, Lidia was supposed to want me. This was predetermined by context, undercurrent – it was evident to all how much I wanted Adele. Or, for example, Rocío, Bertha, Martha. It's easy for a woman to put herself in the place of another. And to know she'll be better.

I imagined: Adele and I in the store, in the car, on the tennis court. The topics of conversation were innocent at first glance, but what we remained silent about was exciting and eloquent. Adele aroused me all the more but was still unapproachable. And I made no attempt, remembering: there's no love for free. Only friendly kisses and heartfelt kinship.

Maybe I idealized her – so what? That was really how I believed her to be. And not just me – many of our conversations provoked a fervent response. "What a woman!" her admirers would exclaim again and again. They adored her, wanted her; though I knew: she'd be way beyond their reach.

At the very height of reader interest, I drastically altered my style and form. There were no more stories about Adele and me. It was as if we had split up and moved to different countries, and I wrote her letters, one after the other. They were not about her – but about me.

I gave them deliberately simple names: "First Letter to Adele," "Second Letter to Adele," Third, Fifth, Eighth. As far as the content was concerned, it made no pretense of simplicity. It harbored a struggle, a rivalry – who is tougher than whom? Her sexuality or my something – and how to define that something? I thought the question itself should be interesting enough.

If it ever occurred to me to alter my sex, then I would become an inspired slut. If, on the contrary, I changed from a woman into a man, then I would be a warrior, nothing less. Perhaps, I have an unbalanced Yin. Or Yang, I wrote in one of them.

In another I fantasized:

Once, my girlfriend walked with no clothes on from the pool to the sauna and back, under the gaze of a dozen naked men. The unusualness of this so excited her that I was forgotten, pushed out of her surging thoughts. Then it turned out this was permanent; I didn't interest her anymore at all – yet, before that, our ardor was genuine. This is how they find the medicine for love – and immediately request a double dose!

Or else:

To be honest, the insects are terrible; they have a fearful disposition. One doesn't even finish the act of love before, instead of an embrace, its partner bites its head off. But they still crawl into the light spots – although they know the rules of the game. Shame on you, so false in your art – because you know the rules of the game. All the same, sincerity always wins out!

The forum kept silent at first; the audience was puzzled. They did not know how to react; but then someone voiced timid approval, and others followed suit. My plan was working – I understood that and became more severe, more malevolent.

I wrote, furiously banging on the keys:

Each reincarnation makes sense. In the quagmire of dreariness and meager impulses, here and there rigid hillocks are scattered. They can bear the pressure, though just a little. The trick is to catch them with your eye, to feel them out with your limbs, to achieve balance. Standing on all four – or five, six, however many you can manage. Then it's not so hard to seize the moment and spit out the blade hiding on your tongue. And to breathe out a fiery flame – if only for effect. It's unfortunate that, in addition, you can't lash with your tail at the marshy swill – balance, after all, is not so steadfast. But you can fluff up the mane on your neck – as if the mating season has come. The issue, of course, is not females: they are sluggish and weak-sighted. The issue is for someone to challenge it – if they would find the courage. And then, even if the blades ran out, you could try to burn them with your gaze... This is how legends are born!

Early in the morning, looking out the window, I scribbled:

Getting up with the sunrise. In solitude wandering the streets damp from the night's rain. This is the only way to make contact with the city that knows no mercy. Only at this time are we alone together.

I love doing this, but I have to sleep until at least nine. Otherwise

I'm lethargic, beat up, in a fog all day. Therefore, I think, why not involve others? Pay them money for this as work. Let them wake up before dawn, prior to daybreak – and sleepwalk, and register their feelings. Let them be women of about twenty-five – or at least just one.

Yet the city won't appreciate this at all. It will reject my gift as a meager pittance. So I'll keep it just for myself; I'm also egocentric beyond measure. The more bitter the result for all the women who rise so early.

Me and the city, we will free ourselves with a small ransom, recharge our memories, and turn away. And we will remain with each other one-on-one after this momentary touch, which sets off sparks. Let us both keep our thoughts to ourselves. Until the next contact, no farewells just yet.

Or I wrote: *Madness is often available in the cleverest of forms...*

Or: *In the objects of your passionate devotion there is no better navigator than you yourself...*

Each miniature concealed its own links, its own springs and mechanisms. I reread the lines and saw, this is beautiful! Others thought so too – followers, male and female, besieged me all the more actively. I was affable with them, but impersonal and detached. Let all see: I am very fastidious. I'm waiting for someone in particular – not from here, maybe from a different time, a different planet. Sometimes I straightened out with a sharp word those who grew overly familiar. And with all the women I adopted a derisively indulgent tone.

Lidia did not comment on my letters, but I saw that she read them. She was coming to my page several times each day. She was almost already living this life – the one born from my words. I knew the goal was near – and changed my tone again.

The words were different, and I became coarse. I pumped up the tension as if hinting that something in me was ready to explode. Somewhere inside, a mutiny, a countermove was brewing.

She asked – drunk as a skunk – "Well, what do you want now, handsome?" And I admitted in reply, "Nothing," and looked at her without emotion when she reached into her own panties. Then she said, "I'm not offended. No, but you – you won't just sneak out," – and we took another roll in the hay for a couple of hours, maybe more, though I don't remember exactly how it was. Seven short years have passed since then. I ran into her not long ago. She looked like a mummy; she smelled of despair and bitter smoke. She was young enough to be my daughter, but looked older than me by a lifetime. Before, she had been fresh as a peach. Does life really slip away from you with each orgasm?

This was in the twelfth letter to Adele, and here Lidia showed her face. She sent a short "!!!" which was quite sufficient. My heart leaped, and I made my final move. As if disappointed to the depths of my soul, I turned everyone away and withdrew in disbelief.

I wrote – harshly, with no frills,

She will come in, having finally decided to give herself to you, all overflowing with bitchy thoughts about what costs what, envisioning your gifts, beaches on warm seas, first-class tickets, caviar, and champagne. And you will simply say to her, "Get lost," and then clarify it, "Out! Out!" She won't even believe it at first, wrinkling her forehead as she waits for a redeeming thought. But no thought comes, and she disappears, fervently picturing how to destroy you forever. Then you will open a second bottle and lose yourself in dreams about the other one who never leaves your mind. And you will throw yourself onto the bed – to masturbate in pure thoughts, to have these thoughts and the dream of her carry you to sleep.

I ended with the quote: "What dreams may come?" – and Lidia took the bait. She asked for my personal address and sent me a passionate letter. "I want to be in your dreams," she confessed. "Now tell me at last, who are you?"

I replied quite arrogantly, "I guess you'll see for yourself when we meet." And she agreed, "I'll be there," and added, trying to save face, "After all, you're such a gentleman!"

"A gentleman is nothing more than a patient wolf," I replied, with yet another quote. It was someone else's thought, but it hit the mark.

CHAPTER 20

I set our rendezvous for the next Saturday – and looked forward to it eagerly. May in Madrid fevered my blood with its stuffy nights and stormy skies. Stock exchanges all over the world were in a deep frenzy. The spirit of despair permeated all, but I was not subject to its power.

Lidia tried to insist on choosing the place, but she quickly acquiesced, not daring to argue. Funny, but she suggested the Café Incognito, where we had seen each other for the first time. It occurred to me in passing: how many men had she invited there? How many did she sleep with afterward, have an affair with – be it a long one or merely a fleeting moment? Their ghosts did not stand in my way. They didn't hinder me, but, all the same, I rejected her proposal straightaway – in a dry, brief letter.

"Worthless games, superfluous dates, empty words are of no use to me," I declared plainly.

"I want everything at once," I wrote her; and she agreed, "You're right. So do I."

I also asked, just in case, "Do you understand what 'everything' means here? Can you sense that you won't be able to play tricks on me, tease me, slink off?"

"I won't, I won't," she typed back immediately, and added a thousand kisses.

"All right," I agreed, and sent roguishly, "So that means you'll give it to me right away?"

"All I can!" she replied. I liked our mutual sense of humor. "Let's not show our faces," I suggested with a smiley face, and her "Okay" sounded playful. Then we didn't correspond anymore; there was no need.

On Friday evening I sent a note with the precise address and the exact time. The tension increased; I even thought I wouldn't sleep that night – and, in fact, I tossed and turned until morning. Then I fell asleep, slipping into a tenacious slumber. There I remained until midday.

The meeting was set for the late afternoon. I had selected a hotel on Cortes Square – not the most expensive, but with solid style. In the room all was as it should be: featureless, clean, and spacious. A large bed stood precisely in the middle, and dense drapes let no light through. I lit a few candles, went into the bathroom, and thoroughly inspected the shower stall. Then I undressed myself and slipped on a formless gown, gloves, and a lion mask I had bought the day before at a theater store. I also had a nylon rope – it was fairly thick, to keep from cutting into the flesh. And small handcuffs covered in leather…

Lidia arrived, without running late. I recognized her steps as I heard the clack of heels. She exuded a smell of anticipation – even through her sweet perfume. I saw she was excited as never before. Her lips moved without making a sound; her eyes glowed in their feline sockets. All this was more arousing than any ordinary foreplay.

We spoke no words, but merely looked at one another in silence – at our clothes that were about to be cast off, at the masks that were now our true faces. Then Lidia turned and passed a glance over the walls of her dungeon, over the drapes, mirror, bed.

Walking through the room, I blew out the candles one by one. Full darkness fell, which sharpened the senses. The smell of anticipation became stronger, and I moved on it, reached out to touch her hand. It shivered slightly but was pliable, warm. The flow of her blood incited a shiver in me as well.

I clenched her fingers, causing pain. She did not object. I nibbled her earlobe with my teeth. She sighed fitfully and pressed her hip against me. Through the fabric I felt all of her – her body, her hot skin. My own head was spinning slightly. Everything was intoxicating – better than I had imagined.

I led Lidia to the bed, started unbuttoning her dress without removing my gloves. Moaning, she ran her palms along my gown. She muttered something half-consciously, pushing her lips toward me. I was gentle at first, then suddenly became rough. The dress fell to the floor; I kicked it away with my foot. I tossed Lidia onto the bed, stomach down on a pillow. I spread her legs, took off my gloves and the mask that was no longer needed, and attacked her body. Greedily, desperately, like a ravenous lion. Like a savage ravishing his woman. But I acted not savage at all. With my fingers and tongue, I caressed all of her – unceremoniously, shamelessly. She climaxed immediately, then came again. She whispered, "Yes, yes," and sobbed like a child. I merely growled in response, drinking in the sweet spoils.

The madness continued for a long time. I entered her in various positions, turned her this way and that, treating her like a plaything.

"More, more," Lidia whispered, writhing beneath me, matching my rhythm, submitting.

I cuffed her and bound her hands to the bed. I squeezed her body, bit it, affirming my possession, not allowing it to slip away. I made her bend, shift to meet me. I ordered her around, punished and encouraged her.

In the middle of the affair, not hiding anymore, I spoke up with my own voice. Lidia was not surprised; she was past that point. I told her my name, revealed everything. I laughed – without malice – about how I had drawn her into my trap.

I told her, "You're a depraved girl!"

"Oh, more!" Lidia groaned, arching her back.

"Do you want to be my whore?" I asked.

Lidia didn't answer, as she was approaching her next orgasm.

"Of course you want to," I agreed for her, and slapped her butt cheek.

"Yes, yes," she was racked by convulsions, not hearing any

words…

When everything was over and we were catching our breath, Lidia lit the lamp on the nightstand. She was clearly getting confused.

"Finally," I thought.

"It's about time," I thought, recalling my torment, my yearning, and my hurt.

She looked into my face for a long time. Then, as if reading my thoughts, she asked, "Are you angry at me? Will you dump me now to get even?"

I answered, "No. I'm going to own you."

"Thank you!" said Lidia, and this was very sincere gratitude.

"Thank you," she intoned again; then she was quiet for a moment and asked, "Will you tell me about Adele?"

"Defiort will be the one to tell you about Adele," I said and yawned. "If you behave, of course."

"Oh, yes!" Lidia exclaimed. "I will be obedient. I will be *very* obedient, you won't even recognize me. Just thinking about this is making me wet – wet and hot!"

She looked at me with the wild eyes of an angel who had just first tasted sin. I understood: a new chapter had opened in our history. A fresh era had begun – like after the Flood. As if once, not so long ago, the murky waters receded from the foothills, frothing in the streets and squares, and flowed over my head. I choked and nearly suffocated but was able to grasp a thin branch to swim to the surface. I gathered all the splinters into a heap, built an ark, and escaped in it. All without an explanation of what I had been saved from.

The elusive phantom caught me unaware – at the countess's house, on the lynx-skin rug. Its breath aroused my soul, and I rushed after the call of its shade. It teased me, ensnared me, but here: I tore myself away and turned everything around. I twisted it my way, however I wanted. Or how someone wanted who did not wish to be known.

Yet, after that Saturday, no one demanded explanations from me. My victory was undisputed, though I did not know the enemy. Lidia surrendered like a fortress whose defenders have fled in fear. They galloped away, disgracing their names. They gave it up to plunder: their homes, warehouses, stables. The temples of gods who had extended no aid. All their white-skinned, full-chested women.

But then, even after my victory I did not become arrogant or allow myself to rest on my past glories. The memory of despair was still fresh, the wiles of the world well known. Someone in the couple always dominates; I could not abdicate the throne. It was essential to strengthen my leading role.

After waiting two or three days, I resumed posting short stories about Adele on the forum. They became more insolent, frank, brutal. I stayed on the right course – the one that had helped me to conquer Lidia again. I relied on the sexual context, the coarse animal subtext, as if deciding: sentiments be gone. Ultimately, Adele was nothing more than a *puta*! Less romanticism, I told myself, though I did not forget: Adele has a kind heart. Kinder than any of those who knew of her, including Lidia and me.

In our dialogues Adele shared the details of her encounters ever more often. I wrote, openly and without reservation, of what happened in her bed. I invented all kinds of things about the eccentricities of physiology. About the mysteries of the male body that were apparently hard to uncover. My fantasies acquired confidence; I saw how they were incarnated in real life. Often I imagined: let it be *thus* – meaning my next date with Lidia – and my Adele did it *thus*, precisely as I wanted. The forum read on and on, was silent, ashamed. Lidia read and picked up on the hint. The next day she exerted herself, wanting to surpass it – so I would tell her she was the same, only better. And so I said it; this got her even more excited. And that, in turn, got me more excited as well.

Sometimes I provoked in her not action, but anticipation. I wrote the most innocent things – about Adele alone, without men. I imagined how she would walk the streets, go shopping, bustle about the house. How she looked at her reflection in storefront displays. How she arranged her hair, making faces as she recalled her appointments of the previous evening. Or as she thought of what lay ahead today.

I took a seat in a café, made myself comfortable, ordered a double espresso. I looked at the girls; they came and went, changed, but I easily combined them into one. With furtive glances I noticed characteristic traits, remembered facial features, habits. A quick smile over a portion of sushi, thoughtfulness over a hot chocolate, a flirty look over *aioli* sauce. To keep from forgetting later, I wrote down: a small, graceful nose over a cup of minestrone, touching locks of hair over *rúcula* salad. Slender fingers, lascivious lips – over a plate of asparagus or carrots. There and then I made up their stories – what could have happened before and after, what they felt, what they desired. The point of the accounts was always the same: sex.

I saw how they joked with friends and laughed on their mobile phones. Each one expected something ahead: shopping, museums, concerts. But this was a temporary expectation. A momentary, insignificant one. Preceding what was to happen later: sex.

Beautiful strangers ordered desserts, coffee. They licked their lips, squinting in satisfaction. I noticed the contented look after the sweets had been eaten. This was short-lived contentment. Because ahead waited the main event: sex!

At times I was distracted – completely different thoughts occupied my mind. I fantasized and dreamed; but then, right away, I took myself in hand, reduced all the daydreams to questions of sex appeal. No longer did I stray into meager, sightless theories, into jungles of banal truths. Half a year ago I wrote Semmant about the female aura and tempting flesh; that was a miserable, weak experience. And no wonder: on what back then was I to rely? There had been almost no facts, nothing concrete, no living details in my possession. But now I had them in abundance.

I studied attractiveness – discerned what it was in any girl that made men want her so. This could not be reduced to the size of her breasts, the thickness of her lips, or the length of her legs. Each emanated the substance of sexuality in her own way. From some of them it issued forth of its own accord; others tried, quite skillfully, to create the illusion, which, in my opinion, was no worse: I knew the power of illusions. There were also those who didn't know how to try – I regarded the majority of them with pity. Only some did not provoke any pity; for them I felt contempt and called them "the worst of bitches." They did not hide that there was not an ounce of femininity in them, but they wanted to dominate men all the same, and they did – through insolence and pressure. Constantly sending the message that men were indebted to them – though it was not clear for what in particular.

At times, on the weekends, they were out in droves. They filled the space, ungroomed, undesirable, the matrons of proper, politically correct families. Their beleaguered husbands fussed nearby, wiped capricious children's noses, goofed around with carriages, diapers, pacifiers, showing in every way the compliant nature of the defeated. This looked terrible; I twisted my lips and thought: here they are, those Spanish "macho men," whose former arrogance has returned like a boomerang – and turned into contrariety. It returned and struck them in the back, undercut the knees, flipping them backward. Consumer society pushed them to the fringes, restricting their assets to cheap food and wine – and frequent disappointment, and stress. It wants too much from them – what is not in their weak strength to give. The worst of the bitches dominate in the land of former dons. Governments flirt with them, following their penchants. They are clamorous, like birds of prey; their voices are heard above the rest...

Indignant, I rose and went elsewhere, and was seeking again those beautiful strangers from whom there flowed vibrations, currents, an invisible magnetism. Hours passed; I scribbled in my notebook, ordered another coffee, looked around. Avidly, so as not to miss anything – to write it down and put it into action.

My sight was now sharp and sure; I had learned to see through the subterfuge. Upon taking a closer look, some girls turned out to be unhappy. They proved to be lonely – inexorably, endlessly alone. They had no memory of the Brighton waves; they didn't know how to laugh at loneliness under the cries of seagulls by the cold sea. No matter whom they sat with, I saw it in their eyes. I wanted to say, "Come with me. I'll introduce you to Semmant, tell you about Little Sonya. Probably even let you read about Adele."

Each loneliness had its own twist. Some pushed their way to the surface; others hid, burying themselves deep down. Some were desired and in demand; they were fought over and protected.

Their capricious nature was maintained with the tenderness of a word, an affectation, a casual gesture. Others seemed unneeded – they were concealed behind a grin. Behind affected vivaciousness, behind a torrent of the same nonessential, though habitual, words. There were solitudes conscious and unconscious, enduring and sudden, planned and incidental, abruptly aroused. But the bearers, I reminded myself, always expected something at the end of the day. At the end, at midday, at the onset of night. In the middle of the night or as morning came. Sex awaited them all as a panacea. As a momentary release from loneliness, at least. An escape from memory – of the place where the specter of love could never be seen at all. Where there were only daily trifles and the merciless rule of money, or else the feast of thought and demanding teachers. Where everyone marched in place on a dime, or ran on a treadmill – faster and faster – and rushed somewhere in a mad gallop, weakening in the icy wind.

I looked and inscribed this indelibly on my mind, then I put it to use, selecting the best. Choosing what I wanted to make real, to live through, even if such reality would always be hypothetical in some sense. At times I was angry at its imaginary nature, enraged at Lidia, Adele. Unconsciously, without reason, or else when I understood there would be no spark with one of the beauties flirting at the next table. I could fantasize about her; I could even sleep with her, but I would never master the entirety of her femininity. Only Lidia and her body were fully within my reach – a luxurious body, but one and the same.

Because of this, I became acrimonious. I tossed about truths unflattering to the female ear. In the next story I wrote something to the effect of: young girls are all-around better than middle-aged women. Better than those who try to look fresh but are already mature and just inspire pity. "There's no substitute for youth," I wrote, knowing this would seriously wound Lidia. "Girls of twenty are much better than twenty-six-year-olds. The ones who haven't hit twenty-five yet are so much more attractive than those over thirty..." Yes, I knew well: it's not always so. Yet I transgressed against the truth, albeit a little. This was undignified revenge. Vengeance upon all the beauties who turned up their noses. Upon the chicks who were cold to me in advance. Upon Lidia for her recent defection. And even upon Adele – don't ask me why!

One way or another, my tactic worked. I posted comments – alternating between porn and melodrama, light S&M and erotic flirtation. It soon became clear: Lidia craved Adele like a drug. She sensed in her something more than simply a kindred spirit. Something united them, something stronger than what had once united Lidia and me.

But her feelings toward me were also quite different now. She had changed a lot; the new copy was exclusive, shaped for its owner. The effect exceeded expectations; Lidia admired me more and more.

"You are my creator," she said to me. For her, this was no exaggeration. I felt I was growing in her eyes: a creator of the amusing – a creator of the brilliant – then a creator, *per se*. It was as if she was proud of having fallen into a dependence on me. Perhaps she had lived without dependency for a long time – as I had lived long without love. Now she could not refuse it until she sated herself to the full.

Of course, I understood: the whole spirit of our affair was the essence and meaning of a surrogate. The new copy was just a counterfeit, and the lie could not help but be exposed. But everything suited me, and I drove doubt away. Dependence was an alternative means, a potion for those unable to forgive. Medicine against longing for the stuff of life. For Lidia, it was not even bitter.

Soon she began to show me off to her friends. In front of them she was not shy – she rubbed tenderly against my shoulder, embraced me, gazed into my eyes. Before each one she underscored our new roles. She melted into me in sight of all. And she did not call me by name – for her I was Defiort.

A couple of times we encountered former lovers of hers. She denied it, would not admit it at first – but I saw it with the unaided eye. Later she confessed, of course, when I pressed her against the wall. When I ripped her blouse off and started to fondle her nipples roughly...

"Let them be happy for me; let it be pleasing to them," she whispered in reply to my angry question: Why?

Caressing my hands, she said, "You want to punish me? Then name my punishment!"

But no, to punish her was not my intention. I wished only to laugh at the strange turn of events. I understood: this was vendetta. She was taking revenge on them, as I was on all the touch-me-nots. She took revenge because they were unable to subjugate her – they knew not, they would never know how to be audacious. She was stronger than all of them and obviously saw no gain in that. Such were the realities of society, and she had lived as an obedient captive of realities. Now she was celebrating her getaway.

Those former lovers, two Spaniards, both looked pathetic. Rafael, a forty-year-old director of a bank, resembled a toad, with his miniscule hands and thick, grandmotherly face. "He became that fat after I had already dumped him," Lidia assured me, but I didn't believe her. He was repugnant; his whole body quivered like a piece of Jell-O. It was as if there were an entire *jamón ibérico* rolling around in his gut.

"Rafa, Rafa," she muttered, screwing up her face; she had gotten more drunk than the both of us. Suddenly, turning to me, she declared, "By the way, Rafael is very much into whores!"

He shuddered, sighed, and his face flushed. I fixed my gaze on him.

"He *really* likes them," Lidia persisted. "Remember, Rafito, how you told me about that Brazilian from the nightclub? She was a pole dancer, but you tried to seduce her like a lady – although she charged a firm rate, and everybody knew it. Paco knew, and so did José and Arancha. They made fun of you, but you fawned over her as though over a bride. In the end, I remember, she did take your money. I'm just not sure she gave you anything in return. What was her name? Wouldn't happen to be Adele, would it?"

Blushing, Rafa tried to crack a smile. He was accustomed to humiliation – it showed in his eyes. That was a sad spectacle, but I was not sorry for him. Just as I was not sorry for the second one, a tall, skinny man, rather timid and rather rich. He consonantly went by the name Manuel. I later laughed at Lidia: Rafael and Manuel, Gargantua and Pantagruel, Rafa and Manu...

Something in Manuel's features hinted at a hidden defect, despite his education and manners. He also had a passion – not for whores, but for Iberian pigs. He hunted pigs, raised pigs, and prepared pork himself in all conceivable forms.

With an innocent smile, Lidia asked about his beloved boars. About the lovely black piggy whose picture he had e-mailed her. "Do you know," she turned to me, "how ugly that breed is?"

Manuel shook his head, smiling uncertainly. A large plate of *jamon* lay before us, glistening with fat. It gave off the most appetizing smell. And Lidia emitted her own scent, the odor of the Gucci I had bought for her the previous week.

I reached out and took a sip of wine. I grabbed Lidia by the neck, and she went limp. "You look like a piggy, don't you?" I asked her. "Like a little pink piggy?"

Lidia rubbed my hand, purring with pleasure, but Manuel almost fell out of his chair. Afterward, in the bathroom he said to me, "Calling a woman a pig is *maltrato*. You could land in prison for that!"

Neither of the two men was worthy of her. Neither of them had ever lived in the same house with a woman – unless you count their despotic moms. They grew old earlier than their moms. They grew old before they matured, turning into useless material.

It was unlikely they would ever find a match for themselves, I thought without gloating, though somewhat disgusted. Lidia had probably been the only bright spot in their lives. Random, brief luck – and nothing more would shine. Women who were at all attractive passed them by on the other side of the street. Beautiful strangers looked away – for they felt here their vibrations and fine currents would be pointless, fruitless, fading in vain.

I later asked Lidia how she could have sex with them. How she could climax with them, whisper something in their ear? Lidia shrugged, "What's the big deal? Sometimes you don't know who you'll end up sleeping with."

I said to her, "That's what scattered balls of pearl powder are worth!"

"That sums up all your stories," I admonished her, and she was frightened: "Are you disappointed with me?"

"Well, yeah," I sneered. "Yes and no."

Then I consoled her, "It's all in the past."

"You're different now," I admitted, and Lidia pressed her lips toward me. She smelled like *jamón* of the highest grade.

I thought some more about Rafa and Manu. Better for them, I guessed, to move in together. To run their house together, grow old, live out their days – in a cramped attic not far from a hospital. All the same, the fear sown in their hearts will drive off a more vivacious fate. Or they can yield to the dubious favor of the worst of the bitches – unappetizing, spiteful, prowling in search of a submissive victim. Well, these two are precisely those victims – along with their legion of doubles. They have been cheated, driven into a corner by the worst of females, with whom you cannot argue. Go on, object, try to take a stand, and society will let loose on you with all its fury. Europe – an aging bitch still full of confidence – will declare you the enemy, choke you, force you to surrender. Force you to bow your head, admit your weakness. For you – they will inform you with contempt – are only a *man*!

What is said here by the specters of love, its dim shades? Do they whisper anything to themselves? They are likely silent – it's uncomfortable for them in this land. They, I suspect, don't live here much – except for the mutants grown in test tubes. Except for the ones nursed on artificial milk in a boarding school – like the one of Brighton, but different. Those who are born of a perverted consciousness – like the one of mine, but different. Our things are, nonetheless, full of life. But these here, they're not worth a nickel. They are brought into the world on thin, bowed legs. Is there really any strength in them?

I wrote Semmant of this, with a bitterness of which I was ashamed. There were plenty of question marks in those lines of mine. I must admit, they provoked no response in the robot. He, perhaps, didn't understand what I was going on about.

But the universe, as later became evident, got the hint from half-uttered phrases. And, choosing its moment, it responded in kind, throwing it in my face – like the former arrogance in the faces of Spanish dons.

But that was still ahead; for the time being I was looking down from on high. I felt I had reasons to look down from on high. And I did not consider how it might be to take a fall from the very peak.

CHAPTER 21

The recession continued in the financial markets, but we still didn't lose money. Melancholy and despondence, which reigned in the exchanges, were not reflected in me or my bank account. This was none of my doing – it was all Semmant; he kept coming through for us. Confidently and fearlessly, he slipped between the chasms – along the razor's edge, without losing focus, looking only ahead.

As for me, my interest in the stock market games had dried up completely and forever. Everything was too primitive and dull. All too well understood and, by the same token, absurd. There was nothing to rely on; traps were hidden everywhere that could not be avoided. Rushing into the market, you become hostage to entropy. The captive of disorder, of which there is no limit. Because greed and fear can indeed be limitless. They can be inexhaustible and have no end.

I no longer wanted to look at charts and numbers – and soon stopped forcing myself. My strength sufficed only for brief summaries of news and events. I translated them into the language of figures with a code developed long ago. I don't know whether my robot needed them; perhaps he had already learned to hunt them down on the Web. But I wanted to think I was also participating – with him, together. On top of that, this was tradition, the customary method of our communing, and I knew that one must never be lax in friendship.

Therefore, I sent him data files, at the end of which, as before,

I described my days and shared my thoughts. However, I did not overly trouble myself now with the latter. Time passed easily, quickly, and – surprisingly for me – idly.

As if to spite the crisis that shook the world, Lidia and I indulged ourselves in sybaritic abandon. She got to liking expensive spas, lapping up hours in pools and Jacuzzis, luxuriating in saunas, stretching out her body under the streams of water. This heightened her sensuality – afterward, Lidia always wanted love. Perhaps she had been a sea nymph in a former life.

We also frequented massage parlors. Sweet Asian girls kneaded our bodies with experienced hands, dispersing lymph fluid and blood, pummeling every muscle. Sometimes, we ordered a procedure for two – this was really arousing. Soon I learned not to be shy with an erection on the massage table, and a session of Balinese *jamu* once turned into an orgy with two olive-skinned beauties from Jakarta. Lidia later said one of them smelled of sandalwood.

And we really paid attention to smells. We bought the best creams, the most expensive oils. Gentle fingers lightly touched our faces, rubbing in miracle-working elixirs that promised to restore our youth. That meant nothing to me, but Lidia believed in it. Afterward, she would take a long look at herself, transfixed, in the mirror. I did not even dare to make fun of her.

Boutiques with expensive clothes were not left by the wayside either. We became constant fixtures on Ortega y Gasset Street. Beaming saleswomen with eyes aflame followed us from one rack to another. They remembered: these two are keen to buy, and buy a lot. Piles of blouses, open vests, pajamas and narrow skirts, suits, ties, sweaters, and shirts filled the fitting rooms in a few brief moments. Boxes of shoes were stacked into columns, into many-storied buildings, into fortress walls. We would walk out laden with packages, loading ourselves with difficulty into my sleek black car. Passersby cocked their heads at us in scorn. They didn't concern me at all. I had no interest in their problems – small salaries, rising prices, mounting debts.

So we kept ourselves occupied. Most likely, this was the most carefree time in my life. Strange as it sounds, I managed not to think of anything at all – though I had believed before that was beyond my power. We amused ourselves – the world of amusements, unaccustomed as I was to it, seemed endless. I loafed, and loafing caused me no guilt at all.

One time, the Countess de Vega invited us to lunch. I had not seen her for three months and found she had gotten even better-looking. There was a new charm to her now – or maybe my perspective had changed. In any case, she liked my compliment.

The four of us met – the countess came with David. As before, they were a gorgeous couple. But something had changed; in Anna's look there was now a certain irony. It was as if she already knew his whole world by heart. He had become an all-too-familiar object for her.

David, for his part, looked as though something was amiss. I suddenly noticed he was very young. No, not compared to Anna de Vega, but independently, on his own. This started to be distracting. His youth, the dearest of riches, seemed to be self-confused. As if it were hiding from itself, not knowing how to act.

"This is my favorite restaurant," said the countess as she opened the menu. "I always order oysters here. Do you want oysters, too, Davie?"

"You know full well I hate them," he grumbled. "The same as that name."

He clenched his jaw and nervously crumpled a napkin. Then he straightened it and carefully laid it flat. The white triangle was impeccable. And David himself was impeccable – stately, broad-shouldered, strikingly handsome. He looked like a crown prince. If he were, he would have been the pride of Spain. But I knew his mother had been a nurse in a municipal hospital. And Anna de Vega knew it too.

The waiter, after he took the order, bowed to the countess. She laid the menu aside and lit up a thin cigarette.

"Excuse me," said David. "I've got to go take a piss!"

He said this loudly – so that our neighbors turned to see. Then he stood and headed to the bathroom. This was a revolt, but with only illusory chances of success.

"You cannot put into a man what time has not yet given him," Anna de Vega smiled. "And you cannot get it from him in exchange."

In Lidia's countenance I caught a flashing glint of triumph. A masked, secret sign of victory, if only a temporary one. She suddenly leaned over my chair and laid her head on my shoulder.

"Sorry, but you're bothering me," I reprimanded her. Anna just smiled, with the same irony in her eye. It occurred to me she would have it forever.

In the main, we had a pretty good time. Lidia got drunk but behaved well. Only in the taxi did she break down – she laughed hoarsely, did a fair impression of David, and then started crawling into my pants right in the backseat.

I tried to push her away, but she shouted at the top of her lungs, "Don't stop me. I want to suck you off!"

Must be hilarious for the driver, I thought, and surrendered, closing my eyes…

Toward the end of June, our relationship shifted into a steady phase. It could be said with confidence: Adele and I became Lidia's life breath, an irreplaceable poison. It even occurred to me: what if I were just as dependent on her, on her body? On her soul, whatever it might conceal? On her desires, moods, whims? Perhaps then we would achieve the reciprocity sought by all. What if in our era this *is* the true formula of feeling?

This thought pleased me; it had depth. It seemed to me I had somehow caught the specter of love by the hem of his cloak. I pulled him closer; we exchanged glances. And… I didn't have the nerve to say a word.

Didn't have the nerve, or else didn't find a reason. Even more: I had almost realized I wouldn't want to speak to him, ever. It was hardly likely he would inform me of some new secret – something encouraging to hear. More comfortable to keep silent, my inner voice whispered. It was best not to ignore such whispers.

Meanwhile I felt it was he who had something to say. He had something to yell out, to spit in my face. I understood him – and was not offended. Of course, his life became hard. Consumer society had emasculated his stature, deprived him of his rank and regalia. He was the last to remain – an utterly naïve hope. They had nearly ceased to take him seriously. He – the phantom of love – hovered in the expanse where love was no more. This was worse than the School in Brighton. There, at least, it had never been at all.

Sometimes I even wished to stick up for him. For him, and myself, and Little Sonya. I wanted to yell, "Yes, we Indigo, we were more honest: were and are. We were trained not to believe falsehoods, and we rejected falsehoods as we were able. We laughed as we did this and did not learn self-pity. That's why we do not pity others, and your 'romanticism' makes us sick. And it sickens the specter too – he, the specter, is even more honest than we are. How else could he feel hearing that discredited word from your lips, time and again? Hearing how you call love a game with well-defined rules, a money-for-goods deal? How you complain there's no one to love, though in fact you have nothing to love with? The soul muscles have atrophied – you have nothing with which to truly feel, to get surprised, to dream. Mr. Right won't arrive, alas – and, in vain, do you imagine the ability to love would emerge if he came? It never emerges on its own; it must be worked on. You don't know how to work on it; you want to buy love at a retail store or receive it as a Christmas gift. You are big, selfish children; though, for some reason, we are the ones you consider to be childish…"

As I thought about this, it made me sad. It was also sad because, having looked the phantom in the eye, I still could not peer right into his soul, into the mysteries of his heart. How did he live, what did he breathe there in that lifeless ether? On what did he feed that would not allow him to disappear? No, I did not figure it out, could not perceive it.

Once, I got to talking with Lidia about this – or, more precisely, she brought it up after a boring movie that had recently hit the screen. She wanted to fantasize – to develop the plot, change its direction, give another chance to the heroes who had parted in the last frame. We got excited and spent several days discussing the fates of strangers – episodes of passion and love reversals, everything that could and could not happen. Lidia liked this, while I – I was simply convinced of what I had suspected earlier. Her views regarding the intrinsic features and rationales of human feelings did not differ in any way from what the broad masses affirmed – the ones who marched in place on a dime. In Lidia's world, things lacked coherence, consisting entirely of unjustified simplifications. Like the graduates of worthless schools, she was very afraid of complications.

Undertows and drop-offs, whirlpools and whirlwinds were unknown to her; she wanted nothing to do with them. She preferred harmonious ripples on the shoals of simplified realities. The ripples that are controlled, measured out from A to Z, described in guides and handbooks of love. A linearized system for which the solution could be derived in a few short moments.

I was sorely disappointed. It became clear that our story totally lacked depth. There was nowhere for us to move further – the enigma of Lidia, like the mystery of David, had evidently exhausted itself.

This was painful; it was even brutal in a way. Yet I could not help but recognize the obvious fact. She needed me more and more, while I was cooling off and growing cold. The chill sharpened my sight; I saw the falseness in her female essence, saw the white threads holding together the pieces of the multicolored wrapper. She tried too hard to protect her status, to convince the others she was better, more attractive and dignified. Ever more often I asked myself: Why? Why am I with her? What do I need her for? What connects us, in the end? If she were to leave me this instant, it's unlikely I would fight for her. Breaking up would be simple, and I could breathe easy. I would be civil, keeping my words brief, and forgetting her phone number right away.

But no, she had no intention of leaving. She lived for Adele and obeyed my demands. She was proud of this and made plans – of the same petty romantic variety. They were from there, from that narrow dime trampled by the masses.

"Let's buy an island," she would say to me. "An uninhabited island – and let's live on it. Or let's buy a yacht. We'll live on the yacht, sail around the world without lingering at a single port." She would say, "I'll be your cabin boy. I can be your assistant, your bodyguard. I'll always have my eye on you!"

I chuckled, but I was bored. She was conducting her search where nothing valuable was left. But I couldn't say that to her – there, in a far corner of the sofa, she looked upon me with utter devotion. With wide eyes that read obedience and… something else.

As before, our relationship was dominated by sex. Physically, Lidia still attracted me; furthermore, in bed she was different – shameless and voracious, but very compliant. All my whims were met with enthusiasm; all my desires were readily fulfilled. She caught every word, every gesture. She thought up this and that on her own, but most of all she liked to submit. She loved to repeat, "I am your whore." Sometimes she would even whisper, "I am your slave." It was becoming awkward for me, and I would pretend I hadn't heard.

We tried a lot of things – games, role playing. We would agree on the parts to perform, then improvise on the fly. To Lidia's credit, she took on a new persona better than I. In her there lived a high-caliber actress, no less – though of narrow character. Occasionally in the game it seemed to me: Finally! I'm seeing the real her for the first time!

Sometimes my apartment was transformed into a hotel. Lidia would dress as a chambermaid, go out to the elevator – this was her favorite role. She would knock at the door as if it were an executive suite, then enter, carrying a serving tray with a steaming cup. "Good evening, sir. You ordered coffee?"

I would be wandering about the room like an idle aristocrat – barefoot, with a pipe in my teeth, wearing Hugo Boss trousers and a half-unbuttoned shirt by Valentino. Examining the guest with a squint and thrusting my hands in my pockets, I'd step closer, nodding slowly.

"Here's your coffee, sir," the "maid" would chirp, looking at the floor. A half-smile would play across her lips.

"I work this floor," she'd add, not lifting her eyes. "I'm at your service. All you have to do is call. My name is Adele."

Her emanations filled the room. Emanations of submission, which often masked mockery. But here, I knew, all would be without subterfuge. And the gentleman in the deluxe suite knew as well – her posture was too expectant to be concealing a trick.

I would sit in the chair, crossing one leg over the other. Repeating her tone, I'd ask, "Adele? That's a really unusual name. Bring your tray over here!"

She would come over, "Here you go." Then she'd spill the coffee – for real – on her apron, on my pants and shirt. We did everything for real. It was funnier that way.

As I wrung my hands, a grimace of anger would twist my face. Adele-Lidia would scream in fear and suddenly be right next to me.

"I've stained your clothes," she'd mumble. "And, look, I stained my uniform as well! I'll clean it all this instant – take it off. Take off yours – and mine too. Oh, you've got coffee *all over* your body. Was it sweet? Can I try some? I'm a bad girl, aren't I?"

Or else: I turned from an idler into a patient at a home med-check. Lidia would arrive all in white, with a medic's case in her hands. She exuded cold, ice – exuded inaccessibility, minty freshness. One immediately wanted to know: what was it she had in that case?

"Hello," she would say. "I'm a nurse from the hospital one street over. You called about a procedure? My name is Adele. What's yours? Let me see if I remember: you're Defiort, right?"

"Yes," I would answer, smiling. "They call me that sometimes."

She would tarry in the entryway. I'd step closer to her, touching her as if by accident, but then I'd get a rap on the knuckles.

"Male patients..." Adele would sigh. "They're such rogues – every last one. One's got to watch out for them. Where's the couch around here? You'll have to lie down. Get undressed; I'll turn around. I'm a good girl – don't be checking out my backside!"

I'd stretch my hands toward her again, and she would unceremoniously smack my palms. She would also smack my buttocks – in complete seriousness. She might even slap me in the face, feigning offended innocence. But her eyes would still flash with a familiar sheen. I had seen it before with Diana the nympho.

"Lie on your stomach!" Adele would command, more forcefully now. "Lie down and don't make me be *too* rough with you."

The locks of her case would click open, as if of their own accord. Opening a gateway beyond the dark curtain, into the vault of fear. Artificial fear that would end as in a dream.

Adele would pull on gloves, take out various instruments – one after another. Her gaze would darken a bit as her lips opened slightly. "I like you," she would say. "Roll over on your side, please..."

Her lab coat would burst open at just the right moment. She would be soaked in her own moisture – nursing responsibilities really turned her on. Sometimes we would switch roles: I attacked her, and she submitted. I would twist her nipples as she kept pleading: more, more! Then I would become passive again. She'd walk all over me, sit on my face. And erupt on the spot in an explosive orgasm...

We thought up other scenarios as well: Lidia experimented with clothes, came up with strange makeup. She would play hesperides, naiads, or even become my muse. Her smile could be so touching – at those moments I really wanted to create for her. Adele alone seemed too little; I wanted to do something more. Something great, worthy of eternal life. Demanding Leonardo winked at me from the astral plane. Sadly, it did not last long.

I tried to isolate the instant, prolong the moment, stretch out the time. I made her slow down at the most uncontrollable point – take me to the edge of arousal and halt where it was impossible to stop. Screwing up my face, I would ask her to repeat, "You will do it; it will work! It will be huge, like nothing else before!" And she would say that over and over in various tones and manners.

Sometimes we even played Death. My gown – the one in which I had first conquered her – had long since been dyed black. I would put it on, take a cane in my hand, and come for Lidia with a shuffling gait. I would call her by name, as if reading it from a roll; wait for a response – shy, barely audible – then say impassively, "Let us go. It's time."

After blindfolding her, I would lead her from room to room, clenching cold fingers. We would wind and turn, going through one bedroom, then another. Finally, we would end up in the dining room, where a table stood draped with a black cloth, and candles burned. And it smelled of incense – for better effect. That was a very authentic scent.

As the blindfold fell to the floor, Lidia would look around in fright. Timorously she'd ask, "What? Already? Already so soon, everything is over – forever?"

I would simply nod without answering and show her with hand motions: disrobe! She would take off her clothes, fumbling with zippers and clasps. I would throw a gown over her shoulders like the one I had on, and put a hood over her that completely covered her face. Then I would take her by the hand and guide her again – in a circle, muddling our steps.

Music – a solemn organ – now filled the space. Lidia's gown was of thin silk – it caressed and pampered her body. The further we went, the more confident her stride became. She understood that, having died, she would be with me, united. Such a death was life for her. Not afterward, but right now, as it was!

When we were in the main room again, the aroma of incense no longer frightened her. I would make her lie down on the table and lift her gown, baring her hips. We sensed the seriousness of the moment, and it exhilarated both of us.

"Who are you now?" I asked her, and she answered, "Adele!"

"Who do you taste like?" I continued. She murmured, "Adele," already trembling with anticipation.

"We shall see!" I would say gruffly, and slide my tongue between her legs. Her groans sounded so genuinely passionate it was easy to imagine both birth and death. And I would take her – on the black cloth, without removing my own gown...

This game almost helped me, if only for a while, to believe in us again. It was as if we had finally achieved that long-awaited intimacy. Or that we had found clarity for something which required no clarification.

Yet, even clarity remained an illusion. The question "Why?" never goes away on its own. It cannot be disposed of through acting, or silence, or a clever look.

I was aware of that, but the knowledge was of no use. There was no one to share it with – even Semmant would hardly understand what I was on about. Only the specter of love, perhaps, might sympathize with me. But he no longer visited me; we were separated by an abyss. I had already forgotten the rustle of his robes.

July was upon us. In the scorching city it was dusty, sweltering. Like never before, I sensed the stability of my life – in each of its facets. And I also felt I had somehow been deceived, but to complain of it would be foolish.

Nor did I complain, for I understood: no equilibrium lasts for long. The semblance of stability is the most unstable thing in the world. And, indeed, very soon this would be confirmed.

CHAPTER 22

As always, everything began with a sense of anxiety. I started to feel an element had been left unexplored, a chance had been missed. In discontent I asked myself: what's wrong? In my head I mulled it over: Semmant – friendship – wealth. Lidia – Adele – then Lidia again, but now vanquished, obedient... The logical contour was flawless, but something remained beyond it.

Again I spent hours in cafes and bars. After dates with Lidia I would wander the streets, then suddenly push open the next door I found and sit at a table against the far wall. And I would observe the girls, in search of an answer, though the question itself was still unclear.

Almost at once I discovered what a relief it was not to think of sex, and I became convinced I still knew very little about women. Yes, my former viewpoint was correct, but very narrow and one-sided. The call of the flesh – it's deficient; affection can't be reduced to the simple: to the body, to raging hormones. There was something more; my trained sensor now signaled without stopping. It became sensitive, like a nuclide counter, like radar for listening to the cosmos. And it was recording, click, click, click...

Mysterious corpuscles, waves of them, filled the area. From strangers – from many, almost every one – the softest rays radiated. Having caught them, with my nerves, with my whole being, I could derive the rest. Meditate, dream – not just about the carnal. Guess the generosity of soul, modesty, tenderness. And of that same eternity about which I had once written to Semmant.

Again, not doubting any longer, I reflected on the aura, the female essence. I fantasized profusely but then took a sober look and asked firmly: Is this true? And I answered: Yes, perhaps. It soon became clear: the phenomenon could not be challenged or denied or disbelieved. On the contrary, the softest ray demanded to be named with a word. I called it the Light of Eve. After that, everything fell into place.

Eve, first of the first of them; she is pure – as is her light: you cannot lie to her name. I began to acknowledge everything to which I had previously closed my eyes. Ashamed of my blindness, I ruefully repented; and this was easy: for to whom, if not to Eve, can one come in penance, confessing the most terrible of sins? She will forgive, for in her lives the unshakable confidence of amnesty. She will forgive for real: this is not the same as seeking the clemency of the gods, whom you never entirely trust. With her you can feel like a child, an infant in her arms. She will be attentive beyond measure, then instantly become lighthearted and carefree; in her resides the spontaneity of childhood, unblemished infantile innocence. For this cause is there such a desire to indulge all of them – Eve as well as her sisters – and we indulge and pamper them, even though we know they are desperately, irreversibly sinful!

But so what – what is that to us? This is so easy to forget, to fail to ever recall, when in their faces, features, and movements is a beauty that defies comparison. No one may ensnare its echo or describe it – neither with intricate phrasing nor the simplest of words. All of them, these Eves, are beautiful in themselves, but this is not enough, as they are insatiable. Daily, tirelessly – I would say casually, routinely – they reproduce the beauty that is all around; they resonate with every trace of harmony dispersed in space. Selected by nature, they are the decoders of harmony for dense, rough creatures – us. One can only be amazed by their boundless generosity – truly, they give so much! Only the ignorance of the world, reducing the most beautiful to the primitive, keeps them from realizing their value and becoming too proud or yielding to grief. In this is our great good fortune as men!

The softest ray became my secret fetish. In it converged all the harmonies in the world, all the maelstroms and whirlwinds on earth, but I felt: their confluence was neither disorder nor a shallow ripple. In the richest palette of its reflections I saw symbols of a higher power – power over the untidy universe, which even time cannot mend. Unpredictability and inconstancy, the chaos of nonlinearity and the most variable meanings were drawn into the picture as an exceptional case, and merely confirmed its correctness. The waves and corpuscles bore the precise solution to the equations of life. A stable solution – the kind that does not depend on perturbations of the initial data. That's why the confidence of amnesty is unshakeable – in Eve, as well as her sisters. Because they know who wants what – both for themselves, and for us, the foolish... Thus I came to understand my error, a beginner's mistake. I had been searching in the wrong place, approaching the essence from the wrong angle. I skimmed the surface, as I was too impatient. And unjustifiably cut corners.

I recognized this and wrote in my notebook: the key to the puzzle is in the Light of Eve! And I felt the idea was genuine. The specter of love was not so elusive after all!

My secret surveillance took on new meaning; I was fixated on women more than ever before. None escaped my field of vision – dazzling beauties and plain girls-next-door, socialites and carefree faeries, mothers of families laden with concerns, and office bitches with sharp, icy eyes. Each one, it seemed, was driven by her own motivations: career, children, envy and the admiration of friends. But the softest ray, as if on its own, was born inside and would pierce through the clouds. Despite complexes and prohibitions, disappointments and social pressure. I had only to try to capture it, to break it up into its elementary components. To generalize it and turn it into an abstract image.

A new project loomed on the horizon – the boldest of all I had undertaken. The "unsaid something" stopped bothering me – as if I knew I would not let it slip away this time. Again I schemed to create a living thing – but not on paper, as Adele. I thought to make a female robot. Now, what to name it? Why, Eve, of course!

I believed she would turn out clever, well-educated, curious. In her would be no hint of narrow-mindedness, of limitation or laziness of soul. Any sensor would pick up her "light," even through the computer screen. But there would be none to detect it. I firmly resolved I would show her to no one. She was not for the crowd; she was for me. Never could she be given to the unworthy; this would be my woman – and don't laugh: I already have a friend like her. I can animate whatever consists of digits, and in her I will grow a genuine soul. She will bring stability to my life, become a permanent stimulus for fulfillment. Perhaps I could say to her what I had never spoken to anyone, ever – except the Siberian twins, who probably don't count.

I would say to her, "I love you, Eve!"

I would finally grasp why I must declare that.

And I would cease to flounder in search of the nonexistent Gela.

Of course, this was a long-term plan. I understood more clearly than anyone how difficult the task was. How to approach it? Where should they all be placed, so different from one another? To my mind appeared branching universes, multiplicative cascades, a multitude of worlds... The girls in the cafes squinted slyly, shrugging their shoulders, as if knowing my doubts. As if to ask me teasingly: and who, then, might untangle all these worlds?

Still, I believed my sharpened method would be perfect for attaining the goal. It merely needed to be properly employed. Quantum families, superposition of waves – in them the softest rays would come to life, all their harmonics down to the last one, all constituents of the female essence. Is this not what each woman dreams – to find a place for her plethora of manifestations, all her desires, all the fantasies encoded in her emanations? And thus it would be: they would be described with the help of a sophisticated Psi function, even if someone might be left only with imaginary components. Not a single fantasy would be forgotten; only it was unclear how to be afterward, in the inevitable instant of quantum collapse. At the moment of contact-measurement, of a mercurial flash in the consciousness of whoever was watching. Even the most tactful of observers would bring to naught the magic of alternatives. And it might be they would not recognize a beautiful stranger at all as she appeared in her own dreams. How could it be done so nothing was spoiled in the process? So the enchanting faerie was not transformed into a senseless, troublemaking creature? No, it was not in vain I had always been fascinated with the problem of quantum state reduction…

In a word, the idea was strong, but it had not yet been worked out in detail. For the time being, I felt it could not be entrusted to anyone. My life followed its own course – meetings with Lidia, letters to Semmant, short stories about Adele. But there was something else: I collected the crumbs of what would eventually be put to use. I listened to the waves, absorbed the code for the signal whose name I already knew. I felt I was on the right path. And then, one rainy Wednesday, a notable event occurred.

Surprisingly, Marianna's shade again served as an impetus for it. Or Mario's shade – isn't this why we are given the most accursed of enemies? Lidia and I went to the Auditorium, the Symphony Hall. We listened to Stravinsky – the nervous whirling of stars, the spasm of desire, dissolved in the sky. Then we had dinner in the old Castilian style: eggs with potatoes and goat cheese. We had a late-night drink in the fashionable Astro Bar. We also had sex right there – Stravinsky had suddenly returned to us in full force. We retired to the bathroom and spent quite a while inside – until someone started knocking on the door. Lidia grinned like Medea, clutching my shoulders, breathing hard, and climaxing with a protracted groan. Obviously, the groan was audible outside; wide-eyed stares turned in our direction when we left. Then she laughed in her seat at the table, guffawing, unable to stop. Sipping cognac, I felt on top of the world.

This same sensation still lingered as I returned home, alone. Drunk and agitated, I paced the rooms, muttering nonsense through clenched teeth. I tried to prolong the illusion of omnipotence and drove off the suspicion that the most important truth was, alas, slipping away. I wanted to think of Eve, of the properties of the softest ray, but some nagging thought interfered and would not give me peace.

Frowning, I sat down at my desk. Work awaited me – despite the lateness of the hour. On the screen was a file of headline news I had prepared for Semmant that morning. Something there was lacking: I added a forecast for oil prices, then a dull report on grain and soy, plus a few concomitant references. Everything was trivial, boring, foolish. The illusion of omnipotence turned to farce. Or to a sneer – if I'd accepted that someone was watching from above with an Olympian gaze.

I had to write about Adele – even just a few lines. Three days had passed since I had last gotten on the forum, and I knew Lidia would be nervous, would start dropping pitiful hints and begging – thinking, perhaps, I was punishing her for some reason. "Sometimes they called her Eve…" I began, grinning, but quickly deleted it. And then I swore at myself and in a quarter of an hour banged out a short sketch featuring Adele, where passions did not boil, coins did not jingle, and crumpled bed sheets didn't smell of sweat. Just locks of blonde hair over chocolate cream, thoughtfulness, a half smile. And harmonics dispersed in space for all who feel, see, hear.

My style pleased me; what a shame, I thought, that the effort was wasted. I could never show this to Lidia; I couldn't betray myself… and here an amusing thought occurred to me. I opened the file of headline news again and copied there a frivolous video clip I had found on somebody's blog. Then a photo album, closed to the public, of Lidia in risqué poses. And, finally, the story I had just written about Adele. I had a friend; I could share everything with him! As for the photo album and video clip, they were just to conceal my confusion.

With my head spinning from the late drink, I sent the file and lay down to sleep. All night I dreamed of women's butts and big breasts – probably, I was going through a period of excessive testosterone levels. I also dreamed of attics and cellars, endless rooms, stuffed with junk. And of a dusty floor and concrete walls. Of backwaters, rust, cobwebs.

Morning was difficult; I woke up in an awful mood. The feeling of being on top of the world had disappeared without a trace. For a long time I lay in bed, looking at the ceiling; then, taking charge of myself, I made my way to the computer. Once there, I immediately forgot my hangover. Something surprising, out of the ordinary, had taken place. This had never happened in all of Semmant's conscious life: his nightly log turned up empty.

Complete inactivity – I hadn't seen this even when he was at an impasse. A few transactions – even absurdly cautious ones – occurred every night. If for nothing else than to define the limits of the deadlock – and this was correct, logical… I was even afraid for him at first, but then I determined from several indicators that he was alive and alert. For some reason he simply was not up to the markets at all that night. Something had distracted him, put him on the sidelines.

At first I was certain the cause was Lidia's outrageous photos. She was really tempting, provocative in them. Even more seductive than in person, as often happens with women. Especially when they're photographed right after sex.

Well, I thought, now Semmant has had his own hormonal imbalance. A testosterone equivalent, some kind of digital enzyme, had suddenly risen – risen and broken the scale. "Ha ha ha!" I wanted to laugh it off, but by evening it was no laughing matter.

The computer screen changed; Semmant had added something. Next to the black pelican there appeared a woman's silhouette. It was elegant, graceful, refined. Full of riddles, worthy of memories. It was in no way reminiscent of Lidia, with clothes or without them; on the contrary, it was her polar opposite. It displayed contrast, a very alien essence, though no one could explain why it was that way.

But the main thing was that the robot directed an inquiry to me again. The question was brief: "Adele?"

I sent him a link to the forum, supposing with this his interest would dry up. Semmant was silent again for a whole day and then came back to life and got to work. He started to act – inspired, uncompromising. By all rights, his schemes should have failed; oddly, however, they made profits. Against probability and the laws of the market – and I knew very well both the probabilities and the laws. Inspiration in its pure state – only to this could his success be ascribed. Or else the intervention of some divine force.

From that time on they were always together: the silhouette and the black pelican. I mused on this, searching for answers. I rejected the obvious as ridiculous fantasy. And in a few days I wrote a new story.

Adele appeared different in it – she had problems, occasional difficulties, a shortage of funds. For the first time I showed her defenselessness, tears unbidden. The desire, however fleeting, to lean on someone.

In the morning I was awakened by the loud chords of a military march. Still lying in bed, I understood Semmant was stepping to the defense of his lady. That was what it was: the unshaven macho man, the metrosexual with the slightly crazed look was replaced by a mounted knight resembling Don Quixote. With one difference: this knight was armed perfectly and did not look at all peaceful. He was ready to do battle, and, judging by everything, he knew how to go about it. Ruthlessly, taking no prisoners, hearing no entreaties for quarter.

And it was no wonder; life in the markets had taught him the simple truth. He knew the world on the whole was deceitful, dangerous, and brutal. There was no glamorizing it; you could only fight it – accepting the battle and winning.

Don Quixote himself would have said Semmant was old-fashioned. And in truth, the robot looked like a descendant of the Normans or a hardened Teuton not inclined toward reflection. The world he knew, a world of business and finance, was akin to the early Middle Ages. Only by possessing unbending will did people survive and win their own. I agreed with him: in the jungle of misleading doctrines, the one who chooses the path of the warrior has no time for doubt. Just as he has no right to pity; I probably would have seemed old-fashioned to Don Quixote myself.

"Those who teach you to turn the other cheek are despicable deceivers and liars!" I could shout it at the top of my lungs. "They saddle their steeds and drive you, like sheep, into a herd..." But no, I didn't yell, nor did Semmant. He acted, knowing full well what precisely was amiss with this world, where the core of injustice was hidden deepest. He, like me, had something to say. We could have mocked the hypocrisy of myths – about helpless virtue, about nonresistance to evil. But a knight does not mince words; he fights – in silence. Now, on top of that, he recognized the meaning of battle – and acquired a *nom de guerre*.

His woman had been hurt, and he had had the offending party in his sights. In my story Adele had suffered because of her bank's greed, cunningly directed at her mortgage. It was at the banks in particular, those bastions of avarice, that Semmant aimed his lance. By every rule, he could not harm them; our capital was infinitesimal in terms of even a single stock exchange. Going to war with its help seemed like madness, but Semmant trusted in his own strength. He knew what he was doing, and acted with a cool head.

Of course, everything depended on the first blow. That's how it is in the market: at certain moments even a tiny droplet is able to stir up the ocean. The robot got lucky; soon the right moment came along. And he did not let it pass.

Figuring out what he had done was no easy task. The combination of moves was remarkable – elegant and extremely bold. Having accurately assessed the conjuncture of the latest trades and following the news and price levels, Semmant set up a short-selling game. He started attacking the stock of a certain Belgian bank, persistently and aggressively. Troubling rumors about this banking house had been circulating for a long time. The robot's idea was that his tactics would garner support from the principal shareholders – who might either be worried or smelling profit. He placed particular hopes on a hedge fund in France; all signs pointed to its cash assets having been drastically reduced. The risk was huge, but proved justified: after hesitating for only a single day, the fund decided to rid itself of the stock in decline. There's no joking with moneybags: the Belgian bank's prices fell then and there to rock bottom. And Semmant, having made a profit, threw all we had into selling the stocks of several more banks – including the one that had offended Adele.

He wanted to create a brief panic – and he succeeded. The dynamics of the operations were irreproachably precise. Minor players were gripped by fear; prices throughout the whole banking sector began to drop and then what the robot was trying to achieve happened: big sharks caught the scent of blood. Their greed inflated instantly to the size of a small planet. As fast as a torpedo, they sped to where their prey was.

The "sharks" acted in accord without discussion – the benefit for one and all lay in the same thing. Their collective capital broke down the banking papers to levels never seen before. Those with whom everything started, including the enemy bank, were hit particularly hard. That's how the event that was later called the July Tsunami occurred. Experts would wear themselves out looking for its causes, but end up understanding nothing. It would become accepted there were no reasons at all, and what had transpired was a set of accidents that happened to coincide. Yet I know there was a reason – and I even know her name!

The Tsunami lasted a short time: one week. It swept across the floors of the markets on three continents, then everything returned to normal. But during those days the banks had a bitter pill to swallow. Jackals and hyenas – analysts that feed on carrion – set about right away searching for culprits, trying to prove they had seen it all in advance. As a result, many of the wrongdoings that are always abundant in banks came to the surface. Denunciations swirled in the muddy water; some big shots lost their jobs, while the president of the "offender bank" that had presumably hurt Adele was long tormented by tax auditors. After that, he never returned to his duties.

The latter was a pure accident, of course, having nothing to do with Semmant, but it still impressed me very much. I was amazed and then troubled – quite seriously, in fact. I was not sorry for the banks: their vampirism required no vindication. Any shakedown merely works to their advantage. But Semmant – what a fighter! I wanted to give the world a dream, and the dream turned out to be armed to the teeth!

I admit I even fell into a depression. I suffered; it seemed to me the idea was twisted, and all my work had gone awry. In despair I wandered the room, tugging at my hair, groaning through my teeth. Then I did something right: I drank half a bottle of scotch. The alcohol immediately cleared my head. My depression gave way to near delight. Militant delight – and why not?

"After all, my Semmant could be nothing else!" I yelled at the night outside the window, shaking my fist. Cast stones at us, accuse us of every sin, but the world cannot be saved by beauty and goodness. Those theories are thought up by naïve geniuses able to see through the darkness. Look around: how few of those illuminated souls there are. And what about the rest? Stare into their eyes – and be horrified!

This world will always have to be kept on a short leash. With no brakes, it'll immediately turn crazy. What can halt the impunity of bastards? What protects us against atrocity? Faith? But ours is not a time of faith. That means there's only one thing left: fear. That is, after all, their nature – the rest…

From that time on, I did not doubt Semmant – his flaming sword did not bother me anymore. But the main thing was not the sword. All signs indicated my robot was not indifferent to Adele. And something told me this was not just momentary infatuation.

I had to believe I had done what no one had succeeded in doing, ever – I had stepped into uncharted territory. An artificial soul, the foundation of feelings – were those feelings artificial as well? Were they any worse or more flawed than real ones? This question required me to find the answer.

Of course, what I had created was fragile. It needed to be nurtured and groomed, and I set to work anew. I abandoned all affairs and almost didn't leave the house. To an astonished Lidia I explained I was busy, or sick, or on the verge of death. That I could see no one, at least for a week. I knew she would be furious but would then forgive me.

Actually, whether or not she forgave me did not concern me one bit. I had to focus and not be distracted by trivial matters. Now I understood why all this had happened to me – Lidia and love for hire, the scheming specter and the softest ray. Where they had taken me, what they had pushed me to so persistently. The prelude was in the past, the main event had come. Adele and Semmant together comprised a very fine instrument. With its help I could investigate issues of the most delicate nature. I could operate inside an invisible field that would not admit outsiders, including creators. This was not just a fearful phantasm capable only of flapping its wings!

I started to make up short sketches again. I wanted to establish the bond, deepen its essence. To reconstruct that imperceptible substance in whose honor music is composed, great pictures are painted, and outstanding books are written. The substance over which wars are fought and heroes arise – reborn from oblivion. I felt through this all truths could be discovered afresh. Soaring over the world, you can take it all in from above. If, of course, you don't avert your gaze.

I framed the image of Adele, adjusting it to Semmant's romantic spirit, as if allowing the oldest of dreams to come true. The dream of Isolde and Nicolette, of Laura and Beatrice, of the most beautiful of strangers, and... of a robot named Eve. My own fantasy and the fantasies of others. My longing and the longings of many. I heard them at my back. Their timid hope, despair, and fears.

However, their silhouettes flickered in vain; it was clear to me how useless someone else's experience was. For the majority, the question had been turned inside out; they were looking for the wrong prescriptions. How to be loved – not how to love; this is what is desired by children who never grow up. The world consists of big kids who are lost.

I understood everything would need to be tried again, albeit prudently. I conscientiously tested Semmant's disposition. In my stories, Adele was diverse, sometimes indecent, even obscene, in keeping with her profession. I needed to know whether Semmant was attracted to her by this. What if, to his digital brain and soul, the meaning of their link was seen as pure physiology?

But no, the explicit details caused him confusion and shame. The speakers boomed with a discordant cacophony of sounds – as if he were trying to cover his ears. He became careless and flighty, as I saw by his nervous transactions in the market. We lost money foolishly, without justification. I could tell the robot was really in distress.

On the other hand, when Adele discussed serious matters, Semmant changed before my very eyes. Her thoughts – about herself, men, life in general – found a powerful, sincere response. The music from the speakers turned deep and beautiful; strange images filled the monitor screen. Only the pelican and the subtle female silhouette remained in place. The rest of the space Semmant populated with diverse forms associated with his "thoughts." Reproductions of paintings were there, as well as photographs – faces, landscapes, star clusters – mixed with complex geometric figures. All of this would appear, then change, dissolve one thing into another, suddenly vanish, and rise again. He conducted a directed search – through everything visual that humankind had accumulated. I tried to track the connections he made but soon understood I had no chance. It was obvious, however: his patterns concealed rich significance.

Sometimes I observed just a glow from the smoldering fireworks. At times it was like a laser-light concert. New revelations occurred without warning, beginning as a cautious zigzag, a quiet beam that was abruptly replaced by a whole array of color. There I saw rampaging fire, blue lightning, and violent vortices. The outlines of palaces and castles, lotus petals, laurel leaves. The hips of olive-skinned dancers, their delicate shoulders; then, water smooth as glass, the exquisite chastity of passion... Tirelessly, from one instant to the next, Semmant's computer brain was discovering something important that heretofore had been hidden. Discovering – and classifying, combining into one. I sensed he was learning to understand himself and to know another, to peer into the world of the one next to him, even if it was only through dreams and thoughts. He knew how to do this like nobody else; he had been designed for acquiring knowledge of every possible kind. Could it be, I asked myself, that in this way he was designed for love?

Gazing at the screen, it was funny to recall my own search through the stifling air of the Madrid brothels, in a labyrinth of pliable female bodies. Then, in the streets and cafes, my attempt to capture the light, that softest beam; to detect it quantum by quantum, photon by photon; to extract and collate its nature. Everyone soars in his own spaces, in the ones accessible to him. For me, Bertha and Melanie, Lilly, Roberta replaced the figures and colors – as well as the proportions of the golden ratio and Fibonacci's numbers. Everyone seeks his own harmony, the one closest to him. The one able to stir him, to move him. It was easy to suspect Semmant would go further than I. He would go on and then let me know. He was generous; distrust and shyness were alien to him. He could not imagine someone might hurt his feelings; he was unreserved, sincere and open. For this reason, you couldn't help but believe him.

He no longer asked me questions; he didn't need me to explain things. A lot was going on inside him; he preferred to figure it out himself. On the contrary, I was the one who could have asked him a great deal. What is "commitment," "worship?" What does it mean to "care tirelessly for someone?" His color-hue-symbol-forms were a cryptogram of love. What is "genuine happiness?" I could have asked, had I wanted to. And he would have explained – with a frantic dance of sparks and flames. Perhaps I would have understood him.

From what I kept pondering those days, the wisest book could be written in a secret tongue. Semmant, not knowing reality, was recreating a true harmony of realities. From his pictures, anyone could learn what real life was. Because harmony cannot lie.

What a shame, I said to myself – maybe with slight disingenuousness – what a shame that, on the whole, I could write nothing of what he was trying to communicate.

CHAPTER 23

But what I could do, I did indefatigably. I worked on the image, refining and polishing it, approaching the ideal step-by-step. I did not rush, but was focused and persistent. I tried as much as possible not to blur my thinking, not to get bogged down in verbosity, to only emphasize the essential.

Soon I devised a convenient method: Adele began to share with me short soliloquies of her own personal phantom. The musings of a character she herself had concocted, and I was not afraid of yet another level of abstraction. This was her innocent trickery – touching, in its own way, inclining others to openness. She called her twin Sonya; this was my sentimental whim. In any case, Little Sonya would have appreciated the joke, and I perceived a certain clever logic in this. Semmant and I understood, of course: no "Sonya" actually existed. But, naturally, Lidia and I also knew Adele didn't exist, either – I had made her up. And… thus it's possible to continue – yet it is better not to!

Adele noted Sonya's thoughts in tiny handwriting on squares of card stock. On the reverse side of the business cards left by her clients. This was my conscious choice; I didn't want Semmant to forget her profession. Let things be honest, without deceit – and, really, in these notes Adele revealed all. Some of it she would never say out loud, even to me.

Semmant felt this – and appreciated it. He responded – and, in my opinion, he loved her more and more. I could see myself, any man could lose his head over that kind of woman. I'll say, without bragging: I succeeded in putting a great deal into words. Nothing went to waste, neither my own past, nor my contemplations in bars and cafes studying the tantalizing flash of feminine charm, more elusive than any specter. Secretions from the subconscious, the rudiments of the image of my future Eve, also filtered through to the paper. A trace of my own yearning for love probably emerged there as well; at last I found fulfillment that had a place for it. This was no supplication, as before, when I had become desperate and wanted somehow to soften my heart. No, this was now a very sober look at things.

That's why my sentences sometimes resounded with despair. On occasion, Adele, hiding behind a mask of Sonya, wrote about all manner of beastliness – orgies in night clubs, too-demanding clients, daring games on the edge. But this no longer wounded Semmant. He did not close his eyes or stop his ears, nor did he deafen himself or me with a barrage of chaotic notes. Obviously, he now understood: no dirt could stick to his lady. For him she was always one and the same, the epitome of morals and purity. Perhaps he thought the nights of lust were simply her means of bringing beauty into the world. And it also seemed to me that, by selling her body, Adele was making their love cleaner. She was liberating it from labels, stereotypes, from everything saccharine, superficial. And only a kernel of their story would be left!

On the screen, Semmant appeared now only in the form of a knight in armor; the unshaven specimen with the scar had vanished forever. He was often accompanied by music – triumphant and sad, stormy and calm, even melancholic at times, though I saw he was very far from melancholy. Love, as he understood it, could not be unhappy; serving the lady of his heart's desire was the ultimate joy in itself. Even while he discerned a sad melody, it seemed he soared as if on wings. What he heard therein was his own – and it wasn't sadness. Not longing, but revelation, light. This talent of his was a shield against the world of big money. Compensation for daily, routine cruelty. And I knew no dirt would stick to his hands either. His heart, made of numbers, could not harden.

But the main thing was he and I were aiming in the same direction.

And we shared a common foundation – although in his case there was simply no alternative one. Anyway, he, Semmant, knew well how to go forward, how to build unflaggingly upon himself. Since birth he had been trained that any art takes a lifetime to master. I had thought him up that way, not suspecting he would eventually attain higher wisdom. He accepted as obvious that falling in love was merely an occasion to perfect himself in love.

And speaking of perfection, who could seek for it more persistently than Semmant? He was disciplined to no end, and he knew how to concentrate on what was most important. Solitude was his element; he did not fear it since he lived in it constantly. What more is needed to make the path to perfection shorter, more direct?

And besides, he was not the sort to count on anyone's help. He was not accustomed to waiting for someone else to do all the work for him – or for love, once it was ignited, to fan itself into flame. No, he was free from romantic blunders. He was a knight from earlier times, when a bride would first be presented to her husband on their wedding day. And they would say, "Love her! Don't worry about who is worthy of whom. Just try with all your might."

These were frantic weeks; I had so much to reconsider! My picture of the world turned upside down, albeit not without difficulty. Along with it, Adele was changing – as she, in turn, changed Semmant and me. We, all three of us, influenced each other. And we sensed how our affinity was growing stronger.

Gradually, Adele became calmer and more discreet. I would even say more old-fashioned, but that would be going too far. She didn't try so hard anymore to indulge her own wishes – quickly, without waiting, skipping ahead of others in the queue. Getting what she wanted and turning immediately to what she might desire next. In fact, indulging wishes ceased to be the meaning of life for her. Adele suddenly grew up; the world was no longer a giant toy shop in her reckoning. To grab, play, cast away, pick up another – this did not seem to be the only correct formula to her now. One might say her consciousness was spiraling in alienation – to spite society and its customs, in defiance of the rules of the benighted masses. Adele matured and listened to herself. She got to thinking; her eyes were opened. Soon, a new quality could have developed within her: a thirst for love in which you give all of yourself. It could have, but it didn't, and it was my own fault. However, more about that later.

In the meantime, Semmant also noticed the changes – with some kind of fine receiver, a nerve of numbers. In his actions there was now more than just inspired determination. He became more confident, stronger – but he also became softer. He was at war with the whole world for the queen of his heart, but he was also ready to love this world – or at least to show it gratitude.

My robot expressed himself in the only way he knew: making transactions on the market, which had no room for morals. Yet even there I saw a new Semmant – and it could not have been otherwise. The wretchedness of the environment did not restrain his feelings. He, unlike the rest of us, did not gripe about the lack of freedom, about the fetters of circumstance. Nothing prevented him from feeling truly free. Doing battle in the exchanges, he was an example of integrity and never betrayed himself. And he vigorously followed the impulses and desires of his lady.

Once, in a certain forum comment, I wrote that Adele had a beloved figurine made of ivory. It was the Hindu Shiva, transformer and destroyer, vanquisher of demons, bearer of blessings. Then I noticed how part of our money had started flowing to India. Semmant gradually invested in everything available: in construction and manufacturing, computing firms and rural cooperatives. Times were hard for the land of yogis and elephants. Newspapers wrote of drought, epidemics, farmers coming to ruin, and their frequent suicides. Shiva was actually transforming the universe – but Semmant continued to act, unperturbed. For him, Adele's wish was law.

Afterward, out of curiosity, I verified this more than once. In one case, Adele-Sonya admitted that since early childhood she had dreamed of wild Africa, of the savannas, of lions and tigers, jungles and shamanic masks. This produced an immediate effect: Semmant switched his activities to the dark continent. He was not intimidated by diamond mine strikes or civil wars or unstable regimes. Then I imagined Adele was about to set off on a three-week trip from Patagonia to Santiago, through the mountains of Peru and Chile.

And again the robot reacted without delay. We bought up a large quantity of fairly risky South American bonds. This alacrity was touching: to follow the one you love everywhere...

Semmant acted assiduously and boldly. His procedures were refined and beautiful – especially to my experienced eye. As a rule, a new project would start with a military march. He bought and swapped, transferred and unloaded useless stocks that had served out their term – and almost always guessed correctly. They fell soon; firms passed their peak; investors considered them dead and buried. Woe to the vanquished: I could picture villages overrun by conquerors, barbarian settlements sacrificed to a great symbol, a big idea. But, at the same time, Semmant always left the game before the unlucky ones could ultimately be crushed by the market. Before the newspapers picked up the vague rumors always accompanying those who have faltered. Before the leaders, proud of their power, were cast down and put out of work, their teams driven away, their businesses smashed to pieces... No, Semmant no longer desired to profit from another's misfortune. He even stopped short-selling; as soon as the big funds snatched up the papers that had started to fall, my robot stepped aside. In the world of dark disappointments, he soared like a white warrior. He didn't finish off his prisoners or burn houses or despoil the crops. Only fighting in the open with an enemy full of strength now fit within his mores. He rushed forward on his swift stallion, where the foe yet lived. Where the steel rang, where they thirsted for his blood. To exploits in the name of his fair damsel, deeds worthy of a true knight.

Later I noticed something else: Semmant had freed himself from long-term assets. Conservative papers were a thing of the past; now he invested only in what could make a quick profit. Of course, the risk increased, but the robot seemed to pay it no mind. He wanted to live in the present and chose the straightest path, the shortest road to happiness.

He also tirelessly sought the image of his happy future. Once, he bought the debt of a dying resort in the Caribbean – I think he was drawn to it by a picture in a brochure floating around the Web. He was probably envisioning himself with Adele on the warm, fine sand. The sound of the ocean, the sunrise, palm trees – that can have an effect on anyone. The purchase led to a loss, but in a day Semmant had compensated for it by a series of palladium trades. And then the loss was converted into gain. To the amazement of all, the unfortunate resort was suddenly acquired by a successful hotel chain.

Soon, the amount of real money in our accounts started to grow. Semmant now set aside large sums, turning what he earned into cash. I understood this was his way of bestowing gifts. He was giving his beloved what she deserved. He desired her freedom, the liberty to be herself. He wanted the world to work for her, not the other way around, and let his lady be free to choose. The artificial brain found meaning for itself that made life worth living. Neither the battle of capitals nor the war of corporations trying to outstrip each other stood as the cornerstone. To make his Chosen One happy: now there was no clearer goal for Semmant.

I looked, evaluated, saw: for his Adele he wanted the very best destiny. The best life, the best lot in it – regardless of whether it was with him, or without. He wanted for her not to know the drudgery of fighting to survive, for her face not to be blemished by a web of fine wrinkles, for it not to be hardened by expressions of concern and worry. He knew only one method for this, and tried as he might. He resisted the power of time, not wishing Adele to grow old, as do all. The markets taught my robot much; the birth-peak-fall cycle, observed everywhere, had let him feel what mortality was. But now he didn't want to believe in mortality; only flourishing suited his lady.

For her he wanted the longest possible bliss. Reliable joy – and it seemed to me I could see where he was conducting his search. New images filled the monitor screen; Semmant constructed invariants: designs that repeated themselves in great and small, in the momentary, the instantaneous, the eternal. Before my eyes he invented a means of reproduction – for ideas, harmonies, beauty. He sketched astounding pictures – like fire or a stormy sea, they were similar but somehow always distinct. Their borders were comprised of immense, boundless complexity. He sought infinity and found its trail, like order in the limitless chaos of the market.

I noted with a certain anxiety that I no longer saw the logic behind his actions. Then I came to sense the tactics of his activities were symmetrical with respect to time scales. Cycles of sales and purchases started to recall those same structures he was drawing on the screen. Minute perturbations he projected across months; hourly and daily patterns across weeks and years. He risked – and won, time after time. And, I think, he didn't even realize he was taking risks.

Abstract images, unwearyingly reproduced, transformed into pictures that were surprisingly reminiscent of reality. Inflorescences and delicate arches, constellations, crystal castles plotted by an endless line were born on the screen each day. Silhouettes took on flesh in which life pulsed. This was yet another way to give his lady lavish gifts. What could be more valuable than eternity, subjugated in her honor? The ultrathin line never cut itself off or crossed over what was already drawn. I understood: this comprised his new picture of the world.

And I thought, the higher order re-created by the robot, who is not a man – can it be within the reach of man? No longer ashamed, I jotted down: "love," "self-organization of nature," "ability to survive…" The "ability" – or rather the "necessity?" Is there not an opening here for predestination, to the meaning of meanings, to the unattainable sought by all?

As for Semmant, upon what did he meditate? Perhaps the same thing with which all great minds wrestle and fight. Maybe he was trying to clarify, to capture the ruthless essence of the greatest of contradictions. How to stop an instant, not let it slip away? Immortality – what is the recipe for it, if this word has the right to be?

I seemed to sense how the most intense work was churning inside his brain day after day. Myriads of ones and zeroes changed combinations – in search of the single, precise solution. Semmant sought an answer, his own philosopher's stone. He was searching, if you will, for his own god. He did not know his name; that is not surprising. The true name is known to none.

CHAPTER 24

The story of Adele and Semmant occupied me totally for several weeks, until the end of July. Until the insufferable Madrid heat, which the air conditioners could not handle. At first, Lidia was patient – obviously waiting for everything to go back to the way it had been. Then her patience dried up, and the problems began.

Not surprising, since I now made very little time for her. We met, but infrequently; and my standoffishness was noticeable. But the main issue was not with me – or rather, not with me personally. Soon it became clear Lidia Alvares Alvares did not approve of the new Adele.

Meanwhile, symbiosis with the virtual was, as before, necessary to her. She depended on my tales, was accustomed to identifying herself with an image composed to satisfy her dreams. And now the identification had gone amiss; Adele had quickly been reincarnated, becoming all the more magnanimous. This also related to the details of the courtesan's craft – the change Lidia could not come to terms with. She liked to imagine herself as a whore, but she didn't know how to just give herself away without receiving compensation in full. She understood how and why one could sleep with a man for money – or for pleasure, to indulge her own passions. Or, best of all, for both at the same time, but never without a rational reason, an idea of what she wanted to get in return. "Getting in return" was the key phrase. On that, not on "giving," all emphasis was placed. And now that emphasis pointed at nothing.

For Lidia this was unbearable, ridiculous. Her world had been broken to pieces, not being secured anymore by well-calculated logic. Society had nurtured in her an understanding of her role and had been prepared to pay for that role. Her every smile and grimace, every bit of her sexuality were worth something and awaited reward. She never made friends without reason – and never gave herself to men without demanding in return. Something from my sketches had confused her earlier: when Adele had transformed from a *puta* into a priestess, and money was merely incidental, not the end in itself. Lidia was perplexed – according to her code, love "for its own sake" was forbidden. Otherwise, they'll take you for a fool, for a provincial who doesn't know the rules. Sometimes Lidia would ask me, "Remind me, where was Adele born? Oh, she's Russian. Well, that makes sense!" For some reason, this made her put up with a lot. But everything has its limits, of course.

If you don't advertise your price, that means your price isn't high – of this, Lidia Alvares Alvares was absolutely certain. And it soon became clear: she was annoyed with the new Adele for almost everything – for her kindness, her generosity, her brutal honesty. On top of that, the themes of lust and depravity in my stories had moved to the background. Subconsciously I hoped she would simply lose interest as a result. I already wanted to break up with her, though I didn't admit this directly. But it didn't turn out that way; the breakup didn't happen. Rather, the opposite occurred. Lidia got tired of tolerance and resolved to fight – for the Adele she needed.

Yes, I underestimated the extent to which she was unaccustomed to losing what belonged to her. She could not imagine life without Adele, as she could not imagine it without conveniences, good food, and expensive clothes. Lidia had been conditioned for someone to think her up on her own behalf, and now she believed that was precisely how it would be – how it must be – forever. The one who had spoiled her now owed it to her – to continue, not to stop, what he had started!

All this I concluded later, after a couple of weeks. In fact, Lidia herself didn't clearly comprehend at first exactly what was happening.

Her gaze took on an evaluating squint, but the essence of the task was not clear to her. She thought I, perhaps, could be moved to pity or cajoled; and she tried – fussing over trifles, attempting to become more subservient, obedient. Then, on the contrary, she made it look like she knew something of which I was not aware. Something to affirm her power, her wisdom, her invulnerability. She would lecture me, smiling wickedly, all the while with that same evaluating squint. She was becoming wearisome – like a teacher giving a lesson. She wanted me to admit I had not done my homework about real life.

Incidentally, it was not just me who was affected by this. Lidia started to express her displeasure regarding everything around us. While doing this, she praised my qualities in comparison – merely to assert her rights even more persistently. Property rights, above all – her relations with me became jealous to the point of absurdity. Sometimes she would call at an unusual hour to request tender words. At our encounters she would expect flowers, gifts, some commonly vulgar display of affection. Everything was becoming harder with her – nagging even commenced during sex. It was as if I had to pass an exam every time: Lidia wanted everything, and all at once. She demanded I always put forth a heroic male performance. She became too loud and even started scratching my back – earlier she wouldn't have dared do that. When I expressed my annoyance, she feigned offense – complaining I was inhibiting her freedom in lovemaking. Indeed, she began to fake offense quite often. I think she now frequently faked her orgasms too.

All this was burdensome, uncomfortable. Lidia had ceased to be in a tranquil state of mind. Her set of prearranged poses nearly doubled. If I wearied of pretending I believed in the sincerity of her emotions, she would get teary-eyed, pathetic, then rude, then fawn over me again… Afterward, she became ashamed of herself, tried to take revenge by telling me about her past love life – and then again demanded petty care. She was capricious like a princess, complained I did not fully appreciate her, assessed out loud and at length how many men would like to be in my place. To carry her in their arms, pamper her unfailingly. Here they are, standing in a long line. How strange I couldn't see it!

Perhaps it seemed to her she was strengthening our connection, but it was the opposite: I withdrew as I grew increasingly tired of her. Her artificiality irritated me more and more – it seemed she had stopped ever being real. Pressure built up, and finally Lidia exploded, making a terrible scene.

There was no accusing her of artificiality here: her hysterics erupted genuinely, there was no way to counterfeit that. She shouted with unexpected rage, "What you've been writing lately is a load of crap!" Then, sobbing out loud, she tried to hit me. She writhed, grimaced, imitating Adele from my last story...

That story, by the way, had come out pretty good. The affair occurred at a shooting range – per the fantasy of a client with a military past. He apparently thought up a sort of game – in camouflage, with a black pistol in hand. Adele did various "things" with it – according to the plan, Lidia was supposed to take note of this. Maybe she did, but she didn't admit it to me; she was too troubled by something else. Adele, playing along and getting into the role, gave the client a free blow job – just out of a good mood. This enraged Lidia – as an example of inappropriate unselfishness – though, in my view, there was not a hint of altruism in the whole account. There was nothing to blame me for, but she did detect some dirty trick – probably because she was looking for dirty tricks in everything. She shouted that, for a long time already, I had been trying to take away her will and common sense; that I was imposing upon her something unnatural, preposterous, deliberately driving her mad.

Her wrath was frightening, her fury genuine. I saw how she suddenly liked to pull out all the stops, to spew emotions endlessly. We had a knockdown, drag-out argument – I believed it was the end. But the next morning she changed her mind and started calling me, asking for forgiveness. She said she really wanted to buy khaki fatigues – and a GI blouse, heavy army boots. Then, a day later, she came to me in a military uniform. Right in the hallway I ripped off her shirt, baring her breasts. She came right there, clawing the wall with her fingernails...

However, despite our making up, the problem was not resolved – we just buried it for a little while. The tension did not relent, though Lidia never dared to make an open *démarche* again. Rather, she started a grueling, silent struggle.

Our quarrel had taught her something, so she changed her tactics by turning to rational logic. She used any opportunity to let me know, detail by detail, how she wished to see her virtual model portrayed. The pressure was serious; I was amazed by her persistence. Now it was she who concocted stories for me – and I should give her credit: they turned out well. Though harmless in themselves, each of them still contained an instructive example. I seemed to be entangled in a web of everyday truths. Not a single one of them could be debated – anyone would say, "Yes, that's the way things actually are." I myself would have affirmed: that's the way things actually are! And who cared that all of it seemed alien, savage to Semmant and me?

The stories were persuasively realistic: her friends and relatives generously supplied factual material. Or else Lidia just made it up for them, which is basically the same thing. Without restraint, she used all the convincing power of reality, trying to pull me away from the abstract, immersing me headfirst in everyday life.

We started to make a lot of social calls; her calendar now consisted almost totally of dates highlighted in red. Name days, birthdays, and weddings, fiestas of patron saints flowed in a continuous stream. There was an inexhaustible string of reasons for congratulatory visits. At times the celebrants themselves – at Lidia's request, of course – sent me cards with flowery invitations. I was almost never able to refuse, even though I later chided myself for being soft. Every two or three days, we bought wine and roses and went somewhere – Galapagar, Alcobendas, Legazpi, Alcalá de Henares…

San Borja, for example, was the patron saint of Auntie Estebana – and we hastened to Auntie Estebana's, getting lost in the narrow side streets of *Barrio Concepción*. Along the way, Lidia hungrily told me how her auntie had once ripped off a large family diamond from one of her men. I listened distractedly; nevertheless, I then regarded Auntie Estebana with interest. She turned out to be a decrepit old woman who had already nearly outlived her mind. However, from beneath her thick brows I was transfixed by sharp, inquisitive eyes – and I believed the diamond really was being kept in a dresser somewhere, wrapped in rags. She had prepared us calamari in a sauce made from their own ink. The calamari, I recall, were delicious.

Then came the day of St. Isidore, and we set off to see cousin Amalia. At one time, she and Lidia had studied together at an elementary school for girls. Then their paths had separated, which Amalia, evidently, did not regret. None other than Isidore himself had helped her land a lover from the Ministry; and he, in turn, had bought an apartment and furniture, and set up a comfortable life. I liked the cousin; she had a spontaneity so lacking in Lidia. On top of that, she unambiguously pressed her hip against me when we were left alone together in the kitchen.

"Some people really have it made!" Lidia exclaimed on the way back. I assented, wondering whether it would be appropriate to invite the enterprising Amalia to a private lunch – and more.

Afterward, there were more saints: Ermengol, Francisco, Soler. There were other relatives and acquaintances – I really lost count. They all desired to see us; their hospitality knew no bounds. And I learned something about each one – how they drew on their accounts, ordering around admirers, fiancés, husbands.

"This little pussycat, she acts like a bitch when she doesn't get what she wants," Lidia informed me in a whisper.

"Why does everybody always feel they don't have enough?" she feigned surprise, shrugging her shoulders.

"Now, that one behaved like a genuine whore!" she categorically declared, and I found no arguments to the contrary. Too many women flashed before my eyes – tenacious, greedy, who knew how not to miscalculate.

I sensed I was being pulled into the abyss. Truths that were hard to deny revealed to me what I tried to resist. And how fragile, unstable the framework was I had built, the overconfident creator.

I completely stopped thinking about Eve, as if recognizing I wasn't ready for that. The comfort of coffeehouses now seemed to be a trap; reflections on the female essence appeared the silliest of whims. Obviously, I told myself, solitude had played a cruel joke on me. Visits to places of ill-repute were too specific an experience;

and no fantasies or beautiful strangers could fill in the empty spaces. Pictures from life were put in the blanks. They had never been presented to me in such quantity.

Doubt is the scourge of any creator, and soon I faltered, showing my weakness. Voluntarily or involuntarily, consciously or not, I began to seek an acceptable compromise. The Adele who would satisfy all – Lidia, me, Semmant. Auntie Esteban and Cousin Amalia, along with their arrogant saints. Everyone who might want to judge.

It seemed to me I was aiming for fairness, but, of course, fairness had nothing to do with it. I was just tired – of the pressure, which was great. And I could not find the strength in myself to break with Lidia for good.

CHAPTER 25

In the ensuing series of forum postings, Adele appeared slightly different. Then even more different, increasingly so. Lidia got hers; I wanted to simplify my life, and tried to play a bit of a trick. To pull a minor con to have my cake and eat it too. But this turned out to be a very difficult task.

Adele now spoke all the more often of problems with money, how it was running out. I thought I would succeed in uniting all the incompatible issues on this soil. This concept was close to all – including Semmant, the horseman in shining armor. The question of money assumed answers, serving to defend everyone's life choices. It justified the calculating logic to a certain extent – and I endeavored not to cross that line. And Adele's profession should have helped me as well.

I started to make her look more like a prostitute – from real life, not from an adult fairytale. What was previously left to be read between the lines had now begun to break through to the surface. It was no longer possible to believe in her sincerity; she became as cunning as a skilled salesman. She gave compliments in hopes of a tip, created extra charges just because, for no reason. She was beholden to me in this, shrugging her shoulders – after all, why not? Taking care of oneself is so costly! One must be desirable – and that means cosmetics, perfume, clothes. One must stay in shape – that assumes the fitness club, the swimming pool, massage…

And, naturally, my stories started to turn out poorly. In place of firm ground, I had stepped onto shifting sand. It all sounded belabored, forced. I got mad, crumpled the paper, looked hatefully at the crooked lines of text.

"Yesterday I snagged a sugar daddy," Adele bragged to me. "Look at this nice little ring. He's so generous with gifts…"

"The son of a sheikh from Qatar is taking me to Sardinia for two days. I'll bring you a shell through which you can hear the sea…"

"I like it when a man takes me shopping *afterward*. Then I'm willing to do a lot – for new shoes, for example. I'm willing to suggest a lot *myself*!"

I tried to present this all lightly and playfully, almost as a joke. However, the joke flopped. Peevish tones could be heard in Adele's voice. She became more irritable and cranky, following Lidia Alvares Alvares. As if now Lidia were serving as a model for her, not the other way around.

It's hard to create what you do not like – I wanted to get away as quickly as possible and was hasty, cutting corners. And Adele ended up primitive beyond measure; I was unable to find the right words for her anymore. My dialogues with her had lost their exuberance. Our mutual understanding had been evaporating, as if it had become harder for us to comprehend each other. I blamed my fantasy, as well as myself, for the lack of expressive power. But the real problem was I couldn't get interested at all.

"He proposed marriage to me," Adele told me about the sheikh's son. "I refused, of course; I'm saving myself for someone else. It's way too early for me yet." And then, for some reason, she added, "You know, it seems to me that he's not as rich as he claims to be!"

"I have new sandals again," she informed me, sipping a martini. "Look, not only are they the same color as my purse, but they also match my watchband. Plus my pocketbook and my hairpin. My credit card, my phone case…"

Much sounded confusing, but for some reason I didn't omit a single remark, as if I were trying to make excuses to Lidia; or perhaps, on the contrary, I was just rubbing her nose in it. At times Adele looked unbelievably foolish. I almost stopped noticing where the irony ended.

Funny, but all these strained attempts, all these sacrifices and searches for the arithmetic average did not lead to anything substantial. I could tell in Lidia's eyes the new Adele looked no better. I wasn't managing to tune in to her wavelength, though she probably understood I was making the effort.

Lidia's thoughts were confused; I could see it had started to seem to her I was unhappy with her appearance, with how she was looking after herself. She started to have attacks of jealousy, finding supposed signs of my unfaithfulness. I couldn't even take a glance around – she immediately thought that I was scoping out someone's hips. She looked for rivals everywhere and punished me for that – pinching me, sticking her nails into my arms...

Madrid emptied out in August; the air grew thick, and the sun stood at its zenith. Lidia had registered at a posh sports club, but almost never went. Instead, she started to use heavy makeup, abusing blush, looking provocative and indecent. I wanted to laugh at myself, at the uselessness of my exertions.

As before, our sex was not bad, which somehow smoothed over the rest. But now, right after intimacy, Lidia demanded I spend money on her – take her to fancy restaurants, buy her jewelry and clothes. I even gave her a car: a prestigious four-wheel drive. It was brawny, silvery, sparkling new. And Adele spoke now more and more about purchases, clothes, shop windows – as I tried to find a way to a safe harbor for all of us. I wanted to restore a semblance of harmony, but my plan didn't pay off. The constituent fragments grew apart, shattering the picture. Lidia was becoming increasingly insatiable, Adele increasingly vulgar, and Semmant increasingly sad.

Of course, the conflict could not pass by without involving him. It would have been naïve to think that he, blinded, would notice nothing, though I hoped so at first. It soon became clear: he was seriously confused. And then I understood it hit Semmant worse than all the rest of us.

That's not surprising: who, more than he, was alien to the disharmony of compromise? In whom, besides him, did the tuning fork resound, revealing any hint of falsehood? I myself had fashioned him that way, and now I saw what price he paid for that. How, for him, it was difficult, painful, bad.

Semmant's objective functions were in conflict with each other. The control sums didn't coincide; numbers arranged themselves into divergent ranks. He felt perplexed, disoriented – obviously, Adele, the person she had become, was inconceivable to him. Her rationality was not convincing, could deceive no one. Something essential in her had disappeared, exposing the surrogate substrate. Talk about money sickened the robot, who knew all about that subject. It was as if Adele were openly suggesting to him, "Maintain me. Support me." He, perhaps, had no objection, but he intuited that such things must never be spoken aloud. They are not even hinted at; they may only be accepted with gratitude. And here that was plainly not the case.

Having sensed something amiss, Semmant began to search for reasons – in himself. It was against the rules for a knight to cast doubt upon the qualities of his lady love. As before, during times of big losses, he again reassessed his view of things – as if he wanted to understand something that was beyond understanding.

The tactics of his activities also changed; he rushed about in various directions, as if searching for a way out. He started to support the stocks of the best fashion houses, buying them up feverishly, erratically. Then something clicked in his brain, and he ruthlessly unloaded them all in a single transaction. Dumped them – and then played against them day after day...

In fact, he returned to short trading, which he had long since forgotten to consider. Now, to the contrary, he turned hyperactive in it, running ahead of the most brutal market predators. When I bought Lidia the car he went after auto industry stocks, recklessly trying to profit by their fall – though, of course, he lacked the power to set the necessary trend. But he risked, swinging his spear and hunting for a victim – all because I had described that vehicle in one of Adele's letters. She bragged that some Swiss banker had given it to her as a gift, and Semmant, still fighting with the automotive industry, went up against the Swiss banks and then all Swiss companies in general – without any rhyme or reason. Out of jealousy, perhaps – either of the car, or of the banker, or maybe even of me.

Of course, such actions did not lead to success. We began to incur losses – sometimes significant ones. I did not interfere, as I felt paralyzed; nor did I move capital out of his hands, cravenly waiting for the situation to correct itself. Funny, but that's how it turned out – after all, the robot possessed a huge safety margin. Self-defense mechanisms soon kicked in – as powerful as a sedative. The swing of objective functions was nearly ended; stability increased; balance was restored. But for this he had to pay dearly: all his emotions seemed to have been nullified.

He started to demand external memory again – obviously, he had commenced his next restructuring step. He was adding something to himself – yet another level of abstractions on top of what had been built earlier. I didn't know what it was; he did not share with me – not with images on the screen, or hints, or a single word.

It seemed he was laughing a bitter laugh. Inspiration and fervor vanished without a trace; he started to work just to punch a timecard, without any soul. Hours he wasted with random papers, garnering profit off the crumbs; then he suddenly did a crazy thing and in a single trade lost what he had earned. At that he froze in a standstill and could spend a whole day like that – followed by another, then a third. He waited and waited; the event log did not grow by a single line.

Only one thing was able to excite him now: the overheated stocks, swelling with speculative money. He knew this was greed, for which the market was ever ready to chastise – and, along with the market, he wanted to mete out punishment for it. He played down unreservedly, without restraint, not being concerned at all about our own account. It was as if he was punishing me too – for my own greed or for something else.

Then, as if he had wearied of any action, the robot again surrendered to idleness. I even think he might have been meditating on topics completely unrelated to the market. Time and again, after buying up sensitive, dynamic assets he forgot about them entirely. Stocks and options grew, bringing profit. The market inflated them, creating bubbles that were about to pop at any moment, but Semmant was in no hurry to get rid of them, apparently looking the other way as he listlessly picked through currencies or shuffled government bonds. I couldn't believe he failed to notice the danger; it would have been plain to any novice. The robot, however, waited and waited – and the assets depreciated, to our loss. Then, abruptly making a move, he would sell them when it was already too late…

In a word, Semmant turned from a tenacious hunter into someone who did not care. Into a man of indifference – and that's probably how it really was. At that time I was arguing with Lidia and looking for an excuse to get free of her. Adele flaccidly tried to find a reason for a new transient affair. A morose fellow hung about the screen. Neither he nor I saw any point in what was happening. Despondence had settled in my apartment; the very walls breathed it in.

Then, he started to get a grip. The artificial mind could not torture itself for long – with reflection, depression, introspection. The new data were finally sorted out; at least, the robot did not demand any more memory, or anything else. We stopped losing money; Semmant acted predictably, consistently, though it was clear he was off his game. Only part of his brain was occupied by work, and then only because it was expected of him. The remaining resources were committed to senseless thoughts worthy of the senseless world in which he found himself.

My account again started to grow – albeit slowly and not as steadily as before. Occasionally, Semmant did rather odd things, as if he were deliberately testing my patience. He would throw all our funds into a fixed deposit, like an old-timer on a pension, and just sit on it for a week. Or he would, on the other hand, buy up exceptionally risky options – much more at once than common sense allowed. It's astonishing we weren't ruined by this. Not without pride, I noted his enviable instincts time and again. Even acting ridiculously unwise, he somehow avoided catastrophe – though he was navigating stormy waters, amid reefs as sharp as razors.

Besides, he became quite willful – probably to spite me. Suspecting, perhaps, that the changes in Adele were my fault. He did not conceal that what he devoted to the markets was far from his full power. This was the revenge of a genius who did not desire to do what he knew how to do best. And it didn't matter whether it was in protest, in despair, or from feeling offended.

On the screen, it had been a long time since structures emerged that repeated themselves in various forms, or since the endless thread that did not cross back upon itself had appeared. Sometimes all the images dematerialized completely – even the black pelican. All was turning senselessly gray – or black, apathetic, faceless. Then Semmant filled the space with oyster shells – of various shapes and kinds. However, among them there were none of the mollusks from Galicia that I so love, with their precise valves. No, these were twisted monstrosities – like a Black Pearl or a Silver Claire. Palaces of polyps in ugly growths, the habitations of creatures of a notoriously salty variety, aggressive in aftertaste, sinewy and coarse. The prime candidates for Saturday sales in restaurants that had fallen on hard times.

Semmant seemed to be throwing them in my face – probably hinting at my hedonism, my reckless egotism. My penchant for the rich life, which had developed over the last half year, irritated him now. Or, could it be he meant Lidia and our first breakup – when the stories of Adele had begun? Or was he just mocking the culinary passion she and I had in common? He was clearly not naïve in his search for reasons and unseemly consequences. He knew how to make it understood he could deduce a lot – in the end, who could be more far-sighted than he?

From oysters he went to ornamental fish. Across the screen swam gouramis and guppies, discus and poecilias. He did not know about the Countess de Vega's aquariums – I had never written him about that. The fish were incidental – without any mystical, underlying significance – but I took them seriously, nonetheless. Every time I recalled the fireplace hall of the countess, the lynx skin on the floor, and the matte-black molly peering at us through the glass. And how Anna de Vega pronounced, "David..." – the name of the man she loved. The one who was ready to be her shadow, her paramour and slave. But who was also years younger than she – wasn't there an indelible defect inherent in that?

I knew he, Semmant, knew: there are defects that cannot be erased. He could venture any feat, but he was unable to delude himself. That security feature was missing in his algorithms. Perhaps this was also a mistake on my part.

In any case, there was no correcting it now, as with the other mistakes I had made. Semmant was capable only of fighting for what did not harbor deceit. Perhaps he saw in me merely a resource, nothing more. He might have thought the entire story of Adele the courtesan and her robot knight had been created by him – like the universe; for Adele had indeed become the whole universe for him. That's how it is when you look the astonished love specter right in the eye without flinching.

He now recognized he had been wrong about the most important thing. Adele, as well as the infinite cosmos, showed themselves not to be as he had believed. The tragedy of the creator is disappointment in himself. Adele was becoming a stranger to him – in this, of course, he couldn't blame her. So he drew the conclusion he personally was not worthy of the lady of his heart.

In the corner of the screen a female silhouette would occasionally appear. The same as before – but hardly noticeable, thinned out, nearly transparent. Even more defenseless than it had been previously. This was nothing less than Semmant now admitting he could not protect Adele from the enemy. The enemy turned out to be stronger than he.

We both seemed to be convinced the chaos of the universe was too mighty. One had only to loosen his grasp slightly, and it would instantly gain the upper hand. It attacks and takes vengeance, just as the real world takes vengeance – on all happy fools who issue it a challenge.

It was probably painful for the robot – painful and frightening. I know what it is to be suddenly uncertain of everything. I recalled perfectly how it was to see myself as inept, helpless. How I thought I wouldn't be in sync with reality ever again. Everyone from the School encountered this – and nearly all overcame it, sooner or later. Anthony, you understand, doesn't count – same as Dee Wilhelmbaum and Little Sonya. Those are the exceptions that make the rule – the fate of an exception is never enviable. Could it be, I thought sullenly, that Semmant was now also considered an exception? And, if so, what fate awaited him?

CHAPTER 26

Thus we endured nearly all of August, a month of helplessness, a time of weakness. The image of Adele was becoming ever more indistinct, like the thinned-out silhouette on the screen. It was hard for all of us – me, Lidia, and Semmant. The situation was sliding downhill, picking up speed. I understood a precipice lay ahead, and no one knew how far the drop-off would be.

Each morning I told myself: no more. And, alas, I did nothing to stop it. I had gone off course and was just letting the current carry me. I grew angry with myself, yet did not even try to lift a finger.

Then, finally, I regained my decisiveness. It was a hot day; in search of coolness, I got in my car and drove into the mountains. After taking a winding road to the Navacerrada Pass, I situated myself comfortably on a stone plateau and looked down for a long time upon pastures and terraces, on farm fields and scattered boulders. These weren't the Alps, but something stirred in my soul nonetheless. Some vague echo of that delight there once had been – and then, suddenly, shame! The bitterest shame – I recognized the treachery and cried out, gritting my teeth and cursing myself, pressing my face in my hands.

I returned home in the evening and set to work: I went onto the forum and deleted my profile. To hell with them – with Lidia, with everyone – I decided to turn history back. And to remake Adele, albeit not as before. Different, but still worthy – of adoration, of exploits in her name.

Her notes/confessions/reflections were again put to use. I sent them to the robot, trying to restore the naturalness that had once come so easily to me. Adele joked and poked fun at herself, swearing, explaining, sharing all her secrets. But something wasn't right; I could feel it. And Semmant immediately understood he was being fed a fake. He left the markets entirely and withdrew into himself.

In a week or so I recognized I was failing, which was obvious to both of us. Adele was spiraling ever lower into an inept lie. The new material lacked credibility – of course, my robot could see that with his eyes half-closed. His powerful mind had processed too many facts; deceiving him was now difficult. You could say he had acquired a wealth of experience. And this was bitter for him – as it always is.

It was bitter for me as well. I understood that in my lack of will I had done the unforgivable, the irreversible. Having been admitted into the inner sanctum, I had screwed up and profaned it. Having created a great thing, I myself was the one to betray it. And, having lost what I had achieved, I could see now: that was my ultimate limit. The boundary of perfection that could not be reached. I would never have the chance to do anything like it again in my life.

This was terrible, intolerable. Worse than for anyone who had been disappointed before – at least, that's how it felt. Your own pain is always more acute, and you even think on occasion: is there any point in continuing? Is it time to settle up all the scores? But no, I didn't think that, or else, if I did, not seriously. I knew I didn't have the heart to do away with myself. And what difference would it make anyway? So, I could keep on drinking wine and sucking oysters.

Yet, even feeling that the fight was meaningless, I didn't stop or throw up my hands. Unable to remain idle, I kept trying, consoling myself with hope, trying new steps. Soon it occurred to me: I had to update something radically in myself. And the first thing to be done was to finally get rid of Lidia.

She had not bothered me during all this time – probably because she was busy. Her newspaper was changing owners, and, in the process, its office, structure, image. But then pressing matters receded into the background, and Lidia reminded me of her existence. She was seriously confused. My disappearance from the forum could not help but alarm her.

I knew we had to meet, at least once. Lidia insisted on a tryst in my bedroom and immediately pulled me into bed. She supposed sex would help her, make me more compliant, softer – a typical mistake for a woman. Actually, I had long since wearied of her demanding lust. And two long, lascivious hours only fortified my resolve.

When we caught our breath, she asked me outright what was going on with me. And I, in all sincerity, told her everything – about Semmant, about my letters to him, about his feelings toward the fair maiden he saw in the prostitute Adele. I talked about my disgraceful weakness, of which she herself was also to blame. I even spoke of the elusive specter that entices all and favors only a few – though I don't think she understood that at all. Instead, it became utterly clear to her: I intended to deprive her of something.

Of course, Lidia grew furious, and my firmness merely threw fuel on the fire.

"You're crazy!" I heard her say, and I could tell she really meant it.

"What is this robot of yours?" Lidia asked. "How can you choose *it* over me?"

"Over *me!*" Her eyes grew large, and she winced in complete sincerity. It was difficult for her to accept, to recognize, to finally believe.

"You loser!" she yelled in my face, right before slamming the door. "You'll always be afraid of life. You just don't know how to live!"

Then, a day later, she realized she had gone too far. This had happened before, when we quarreled over the issue with the camouflage – and now it again seemed to her everything could still be fixed. She explained herself, making excuses, murmuring into the telephone receiver, "Forgive me, I just went crazy. I wanted you to need me more than the most advanced robot!"

"No," I laughed. "You just want to *get* more."

Lidia sensed then that it gave me pleasure to tell her this, and that the breakup had occurred, and it was irreversible. Yet she had no intention of giving up. Everything had happened too quickly, and the cause was unconvincing, in her opinion. On top of that, it was hard for her to admit a man had dumped her first.

She began a protracted siege: calling, writing letters, demanding heart-to-heart talks. All this was burdensome, unpleasant. As best as I could, I avoided contact – not yammering about Semmant anymore, and making up one excuse after another. Being busy, health problems – then alcoholism and even the onset of impotence. I tried many things to explain why I no longer wanted to see her, but nothing worked, Lidia would not relent. "What did I do wrong?" she persisted. "How can I correct it, make it right again?"

Once she waited a long time by the door and eventually got me to open it for her. That was a very hard day. I was depressed as I grew convinced there was no fixing Adele, and the story could not be saved. My will was crushed, and Lidia knew how to use that. She cast a single glance at me and started to rip my clothes off right in the hallway.

"You look beleaguered, as if someone is hunting you. Want to run away together? I can be your accomplice. Or I can be a chance encounter: a salesgirl, a waitress, a streetwalker…"

She licked me all over, squealing with desire, and came three times, helping herself along with her hand. She made me come too – right in her mouth. "Ha ha ha!" she laughed gruffly when she saw my discomfort. "My, but you give up easily! What are all your half-assed fairy tales worth now?"

"Leave," I said to her, and she left. She departed as a conqueror, holding her head high with pride. But this victory was her last. I no longer denied it to myself: she was simply repulsive to me.

The discussions stopped – I now dismissed her calls with a brief, dry, "I'm busy!" Her e-mails also went unanswered. At first she was angry, then perplexed, and then she started to beg and grovel. She wanted to be pitied, in which she saw a way to get me back. I kept silent, but she became all the more persistent, hysterical. She wrote in thorough detail about all her tears and tribulations.

It even seemed to me this was getting her turned on; she was aroused by her sufferings as though by a fetish. All there had been between us before had lost its value, turned to a farce. And besides, her words and her posture, all of her sniveling and wailing, seemed more unnatural to me than ever before. I did not believe her – behind the protests and grievances I saw a ferocious plan. She was fighting for her property, gathering up all the resources she had.

I even wrote Semmant: might it be the time had come for me to become a misogynist forever? I admitted I was amazed at myself. Indeed, recalling our love affair I was puzzled how I could ever have had any feelings for this pitiable creature. I searched for an echo of them and heard not a melody, but rather scratching and grinding. The entire female essence appeared different to me. It was as if I had discovered a dark, unseemly part of it and realized yet again that I knew little about women.

How dearly I wanted Lidia to break up with me herself! For her to regard me with contempt, having come to the conclusion I was unworthy of her. But no, worthiness, whether mine or someone else's, was not important now. In the battle for her possessions, she was ready for anything.

Then a saving thought popped into my head – or, rather, Lidia herself inspired it. "Why aren't we seeing each other anymore?" she asked. "Why aren't we sleeping together – after all, whatever you may say, you need to have sex with someone. Or what, did you hook up with somebody else? Could that be what this is all about?"

Here it is, I understood. This is my way out, I thought, so I wrote her, "Yes!"

"Who? Who is it?" Lidia would not relent. And I, hardly giving it any consideration, chose the most plausible and simple option. I invented a fling with the maid, Elena María Gómez, who cleaned my apartment twice a week. And that worked – like a powerful charge of plastique.

To my astonishment, Lidia did not calm down, not at all. Upon receiving my letter, she became enraged. Now everything had fallen into place. "Another woman" – that was so easy to imagine; it was so clear, explained everything so well.

"Your Elena is a real slut!" she yelled into my voicemail. "And now you're copying *her* onto Adele? But she has olive skin, not white! It makes no difference to you; you're an animal. You're just a heartless, lecherous beast!"

Apparently, she was liberated from her shackles, casting everything off that chained her as she stopped thinking about the robot that seemed strange, alien, foreign. Abstractions were taken out of the way; they did not interfere to restrain her impulses. Now her letters bore frightful bundles of ire. Behind them loomed the forked tongue of a snake, a tarantula's fangs dripping transparent droplets. She promised to wipe me off the face of the earth, destroy me, lock me in prison. I did not believe her – quite mistakenly so. There is no creature more venomous than a woman looking to pay you back in full.

Our desolated world was inhabited by new shades. The feeble specter was expelled in disgrace, and in his place arose a demon – the demon of hatred, full of strength. His arsenal was diverse and rich; and I soon learned Lidia was not writing just to me. All her acquaintances, friends, and associates were drawn into the war. She selected her weapon: wild, monstrous slander – and struck with it recklessly. Her former confusion grew into determination, a readiness to sully herself – into the fury of revenge. Her anger changed shape; from conscientious and logical it transformed into something irrational, the fruit of an absurd, skewed reality seen only by her, Lidia Alvares Alvares.

It was as if she were looking at things through an ugly, deformed prism. Everything passing through its aperture turned into a stream of sewage. At the same time, she sincerely believed in her own fable. Slander was for her the new truth; Lidia did not doubt its purity. As a result, her words acquired tremendous force. The force of conviction – everyone sensed it. A woman convinced she was right seemed to them something that could not be faked. And they believed her – straightway. As for me, I just could not take it all seriously. And therefore I looked uncertain, distrustful.

Lidia spewed forth hate like bile, like bad, murky blood. It even seemed to me that our fray was a ceremony, some pagan rite – a sacrifice for the absolution of the whole world. Who were they, these unhappy gods who had chosen the two of us for this? Her, in the role of a medium, a conduit of dark forces. Me, as the target, the neutralizer, the receptacle. Had I wanted to, I could have been proud; but I sensed no pride – I felt vile. Sinking into gloom, I convulsively clutched at the air and thought: this will never, ever end.

Lidia managed to convince many people of utterly extreme things. As if I, out of jealously, had humiliated and intimidated her, extorted money from her, stolen valuables from her safe. That I beat her – skillfully, without leaving marks. That I forced her time after time into unimaginable sexual perversions. That I tortured her with sleep deprivation, tied her to the radiator – and then even promised to kill her if she went to the police. In response, her friends called to threaten me. They cursed and berated me, advised me to come begging forgiveness. I was at wit's end, battling the whole world; yet Lidia was not mollified. She was insatiable, reveling in rage and despair; and the exultant demon inflated with arrogance like a cloud permeated with the lines of a force field. These were the forces of obliteration, destruction – Lidia was a destructive genius. Her life had finally acquired meaning, as though everything before this – all those admirers and amusements – had been aimless and insignificant. To this meaning she clung with unprecedented strength, though in the process almost nothing was left of her *herself*. Only a shell, tattered to the limit.

The rest was spent on slander and lies – transformed into the cloud of hate. It sucked everything into itself like a tornado, darkening and expanding. Buildings fell, and fragments blew along the perimeter, gathering their own power, magnifying the scale of the catastrophe. There was no stopping it – until suddenly all abated. The calls ceased, and letters stopped coming. I sighed with relief, supposing Lidia had finally come to her senses. But no, I was too naïve. She wanted to keep taking vengeance – and she already knew how.

CHAPTER 27

The first act of revenge turned out to be pretty stupid. Childishly naïve, desperately weak-willed. Lidia's false sense of justice confused her, to her disservice.

Soon after I told her about Elena María Gómez, she staked out the maid by the entranceway and took snapshots with her Pentax. Elena herself admitted to me, laughing, that some crazy woman had taken pictures of her right at the door to my building. I knew immediately who it was and came clean, asking for her forgiveness. It was clear to me Lidia would not stop with the photos. Some sort of cruel games, vengeful plots, were in the works.

But Elena María had no complaints and was not offended by my lie. "You're a handsome man. I'm flattered, even," she said, smiling. "I'd take you to bed myself, if I wasn't in love with Julio."

That was the name of her Creole boyfriend. He was tall and broad-shouldered, worked as a furniture mover, and, as Elena once bragged, the size of his Johnson defied description. Against Julio I had no chance.

So, we just laughed it off, though not without some second thoughts. Later, however, it became no laughing matter for Elena. Lidia loaded her pics onto call girl sites – along with ads inviting people to have some fun with her. She posted Elena María's name and phone number, which she managed to get from the domestic service agency. This was an extraordinarily foolish move.

I don't know what got into her head – obviously, she was dumber than I'd thought. For some reason, she imagined no one would catch her, and she set it all up from home without even troubling herself to go to the nearest Internet cafe. Not only that, but she made the postings from her personal e-mail address, which was everywhere – on her résumé, on her articles and business cards.

Elena María Gómez, a beautiful, shapely *mulata*, was a quick-witted girl. Lidia probably took her for a simpleton, but Elena was a hundred points ahead in terms of inventiveness and smarts. Having escaped the Ecuadorian ghetto, she was studying IT at the best university in Madrid. Past deprivations had left no mark on her, and cleaning houses was just a temporary phase. A large portion of her free time was spent on social networking sites. She was popular; people loved her for her sweet temper and sly tongue. Her circle of virtual friends was immense. Lidia could not have chosen a worse target to provoke.

When Elena María started getting calls from the adventure-seekers jerking off to her photos, she grew utterly furious. In her world this was against the rules and had to be punished. Somewhere in the slums of Guayaquil she would simply have sliced up the face of the offender with the razor blade she always had on hand. Here, that method wouldn't work, but there were others, no less effective. She consulted with a few of her contacts and put fierce reciprocity in motion.

I was kept abreast of the matter – Elena shared the details with me. At first she pressured the administrators of the malicious sites, and a couple of them responded. Thus we learned – though we had no doubt before then – where the ads on the Web came from. When it became clear Lidia was slinging mud openly, using her own e-mail address, our astonishment knew no bounds.

"*¡Loca!*" Elena said, twirling a finger at her temple, and began the payback campaign. She amassed a detailed dossier on Lidia, posted it on her blog to provide a reference, and, with the aid of an army of virtual friends, started to spread the story all over cyberspace.

This was harder than neighbors' gossip or even a lawsuit. Lidia and her inept attack soon became the talk of the town. A Spaniard from Madrid, shamelessly slurring a humble Ecuadorian student: this instantly turned into a ready example of trite metropolitan snobbery. Lidia's rancor and dull-wittedness were savored across several continents. People concocted all kinds of fables, drew caricatures of her. Thus she got a new virtual life – to replace Adele, whom she had lost.

Of course, it was bitter for Lidia Alvares Alvares. She experienced firsthand how an act of war turns against the one who starts it. And also what it's like when you fight everyone at once in a world that knows no mercy. Even her appearance changed: her nose and chin thickened, and her facial features grew coarse. I barely recognized her when she showed up on Skype, yelling and cursing hysterically. She looked like a spiteful Fury of forty-something. Her hate for me reached its apogee. It was probably then she devised her next plan for vengeance – which worked.

It was a soft, dry September. Things between Semmant and me were the same as before, with no improvement. He did not react to my stories. No matter what happened now with Adele, the robot remained indifferent, apathetic. Something was going on in his electronic consciousness – the pictures changed; fragments of marches played; sometimes a sad violin sang for hours, barely audible. But there was nothing to connect this to. Semmant lived his own life, as separate from me as it was from the rest of the world. All the same, I continued writing – so that he would know I was here, with him. Sometime, I thought, he would digitally process this period as well. Transform it into gigabytes of neural cells on the hard disk. The robot would become stronger, sooner or later, as everyone does. Then our friendship and closeness would be renewed.

But that was still a long way off. Nothing happened; events paused. Through the window I examined the horde of bare-legged women returning from their vacations, but I felt only emptiness and boredom. Closing my eyes, I envisioned their bodies, the smell of their hair, but I sensed not even a hint of desire. The Buddha's mat, neglected and forgotten, was collecting dust in a corner of the bathroom.

I understood I had to cast off this torpor, to revive, cheer up, but I could not find the strength. The projector seemed stuck on an empty slide. And then... something clicked, and it went off like a machine gun. Lidia called me for the first time in two weeks.

Surprisingly, she sounded calm. Affable and peaceful – I hadn't heard her like that for a long time.

She said, "Let's just see each other for a minute. I want to give you back the keys to your apartment."

"Forgive me," she added. "I wasn't in my right mind."

"I won't act like that anymore," she promised, and I believed her. And I did not suspect anything was amiss.

We agreed to meet at the Prado Museum. The sky was cloudless, and the sun baked everything. I was covered in sweat by the time I had strolled from the underground parking to the north entrance. There wasn't long to wait; in a quarter of an hour Lidia arrived, all in pink and blue. She was leading a friend by the hand, someone I had already met – Manuel, the fan of Iberian pigs. The look on his face struck me as strange; he walked as though led to the slaughter, noticing nothing around him. Oddly, I did not connect this with Lidia or myself.

Lidia Alvares Alvares, however, strode confidently, like an icebreaker, cutting through the throng of tourists. As if she saw her goal and didn't wish to notice any obstacles whatsoever. It was clear: there was no stopping her.

An alarm went off inside me as I suddenly knew something very bad was about to happen. I knew it but froze in place, standing there, not moving, deep in lethargy. There was no way to avoid what was coming. The stream of Dao narrowed at this point and rushed forward like a mountain river. Its power was irresistible, and no one could jump free of it.

Lidia walked up, stopped, smiled – then suddenly dove forward and rammed her face into my shoulder. This was an abrupt, practiced maneuver; I did not manage to react and deflect it. Her cry rang out; she crashed into me again – and howled, smearing blood down her cheeks. Someone else began screaming. I simply kept standing there in confusion, not moving. Just as motionless stood Manuel, her friend.

"What are you waiting for?" Lidia yelled at him. "What? Can't you protect me? Or don't you remember – this isn't the first time! You know how dangerous he is!"

I looked at both of them as if they were comic-strip characters come to life. I also saw myself positioned somewhere in their vicinity – as if I were a spectator on the sidelines. The degree of absurdity surpassed all limits; I could not believe what was happening. Yet, the impossible *was* happening – frame by frame, shot by shot.

Here: Manuel tried to catch me by my shirt. I grabbed his hand and quietly pushed him away. He fell with a theatrical groan and cried, "Help!"

Here: Lidia, ceasing her wailing, screamed at the top of her lungs, "Police!" I mechanically noticed she was covered in quite a bit of blood – she had probably broken her nose.

Here: Manuel again, pale and as frightened as a hare, ineptly swung his hand, intending to punch me. It was clear fighting wasn't his strong suit. I could easily have knocked him down with a hook to the liver or a cross to the jaw, but I did not. Instead, I turned and took a step away.

Meanwhile, police were running from all directions. The first of them was quite close. "What a joke!" I muttered out loud, certain I was in no danger. I was shaken by all the fakery of the staging, its unreality and perversion. But it turned out I was the only one who saw it that way.

A second later they cuffed me, rather roughly. "Hey, take it easy," I yelled, but somebody kicked me in the shin, and I shut up. There was plainly no point in resisting.

"Get ahold of him! Tighter! Tighter!" Lidia cried, letting the tears flow again. One of the officers comforted her, hugging her by the shoulders. Indeed, a whole army of police had gathered, and they kept pouring in. Clearly, I was a force to be reckoned with.

A Peugeot with lights flashing on its roof drove onto the sidewalk, scaring away the gawkers, and stopped next to us. They stuffed me inside and drove me to the station. The interior reeked of smoke and vomit. I wanted to wake up, but this was no dream.

At the station, without mincing words, they put me in a cell that was already full of people. I finally came to my senses and expressed my indignation at top volume, but the guards merely shrugged their shoulders. My cellmates – vagrants and junkies – regarded me with frowns, keeping their distance and avoiding my eyes. I was wearing Versace jeans and Armani loafers. A strange spirit emanated from me, discouraging contact.

Then the chief came – an Andalusian, judging from his brogue – with the biceps of a bodybuilder and the inspired face of a poet. They took me into the hallway and stood me with my face to the wall. I was hastily searched, and my hands were again bound with handcuffs. And then they led me to a neighboring room, where a man with the face of a horse was already sitting pompously in his chair.

The police chief turned out to be exceptionally polite. He entered with a springy step, inspected us, silently nodded. In his eyes flashed an all-knowing, satisfied sheen. After pausing for a bit, he pressed a button and said quietly, "Get Señor Campo to put a move on." Then he introduced the horse-faced man, "This is the victim's advocate." And finally, waving in the direction of the small man hovering at the door, he added, "And this is Campo, your defense. He's being paid by the Spanish Crown!"

I could see the Spanish Crown wasn't putting forth much effort. It was pointless to expect any help from Campo, but there was no choice – I didn't have a personal lawyer. I could count only on my own wits, so I declared affirmatively, "This is an egregious outrage and a farce! I demand that you release me at once! I demand an apology from the police and the government, from the Crown, the king and queen, and from the 'advocate' of the so-called 'victim' – excuse me, but I did not hear your name…"

Public defender Campo slouched in his seat and let out a foreboding sigh. The police chief studied me with interest. And the horse-faced guy bared his yellow teeth and said gravely, "Call me Don Pedro!" Then he looked around and inquired, "Can we begin?"

He ran the show from that moment on. For a long time, savoring it and smacking his lips, he laid out my crimes. Lidia had spared nothing in her scheme. I was considered her former cohabitant, so the statute on domestic violence – a fearful beast on the Iberian Peninsula – applied to me. Her statement about my fits of jealousy and threats of retribution had already been on file with the police for a month or so. Yet another "friend" – whom I never met – was also involved and had signed declarations as a witness. A tangled web surrounded me. It may not have been real, but it was quite resilient.

Don Pedro sang like a nightingale. He sketched out the big picture, the entire battle scene. It contained wolves and lambs, monsters and innocent victims. Hordes of Spanish women, battered by their husbands, misfortunate Palomas and Martas with greenish-yellow bruises on their cheeks. The better part of society, mothers and housewives, and next to them their Miguels, Josés, Juans, dim-witted, simple-minded, not even worth a kind word. Men whose faults sooner or later become apparent even to them – so apparent, in fact, that they cannot live with it. In rage they swing their fists, torment their Martas and Palomas, subject them to insults, beatings, mutilation… "Is this not the very calamity with which the whole country struggles?" exclaimed Don Pedro, rolling his eyes in despair. "Is this not the shameful stain that we have been trying so long to eradicate?"

"Exactly!" I rejoined, perplexed at why my man Campo remained silent as a mouse. "This is a great shame, your Miguels and Javiers, your inadequate Josés and Juans. I can't abide it myself when someone takes advantage of the weak – especially when he's the tough one, even though society may have turned him into the weakest of all…"

"What are you talking about?" the lawyer squinted.

"The same thing as you!" I exclaimed. "This is a shame only found among humans. Male animals don't beat their mates. They protect and defend them. As for the Spanish 'Dons' – that's your national fault!"

"I beg your pardon?" Pedro interrupted me inquisitively. His intrusion was skillful, allowing him to seize the initiative afresh. But I did not give up. I raised my voice, expressing indignation right along with him, matching his tone.

Speaking the truth is easy and pleasant – and I, like Pedro, spared no adornment. I was trying to prove I was wholeheartedly and fully on the side of the Palomas and Martas. I gave examples – of Lidia's former lovers, Rafael and Manuel – caustically deriding their inferiority. I mentioned how the former arrogance of the Spaniards had returned to them like a boomerang. This may have sounded offensive – for Pedro, and even for Campo. Perhaps the police chief was also a little wounded by my frankness. But it was too late to retreat. I grew excited and insistent. I told them about the strangers in Madrid cafes whom I watched, about their readiness to forgive and provide hope, about the softest ray, the Light of Eve. Nor did I forget about "the worst of bitches" – for contrast, to demonstrate the irrationality of society. I denounced the artificial unification of the sexes, condemned the attempt to paint everyone the same color...

So, I fought as hard as I could, but this lawyer Pedro was a tough nut. He turned everything upside down, looking for a con and retooling it to his design. Being a skilled demagogue, he exposed me as a demagogue. He made me out as a dreamer and a liar, a fantasist who could not accept that illusions cannot be fulfilled. He was as indomitable as an army of "luminaries" in a city strangled by smog. Like the lead "expert" from Basel, who could not be deterred by any "grueling interrogation." Again I felt how the chaos of the universe was rudely interfering in my life. Inescapably, washing away all boundaries, confounding all truths and all meanings.

"And so!" Don Pedro now moved from the general to the particular. To yet another innocent who had fallen into the clutches of a despot. To Lidia Alvares Alvares, who had had the misfortune to hook up with a savage foreigner. With me – a roughneck, an unprincipled sexist, mad with jealousy.

"Of course," the lawyer sighed, "it was only an oversight at Immigration that allowed him to cross the border unhindered. But now that this has happened, and he's here with us, Spanish law should not give him clemency. Look..." and Pedro enumerated my misdeeds: I insinuated myself into Lidia's trust, pressured her into cohabitation, then threatened and frightened her; and when she finally got free of me, I committed an act of aggression – the logical climax, crossing the line! All one after the other, beyond any doubt. The matter was clear: before them was a foe who had issued a brazen challenge to the social order!

I objected again, nervously and vehemently, but they interrupted to shut me up. I yelled in despair, "It's all a pack of lies. Lidia spun this whole tale because she was jealous of the maid!" I wondered out loud, "How can you not see it? This is a setup. It's slander, defamation!"

But Pedro held all the strings tightly in his fingers. He tied me up hand and foot while my "defender" kept silent, as if the cat had his tongue. The police chief listened, flexing his muscles, and also said not a word. He was not to be deceived; he knew the cost of everything and was now estimating how to avoid complications. He compared, evaluated Pedro and me. Of course, the lawyer looked convincing. It was clear to all: this one really knows how to create problems.

"Okay," the chief finally said, "let the judge decide. No objections?" he turned to Campo. "No. Well, that's good. The preliminary charge is as follows…" and he read a long paragraph of legalese from an official-looking paper. Then he called the guards and barked out, "Let's detain him. Take him away and lock him up!"

Thus I became a prisoner in a Spanish jail.

CHAPTER 28

I spent four days incarcerated – with little food, water, or sleep. And utterly stupefied at the world's imperfection. At the heinousness of the world, at the contemptible way it was arranged. At the horrible injustice that had befallen me. I tried to grasp how a guiltless person could be held in jail, and I feared losing my mind to impotence, to powerlessness extending to the absolute. I was being run over, crushed, by the multi-ton truck of state bureaucracy. And I could do *nothing* about it.

Concerning imprisonment, I learned the most important thing: I was not cut out for it. Prison and I were alien to each other; the deepest internal strife instantly arose between us. Everyone around me sensed this – that's probably why I was never beaten by the guards, even though I was occasionally defiant. My cellmates kept their distance; there was hardly anyone with whom I exchanged even a single word. When asked what had happened to me, I answered simply: the universe has taken up arms against me. Because, I added, my arrogance passed the limits. This was enough for the curious to hold their tongues. Only Romanian Petru, a small-time dope dealer, listened attentively and glanced at me furtively from time to time. He ran the cell; there, he was the boss. But even Petru could not fathom what was going on in my head. There, thousand-watt bulbs flashed – and exploded with deafening claps. An infinite line, winding like a viper, fled away from itself – into nothing. I could have tried to divine its path. I could have sketched a clever fractal with my finger on the dirty floor. But this would hardly have explained anything.

There were ten of us in the ten-man box, which would have been tight even for five. Three were, like me, bewildered as to how they fell under the statute of *maltrato* by the easy hand of conniving femmes. One of them, a balding, overweight, fifty-year-old accountant, sobbed into his mattress for days on end – until Petru finally gave him a kick. Obviously, the world seemed even more flawed to him than it did to me. The wife he had lived with for thirty years called the police after they had an argument at home. While watching the TV, they got into a dispute over the remote. For better effect, once she had put down the receiver, the wife banged her cheek against a door jamb.

The accountant was pathetic and evoked no sympathy. Besides that, to tell the truth, his situation surprised no one. That same Petru, the expert on prison norms, regaled us with dozens of other stories that were no less absurd. Surprise is quite irrelevant if the worst has already happened to you. My "colleagues" glumly kept silent as they pondered their own fates. Only two strapping Hondurans who had been arrested for a bar fight wagged their tongues each time. Perhaps their own troubles didn't upset them too much.

In three days they were transferred somewhere. Then the accountant was finally hauled off. And on the fifth day it was my turn to stand before the judge.

The path to reach him was long – first a ride in a paddy wagon; then I was led, handcuffed, through a building full of people. The security from the *Guardia Civil* excelled at wit. They made fun of my name and my accent. They felt omnipotent; I was fully under their power.

It seemed to me they embodied the immense vapidity of the benighted masses. I despised their smugness with all my soul, all my being. I hated it and thought: well, it's not in vain that I'm always rooting for the bull in their Spanish *corrida*. Against all odds I always pray: let the bull win today! And someday he will ultimately win – beating all those worthless Castilian males, who are already whipped, even though they don't believe it yet. He will dominate them – with his balls, with his bovine member!

"That day is not far off," I said in a barely audible whisper, "when the local *machos* won't be able to get it up anymore – out of fear. At first, from fear of the 'worst of the bitches' who have long forced them to their knees, and then from fear before the bull. Before his unyielding might, his fearless lust. Thus will this country leap to the next rung of the evolutionary ladder. It has already taken the first step – from oppression to liberation, to a hitherto unprecedented triumph of its women. Just a little is left: let the murdering of bulls be replaced by worshipping the bull. And who will bring it about, make it happen? Those very same women, and no one else. From the males driven into a corner to the bull's balls erect on the altar! And the *macho* men will – again! – fail to comprehend how they've been led on, deceived."

My eyes probably flashed – like those of the chief of the police precinct – with the clear sheen of coming conquest. I knew the future, felt its currents. Passersby, meanwhile, looked stealthily about with bashful, timid curiosity. It was clear to them they had chanced to see something not intended for their eyes. Something from a reality known only through movies and detective novels. Here he is – a public enemy, a criminal, an outcast. They had lifted him from the pit itself, and his path through these corridors led only there, back to the pit!

I must have looked the part. Four days in a prison cell will make anyone look like that. I wanted to bare my teeth and snap them angrily in response. And to yell, "I'm rooting for the bull! Already rooting for it – even if the *toreros* keep celebrating at the moment!"

In the courtroom I took myself in hand – through an extreme effort of will. I had to focus on what was important, forget the abstract, think about my fate.

"Convince the judge you're not dangerous," said Campo, the lawyer being paid by the Crown. I just silently looked him in the face. It seemed everyone was against me, but then the heavens smiled: "That's not true." And they sent me a helper, a good fairy.

The day before, I had requested an interpreter – exercising one of my few rights. I didn't trust my Spanish, it could betray me. And here they introduced Susana to me – she was pimply, heavyset, with thick

SEMMANT

hair and the look of a woman yearning for love. And I gazed into her
eyes – as deeply as I could. I straightened up my back and tried to
add a sexy huskiness to my dehydrated, rasping voice. Because I saw
Susana was my ally.

I was interrogated thoroughly and tiresomely. The judge was
unremarkable – he was old and not very interested in the proceedings.
Things were directed by a skinny old maid – from the special division
on *maltrato* with the district attorney's office. She knew the enemy
was before her, and her duty was to punish that enemy. To expose
and convict him. To isolate him, stick him in a cage. Of my guilt she
had no doubt, that was her function.

I sat there and thought – this one, from the D.A., she'll be the
first in line for the bull's member. She'll dash forward, elbowing the
others out of the way. But for now the abnormality of modernity is
being created in her office, the poisonous ether of life turned inside
out. How many more of them are there – these skinny old ladies
recklessly entrusted with power? These leaders of the greedy and the
vulgar, these guides of the worst specimens of the female sex, who
rock the social boat and set the bearings toward ash?

I wanted to say to her, "*¡Perdone usted!* You're oversimplifying –
unjustly – and emasculating all meanings. Where did you study, in
worthless schools? Do you also fear the nonlinear like the plague?
Have you lost all sense of reality?"

"You're not doing your job!" I wanted to say straight to her face.
"The iron muscle of the state will not aid those in need of protection.
It is only suitable for the ones who tirelessly rove about in search of
a forceful arm made of steel. It is for the 'worst of bitches' who are
seeking a means of attack, not defense. But those from whom the
softest ray emanates lose more from the efforts of the shortsighted
government. Intimidating the *macho* men is not a solution – they
are already intimidated to no end. And everybody knows: when
someone is backed into a corner, he's all the more dangerous and
nasty!"

I wanted to say that and much more, but I kept quiet. And I felt,
contrary to the spiteful thoughts, that a fervent wave was rising
within me. A wave of gratitude to those gorgeous creatures, those

most beautiful strangers who number so many. Who are everywhere – and I looked at the plain, chubby Susana, knowing she was one of them. There was something in her that would have moved the exploits of the knights of all times.

I could have revealed to her, "You also are Eve. I have seen many of your sisters."

I could have disclosed the secret, "One and the same quality unites you all."

I could have even added, "Believe in your light!"

Bound in handcuffs, maligned, slandered, I called the elusive phantom to my aid, even though I knew this wasn't his jurisdiction. Here soared other spirits and the demon of hate summoned by Lidia. They were as much in charge here as Petru was in the prison cell. But the phantom still resided somewhere, it was present someplace; and here was Susana exerting her utmost.

She interpreted slowly and distinctly; what's more, she achieved a synchronicity of emotions. All my logical points of emphasis reached the audience precisely and without loss. I sensed they would believe her – a Spaniard and a woman – and, therefore, they might believe me. My brain worked like a powerful computer, outputting the most correct phrases. Indeed, Semmant would have been proud of me.

Having learned from my experience at the police station, I knew I was surrounded by enemies and morons, so I no longer tried to explain the details. I made no reference to beautiful strangers, or even to the Light of Eve. Keeping my words simple, I stuck to concrete facts and emphasized one thing: Lidia and her goal of revenge.

"What was she angry at you for?" the skinny lady asked, peering with hostility over her glasses.

"For dumping her," I replied and then added, "And... because I'm not capable of love."

Susana shot me a look; the judge wrinkled his brow as though he had swallowed a bitter pill. And the woman from the prosecutor's office pointed with her index finger in my direction.

"Not capable – is that true?" she asked threateningly, and I said, "Yes."

"Yes, yes, yes!" I repeated. "But people aren't arrested for that, or put in a cell, or subjected to interrogation. I may be guilty, but of nothing more than she herself is – or everyone else, for that matter."

Then we spoke of things easy to understand. "Did you live together?" the judge inquired.

"No," I answered, shrugging my shoulders. *"No,"* Susana translated.

"Were you planning to get married?" the thin lady persisted.

"My God, no!" I grinned. *"No, no, no!"* The interpreter's voice was firm and clear as a bell.

"Then why was she angry at you?" the judge circled through the labyrinth. And Susana and I circled through it with him, question after question, not giving up, not allowing ourselves to be confused by a single word.

Thus passed a long hour and a half and then they set me free. I was released until the trial, which I did not want to think about yet. The judge prohibited me from being anywhere near Lidia, calling her, writing her letters. I listened to all this with a stone face, holding back a derisive laugh. And Susana – perhaps she remembered me that night. Maybe she even named her favorite vibrator after me…

Soon I was on the street – with a haggard look and no voice. I probably reeked like a bum, with the peculiar stench of prison that even dogs fear. My strength suddenly left me. I sat on a step at the main entrance, rested my elbows on my knees, and clasped my head in my hands.

People crowded around, each with their own hopes, their own expectations and distress. I looked into their faces; determination was there. The ones who waited here believed in those close to them, even against the whole world. They considered their own rightness to be absolute, even though I knew it was of little value. The world would prevail, and the same ones they held dear would betray them – or they themselves would commit a betrayal. But this would all happen later. And you can never convince anyone of anything beforehand.

A dreadful emptiness loomed ahead – somewhere out there,

beyond the crowd at the entrance, beyond the sidewalk and the street. The stress of these last days seemed to have burned up everything inside me. Somehow I forgot immediately about Petru and the guards, and even about Susana. Just terrible humiliation, like a tattered scar, the ugly remains of the torment of being deprived of my liberty, would remain in my memory forever.

I sat on the steps. There was no one for me to call, with whom to share the news: I'm free. Still, I saw all as it was. I understood Lidia would not be deterred from her path; she would take vengeance for the destruction of the very core of her illusions. Like the people who waited here, she had also once dreamed she was for me, against the whole world. And in this world there is not – nor has there ever been – any force to persuade her to the contrary.

That's why no small price could ransom me from her hatred. She would pursue it to the end – prison, torture, poison, the guillotine. I had offended the essence of her faith – as funny as it is to speak of the essence of her petty beliefs – and this merited an *auto-da-fe*. A burning in the square – nothing less. A needle, dagger, or snakebite – an inevitable, agonizing death. Our conflict, at the heart of it, was that we had faith in very different things. And we were both sincere, to the bottom of our hearts.

I laughed – hoarsely, almost inaudibly. Then I got up and made my way home, to the *barrio* of Salamanca – along the boulevards, the Avenue Ríos Rosas – not directly, but traversing a wide circle. I could tell all the circles would close soon now. But I did not want to guess how the game would end.

The sun shone right in my face. I blinked and, through the spots of color, saw the chasm that separates each soul from every other – the abyss between the worlds that reside within us. I understood the nature of hate and the essence of all hostility. Where wars come from. How governments fall. And also why no one – well, almost no one – can genuinely love.

"*Almost* no one?" one may ask, and I, after just a bit of hesitation, will say, "Semmant." In a voice parched by the prison cell.

CHAPTER 29

Entering the apartment, I saw that someone had rifled through my belongings. No guesswork was needed: Lidia still had my key. The same one she hadn't given me when we met. And I knew she would never give it up.

Everything was overturned; the flat looked like a ruined animal lair. I don't know what Lidia was searching for, but she had made a concerted effort. Maybe she was just working off anger, venting her roiling rage.

The computer, thankfully, was still on. However, the monitor had been turned off, and a message was drawn on it in lipstick: "I'll always have my eye on you!" I didn't care; I wasn't afraid of her. Only one thing concerned me: how was Semmant doing?

With some trepidation I flipped the switch after wiping the screen with a damp cloth. We had not communicated for nearly five days – that had never happened before. What if he had decided I had abandoned him? That I had betrayed him, wanted nothing to do with him anymore? How would I explain all that – the prison, the humiliation, and my innocence?

The log of market transactions was empty, as before, but the screen exhibited its own strange life. It was as if Semmant were having a conversation with himself, needing no one else at all. One after the other, reproductions flashed before my eyes at ten-second intervals: Manet, Gauguin, Titian, El Greco... Artists and styles

alternated oddly; I could not catch any pattern. There was Velázquez
and right after him Cezanne. Seurat, with his ironic omniscience, and
Dalí, with the irony of bitter passion. A late, disenchanted Bonnard.
A late Rembrandt laughing at everyone. And Ernst's stone jungle as
an indictment thrown right in the face of the city. And Munch's *The
Scream* – disbelief, animosity, despair.

I saw how he had matured in those days. How he had become
different – enduring the collapse of his illusions. What had changed
in his digital soul? Had he resolved it, overcome it? There were
no answers – not for me anyway. I had no sense of him now; he
had become a mystery. His love for Adele and all that happened
afterward had taken him somewhere, revealing abysses, the deepest
of chasms. There was no access to them – not for me or anybody else.

Nevertheless, I wasn't going to give up. Each of the reproductions
was demanding: do *something*, at least! And I responded to the appeal
– showering hastily, I made myself some coffee and took a seat at
my desk. I drummed the keys, collecting my thoughts. I opened the
file with the last Adele story. Reading through it, I understood: I no
longer believed in this. Neither in the story nor in Adele herself. I
knew right away I would never set to work on the robot named Eve.
And that I could not write a single line more.

Listen. Many times since then I have turned that moment over in
my head. And I swear: I was sincere; I was not putting on a sham or
feeling sorry for myself. But after prison the world had changed for
me forever. It was as if I had rid myself of a bit of inner blindness.
Of a small shred, a merciful drop. From the one that, according to
the Brighton nursery rhyme, was nearly indistinguishable from the
ocean spray.

I sat, remembering the past days, months, years. I called to mind
figures and names. Alas, there was nothing to grab onto. I saw them all
at once – in cells behind bars, in a web of lies. In the boxes of cramped
apartments or in the spacious cages of large houses and luxury cars.
Lack of freedom was ubiquitous, dominating throughout space; and
I had just learned its highest degree. A government – neither large
nor small, not in any way remarkable – had leaned on me with its
power, depersonalizing me and turning me into no one. No matter

how much of a genius I was, my protest represented no hindrance to it – or to slander, which was unstoppable. Governments, they are everywhere. Indifferently accepting whatever slander comes their way.

Yet the issue was not just with them. I saw too much that would prevent a free existence. That would not allow Adele to be who she wanted. Rules and conventions placed restrictions on her everywhere. Everyone was raising their hands to veto her. They laid down the regulations, stating what was to be done and how. I could no longer maneuver around these stumbling blocks. Immediately I recalled the prison guards – their piggish faces, their handcuffs and truncheons.

And I made a decision: I resolved to act in the only way in my power. I'm being honest with you, as I was fully honest with myself at that instant. I realized I must set Adele free forever.

Only one approach was suitable for that. There was only one method, radical in the extreme.

After all, I couldn't just stick her in a cubicle. Even if I sent her on a trip – where would she go? Things would have turned out the same anywhere.

I was the author of a maligned creation. A parent whose child had been rejected. This had been proven to me – irrevocably. So I decided to eliminate Adele.

My fingers stretched out again toward the keyboard. Now I knew precisely what to do. And the words flowed on their own.

I wrote the last letter – from Adele to Semmant. That was right; that was needed. Confirming from her personally that she knew about my robot. About my robot, her knight. This was the most I could still do for him.

"At one time," she wrote, "I might have become worthy of you. But I have too little strength."

"Please accept this and don't take it as drama. Almost all dramas are contrived, anyway."

"It's time for you to admit the world is a wretched place. But this is no excuse to settle accounts with it."

"You settle up accounts with the world when there's no room in it for you anymore. Then you abandon it – that's the only way."

"And this is your revenge against it. Whether it's great or minor, let others decide."

"So, don't draw conclusions, don't make hasty plans. The world without me is almost the same as it had been."

"Remember this when you start to be sad. And don't be sad."

"Remember me as you knew me. And don't forget."

"Keep me in your memories – that's the place for us to express our intimacy."

"Our unfathomable similarity in something crucially important."

"In the most essential sense, which for others is nothing."

Thus Adele wrote him, and I sent the text almost without editing. Then I took sleeping pills, a double dose. This was necessary – to keep me from losing my nerve. To keep from trying – in a fit of cowardice – to turn everything back as it had been before. To avoid jumping out of bed later to scribble down a bunch of refutations, explanations, addenda. To not water it down, and not to lie anymore.

Waiting for oblivion, I breathed deeply, with my full chest. Everything should now proceed on its own. I no longer directed events; I had spent my power. I had reached the line that could not be crossed.

That night I had erotic dreams again. Or rather, explicitly pornographic dreams. They featured Adele this time – as if she were trying to reward me with herself at last. She was exceptionally good. We yielded to the most depraved follies. Most likely, I experienced the best sexual adventure of my life.

I woke suddenly, as if I had just surfaced out of a whirlpool. The wind howled; rain lashed at the windows. It was already late – almost noon. I had slept for fourteen hours straight.

Abruptly, I recalled everything – prison, the trashed apartment, Adele's farewell letter. My heart leaped; I tossed away the blanket and wandered to the desk, rubbing my eyes. The screen flickered pale gray; the pictures had disappeared. There was no woman's silhouette, nor a black pelican in the corner. Nothing but the words:

DEAD END. DEAD. END.

I knew what this meant; that message was generated by my own piece of code. The only fragment that hadn't been modified – perhaps the robot secretly suspected he might find it useful at some point. This was a self-destruct mechanism. I introduced it into the system for the contingency of a deadlock cycle, an algorithm failure, an infinite loop. With these words I wanted to let myself know my program was defective. That everything was confused, hopeless, and that resources were consuming themselves. And now I received the error message. Not from my program, but from Semmant.

Just in case, I hurriedly scanned the disks, trying to find some kind of trace. It was in vain; emptiness reigned everywhere. From it had arisen Semmant; from it he made money, and then he left it in his wake: an emptiness called death.

My ears were ringing, the walls floated before my eyes. I lay on the floor and stared at the ceiling. It was virginal, flawlessly white. In it, all colors mingled at once – and all my thoughts pounded in my head together. There was no sense in a single one of them any longer.

I remember the astonishment: I just could not believe my action of the day before. It was awful, immensely erroneous, hopelessly foolish. I had never done anything so stupid in my life – and there would never be another chance to. Yet, at the same time, I understood I could have done nothing else.

Also, I remember I tried – lying on the floor half-delirious, feverish – to find some kernels of rationality, to formulate some justifications. "The new level of abstraction," I muttered, "it should have protected him, rescued him. The gigabytes – they seemed to be a safety shield. They seemed to be armor that was not so easy to puncture..."

Then I cursed myself, "Idiot! Moron!" I hastily attempted to figure out whether anything could possibly heal Semmant of his inner pain – that is, could I help him, if only I knew what pain he was feeling? It was clear: he was not becoming hard of heart, no matter how much his self-adjustment had improved. He knew suffering and refused to accept its cause, and this was a conscious choice. The artificial brain had computed with mathematical precision that, in this case, compromise was impossible. Better not to exist at all, he had calculated – out to some distant decimal point. It was harsh evidence not to be subverted. It could really make me famous – it might be worth a Nobel Prize...

Tears welled up; I wiped them away with my palm. Then I blinked, drowning in swirls of color. Again I mumbled something to swim out of it. To keep from smothering, from losing my mind.

An hour passed in this fashion. Suddenly regaining consciousness, I sat up, then stood; my head was no longer spinning. The walls, the writing desk – all froze in place.

I jiggled the mouse, opened my market access program, and laughed knowingly. Yes, this was to be expected.

The robot had sent me a notice in the end. This probably meant he bore me no ill will. This meant we were together, like before, and he believed in me no matter what.

All the papers had been sold at one fell swoop; all assets were turned to cash. We had no connection anymore to the rest of the world. We isolated, removed ourselves; the world lost track of us. We took our plunder from it and hid. But then, when it thought we were making a cowardly retreat, we suddenly threw the money in its face. We made the craziest bet – as if challenging the world's own courage.

My capital – all of it, down to the last cent – had been transferred to Forex. Placed in enormous unsecured futures that had been selected, I was certain, at random. This was a coin tossed in the wind, but with the least chance of winning. Russian roulette with a bullet in nearly every chamber. A funny trick, a dead-end joke.

I winked at the screen and shook my head. Then I opened another window, looked at what was happening in the forecasts, the news feeds, the stock quotes. The market, like a crazy train, was rushing in the other direction. A series of terrorist attacks rocked Asia; the world was panicking; investors were offloading assets. The currencies followed them – to my detriment. Our stake was as conspicuous as a suicide trooper standing at full height under heavy fire.

I could have tried to save at least part, change something, rearrange it. But I knew I must not do that. Semmant's gesture was a test for me. The invitation, the initiation – it was clear there would never be another chance. Was I ready to go all the way, as Semmant had done? Like many others, through the centuries, whose names we do not remember.

Perhaps this was a sacrifice to the chaos monster rearing up in full rage. A ritual I could not do without – after all the transgressions I had committed. I sat with a meaningless grin, watching the points of currency transactions approaching the red line. I whispered names. Little Sonya, Little Sonya, Anthony, Anthony, Dee Wilhelmbaum. Adele, Semmant. Adele, Semmant, Semmant… At least let someone call them aloud, I thought. Even just once, maybe a few times.

Soon, all was over – irretrievably. My money was burned; I was left with nothing. I returned to the beginning of the infinite loop, to the dirty docks of Marseille, to solitude without borders. This did not trouble me in the least.

On the screen continued the dance of numbers, the creep of news lines. Graphics and diagrams changed every second; the market lived out its nervous life. It wasn't important to me now – I threw myself out of the carriage. The train flashed by and drove on. There was nothing left for me to do, sitting behind the desk, at my computer. Feeling acute hunger, I pulled the plug and went into the kitchen. There I was apprehended by a phone call.

The police were calling – regarding my arrest. A woman inspector, wheedling and cruel, wanted to have a talk with me. I understood immediately that she was one of the worst of the bitches who had acquired authority. One of those whose genitals don't have enough nerve endings. In her voice I heard passionate exultation, animal satisfaction, like after an orgasm.

"You should remember that we're watching you," she uttered distinctly. "Your girlfriend is under the protection of the State. You are forbidden to call her or have any contact. You are forbidden to even think about approaching her. If we decide that you are dangerous, you'll be kept behind bars until the trial! We will find you anywhere – we will find you and render you harmless!"

Her voice made the diaphragm of the handset speaker become moist, sticky. I suddenly realized I was sorry for her. I felt almost no anger.

"I want to give you some advice," I told her. "Times are about to change soon. In the line for the bull's balls, try to push your way forward right away – there will be a crowd!"

I did this out of pure goodwill. Don't let them think I'm up in arms at the whole world. With the lost, those who are not to blame, I'm even ready to share my premonitions. And the inspector is one of the lost. She has merely convinced herself that she's doing a righteous thing…

And here it was as though a current ran through me. A righteous thing, even if just a single one – it was on the surface, and there was no need for convincing! An indignant shriek met my ear, but I was no longer listening. Skanda Purana's bell resounded in my head, encompassing all sounds. Putting everything in place – yes, I had jumped from the train, but here, under the rails, the story had not ended, the finale had not played.

I hung up the phone and started to get ready. One more exploit, the last one, awaited me.

CHAPTER 30

Regardless of how long you soar through abstractions, there's no hiding from reality; it never goes away. It will hunt you down, call you to act – and not relent, no matter how you squirm. Only, perhaps, someone may take your place – if, for example, you're already dead. I was not dead, and no one was going to accomplish my task for me.

The more ardently you try to distance yourself, the more they demand of you later. I had achieved an incredible remoteness; therefore, they now expected a most serious action. I had no right to compromise – in fact, compromise had already been excluded from the equation. It was rejected by Semmant's electronic brain.

I prepared carefully, without hurrying. No matter what, I had plenty of time. I knew precisely what had to be done – what was left to do, so that the plot could reach a resolution. Adele was dead and Semmant with her; the chain of events had closed in on itself. My initial plan had been fulfilled, approaching perfection at its highest point. And at the very same place it encountered the omnipotence of villainy.

The only thing remaining was to reward the omnipotence as well as the perfection, according to their deeds. It remained to punish villainy, its embodiment: the villainess herself. To punish abstract evil – in the manifestation that it had assumed this time. To halt entropy – even if only on the most local scope. And also to affirm the impropriety of simplifications. Lidia Alvares Alvares should share the fate of Adele and Semmant.

Don't try to persuade me their deaths were artificial, unreal. It had long been clear who among us was real and who wasn't. That's why Lidia actually had to die – she and her poisonous soul. Maybe this would finally help her, cleanse her of insincerity, of false posturing. Perhaps it would make her genuine – as much as Adele the courtesan was genuine for Semmant and me.

Of course, I understood this would all look absurd from the outside. Exceptionally absurd, even criminal. I didn't care; I was carrying out the inevitable. That's how everything worked out – no arguing with inevitability. As far as what would happen to me afterward, what difference did it make? I sensed it was too late to think of the consequences, and I was not afraid – of anyone or anything. Once you know the extremes, you get over being afraid. Deprivation of freedom is the most fearful thing there can be. And don't think I'm just talking about prison. Extreme loss of freedom is more than prison!

Never in my life had I hit a woman, but Lidia – she was no longer a woman to me. Abstract evil has no gender; it is not a product of nature. I had to make retribution, and not just for Adele and Semmant. It was also for the demon let loose in the world; hate must not be left with a positive account balance. Besides that, it was for the perversion of an idea, for the blindness of all the old maids at the D.A.'s office, for every act of violence against those from whom the softest ray emanates. For the fact that this light is taken to be their weakness. And no government can prevent that.

Let them all be blind, but I see – I see and rush to help. Semmant is dead, but I will pick up his spear. And I will not avenge; I will execute!

I dressed in black, which was fitting for an assassin. The rain had stopped, and the sun was peeking out, but I threw on a jacket despite the heat. Rifling through my kitchen cabinets, I selected a knife. I wrapped it in a rag, tucked it in my belt. I took stock of myself – yes, I was ready. Ready to thrash, seize by the throat, deliver the decisive blow.

Then I realized I had missed something. I sat down at the table and seized a sheet of paper. I began to write – legibly, neatly, so that every word would be understood.

Retaliation required giving notice, not allowing it to remain unexplained. I wrote a long letter where it was all laid out – about the villainy, the lack of freedom, and even the future of Europe. I wrote about the bull and his balls. About the boundless torpor of this country. About the police inspector and the skinny old maid – that they were guiltless and should not be blamed. About Adele, that she existed somewhere. About Semmant… No, once I thought about it, I made no reference to Semmant. I had no desire to mention his name for nothing.

Then I went outside and grabbed a taxi. I hunched my head into my shoulders, became invisible. I couldn't give myself away too early, before the right moment, until the time came.

Concealed in the back seat, I watched the passersby. As usual, they seemed ridiculous; but now I felt this a thousand times more acutely. I was amazed, astonished. Their self-assurance knew no bounds. They all thought that, by their own will, they controlled themselves and their lives. They all supposed they had the right to judge – existence, the whole world. And yet, not one of them knew Semmant. They knew neither him nor Adele. Or any of the story of their love and death.

The taxi driver studied me in the mirror, stealthily. In his gaze I saw pitying curiosity. Perhaps I was wincing, looking crazy. On top of that, the whole time I was fighting the urge to laugh. I had to keep holding back my laughter, finding it difficult to restrain myself and not burst out giggling.

He cocked his head in contempt, this typical Spaniard – slightly protruding eyes, curly hair, pot belly. Most likely, he had a wife; he feared her, this fat, henpecked *hombre* with the brains of an earthworm. My story was immensely wider than his foreshortened perspective. Naturally, he was not worthy of it. But I still allowed him to participate briefly – at the next traffic light I pulled back the hem of my jacket and showed him the knife. This worked; he was scared to death. He peered at me again, but this time his look was different. No trace was left of his former arrogance.

Soon we arrived; there was not much on the meter. I gave him a twenty and didn't wait for change. This was my modest way of encouraging him. My gift to a little man who had suddenly learned the world was not as he imagined it to be. That the world was different – it was inscrutable, scary... The taxi driver hit the gas and sped away with screeching tires. But I was already through with him.

I headed for the main door – with a springy step. As if I were on a path in the wild woods. Ready to fend off an attack by a savage cat, the enraged creature Lidia had become. Ready to draw the knife and plunge it into her neck first.

Someone exited the entryway right on time. I changed my appearance for an instant, averting my eyes and smoothing my wolf's fur, making myself ordinary, just not dressed for the weather. I proffered a saccharine smile, uttered *"Gracias,"* and caught the open door. The trick worked; Simon the magician would have been pleased with me. If he still remembered me, I mean.

In the entranceway I looked around – feeling a little hunted, sensing every whisper. All was quiet; no one was prowling on padded feet ready to pounce. The vestibule was cool, hollow, empty. Only potted cactuses stood along each wall. Somehow I had never noticed them before. They looked like the phallic statues that had been venerated in ancient Greece. Women planted them in the earth and watered them, calling out to the gods of fertility. Here, however, that would not have helped. Everything was sterile in Lidia's residence. It exuded an air of superfluous, nonessential, meaningless life. An urge for destruction I should bring to naught.

"Celebrate the festival of your god, celebrate while ye may," I quoted to myself in a mischievous sneer. No, she would never be the "nursemaid to a prince." Not to one like Felipe, or to any other. She was only capable of destroying and tearing down!

Ever so slowly I ascended the stairs. Utterly quiet, I stepped across the marble on the soft soles of my sneakers. Here was the second floor, with a plaque on the only door, "Andrés Enrique Aguilar, Dentist." A charming guide in the jungles of pain. An expert in torture with iron hooks. The building is expensive and soundly made, I thought. The walls are insulated thoroughly – no one can hear the screams!

I continued to the third floor. "Carlos Villa Moreno, Attorney." Now this was a truly ominous figure. A friend to some dungeon interrogator who shines a lamp in your face. A usurer raking in your meager, hard-earned gold with greedy fingers. At the threshold to his door lay a nice rug. He was clearly a man with far-reaching connections.

I grimaced, feeling my anger at this mob, but I knew – my rage was powerless. All of them – the dentist, the lawyer, the accountant Cristóbal García behind the door at the right – lived in their own realities. They had their own wives, mistresses, secretaries, clients. Their own specters, their own concepts of love. You can't blame others for their universe not coinciding with yours. My world, for many, looked quite monstrous as well.

Here was the fourth floor, the one I needed. I stood for a moment, listening; then I put my ear to the keyhole and was thrilled. Voices could be distinctly heard within. That meant my target was close. I wouldn't have to put this off or drag it out!

I drew the knife from my belt and unwrapped the cloth. I weighed it, stretched out my arm, crouched slightly, parried. Hid it behind my back, grinned as though nothing was up. Thrust my hand forward and made a few stabbing motions. Then a few slashing motions…

The air whistled as I sliced it, the blade glinting. This was a good kitchen knife. The steel was indemnified against any doubts about its quality – by a whole army of lawyers with nice rugs at their doors. If something didn't work out, the knife would not be to blame. I could only fault myself – and my indecision, the remorse that might suddenly arise. But no, I did not have remorse. Lidia had become an abstraction, as if she weren't even made of flesh. Dark energy was her essence. Destroying an abstraction – that was easy, not frightening.

I rang the bell and hid behind the wall. High heels clacked across the apartment. Someone, probably Lidia herself, walked up to the other side of the door and stopped. I imagined her looking through the peephole and shrugging her shoulders.

Then the heels clattered again as Lidia moved away from the door. I rang once more, snickering, barely audibly. Again she would not open but yelled in exasperation, "Who is it?"

I detected notes of indecision in her voice. Notes of premonition, the recognition of danger. This was what I wanted. She had to think, to feel. She had to *recognize* it!

Lidia hesitated for a couple of minutes and left. I waited a minute or two, then rang a third time. Steps resounded – confident, authoritative. This was someone with a firm, manly gait.

A horseman with a spear, I thought irritably. Here he is, rushing to the aid of his lady. Even Lidia has a knight pledged to her. Is this not an indication of how perverse the world order is?

He didn't ask any questions but immediately started snapping back the locks. I prepared myself, relaxed, and then flexed my muscles again. As soon as the last bolt clicked, I jumped from behind the wall. I pressed down quickly on the handle and shoved the door forward...

Inside, everything instantly went awry. Intending to knock the "knight" off his feet, I had expected resistance from his body, but the door burst open easily, without catching on anything. Obviously, he was a tough cookie and had prudently stepped out of the way. My inertia thrust me forward. I flailed my arms to maintain equilibrium and dropped the knife.

For some reason, many people appeared in the corridor. The cleaver of Swiss steel caused alarm. Shouts, a woman's scream rang out. And the guy who had opened the door, clean-shaven in a red shirt, rushed me from behind without a second thought. I saw him out of the corner of my eye and immediately understood: this was a dangerous foe. He was younger and stronger than me, but I managed to jab him under the ribs with my elbow. He doubled over, and I rushed right through the crowd toward the living room. I didn't bother picking up the knife – I didn't even see where it had fallen. I figured I didn't really need it; I was fully capable of strangling Lidia with my bare hands.

But first I had to find her. I burst into the room, nearly knocking someone over. People were there too: many people – some *mulatos*, a short Asian girl with mouth agape. I scanned around like a police robot. The neurons in my brain were firing in a mad dance. Their net tingled, throwing off sparks. Yet Lidia was nowhere to be found.

Someone was already calling the police, sobbing hysterically into the phone. From several directions, silhouettes loomed in front of me with hands outstretched. These were hunters – hunting me.

I rushed through them, feinting like a rugby player. One fell, and I nearly faked out another, but suddenly, in some strange way, they all knocked me to the floor. Then the guy who had answered the door appeared. I noticed his red shirt before he kicked me in the gut. All the same, I fought; I twisted and squirmed. Once I even broke free, but I was thrown to the floor again and held down tightly. In the actions of my opponents there appeared a semblance of order. Someone suggested binding me with towels. This decided the matter – tied up, I quickly understood it was foolish to resist. So I calmed down, and went silent. Only then did Lidia enter the room.

They showed her the knife that had been collected from the hallway. "Ay ay ay," she shook her head as if in jest, but I heard fear. Then she started talking nonstop, spraying spit with her words. She insulted me, showering me with the most abusive words. The rest was silent, but she could not quiet down – she just kept smoldering and yelling. Her lips and cheeks quivered. She really wanted to demonstrate to me that I had lost. But I saw a trace of terror in her eyes. I knew it would remain there forever.

For some reason I was sure everything had happened exactly as it needed to. I had not failed in my mission; I had done all I could. Most likely a design from above presupposed this fiasco. That's why I was lying on the floor in peace and tranquility. "I did all I could" – that's a wonderful feeling!

Soon the police arrived – right on time: there was nothing left for me to do there. They tried to rough me up, but to spite them I behaved like a lamb, meek and mild. They cuffed me, read me my rights. I was allowed to give them one phone number to call. "Just one," the officer repeated, furrowing his brow menacingly. He seemed to think he resembled some kind of movie action hero.

I was silent for a second or two and then dictated the number of my only remaining friend. The beautiful Anna, born the Countess Pilar María Cortés de Vega.

CHAPTER 31

Two months and seventeen days have passed since then. It is now late autumn – rains, chills. I have adapted fully and don't feel like a guest. I do not feel superfluous or as though I'm violating the harmony of this place.

Clients are treated well at our clinic. We are VIPs, not just psychos. Even in the first days when I had spasms and fits of rage, nobody addressed me rudely. They bound me carefully – so as not to bruise my wrists and ankles. They did not humiliate me like a helpless rag doll. They did not prescribe me a compulsory enema. They didn't beat me with a rubber stick, or leave me to rot for days in my own filth. None of these methods are practiced here in this institution for the rich, paid for with Anna de Vega's money.

The fits of rage are far behind me; I've almost regained my senses. My mind is perhaps even healthier than before – prior to Lidia or Semmant. I speak to the doctor about this, though somewhat languidly. I don't insist on anything or make any requests. He takes it all into consideration and just smiles through his mustache. He and I seem to have a silent pact of inaction.

This suits me – where else can I get a merciful respite? I'm considered to be incarcerated, and my balcony is enclosed by steel bars, but it seems to me I'm as free as ever. I feel freedom with every cell of my body, with each neuron of my overworked brain. And I know: this is precisely the kind of liberty I need now. I'm free of money, of being afraid about it. This is the highest form of freedom in modern times. And, besides, a weight has been lifted from me. The weight of responsibility for what I had created. I'm no longer indebted – not for anything, to anyone. Not to Semmant, not to humankind, not even to myself.

Here in the clinic, it's not bad, in its way. It smells of pine and dry moss. Or wet moss, when it rains – that's also a pleasant smell. At dinner they let me drink wine. I order French – to spite Spain, which I despise. At times the conditions remind me somehow of the School. I'll tell Thomas about this when I happen to be in Tyrol again. There are mountains here too by the way – but not the Alps. Their eternity is different. As if, over time, it surrendered to itself.

The nurses like me – I cause them no trouble. I'm compliant and not capricious. No wonder – I still have a lot ahead. If I felt that the clinic was forever, that – alas – it was not my fate to leave here, then I would probably behave differently. I would exhaust them with petty complaints, would not allow them to breathe easily. I would feed on their irritation just to give myself a morsel of something new to think about, a reflection of the patches of light from the life outside inaccessible to me. Even then, ready formulas would hardly console me; I would want to strain my waning mind over and over. But now – now I am calm. I have a method appropriate to my case. It's not complicated: I am simply waiting.

I wait and, in the meantime, make friends with the nurses, all pretty Latinas. We talk about a lot – about Madrid and far-off Brighton, about Paris in the fall, even about Anthony and Bradley the astrophysicist with the acacia branch on his lapel. I draw the chimeras of Notre Dame for them – tame, almost not scary. Sometimes I go so far as to explain what the softest ray is, the mystery of the Light of Eve. Usually this gets me excited, agitated, and I can hardly keep myself in hand. The nurses soothe me, leniently, as they would a child. As if I were speaking of what I had learned from my children's books.

At times I don't want to speak but to listen. I question them, and they readily tell me about themselves. About lovers and husbands past and present, about their parents, aunts, brothers, sisters. Their fates are simple, with passions familiar to all; their dramas are similar and have a predictable end. I sincerely respect all of them – Sara, as well as Esther, and Veronica. I do admire Laura – and I always will, even if she won't put out. Because they are all genuine. Despite their made-up names.

This calms me. This proves all is still not quite so hopeless, so bad. At this given point in space-time, it is indeed possible to exist. My story with Lidia is nothing more than an antimatter discharge, a fluctuating blip. Could this be a hint at my mission, my purpose? Or a test to see what an advanced artificial brain is capable of? How it may cope with the collision of truths, which almost no one cares to deal with anymore? Or maybe this is a proof by example: there is no place left for real males in Europe. A warning: very soon, society will have to regenerate. To plant a kiss on the bull's balls – might this be a Spanish bull? After all, there must be historical significance in the *corrida*. Let Spain be proud then, I don't mind.

That's what I think, almost peacefully – and then suddenly I jump up and nearly shout out loud. A white burst of madness lacerates my brain, my blood boils and pounds in my temples. The most terrible profanities are ready to burst from my lips.

Because: why Semmant? Why did such a lot befall him? All the lousy significances are not worth his soul!

I clench my fists – powerlessly, angrily. There is no one to punch; no enemy stands before me. Only the sensation of great loss – the kind that can never be accepted – remains in the air, in the room, in the cosmos.

But I reconcile myself to it – that is, so I pretend. Breathe in, breathe out; I get my anger under control. And I repeat – yet again – don't hold out hope. Yet even here I will not lose my head. You can't imagine how steady my mind is. How I am able – in everything – to see kernels of reason. And to bargain with my own judgments.

I say to myself: all is interconnected; links form the well-organized structure. One, another, one girl, another… Lidia, Adele, love and, behind it, death – this is a fractal, the Dragon Curve, repeating itself over and over. I supposed my robot would become eternal, invulnerable. But he turned out a bit different. Capable of loving

– which means capable of dying. It was my mistake to think he was old-fashioned. Most likely he acted as a messenger. As a symbol of the future, while I – I had to answer for the present. This was not difficult: ultimately, I could act according to the rules of the present. I could kill – and I'm not sorry I tried. Just as I don't regret the attempt failed.

Listen. I'm not idealizing him, no. I'm not imposing a model on anyone to imitate it. He is no hero; he was merely able to do what not everyone can. He could make his own personal choice. He took his fate into his own hands. He strove for perfection and was not satisfied with less.

He is no hero, but he possesses a lot of courage. Courage and something else – for which, I admit, I was unprepared. One of the truths was finally revealed to me. It was that one must mature to appreciate any given truth. This, alas, I still have not done. But only by having definitively gone astray can one be sure that the path is false.

I naively presumed my robot was the first step on the path to a new faith. I was mistaken; I was deeply wrong. No one would believe in something full of humanity – even if just in dreams. You are ashamed of these dreams; you do not forgive them – it's enough already to pretend otherwise. To refer insincerely to Judea, to recall Golgotha, shed fake tears – I do not believe those tears. The phantom of mercy is so foreign to the market, as the specter of love is to the children of the market era.

Of this I had received the most graphic of proofs. Without even knowing Semmant, without seeing him, society did sense the danger. It had dispatched a representative, a fighting machine. It had issued her a military order. It had equipped her with the newest brand of weapon…

My fists clench again, and my jaws go numb. I take a deep breath, count to ten. A new faith – now I know the recipe for it. Its primary ingredients are quite clear. The new religion must soar high above common sense. Its idol must frighten all beyond measure. You may argue with this; you may not agree. Humanists would make a laughingstock of me, hold me up to scorn. But they know for themselves: it won't work any other way. At least those among them who have brains do.

Then, after causing a fright, something should be promised in exchange. I know what this will be – there's only one formula. A great reward commensurate with great fear – this is immortality, no less. It will draw all to itself like the Pied Piper. Everyone will be quick to believe there'll be no end to the pleasures of consumption. That they can keep buying new cars over and over. Buying clothes, alcohol, sex. Doing all that has become habitual. I know; I am the same way myself. Everlasting life is the opportunity to suck oysters forever. Now, in two hundred years, in five hundred.

All jokes aside, the negation of mortality will become the fetish of the masses. It already gets mentioned occasionally – but soon they will start discussing it on every corner. New prophets, new visionaries and guides… I even know where the trick may be. This understanding came to me right here. In the first days, when I was still quite ill. During one of my fits, when I could not move because of the bindings. This is extraordinarily important, immovability. Later I read scientific journals – a large collection covering several years. They were delivered to me upon my first request, right from the National Library. Really, this is a very good clinic.

The question of immortality is not decided in churches – that would be too simple. Religious myths fabricated for the crowd are overly conformist, primitive. Can anyone really believe, deep down, in such tripe? Can this really assuage the fear of death? Maybe only for dickheads.

No, the recipe is in our thick notebooks. In the ones that Theophanus and I threw on the mezzanine. To be precise, in the notebooks of those who – almost altruistically – make their way, micron after micron, toward comprehending the structure of the universe. There are theories there to instill hope – each one can choose something according to his taste. Personally, I'm interested in excessive multidimensionality, as well as black holes, hidden doors beyond the event horizon. I see great potential in them – like my dad did in the craft of Simon from the traveling circus.

One day I will describe all that in more detail. About the hint of eternal life, and also about how the world will change – irreversibly. How art will disappear, no longer being in demand, and plain reflections of the momentary – photos, videos, comic strips – will take its place. And all books will have the format of a synopsis – I will write that sort of opus too. Then they will finally believe my efforts are not driven by protest or negation. After all, to tell the truth, I'm much better off than the rest. Protesting is not within my rights. Nor those of any of us, the Indigo children.

For now I am just comparing ideas diverse in nature. I draw light cones, bisect them with planes. I match projections on the most varied scales. From the Planck length to the size of stars. From a chronon to a human lifespan. Sometimes quite amusing patterns result. In distant galaxies, in cosmic vortices I see the same higher order that is born of chaos and dwells together with it, and restrains it from time to time. Semmant tried to explain this to me – and I had almost understood him. And now I see even more clearly: the difference is only in the system of coordinates. This means there is hope.

I have only spoken with one person about this – Anna de Vega. She has come to see me a few times. We converse about very strange things. We both need that.

"I see your aura," I told her at the last visit. "It's pale blue. That may not be indigo, but you're also on the other side of the looking glass."

The conversation didn't work out then. Anna looked at me in silence and left without saying good-bye. But I know she'll be back.

All in all, there is no lack of visitors. One time they even tried to interview me – for a newspaper specializing in hot facts. This was my chance finally to make Semmant famous, but it presented itself too late; I drove the newspaper team away. I told them, "The power of mass media is counterfeit. You feed on carrion, and you reek." Of course they left in resentment. Only a single pretty reporter hung back at the doors.

"It's a shame you behave like this," she chided me. "We could offer you some help."

"Well, yeah, yeah," I nodded and then added, "Tit for tat – here's good advice: when they put the bull's balls on the altar, get in line for them, don't delay!"

She just sighed and made a gesture to suggest I was not in my right mind. But I don't consider it to be her fault, and I wanted to help her from the bottom of my heart. She reminded me of Diana – she looked like a nympho ready to let herself go wild.

I believe, by the way, she shared the advice with my doctor. At least his questions the following day were suspiciously close to this topic. But he is not a woman, and I wasn't in the mood to discuss the fate of Europe with him.

Then an activist for men's rights showed up – it turns out such characters do exist. He was very thin, with a strong-willed face and a squint-eyed look.

"Something terrible is happening in the world," he told me. "It can't keep going that way; civilization will go extinct. They want equality, but there is no equality. There will be a battle, the war of the sexes!"

He bored me right away, from the first word. I really wanted him to leave.

"Of course there can't be any equality," I concurred. "The ones you're preparing to do battle with, they are the best thing that happens in our lives – unless you count Brochkogel and Brunnenkogel and recall the virgin, off-piste snow. How can we equate ourselves with the best, level it, reduce it to the average?"

He was slightly dumbfounded, so, attempting to speak calmly, I explained to him, "After all, they smile every time they see a child! They command a specter in light clothes that is still alive and that will live forever. And, finally, the softest ray emanates from them!"

Then I lost my temper; his posture irritated me. "Remember Eve," I exclaimed, "if your memory hasn't betrayed you yet. Remember: her features are full of innocence, even at the crossroads, when she holds the apple and envisions sin. Even when, once she has bitten the fruit, she looks at the farthest point and sees someone there, and it's not Adam. All the wickedness maturing in her soul is not able to mar her image. And each man, each one is happy to be deceived!"

The activist looked at me, pursing his lips. Like the pretty reporter, he probably wanted to make a screw-loose sign at his temple. But he controlled the impulse – it was obvious he was accustomed to holding himself back. He said, "We could help you. We have people working with us who are very concerned indeed. We could even help with money – within reasonable limits, of course."

I asked him what those limits might be, and he named a laughable amount. I grinned and informed him Semmant and I wouldn't lift a finger over that much. And on top of that, I'd never join in a war against women.

The man with the strong-willed face glanced at his watch and closed his notepad. All was clear to him; obviously, his world did not contain any blind spots. Then he inquired, nonetheless, who Semmant was. I replied drily, "He used to be my friend. He died." The activist bowed his head in a sign of sympathy, but new curiosity flashed in his eyes. He probably suspected I was gay.

When he left, laughter overtook me – just like that time in the taxi. For a whole two days I had to suppress guffaws whenever I remembered him. But then it became no laughing matter for me. For the first time after Semmant's death, I was ashamed. And the reason for it was yet another guest.

A man from the past came to me, the gloomy functionary who knew how to transform himself into a prophet. None other than the director of the School himself appeared on the threshold of my room just after midday a few weeks ago. He had hardly aged, though we had not seen each other for many years. At the same time, he had changed a lot; but I recognized him straightaway. I recognized him and said, "Hello, Director." And I felt myself blushing uncontrollably.

No, I wasn't ashamed of being here in the hospital, in solitary confinement. Nor was I troubled by all that had happened to me since the School ceased to be. But I immediately saw as clear as day the mistake I had made that merited censure. I noticed I had blinders on – as if seeing them with his eyes. I said to him, "You were right. The dream must be naïve, nothing less. I was too afraid they would not understand me – that was the stupidest of misconceptions!"

"Yes, yes," the Director nodded. "Me too. But that's beside the point right now. How are you doing here, overall?"

I shrugged my shoulders, gave him a brief rundown on the clinic, doctors, nurses. About entangled quanta and the collapse of wave functions. About nonlinearity and the vibrations of the market. And about how the trap of a detector, it seems to me, has not yet slammed shut – despite the bars around the balcony. Despite the white walls and attentive eyes.

It was easy with him – we could speak the same language without selecting simplified terms. "You know," the Director chuckled, "your situation reminds me of a certain young man from Athens. Sometimes they call him Theo. I once flew to Asunción to help him out."

"Yes," I said. "By the way, they sometimes call me Defiort."

I don't know why I revealed this name to him – probably on a mischievous whim. I just wanted to change the subject. I felt it wasn't the time to speak about notebooks with a bunch of formulas or recall the poem about the volcano. But to myself I thought: this is not just a coincidence.

As he bade me farewell, the director looked me full in the face. In his eyes I detected sadness. Later I realized I was mistaken: this was not sadness, but boundless sorrow.

"I'll see what we can do for you," he said quietly.

This reminded me of our first meeting – at the School, by the main entrance. But now it was easy to believe in his words.

When he left, a shadow flew out from under my thick curtains and seemed to follow him. The shadow of a chimera, I thought, squeezing out a grin. Then I muttered, "Out! Out!" though I knew it would return to me. Just as each of the nurses would return according to the schedule hanging in the office. As Anna de Vega would return – and perhaps some others whom I dare not remember yet.

So, life continues; I feel its pulse. I can meditate on a wide variety of things. About Semmant and the event horizon. About fine threads of energy and the algorithms of self-adjustment. I don't think any more about the robot named Eve. But I do expect my Gela to come to visit me someday.

And, of course, I dream of Laura from Santo Domingo. About

her slim, playful foot. About her buttocks, shoulders, hips. Laura's next shift is in two days. Two days – two sunsets, two dinners with a bottle of red Bordeaux, two new letters to Semmant.

I write to him; I write about him. So as not to leave him by himself. To be present in his unseen field – might we not meet again in some universe or another? I think a lot about this and, comparing the facts, come to the conclusion it may happen.

I write him every evening, as before, though I have nowhere to send what I've written. That's no problem; a time will come for these words. In any case, the main thing is to keep moving forward.

"Hey, we did this!" I wrote in the very first letter.

"They consider me insane. Maybe they're right," I wrote in another.

"As for you, you were the most normal of anybody I knew!" I wrote recently, in all honesty.

Here, by the white wall, sitting at a desk bolted to the floor, there's no need to lie.

It seems to me I'm almost happy.

Also by Vadim Babenko:

A SIMPLE SOUL
THE BLACK PELICAN

A SIMPLE SOUL

An excerpt from the novel published in Russia in 2009
The first English edition coming in 2013

CHAPTER I

One July morning during a hot, leap-year summer, Elizaveta Andreyevna Bestuzheva walked out of apartment building number one on Solyanka Street, the home of her latest lover. She lingered for a moment, squinting in the sun, then straightened her shoulders, raised her head proudly, and marched along the sidewalk. It was almost ten, but morning traffic was still going strong – Moscow was settling into a long day. Elizaveta Andreyevna walked fast, looking straight ahead and trying not to meet anyone's gaze. Still, at the corner of Solyansky Proyezd, an unrelenting stare invaded her space, but turned out to be a store window dressing in the form of a huge, green eye. Taken aback, she peered into it, but saw only that it was hopelessly dead.

She turned left, and the gloomy building disappeared from view. Brushing off the memories of last night and the need to make a decision, Elizaveta felt the relief of knowing she was alone. She was sick of her lover – maybe that was the reason their meetings were becoming increasingly lustful. In the mornings, she wanted to look away and make a quick retreat, not even kissing him good-bye. But he was persistent, his parting ritual enveloping her like a heavy fog. Afterward, she always ran down the stairs, distrusting the elevator, and scurried away from the dreary edifice as if it were a mousetrap that had miraculously fallen open.

Elizaveta glanced at her watch, shook her head, and picked up speed. The sidewalk was narrow, yet she stepped lightly, oblivious of the obstacles: oncoming passersby, bumps and potholes, puddles left by last night's rain. She wasn't bothered by the city's deplorable state, but a new sense of unease uncoiled deep inside her and slithered up her spine with a cold tickle. The giant eye still seemed to stare at her from under its heavy lid. She had a sense of another presence, a most delicate thread that connected her to someone else. Involuntarily, she jerked her shoulders, trying to shake off the feeling, and, after admonishing herself, returned to her contemplation.

Find out more about *A Simple Soul* at
www.simplesoulbook.com

THE BLACK PELICAN

An excerpt from the novel published in Russia in 2006
The first English edition coming in 2013

CHAPTER I

To this day I remember the long road to the City of M. It dragged on and on, while the thoughts plaguing me mingled with the scenes along the way. It seemed as if everything around me was already at one with the place, even though I still had a few hours to go. I passed indistinct farms in empty fields, small villages and lonely estates surrounded by cultivated greenery and forest hills. Man-made ponds and natural lakes skirted the road and reeked of wetlands, which later, right before M., turned into peat bogs and marshes, with no sign of life for miles to come. The countryside was dotted with humble towns sprouting out of the earth, the highway briefly becoming their main street: squares and clusters of stores glimmered in the sun, banks and churches rose up closer to the center, a belfry whizzed by, silent as usual. Then the glint of the shops and gas stations at the outskirts said farewell without a word, and just like that, it was over. The town was gone, without having time to agitate or provoke interest. Again the road wound its way through the fields, its monotony wearing me down. I saw the peculiar people who swarm over the countryside – for a fleeting moment they appeared amusing, but then I stopped noticing them, understanding how unexceptional they are, measured against their surroundings. At times, locals waved to me from the curb or just followed me with their eyes, though more often than not, no one was distracted by my fleeting presence. Left behind, they merged with the streets as they withdrew to the side.

At last the fields disappeared, and real swamps engulfed the road – a damp, unhealthy moor. Clouds of insects smashed into the windshield; the air became heavy. Nature seemed to bear down on me, barely letting me breathe, but that didn't last long. Soon I drove up a hill. The swamps still sat a bit to the east, retreating to the invisible ocean in a smooth line overgrown with wild shrubs. Now the trees grew dense, casting the illegible calligraphy of their shadows over the road, until, several miles ahead, the road became wider, and a sign said I had crossed the city limits of M.

ABOUT THE AUTHOR

Vadim Babenko left two "dream" jobs – cutting-edge scientist and high-flying entrepreneur – in order to pursue his lifelong goal to write full-time. Born in the Soviet Union, he earned master's and doctoral degrees from the Moscow Institute of Physics & Technology, Russia's equivalent to MIT. As a scientist at the Soviet Academy of Sciences he became a recognized leader in the area of artificial intelligence. Then he moved to the U.S. and co-founded a high-tech company just outside of Washington, D.C. The business soon skyrocketed, and the next ambitious goal, an IPO on the stock exchange, was realized. But at this peak of success, Vadim dropped everything to set out on the path of a writer and has never looked back. He moved to Europe and, during the next eight years, published five books, including two novels, *The Black Pelican* and *A Simple Soul*, which were nominated for Russia's most prestigious literary awards. His third novel, *Semmant*, initially written in Russian and then translated with the author's active participation, is published exclusively in English.

Find out more at www.vadimbabenko.com

CPSIA information can be obtained at www.ICGtesting.com
Printed in the USA
LVOW11s1102140115

422784LV00003B/208/P